THE GIRL IN THE LIFEBOAT

A novel of the Titanic

Eileen Enwright Hodgetts

ISBN: 978-1-7376070-3-8

Eileen Enwright Hodgetts

CQD CQD SOS *TITANIC* TO ALL SHIPS. POSITION
41.44 N 50.24 W. WE HAVE COLLISION WITH
ICEBERG. SINKING. COME AT ONCE. WE STRUCK AN
ICEBERG. SINKING.

CARPATHIA TO *TITANIC*. PUTTING ABOUT AND
HEADING FOR YOU.

OLYMPIC TO *TITANIC*. CAPTAIN SAYS GET YOUR
BOATS READY. WHAT IS YOUR POSITION?

TITANIC TO ALL SHIPS. SINKING HEAD DOWN
41.46 N 50.14 W. COME AS SOON AS POSSIBLE.

BALTIC TO *CARONIA*. PLEASE TELL *TITANIC* WE
ARE MAKING TOWARDS HER.

TITANIC TO ALL SHIPS. WE ARE PUTTING
PASSENGERS OFF IN SMALL BOATS.

OLYMPIC TO *TITANIC*. AM LIGHTING UP ALL
POSSIBLE BOILERS AS FAST AS CAN.

TITANIC TO ALL SHIPS. ENGINE ROOM GETTING
FLOODED.

VIRGINIAN TO CAPE RACE. PLEASE INFORM
TITANIC THAT WE ARE GOING TO HER ASSISTANCE.
OUR POSITION IS 170 MILES NORTH.

TITANIC TO ALL SHIPS. SOS *TITANIC* SINKING BY THE
HEAD. WE ARE ABOUT ALL DOWN. SINKING.

Eileen Enwright Hodgetts

PART ONE

NORTH ATLANTIC

There was peace and the world had an even tenor to its way.

Nothing was revealed in the morning the trend of which was not

known the night before. It seems to me that the disaster about to

occur was the event that not only made the world rub its eyes and

awake but woke it with a start keeping it moving at a rapidly

accelerating pace ever since with less and less peace, satisfaction

and happiness. To my mind, the world of today awoke April 15th,

1912.

Jack B. Thayer III, *Titanic* survivor

Eileen Enwright Hodgetts

CHAPTER ONE

April 15, 1912
On Board the *Titanic*
North Atlantic
Alvin Towson

The *Titanic* was sinking rapidly, and Alvin Towson was out of time. He had come so close to catching her, but she had escaped him, and now she had gained a seat in a lifeboat. For a brief moment, the world seemed to stand still, and all he could see was the stewardess's upturned face looking back at him triumphantly from the safety of the last lifeboat. Paralyzed by anger and frustration, he watched as the boat was slowly lowered into the water. It was not until the sailors took up their oars and the boat moved smoothly away that reality washed over him. If Towson did not do something now, he was going to drown. There could be no reprieve for the *Titanic*. She was sinking by the bow, and her decks were already awash. The night was filled with the dying groans of the great ship and the despairing screams and prayers of the passengers left behind.

The *Titanic*'s stern was starting to rise out of the water, with passengers scrambling and clawing their way up the steeply sloping decks. Towson curled his lip. There was no safety to be found by climbing higher. His only hope of safety, and his only hope of seeing the stewardess again, lay in finding a lifeboat.

The *Titanic*'s lights were still blazing, lighting the dark surface of the water and the pale faces of the passengers in the lifeboats, looking back at the disaster they were about to escape. He could see that the crewmen were rowing for their lives now, pulling hard on the oars and fleeing the suction that would surely take the lifeboats down when the ocean opened to swallow the great liner.

Towson wasted no time in envying those who had found a way to leave the stricken ship, and he resisted the temptation to join the panicked men and women clawing their way toward the illusory safety of the stern. The last lifeboat had departed, and now it was every man for himself and no more nonsense about women and children first. He turned to look for something, anything, that would float, and saw a group of men working frantically on the roof of the officers' quarters.

He squinted to bring his eyes into focus and saw that they were manhandling a flimsy canvas craft, the last of the collapsible lifeboats. They were not wasting time rigging it into the davits and instead were maneuvering it onto a makeshift ramp that would slide it down into the icy water that was already rising up to meet it. He released his hold on the railing and allowed himself to slide down the deck and careen into the men who were guiding the boat onto the ramp. His momentum knocked two of them aside, and suddenly the flimsy boat was within reach. He grasped at the ropes slung along the side and heaved in unison with the desperate remnant of men who still believed they could be saved.

They were doing it. They were going to launch. They were going to be saved. The ship gave a great groan. Towson looked up and saw one of the massive funnels breaking loose. It teetered for a moment, held by the remnants of its guy wires, and then it crashed down in a shower of sparks. As it fell and shook the deck plates, a great wave rolled up across the bow, lifting the lifeboat free of the makeshift ramp and sweeping Towson off his feet into water so cold that he was unable to draw a breath.

Icy water closed over his head and carried him down into a maelstrom of kicking legs and grasping arms. His life jacket dragged him to the surface. He cleared water from his eyes. He was still beside the boat. The wave that had washed the flimsy craft from the ramp had turned it over, and now it was an inaccessible wooden hump presenting its keel to the cold light of the uncaring stars. The ropes were still in place along the gunwale. He could still find a handhold. He clung to the rope while the lifeboat, with air trapped beneath its upturned hull, drifted free of the sinking ship.

He could not say how long he clung to the rope in a blind and deaf panic, with all his attention focused on keeping hold of the rope.

Slowly reason began to reassert itself, and he understood that he was not alone. He sensed movement around him and forced his eyes to open. Lights still burned on the dying ship, and he saw that the hungry sea around it churned with the thrashing of hundreds of arms and legs. Starlight showed him half-frozen men crawling onto the upturned hull, to which he clung in paralyzed horror. Desperate survivors were reaching out to grasp the keel and pull themselves upward. They came up out of the water like creatures rising from a swamp, writhing, groaning, and fighting for space.

He turned to look behind. The *Titanic*'s stern was almost upright and crowded with people climbing over each other to reach the highest point and gain just a few more seconds of life before they lost their grip and plunged down into the water.

The upturned boat drifted among the living and the dead, and Towson knew only one thing—he would have to release his death grip on the rope and fight for a place on the upturned hull if he had any hope of living. He forced his fingers to open. For a moment, he thought he would drift, but he kicked out savagely, leveraging himself upward on the shoulders of those beside him and pushing them carelessly down into the water. Slowly, painfully, he began his climb upward, lashing out at anyone who dared to climb beside him. Now was not the time to be timid. If he intended to live, then others would have to die.

At last he was out of the water, shivering and gasping with the effort but able to grasp the protruding keel. A hand clasped his ankle. He kicked out and felt his foot contact something soft. He kicked again and again until the hand released him. Now he was shoulder to shoulder with other like-minded men, who groaned with pain as they tried to keep their precarious handholds.

A whistle blast came from somewhere nearby, and the men around him, who had been cursing as they fought for their right to live, grew suddenly still.

"It's an officer."

"It's Mr. Lightoller."

He could see the officer now, half out of the water and clinging to the bow of the boat with a whistle set between his blue lips.

"What do we do, sir?"

Lightoller spat out the whistle and spoke with surprising energy. "We stop behaving like savages and act with discipline. Anyone who

9

does not intend to obey my orders can leave now."

Towson had little love for the British, and absolutely no love for the officer class, but he maintained his grasp on the keel. As the officer issued orders and the men responded, he began to feel hopeful. The night would be long, but ships were coming. The radio operator was hauled out from beneath the upturned hull, where he had been trapped in the air pocket. He seemed half-dead, but he managed to release words from between his chattering teeth. Ships were responding to his distress call. The *Baltic*, the *Caronia*, the *Olympic*, and the *Carpathia* were lighting up all boilers.

For one brief moment, the shivering men were united in hope, and then, as if a curtain had dropped on a stage, the lights of the *Titanic* flickered out.

Lightoller's voice came firmly out of the darkness. "Let us pray." Towson had no energy to give to prayer; he preferred to think of revenge, and of regaining what was his.

Lifeboat Fourteen
Poppy Melville

Poppy Melville watched the lights flicker one last time as the *Titanic* slid beneath the dark surface of the Atlantic, and then the ship was gone, and with her went any hope of safety. The starlight, cold and merciless, shone down on the people struggling in the water, and their desperate flailing produced a maelstrom of white phosphorescence. The iceberg, the cause of the disaster, was surely some miles away now, drifting majestically on the current with nothing but a scraping of red paint to show what it had accomplished.

In lifeboat number fourteen, Poppy clung tightly to the child who had been placed on her lap. She held the little boy close, keeping his face pressed against her coat. She could prevent the child from looking, but nothing could prevent him from hearing, and the night was far from silent.

The officer in charge of the lifeboat held up a small oil lantern. Its light flickered as his hand shook. Poppy focused on the wavering light and watched as the officer slowly steadied his hand and found his voice.

"You on the oars," he said. "Pull away. Look sharp."

A man's voice came from the darkness behind Poppy. It was the harsh voice of a man accustomed to making demands. "Turn back. Turn back. We'll pick people from the water. We have room."

The officer spoke quietly but with authority. "If you are not quiet, sir, I will be forced to put you over the side. We loaded this boat with women and children. What are you doing here?"

Poppy turned her head to see who had spoken but saw only a huddle of dark shapes: women, children, and presumably at least one man who was not supposed to be there. Although the man fell silent, some of the women took up his cry, insisting that they turn back.

The officer's face was set in an expression of grim determination. "Pull away," he commanded.

The sailors bent their backs to the oars and set the lifeboat in motion. The cries of the people in the water followed them. The boat moved in a hesitant, meandering path as the oars encountered floating obstacles—maybe deck chairs or tables … maybe people. Poppy looked over the side for just a moment and saw what she had no wish to see or ever remember: arms reaching toward them, trying to grab at the oars as they dipped in the water, and mouths opening and closing in weak, plaintive cries.

A woman in the bow turned her head toward the officer, and the lantern light reflected on the tears streaming down her face. "Please," she pleaded. "My husband. He couldn't come with me. That could be him in the water."

The officer shook his head. "If we go back now, we'll be swamped."

"But we have room," the woman insisted. "We have empty seats. We could take at least another twenty or thirty."

"How can we take twenty or thirty when there are thousands in the water?" the officer asked. He turned his face away from her and called to the sailors in a note of desperate command. "Pull away, and don't stop for … don't stop for flotsam."

Poppy's thoughts were beginning to clear from the paralyzing shock that had gripped her. Now she was able to recognize the officer's Welsh voice and remember his name. He was Officer Lowe, and he had ordered her to take charge of the women and children in the lifeboat. He had a gun, and he'd fired it as the lifeboat was being lowered into the water—fired it to keep frantic passengers at bay. Even in the panic of the moment, she had known him to be right.

The men who had tried to leap aboard as the boat inched down the steep sides of the ship would have tipped them all into the water. From the grim expression on his face, she trusted that Officer Lowe still had that gun and he would not hesitate to use it again.

Although she was certain that the shock of seeing the great ship dive beneath the waves would never leave her, Poppy managed to focus her thoughts on the needs of the moment. Where were the other lifeboats? Where was Daisy? Waiting her turn to board, she had watched lifeboats being loaded and sent away from the sinking liner, but had caught no sight of her sister. What she had seen was passengers complaining bitterly, seeing no reason why they should be roused from their beds and trussed into life jackets. The *Titanic* was a floating palace, and she had been designed to be unsinkable. How very wrong they had been. Now these lifeboats were all that was left of the grand ship.

Poppy peered through the darkness. If every lifeboat was equipped with a lantern, surely she should see other lights. Surely this was not the only lifeboat left afloat. She shook her head. No, she would not even entertain that thought. They were not alone. She was not alone. Daisy was out there somewhere.

"Stewardess."

Poppy looked up and caught the officer's eye. "Are you the stewardess assigned to this lifeboat?"

"Yes, sir. Poppy Melville."

"Very well. Come here, please."

The child stirred in Poppy's lap as she made to rise. Beside her a woman reached out and took Poppy's burden.

"Are you really part of the crew?" the woman whispered.

Poppy nodded. "I am."

"Do you know what's going to happen to us?"

Poppy stood up and straightened her shoulders. "We're going to be rescued. The wireless officer sent out messages. Ships are coming for us. It won't be long."

She picked her way between the huddled passengers and past the men at the oars, observing in passing that some were *Titanic* crewmen and some were obviously passengers. Lowe was standing at the stern. His hand, blue with cold, was grasping the ice-coated tiller. The lifeboat rocked precariously as she tried to find a place to settle. At last she sank to her knees beside him and gasped in shock as the icy water, trapped in the bottom of the boat, swirled around her ankles.

In the flickering light of the lantern, Poppy saw the expression of rigid self-control on Lowe's face.

"Listen carefully," he said. "You are a representative of the White Star Line, and I am trusting you to conduct yourself accordingly. You will not panic or become hysterical."

Poppy shivered as the icy water soaked through her coat and skirt and reached her knees. It would be very easy to give way to panic. Safety in the lifeboat was a mere illusion. If the great, unsinkable *Titanic* could disappear beneath the waves, so could this little boat. Behind them the cries of the drowning passengers were beginning to fade, and nothing lay ahead of them except a vast, cold ocean where starlight glinted on drifting ice floes. The sea, for the moment, was eerily calm, but that could change at any time. What would become of them if the wind increased and waves began to build? Despair would be so easy.

Lowe spoke softly, and the Welsh lilt of his voice was strangely comforting. The light of the lantern showed her a very young face, maybe not much older than her own twenty-two years. "I'm not sure if I am the only surviving officer," Lowe said, "but it's possible. So, now that the noise is dying down …" He grimaced and fell silent.

Poppy nodded her head. He had said what needed to be said.

"Now that it is a little quieter," Lowe continued, "we'll need to be listening for another officer's whistle. Boxhall may have made it into a lifeboat. He said he would try. Otherwise, it's just me."

"What about the captain?"

"He knows his duty," Lowe said grimly. "He is not in a lifeboat. Do you know how many stewardesses were saved?"

"All the female crew were assigned seats and sent to their lifeboat stations," Poppy said. "My sister, Daisy, is also a stewardess, and she is in one of the other boats. Where do you think they are? Why can't we see them?"

Lowe put his finger to his lips. "Keep your voice down. You need to stay calm, and you will need to keep the passengers calm. You do not have the luxury of worrying about your sister. I have to steer, and the men have to row. The passengers are your responsibility."

"What can I tell them?" Poppy asked. "Will there be a rescue ship?"

Lowe gave a slight nod of his head. "A number of ships are coming, but the closest is the *Carpathia*. If only we could have stayed afloat until she came, we wouldn't be ..." His voice trailed away. It seemed to Poppy that the young officer was unwilling to put his thoughts into words. He, like everyone else, was stunned by the speed at which the disaster had unfolded.

"There's one other possibility," Lowe said, "but I would not pin my hopes on it. Some people observed a light on the horizon and—"

"Another ship?"

"I don't know what else it could be, unless it was just a star. We told the first lifeboats launched that they should pull for that light." He grimaced. "I suppose they're all spread out now, and I don't know if we can round them up again and keep them in one place until the *Carpathia* comes up."

Poppy silently scanned the ocean. She was not sure if she was looking for the lights of another lifeboat or if she was hoping that a mystery ship lay just beyond the horizon. At last she saw a flickering orange glow. She lifted her arm and pointed. "There. Over there. Is that a lifeboat?"

Lowe joined her in squinting at the pinprick of light. "It's a flickering oil lamp," Lowe said at last. "Yes, that's a lifeboat."

Although her own common sense told her that the presence of another lifeboat added nothing to their safety, Poppy felt elated. At least they were no longer completely alone, and perhaps Daisy was on this boat. She had to be on one of the boats.

She startled as Lowe blew a long blast on his officer's whistle. Almost immediately the blast was returned.

"Well," Lowe said, "at least that's one other officer. We'll go over there and make a plan. Thank you, stewardess. You have been very helpful. Please return to your seat."

"What will you do when we reach them?" Poppy asked. "How long before the *Carpathia* arrives?"

"A long time," Lowe said, "but maybe we can do some good while we wait. Some of those boats were launched with empty seats." He hesitated. "If we ever reach dry land," he said thoughtfully, "I think questions will be asked about that. Meantime, we'll transfer people out of this boat into other boats, and that way we can go back and see who we can pick up."

"You mean you'll pick them up from the water?"

Lowe could not meet her eyes. "The cries are dying out. Those who are left won't have the energy to swamp us. We'll go back."

Poppy focused on the flickering light as the sailors dug their oars into the water, and Lowe stood at the helm, sending frequent short whistle blasts across the dark sea.

Time crept by. Poppy's wet feet became numb. The stars began to fade. She leaned forward as if she could move the boat by force of her own will. Why were the stars fading? Was it the approach of dawn, or were storm clouds building on the horizon, wiping out the starlight and bringing wind and waves? Their position was so precarious. They were so alone, just a handful of small boats sending out puny whistles of distress. She made out three distinct whistles, which meant that three officers had survived, although the whistle blasts came from different directions, and one of the boats seemed to be far away.

The firefly lights of four of the boats grew closer together. The men pulled on the oars, and Lowe shouted instructions. At last they were able to see the little flotilla by lantern light.

"Three lifeboats and one collapsible," Lowe said. "Where the devil are the rest of them?" He scowled as the sailors abruptly stopped rowing. "What's the matter?"

A sailor spoke up, resting on his oar and squinting ferociously. "Something ahead, sir."

"We can't stop for people in the water, not yet. We'll come back."

"Ain't a person, sir. It's a … uh … I think it's a staircase."

Lowe raised the lantern higher, and Poppy saw the dark shape of a large piece of wreckage.

"Go round, go round," Lowe ordered. "Starboard oars."

Poppy peered at the wreckage, frustrated by the fact that the stars that had been so bright now seemed to have dimmed. She agreed with the sailor: the wreckage was part of a wooden staircase. She had watched the funnel fall onto the deck and send up a shower of sparks and wreckage. It could just as easily be a staircase as anything else, but it didn't matter what it was; what mattered was the fact that a man was clinging to the top step.

"There's a survivor," she shouted. "Do you see him? He has a white shirt."

"We'll come back for survivors," Lowe said. "First we'll offload these passengers."

"But we can take him now," Poppy said. "It's just one man, and we can't leave him."

"Stewardess," Lowe said impatiently, "must I remind you that you are —"

The rest of his reminder was drowned out by pleas from the passengers. They seemed united in their determination to save this one man. In that instant, the unknown survivor became for them a tiny beacon of hope. Poppy watched with bated breath as Lowe weighed the wisdom of taking on an additional passenger. The man could be hysterical. He could be drunk. He could upset the precarious balance of their small craft.

Lowe reached a decision. "Ship your oars," he shouted. "We'll drift down on him. If the poor devil can get in here, we'll take him."

The sailors shipped their oars, and as they began to drift down on the wreckage, the passengers edged across their seats, trying to take a better look. The boat listed precariously. Lowe uttered some words Poppy had never heard before. She thought that maybe the Welshman was speaking in his own language, or perhaps these were the swear words of a sailor. It made no difference what they were; they carried the authority to freeze the passengers like statues as the man from the stairs released his grip on his makeshift raft and eased across into the lifeboat, ending up on the seat next to Poppy.

The flickering lantern light showed her a big man dressed in the remains of a white undershirt. He shivered uncontrollably and only lifted his head once to look at Lowe.

"Thanks, mate."

"Can you row?" Lowe asked.

"I can try."

Poppy could see that their newest passenger was in no shape to row, and she was relieved when Lowe dropped the subject and ordered the sailors to continue to their rendezvous with the other lifeboats.

She soon made out the details of the three regular lifeboats and one unusual small craft with canvas sides. Presumably, that was the one Lowe had called a collapsible. Although all the lifeboats seemed precarious, lost on the vast expanse of dark ocean, the collapsible seemed to be no refuge at all, with water washing over its canvas sides. Another lifeboat, only half-full of passengers, had come alongside it, and an attempt was being made to transfer the soaked survivors from the canvas boat into the stable wooden lifeboat.

The sailors in Poppy's boat shipped their oars, and hands reached out eagerly to pull the boats together, threatening everyone's safety as the boats rocked and water washed over the gunwales. The blasts of Lowe's whistle were drowned by a chorus of questions and wails.

"Who do you have?"

"Is my husband on board?"

"Have you seen my children?"

Poppy uttered only one name as she caught sight of a curly-headed figure in among the passengers.

"Daisy?"

Poppy's sister looked up and grinned her usual careless, unthinking grin. All around her, women were learning the dreadful truth that they were now widows, but Daisy was smiling and waving. Although her whole being was flooded with relief, Poppy could not return the smile. How, in the midst of all that had happened, could Daisy be so unaware of the grief that surrounded her?

Lowe blew a commanding blast on his whistle and cut through the chatter. "Listen," he said. "On my command, we're going to move passengers from this boat into the other lifeboats, and then I will take this boat out among the people in the water to see who can be saved. It will be quiet now ... only the strong ... only the lucky ... only by the grace of God ..." His voice faded. He had no need to explain. There was no danger that the lifeboat would be swamped. Very few people would be in any condition to even cry for help.

With Lowe issuing commands, passengers were moved from one boat to another. When he ordered Poppy into lifeboat ten, she found herself unable to move. The fear that she had been holding at bay suddenly overwhelmed her, and she could not bring herself to even stand.

Lowe's voice cracked like a whip. "Do as you are ordered, stewardess."

The shivering survivor they had plucked from the staircase came to Poppy's aid. "Stow it, mate," he shouted. "She's going." His face was suddenly next to hers, his breath faintly warm on her cheek.

"You can do it," he said. "One last push, eh?"

She steadied herself against his shoulder and shuffled toward the extended hands of the sailors in lifeboat ten. In one heart-stopping step, she bridged the gap above the hungry ocean, and then she was seated beside her sister.

"Well," Daisy said, "that was exciting."

"Exciting?" Poppy queried, her anxiety giving way to anger. "That's not the word I'd use."

"May I borrow your coat?" Daisy asked. "I'm afraid I'm very wet. I've been in the water."

Poppy's questions died before they could be asked as a cry rose from Lowe, standing in the stern of lifeboat fourteen.

"Rockets," he shouted.

Poppy lifted her head and saw green lights streaking up from beyond the horizon.

"It's the *Carpathia*," Lowe said. "We're all saved."

CHAPTER TWO

Pier 54, New York Harbor
Poppy Melville

The *Carpathia*'s horn blasted out the news of her arrival in New York. Belowdecks, out of sight of the watchers on the shore, the *Titanic*'s surviving passengers prepared to disembark. The ship's corridors bustled with activity and last-minute tears and goodbyes.

Poppy ushered Madeleine Astor, the last of her charges, into the Grand Salon. Her work was complete, and soon she would be able to take off the starched white apron that marked her as a stewardess.

Mrs. Astor, pale and waiflike, kissed Poppy's cheek. "Thank you, Poppy. You have been such a comfort."

Poppy wanted to hug the young widow. Mrs. Astor was just eighteen years old and visibly pregnant. When she boarded the ship in Southampton, she had been returning from an extended honeymoon with her husband, one of the wealthiest men in America, and now she was a widow. Poppy had been watching when Mrs. Astor was lifted from lifeboat number four to the deck of the *Carpathia*. She had been the one who held Mrs. Astor's hand as she had finally faced the certainty that her husband, John Astor, had not been rescued. All the money in the world could not insulate her from the shock of her sudden widowhood.

"He asked to come in the lifeboat with me," she said tearfully, "on account of my delicate condition, but it was not allowed. Women and children only, they said. He told me he would be all right. He said he would see me in the morning."

Mrs. Astor's maid came forward to take her arm and lead her

away, but Mrs. Astor was not easily distracted.

"I wonder what they did," she whispered, "after all the boats had departed and they knew there would be no rescue. How did he pass those last few minutes? Did he go to the bar and wait with the other gentlemen?" She gave a small, ironic smile. "The richest men in America, all waiting to drown."

"I'm sure he was thinking of you," Poppy said, "and the baby. He must have been glad to know that you were safe."

"Safe?" Mrs. Astor queried. "Thank heaven he didn't know the truth. We weren't safe, were we? Twenty little lifeboats, all alone."

The maid was now pulling on Mrs. Astor's sleeve. "You mustn't upset yourself, Mrs. Astor. Remember your condition."

"I'm well aware of my condition," Mrs. Astor said impatiently. "If it were not for this baby, I would have stayed with John. They say Mrs. Straus stayed with her husband."

Poppy nodded. "Yes, that's what I heard."

Mrs. Astor continued to resist her maid's urging. She wiped away her tears and stared into Poppy's face. It seemed to Poppy that this was the first time the young widow was seeing her as a person and not as a servant.

"What will you do now?" she asked. "Will you take work on another White Star ship?"

Poppy shook her head. "No. I don't think I want to go to sea on any ship, ever again."

Mrs. Astor smiled bleakly. "I understand."

"My sister and I were working our passage on the *Titanic*," Poppy said. "Now we're going to take our wages and go to California."

Mrs. Astor patted Poppy's arm. "I wish you luck."

"And you too," Poppy said, "with the baby and ..."

Tears formed again in Mrs. Astor's eyes. "He'll never know his father."

"I'm sorry."

Mrs. Astor swiped her hand across her eyes, and the tears gave way to a simmering anger. "Someone is going to be sorry," she said, turning away and allowing her maid to lead her into the Grand Salon.

Poppy breathed a sigh of relief and went in search of her sister. She was surprised to find Daisy sitting on an unmade bed in one of the abandoned second-class cabins, with tears glistening in her startling blue eyes. Daisy rarely cried alone. Daisy's tears were usually a weapon she deployed to get her own way.

Poppy sat down beside her. "It's all right, Daisy. We're safe now. Don't cry. It's all over."

Daisy shook her chestnut curls, and her bottom lip quivered. "I wanted to see the Statue of Liberty," she complained, "but I was stuck belowdecks, looking after Miss Walsh's second-class passengers. It was Miss Stap's way of punishing me. I missed everything, and it's not fair."

Poppy sighed impatiently. There was no love lost between Sarah Stap, the *Titanic*'s senior stewardess, and selfish, scatterbrained Daisy. Poppy loved her sister, but she was under no illusions about her. Daisy was the center of her own universe. Even now she was actually complaining about not seeing the Statue of Liberty when she should be thanking heaven that she had not been trapped on the *Titanic* as it slid beneath the waves.

"You should be glad you're alive and well and able to sit there and complain," Poppy snapped. "Miss Walsh was not so fortunate, and that's why you have her passengers."

"We were all supposed to have seats in the lifeboats," Daisy said sullenly. "I don't know why she stayed on board."

"Perhaps she was helping someone," Poppy said, "and left it too late. It was hard to persuade some of the passengers to put on their life jackets and go up to the boat deck."

"I know," said Daisy vehemently. "Miss Bonelli gave me so much trouble that in the end I just left her to work it out for herself."

"Daisy!"

"She survived. I caught a glimpse of her being hauled up onto the *Carpathia* like a sack of coal, screaming all the time that she was going to drown."

Poppy shook her head. "Really, Daisy, don't be so unkind. We all thought we were safe when we saw the *Carpathia* coming towards us, but no one told us how hard it would be to get on board."

"You climbed the ladder," Daisy said. "I watched you."

"I'm young and healthy," Poppy said, "but I was terrified. It was a long climb, and my hands were numb with cold, and I couldn't even feel my feet. I'm not surprised that they had to haul some of the other people aboard with ropes and nets. Do you think Miss Bonelli will report you for not helping her with her life jacket?"

Daisy shrugged. "I don't care what she says. We're in New York now, and we're never going to be stewardesses again, so it doesn't matter if she complains." She gave Poppy an imploring smile. "Come on, Poppy. Let's go up on deck. I want to see New York."

Poppy caught hold of her sister's arm as Daisy attempted to rise. "Just a few more minutes, and it will all be over," she said. "Be patient, please. Don't draw attention to yourself. We've been lucky so far, and—"

"Lucky?" Daisy interrupted. "We nearly drowned. Do you call that luck? We set sail on an unsinkable ship, and it sank. I wouldn't call that being lucky."

"But we were saved," Poppy said, fighting to physically restrain her and ignoring Daisy's gasp of pain as Poppy's fingers tightened their grasp. "Stop it, Daisy," she said through gritted teeth. "Don't spoil it now by doing something silly. If we can be good employees for just a little while longer, White Star will pay us our wages, and we'll be able to go ashore. After that we can do everything we've dreamed of."

"I don't care about the wages. I just want to get away from those cranky old ladies and weeping widows," Daisy said.

Poppy looked into her sister's sullen, pouting face. "I know you don't mean that," she said. "Try to have some sympathy, Daisy. You'd be weeping if you'd had to get into a lifeboat and leave your husband behind to drown."

Daisy would not look her in the eye. She looked down at the floor. "I know you think I'm being awful, and I'm sorry. It's just that it's been so horrible, and I want it to be over. This was supposed to be our big adventure, and now everyone is so sad. I just can't stand it. All I want is to get off this dreadful ship."

Poppy stood up. "This ship saved our lives," she said. The *Carpathia* was not as large or as opulent as the *Titanic*, but she had brought the pitiful survivors of the *Titanic* safely into harbor. In Poppy's eyes, the *Carpathia*, small, shabby, and overcrowded, was the greatest ship ever to have sailed. She knew she would never forget the moment when the Cunard liner had first appeared on the horizon, bringing a ray of hope along with the first light of dawn.

Daisy spoke in a small, choked voice. "I thought we would all die," she said. "I was so relieved to see you. I didn't know what lifeboat you were in or if you'd been saved. I thought I was going to be all on my own."

Poppy shook her head, resisting the urge to give in to Daisy's threatened tears. Their time on the *Carpathia* had been filled with extra duties, and there had been no time to talk, but she was worried about Daisy, worried about what Daisy may have been doing as the ship had been sinking.

"I was in my assigned lifeboat," Poppy said, "but you were not. What happened?"

Tears spilled from Daisy's eyes as she stretched out her arms like a child seeking comfort. "I don't want to talk about it."

"You had a lifeboat assignment," Poppy insisted. "What happened? How did you get so wet?

"It was horrible," Daisy said with tears flowing freely down her cheeks. "I was in a good boat, but the officer said there wasn't room for me and as I was crew I would have to get out and take a seat in one of those awful little collapsible boats. I don't know how it stayed afloat. Water was coming over the sides and I was sure it would sink."

Daisy gave a long, sobbing moan and threw herself from the bunk onto the floor. "I thought I was going to drown," she wailed.

Poppy raised her eyes to heaven, but as usual, heaven did not give her the strength to resist her sister's tears. Before she could stop herself, she, too, was sitting on the floor and holding Daisy close, not even caring that Daisy's tears were staining her apron. As soon as they were ashore, she would take the apron off and throw it into the harbor. She would never wear an apron or a uniform ever again.

Daisy was sobbing loudly now, and Poppy buried her face in her little sister's hair and allowed her own tears to flow. At long last they were in New York. Their dreadful voyage was over, and she could finally abandon the courage that she had been holding on to for the past three days.

For a brief moment, she indulged in the fantasy that her father would be proud of the way she had behaved as the great, unsinkable *Titanic* slid beneath the waves. She had shown as much courage as any son would have shown. Of course, if she had been the son her father had always wished for, she would not have had a place in a lifeboat. If she had been a deckhand of the *Titanic* instead of a stewardess, she would probably have been thrown into the sea to fend for herself instead of being ushered into a lifeboat. There was something to be said for being a woman, even though her father could not appreciate it.

She took a deep breath and gulped back her tears. It was over now. Fifteen hundred people had died, but Daisy was alive, and so was she. Their father would never know that she, his disappointing oldest daughter, had behaved with courage. He didn't even know that Daisy and Poppy were aboard the *Titanic*. They had used only abbreviated names when they signed on as stewardesses, and they had no intention of telling him that they were now in New York. They had no intention of telling him anything ever again.

Ten days had passed since the sisters had stood on the dock in Southampton, waiting to board the *Titanic* along with the rest of the crew. The following day, when their father may possibly have wondered why they had not returned home to Riddlesdown Court, they had been hard at work as stewardesses. As the *Titanic* had sailed majestically out into the Solent with the band playing and the people onshore waving and wishing the ship bon voyage, Poppy and Daisy were already belowdecks, unpacking luggage for first-class ladies.

Poppy wondered if her father had noticed even now that she and Daisy had not returned from London. If he had noticed, would he bother to look for them? She released her hold on Daisy and wiped her eyes with her sleeve. She knew the answer to her question. Her father wouldn't look. He didn't care.

As she pulled Daisy to her feet, an officer in the *Carpathia*'s Cunard uniform appeared in the doorway. "*Titanic* crew?" he asked.

Poppy nodded wordlessly. The officer reached into his breast pocket and produced a clean white handkerchief. "Dry your eyes."

Poppy took the handkerchief. "I'm sorry, sir." Despite the extreme brevity of her service on board the *Titanic*, she had absorbed the fact that officers were to be addressed as "sir." Why attract attention now by breaking the rules?

The officer shook his head. "Don't apologize. I don't blame you at all for crying. I've watched you ladies at work, and I thoroughly admire the way you've managed to hold yourselves together and care for your passengers. Well, it's over now, so I suggest you take off your aprons and go on up to the stern deck and join the rest of your crew. The *Carpathia*'s crew will disembark the passengers. No need for you to concern yourselves with that."

"Are you sure?" Poppy asked, still wiping her eyes on the

officer's handkerchief.

"Of course he's sure," Daisy said, her tears already forgotten. As she smiled up at the officer, the blue of her eyes seemed to grow in intensity until they were as bright as cornflowers. Poppy also had blue eyes, but she knew they were no match for Daisy's, and she was certain that they were now red with weeping.

Daisy was already untying her apron. "If anyone comes looking, don't tell them where you found us," she said.

The officer smiled. Poppy was not surprised. Daisy had that effect on men. "I won't say a word. Off you go." He stepped out of the cabin and gestured to a door set halfway along the corridor. "Open that service door and take the stairs up. Should bring you out at the right place." He sketched a small salute and departed.

Daisy took off her apron and flung it on the floor. Poppy picked it up.

"Oh, come on," Daisy said. "We don't need them."

"We should wait until Miss Stap or someone else tells us to take them off."

"Don't be silly," Daisy said. "We've arrived. We're in port. We completed the voyage, so now we're not working." She spun around in a circle. "We're free."

"Free but without any money," Poppy said. "We still have to be paid."

"Not really."

"What do you mean?"

Daisy arched her eyebrows. "You'll see," she said.

Poppy shook her head. "I don't know what you mean, but whatever it is, I still think we should go up with the rest of the crew and collect our wages."

Daisy grinned. "Father would be so surprised if he knew that his useless daughters had actually earned money." She squeezed Poppy's arm. "Next stop, California. Once we're there, our problems will be over. I have the name of a film producer. We'll get starring roles."

Poppy looked at her sister. She had never seen her so alight with energy. For a moment, she gave in to the fear that the energy was unnatural and unhealthy. Although she alone among the stewardesses had somehow managed to end up soaked to the skin and had spent the night in wet clothes, the effect had been to brighten her cheeks and her eyes and fill her with feverish brilliance. She appeared to be perched on the tipping point between tears and laughter, and now she seemed to hint at some secret that she was not ready to share.

"You may get a starring role," Poppy said, "but I won't."

Daisy gave her sister a slight shake. "Of course you will. You just need some makeup and a different hairstyle."

Poppy smiled. "I know what I look like," she said. "I'm too tall, and my hair is awful. You're the star, Daisy. I'll be your manager."

They were met by a gust of wind and rain as they opened the door at the top of the stairs and stepped out onto the stern deck of the *Carpathia*. Although the night sky was dark with rain and racing clouds, the *Carpathia* was bathed in light, not only from her own deck lights and the dock lights but also from what seemed like the flashes of thousands of cameras. For a moment, even Daisy was overwhelmed, standing still and staring at the crowd massed along the shoreline.

"Are all these people here because of us?" Daisy asked.

Poppy stared at the mass of men and women. "I suppose they want to see for themselves," she said. She shuddered in revulsion. "They're ghouls."

"Some of them are reporters," Daisy said. "Look at all the camera flashes. They're taking pictures." She patted a stray lock of hair. "Do you think we'll have our pictures in the newspapers?"

"Let's hope not," Poppy said. "We don't want to be recognized."

"We won't be," Daisy said. "I'm quite sure that he drowned."

Poppy frowned at the look of alarm on Daisy's face. Sometimes Daisy's mouth ran ahead of her thoughts. She had obviously said something she did not mean to say.

"What do you mean?"

"Nothing," Daisy said dismissively. "I just mean that we may not be recognized as who we really are now, but one day we'll be film stars, and everyone will recognize us."

A woman in a heavy coat and sensible hat separated herself from the group of *Titanic* stewardesses standing along the *Carpathia*'s rail. Poppy recognized her at once. Sarah Stap, the senior stewardess, had been particularly hard on Daisy in the days before the sinking. She had declared Daisy to be lazy, flighty, and absolutely unsuited to the work of a first-class stewardess. Her attitude had not changed in the three days since the disaster, when survivors had been crowded on board the *Carpathia*. It was Miss Stap who had kept Daisy busy belowdecks as they had approached New York, instead of allowing her topside to see the Statue of Liberty.

"Where have you been?" Miss Stap asked, ignoring Poppy and concentrating on Daisy.

"I've been doing what you told me," Daisy snapped. "I've been playing nursemaid to the second-class passengers, but I'm finished now. I'm ready to go ashore."

"Miss Sloane has coats and hats for you and your sister," Miss Stap said, turning away from Daisy and concentrating on Poppy. "They've been brought aboard by a White Star representative. I hope you are suitably grateful."

"I hope the White Star Line is suitably grateful for all my hard work," Daisy interrupted. She flicked a disdainful finger at the offer of a hat and coat. "I will not wear that ugly hat."

Poppy took the hat and coat from Miss Sloane and handed them to Daisy. "Put them on," she hissed. "Don't spoil everything now."

Daisy looked at Poppy in surprise.

"I mean it," Poppy snapped. "Put on the coat and hat. You look flushed like you have a fever. Do you want to get sick now and have to go to hospital?"

Daisy shrugged into the coat, studied the hat for a moment, and set it on her head at a rakish angle. Poppy was not sure how Daisy had accomplished this miracle, but somehow she managed to make the hat seem attractive, even fashionable.

"Right," Daisy said. "Now can we go ashore? Where do we collect our wages?"

Miss Stap pursed her lips, her expression becoming malevolent. "You're new to this," she said. "You don't understand. Having failed to complete the voyage, I'm afraid you will not be collecting very much in the way of wages."

Poppy's heart sank. They would need every penny they could get for a train ticket to California, and now Miss Stap was suggesting they would not be paid in full. She knew better than to adopt Daisy's confrontational tone. Their old nanny's voice echoed in her head. *You catch more flies with honey than you do with vinegar.*

"What do you mean?" she asked. "Surely we've completed the voyage. We're in New York."

"But we're not on the *Titanic*," Miss Stap said. She looked at

Poppy for a moment and finally nodded her head in grudging approval. "I have observed that you are a sensible young woman, unlike your sister, so let me explain. We are subject to merchant marine law. Our pay stops when the ship stops. Our ship stopped three days ago."

"It didn't stop," Poppy said disbelievingly. "It sank. It's not the same thing."

"Well," said Miss Stap, "we shall see what happens. Perhaps the company will be generous. I am only telling you the letter of the law. The crew knows what to expect." She lifted her head and indicated the men who were huddled along the rail, their weary faces illuminated by the shore lights.

Poppy's work with the *Titanic*'s passengers had kept her separated from the *Titanic*'s surviving crew members, who were deckhands, firemen, cooks, and stewards. Some of them had rowed the lifeboats, but most of them had survived initially by clinging to the few floating remains of the *Titanic*'s deck chairs or by swimming through the icy water to any lifeboat that would pick them up. Once aboard the *Carpathia*, they had been set to work, and only those that were injured or frostbitten had been allowed to rest.

A big blond-haired man with a slash of scar across his cheek and bandaged hands stepped forward. "Fair dinkum," he said. "They owe us."

Poppy recognized the Australian by his voice. He was the man from the staircase, the one who had given her the courage to move between lifeboats. She had not seen his face before and had not known about the disfiguring scar.

"It's not as though we jumped ship," he said. "I'd say the ship jumped us."

The crewmen murmured their agreement. They were moving away from the rail now, drawn like moths to a flame to the small group of stewardesses. Normally, they would not be permitted to talk to the female staff, but today was different. The voyage, such as it was, was over. Poppy watched as her sister preened under their interested gaze. Her actions were instinctive. She meant nothing by them. Upwards of a hundred men were assembled on the stern deck. Daisy was only doing what Daisy always did.

The big man nodded his head to Poppy. She was not sure if he recognized her. They had both been cold, wet, and disheveled, and there had been no introductions. "Ernie Sullivan, fireman," he said, "and Miss Stap's telling you the truth."

"I'm not so sure about that," said another man, pushing his way forward. Poppy knew this man, Alfred Crawford, one of the first-class stewards. Their paths had often crossed as they went about their tasks of keeping the first-class passengers happy.

"We've lost our personal possessions," Crawford said. He nodded his head to Sullivan. "I don't know about firemen, but we who are in cabin service have accumulated valuable possessions, watches and chains, good-quality silver hairbrushes. I have always attempted to equip myself like a gentleman. We should be compensated for our losses." He gestured toward another crew member. "I'm sure that Mr. Brown agrees with me."

Poppy recognized the white-haired man who was nodding his head in vigorous agreement. He, too, had been one of the first-class stewards. "I had a very good set of boar-bristle clothes brushes," he said.

Poppy smiled to herself. Both of the cabin stewards were now speaking with affected accents that echoed the voices of the gentlemen they served in first class.

"Oh, come on, mate," Sullivan said. "They're not going to give us special treatment, because that would mean admitting liability. What do you think would happen if they had to pay compensation for every bit of fancy stuff that went to the bottom?"

Poppy looked at him in surprise. As a fireman, he held one of the lowliest positions on the ship, spending his days shoveling coal into the massive furnaces, and yet he seemed to speak with authority.

"I've been told that the purser didn't open the safe and allow the passengers to retrieve their valuables," he said. "So now the safe is on the bottom, and it's filled with things that are worth a whole lot more than your silver hairbrushes, Mr. Crawford."

Daisy suddenly squeezed Poppy's arm. Poppy looked down, and Daisy winked.

"What?" Poppy asked.

Daisy lifted her head, and her eyes sparkled. "Nothing," she said airily. "I'm keeping it as a surprise, and I'm not going to tell you until we go ashore. Just take it from me that we don't have to worry about money."

Poppy was aware that Sullivan was still standing beside her, but as was the case with all men, he was not looking at her; he was looking at Daisy. Daisy returned his gaze with a fluttering of her eyelashes.

"I saw you," Sullivan said in a low voice.

Daisy frowned. "What do you mean?"

"You know what I mean."

Before Daisy could say another word, Sullivan abruptly looked away and fixed his eyes on two figures who had now appeared in the doorway. "Officer on deck," he shouted.

The ragtag crew shuffled themselves into a semblance of order as two men, an officer and a civilian, emerged from the shelter of the doorway and were buffeted by a gust of wind.

"Not one of ours," Sullivan remarked. "That's a Cunard man. What's happened to our officers?"

"Drowned," said Crawford lugubriously.

"They're not all drowned," Sullivan amended. "I know Mr. Lightoller's on board, and he's the most senior officer. Why hasn't he come up here to talk to us?"

The Cunard officer, who seemed extremely young, held up his hand for silence before ostentatiously unfolding a sheet of paper. "I have here a list," he said, "of *Titanic* crew members who are to report to the starboard-side promenade deck for disembarking. Bring your papers and possessions, and be quick about it."

A mustachioed man in a salt-stained sweater spoke up from the back of the crowd. "Papers and possessions," he scoffed. "We don't have any papers or possessions. We have nothing but the clothes we stand up in. Speaking on behalf of my entire team, I believe that we are owed an explanation. What is this list you're reading? Why are you separating us?"

The officer looked momentarily taken aback. "Who are you?" he asked. "What do you mean by 'team'?"

The crewman's mustache quivered indignantly as he squared his shoulders and puffed out his chest. "I am Charles Joughin, chief baker, and I demand to speak to a representative of the British Seafarers' Union." He waved a hand to indicate the assembled crew. "The passengers are not the only people who suffered from shock and injuries, but they were the only ones who were allowed to rest. We have all been working full shifts on the *Carpathia*. Cunard should pay our wages."

The officer shook his head. "I am not in a position to answer you," he said, "but I will put your request to the appropriate authority."

Joughin looked toward the civilian. "What about him? Who does he represent?" He gave the civilian a challenging glare. "Are you from the union?"

Sullivan stretched out a long arm and took hold of Joughin's elbow. "Give it a rest, mate. You won't find a union representative here. Wait till you get back to England."

The officer raised his voice to be heard above the murmurs of disapproval from the crew. "Order, order. Let's have some order here." His voice cracked and turned to a youthful squeak as he eyed the crew and saw the way they were shuffling their feet and moving toward him.

Poppy watched without surprise. As she had moved around the *Carpathia* over the past three days, she had caught sight of the surviving *Titanic* crewmen and had seen the shock and weariness in their faces. It was one thing for the surviving officers to take their turn standing watch, but it was another thing to ask the firemen to go down into the bowels of the *Carpathia* and resume the backbreaking task of feeding the boilers.

The officer flapped the piece of paper. "I'm going to read this list," he declared. "As for possessions, the Salvation Army has collected clothing for you. Those of you who are going ashore will be given clothing and a place to sleep."

Sullivan's voice cut through the continued groundswell of complaints. "What do you mean? Aren't we all going ashore? What if our names aren't on your little list?"

The officer looked at Sullivan, no doubt noticing the man's broad shoulders and scarred cheek, and returned to the comparative safety of the sheet of paper—his token of authority. "The crewmen named on this list," he said, "are to follow me, and the rest of you will wait here."

Daisy tugged on Poppy's arm. "What's going on? Why can't we all just go ashore and be free?"

Poppy looked across at the dock and the ever-growing crowd lining the shore. "Perhaps they're trying to avoid trouble. We haven't seen the newspapers, and we don't know anything. Maybe someone is trying to blame the crew, and it will be safer for us to wait until the crowd disperses."

"Blame the crew," Daisy repeated. "Why would anyone blame the crew? None of us were steering the ship. Do you know something you're not telling me?"

Poppy thought of the many conversations she had overheard as she moved among the passengers in the crowded salons and corridors of the *Carpathia*. Questions were being asked. Passengers were telling and retelling the story of the sinking, and slowly but surely the wealthier survivors had begun to congregate in groups. She was certain that their recollections were now turning into complaints. Once the shock wore off, the wealthy widows would no doubt be hiring lawyers. She remembered Mrs. Astor's parting words: *Someone is going to be sorry.*

"Someone will have to take the blame," Poppy said.

"But not us," Daisy whispered. "We didn't do anything."

"Perhaps it was wrong for us to be in the lifeboats," Poppy suggested. "Perhaps we took the places of some rich people who should have been saved."

"We were told to take those seats," Daisy reminded her.

Poppy nodded. "Yes, we were, but they've had time to think about it since then, and perhaps saving us was a mistake."

Daisy stamped her foot, something she had done so frequently during her childhood that even now she was an adult, she just couldn't stop herself. "It is not a mistake for us to be alive," she insisted.

The officer looked up, ready to discipline the crew member who was disturbing his reading. When his glance fell on Daisy, he smiled and shook his head. "There are no women on my list," he said.

"Well, that's all right, then," Daisy whispered.

"Get on with it," Sullivan said. "We're listening."

The officer called out names. "Andrews, Bright, Clench, Collins, Crawford ..."

Poppy watched as the crew members shuffled forward. Crawford's face was creased with anxiety.

The officer completed reading his alphabetical list and folded the paper.

"Wait a minute," Joughin called out. "You take Collins, who is nothing but an assistant cook, and you don't take me? I am the chief baker."

The officer shook his head. "Those are the names I've been given. Perhaps you should be glad you are not included."

Poppy saw an expression of anguish take up residence on Crawford's face. "Why me and not Brown?" he asked.

The officer indicated the civilian who had been standing silent the whole time. "I can only tell you what names are on my list, and that is all I know. This is Mr. Williams, who is here as a representative of your employers, the White Star Line. He will tell you of the arrangements that have been made for the rest of you to return to England. If your name has been called, form a line and follow me."

As a handful of crew members shuffled into line behind the officer, one of the men who had been singled out took a decisive step forward and looked the officer in the eye. "What's going on? Are you saying that if we follow you, we ain't going home?"

The officer took a step back. It was obvious that he was uncertain of his authority over these men. He was a Cunard officer, and these were White Star men. It was possible that he also had some sympathy for them. They were a ragged bunch, bandaged, burned, and frostbitten, with haunted, bloodshot eyes.

The civilian stepped forward. He was a big man with a booming American voice. "That's enough," he said. "Do as you're told."

Poppy was surprised to see Ernie Sullivan position himself to confront him. The two men were equal in height and bulk, and Sullivan looked the American in the eye. "What's going on?" he asked.

"Was your name called?" Williams asked.

"No."

"Then you've nothing to worry about."

Sullivan took a step closer. "Why would any of us have anything to worry about?" he asked.

Williams stood his ground. "Some of you will have a great deal to worry about," he said, "so I suggest you listen carefully and do what you're told. The United States Senate has convened an inquiry into the circumstances of the loss of your ship. Some of you have been identified as persons who will be able to give meaningful testimony as to what occurred."

Sullivan turned his head to look at the assembled crew. "Why talk to us?" he asked. "Talk to our officers. They're the ones who hit the bloody iceberg."

"Your officers are under subpoena," Williams said, "but that's not the end of it. They'll want to know about the lifeboats."

"We'd all like to know about the lifeboats," Sullivan countered.

Williams placed the flat of his hand against Sullivan's chest. "Step back," he said.

Sullivan rocked forward on his toes, seemed to think better of it, and took a step backward. "So what happens to the rest of us," he asked, "the ones who have not been called? When do we go ashore?"

"You don't," said Williams. "A harbor tender is waiting at the starboard boat deck. You'll be taken directly to the SS *Lapland*, and you'll set sail for England immediately. You will not set foot onshore."

Daisy's voice rose in a howl of complaint. "No, you can't do that. You can't make us go back." She tugged at Poppy's arm. "Tell him, Poppy. Tell him we're going to California." She pushed Poppy forward. "Tell him."

Poppy shook her head. "Stop it, Daisy. It won't do any good. We'll just have to make the best of it."

Daisy pushed Poppy aside and rushed toward the port railing. "I'll jump," she threatened. "If they don't let me go ashore, I'll jump into the harbor. I'm not going back to England."

The wind tugged at her hat and blew open her coat as she stepped up onto the lower railing. She turned to Poppy. "Come on. We can do it. They can't stop us."

Ernie Sullivan

Sullivan kept one eye on the shore and on eye on the girl clinging to the railing. He understood her disappointment, but it was nothing compared to his own frustration. Signing on as a fireman had been an act of desperation. As he sweated and shoveled in the living hell of the boiler room, he had told himself it was all worth it because this was the only way he could follow his quarry to New York. He had been down below in the scalding engine room, and the rich old woman he was following had been up above, but they were on the same ship, and she would not escape him. He was at the end of his family's long journey, and he was approaching a confrontation that had been three generations in the making. The boiler room had not killed him, and the Atlantic had not drowned him. He could not stop now.

The stewardess had twisted around and was seated on the top railing. She had her back to the water, and although she was still declaring that she was going to jump, she seemed to be seated quite securely. He wondered if he was the cause of her dramatic shenanigans. Perhaps he should not have said that he had seen what she was doing as the *Titanic* was sinking. He dismissed that thought immediately. None of this was his fault. He had seen her effect on his fellow crew members, and he knew her type. All she wanted was attention. Perhaps she thought her threats would make the White Star representative change his mind and allow her to go ashore. Whatever her reason, she was supplying the diversion he needed. He was quite certain she wouldn't jump and equally certain that he would.

He glanced over the rail at the long drop into the choppy waters of the harbor and the small boats buzzing back and forth. The crowd on the shore had their eyes on the starboard side of the ship, where the gangway had carried the *Carpathia*'s regular passengers ashore. The *Titanic* survivors would be next.

Sullivan shivered at the thought of the long fall into cold water and determinedly suppressed the memory that threatened to disable him. He could not think of the paralyzing cold of the North Atlantic or his desperate attempts to make his muscles obey him and propel him to the surface. Against all odds, he had found a refuge among the flotsam of the *Titanic*, and he was still here, still alive. He knew himself to be a strong swimmer, and if he intended to avoid a return trip to England, he would need all this strength. He would be diving into a river, and there would be a current to contend with. What about the tide? Was it running fast enough to sweep him out to sea? Or perhaps that didn't matter. Perhaps he wouldn't last long enough to find out. He could be run down by any of the agitated helmsmen whose boats buzzed like wasps around the *Carpathia*.

He checked again. The girl was still sitting on the railing. One of the stewardesses was pleading with her to come down. The Cunard man was sidling toward her. No doubt he would snatch her from the rail, and no doubt the White Star Line would never employ that girl ever again.

He removed his coat, but he kept his shoes. They would weigh him down, but he would need them to scramble out of the water. He checked the pouch he kept next to his skin. So far it had proved to be waterproof. The documents inside were still safe. He moved away from the crew and the girl, who seemed to be really enjoying being the focus of attention. He climbed the rail and took a moment to look down into the water, checking for obvious obstructions. This was not the time for a fancy dive. He dropped, feet first.

He hit hard and went under. His ears echoed with the sound of a thousand people screaming. *No, don't listen. Put that behind you.* He pulled himself together and kicked upward. His head broke the surface, and he oriented himself toward the shore. A strong current tugged at him. He allowed himself to be carried downstream. He would not strike out for the shore until he was clear of the flashing cameras and the dock lights.

From the corner of his eye, he saw the beam of a searchlight sweeping across the water. Surely no one had seen him jump. He ducked below the surface and swam a few strokes underwater. When he surfaced, he could see that the light had not followed him. It was focused on something a hundred yards away. As he struck out toward the shore, another beam of light pierced the darkness and landed squarely on him. He was pinned for a moment. He trod water as he drew several deep breaths. He would have to stay under for longer this time. He would stay under until he had no breath left. Surely then he would be clear.

The light moved, bouncing on the choppy wavelets as if it were painting a path for him to follow. He wiped water from his eyes and kicked strongly to lift his torso from the water and saw a struggling figure caught in the beam of another searchlight. He knew at once that it was the stewardess. Had she really jumped, or had she misjudged one of her threatening moves? If she'd fallen backward from the rail, she would have hit the water hard. She had been wearing a heavy coat and, like many other women, long skirts and petticoats. Her layers of clothing would be dragging her down. Even if she could swim, she couldn't swim in those clothes. He felt the tug of the current. He could resist it, but surely she could not.

He felt his opportunity slipping away. His family had waited so long for the confrontation he had planned. For as long as he could remember, his grandfather had told him that this was to be his mission in life. He would be the one to claim justice for all that had happened.

I'm sorry, Granddad! Justice will have to be postponed.

The searchlight stayed on him as he struck out across the current, swimming strongly toward the girl struggling in the water.

Alvin Towson

A paralyzing fear of what awaited him kept Towson from leaving the *Carpathia*. He stood to one side as the sad procession of *Titanic* survivors filed past him and made their way down the gangplank and onto the dock. Some of the women still wore their fur coats; some wore only borrowed clothing; some walked; some limped; and some had to be carried. As each emerged, they were greeted with camera flashes and a mixture of semihysterical cheering and weeping from the great crowd that had assembled to meet them.

"That's Mrs. Astor, poor woman."

"I think that's Mrs. Ryerson, and that's her son, poor boy."

An Irishwoman was met with weeping and open arms. A gentleman was welcomed by a bevy of servants. A child, alone and trembling, was handed over to the Salvation Army.

"Are you ready to go ashore, sir?"

Towson turned to look at the *Carpathia*'s assistant purser, who was indicating the gangplank with a firmly pointing hand.

"I don't have my papers."

"No one does, sir, but don't worry. You'll be accommodated. The names of survivors have been published in the newspapers. I don't doubt someone will be waiting to meet you, and if not, the Salvation Army can be of assistance."

Towson closed his eyes as if ignoring the assistant purser would somehow make him go away. It was hopeless, of course. He would have to go ashore and face the music. His name had been in the newspapers, and anyone looking for Alvin Towson would know where to find him.

The lights of New York City lit up the sky just a short distance away. If he could reach the city's crowded streets, he could possibly conceal himself, but first he would have to run the gauntlet of the press corps. Behind them would be the restless, inquisitive people of New York, and behind the New Yorkers would be the men who were waiting to receive the jewel—the price he must pay for being allowed to return home.

The men who waited for him would be standing alone. Even in the excitement of the moment, no one in the crowd would willingly stand next to one of them. They would be big men in dark coats with pockets deep enough to conceal a small arsenal. They would not be happy to find him empty-handed.

If only he could be certain that the girl had survived, he should still be able to save himself. The girl who had snatched his winnings from the card table in the smoking room had no idea what she had. The Matryoshka did not easily reveal its value. To some, it would appear to be nothing more than a badly flawed diamond.

For three days, he had tried to find out whether the thieving stewardess was alive or dead. He had seen her enter a lifeboat, but he had not been able to find her on board the *Carpathia*. The surviving *Titanic* crew had all been put to work: some to stoke the boilers as the *Carpathia* raced toward New York, some to serve meals, some to stand watch—the fear of icebergs had everyone on edge—and some to care for the injured. He knew by the girl's apron that she was a stewardess. The fact that he had not been able to find her did not mean she had drowned during the long, cold night when they waited for rescue. He had heard that the *Titanic*'s stewardesses had been set to nursing the sick and injured and they were not mingling with the passengers or crew. Although he had kept his eyes open studying everyone he encountered on board the crowded *Carpathia*, he had not found her. However, he would not have to wait much longer. If she had lived, she would be going ashore with the rest of the crew. She would not be able to hide from him.

The assistant purser spoke firmly. "It's time to go ashore, sir."

"What about the crew?" Towson asked. "I haven't seen the *Titanic*'s crew going ashore. Where are they?"

"They're not going ashore, sir. They're going straight back to England. There is a harbor tender coming to pick them up."

Towson stared in disbelief. "None of them are going ashore?"

"The officers will go ashore but not the crew. I must ask you to leave now, sir."

Towson's heart sank. What was he to do now? If what the assistant purser had said was true, he would gain nothing by lingering on the *Carpathia*. The girl would not be going ashore.

The officer was becoming impatient. "You need to disembark,

sir."

Towson stood at the head of the gangplank and looked at the sea of interested, eager faces. All eyes were turned toward the sad procession of passengers leaving the *Carpathia*. Some of those eyes were looking for him. How was he to reach the safe anonymity of the city?

As if in answer to his question, the faces turned abruptly away. Something was happening in the harbor. The crowd were murmuring now and pressing forward. No one was looking at the gangplank of the *Carpathia*. He had his moment. He hurried down the gangplank, stumbling on his sea legs, and made a dash for the immigration building.

Once inside the shelter of the building, he expected to be met by immigration officials, but even the officials had turned away. Something of great interest was happening in the harbor. He took his chance and walked silently and carefully past the oblivious officials. He could hardly believe his luck as a world of possibilities opened before him. Records would show that Alvin Towson had not come ashore from the *Carpathia*. Possibly Alvin Towson had not been rescued by the *Carpathia* and had in fact gone down with the *Titanic*.

He was overcome with a sudden disheartening weariness. He had escaped undetected from the *Carpathia*, but his future was still terrifyingly uncertain. He would have to start all over again with no money, no contacts, not even a name, and all the time the fear of recognition would be in the back of his mind. If only he had managed to come ashore with the Matryoshka in his pocket, he would …

A cheer from the crowd drew his increasingly despairing thoughts away from the loss of the jewel. What on earth was getting everyone so excited? He hurried away from the immigration building and slipped in among the crowd of onlookers.

"What's happening?"

"A girl trying to drown herself in the harbor. Jumped off the *Carpathia* and right into the water."

"Drunk!" said a voice behind him.

"No. Probably brokenhearted," said another. "Lost her sweetheart on the *Titanic*."

As speculation rose around him, Towson pushed his way to the front of the crowd. Camera flashes illuminated the dark, choppy waters of the harbor, and a searchlight traced a path from the deck of the *Carpathia* to the swimmers struggling in the water.

"She don't want to be saved," a voice muttered beside him.

"Told you so. Suicide, that's what it is."

"No, no. See, someone's going to save her. He's a powerful swimmer, ain't he?"

Curiosity drew Alvin forward. Why would anyone from the *Carpathia* want to drown themselves now? A small boat followed the path of the searchlight and approached the swimmers. A crewman leaned over the gunwale of the boat and began to heave the girl aboard. The man who had rescued her waited, holding on to the boat and wiping water from his eyes.

The half-drowned, suicidal girl collapsed into the bottom of the boat and lifted her face to the beam from the searchlight. Her hair was wet, and her curls hung in rat tails, but Towson knew her at once. He had found the stewardess. She was not dead, but she was not coming ashore.

He considered his options and found that he had none. If she was going to England, then he would have to follow. She did not know the value of what she had, but he did.

CHAPTER THREE

The Dulwich Club
Pall Mall, London, England
Captain Harry Hazelton

Harry Hazelton, formerly a captain of the East Surrey Regiment, leaned back in the club chair and stretched his long legs. "Wonder what happened to our drinks," he said, wincing as pain lanced through his left leg. The injury had occurred only a year ago, and he had not yet learned to live with it.

His companion at the low table in front of the empty fireplace shrugged his broad shoulders. "It's the Dulwich Club, old man, not Boodle's. Our graduates don't have that kind of money and neither does the club.

Harry looked at his surroundings, taking in the familiar shabby armchairs, the dusty drapes, and the antiquity of the waiter who was now approaching bearing a small silver serving tray. Harry could not fail to notice that the tray was green with tarnish. It would never pass muster at the officers' mess in Lucknow, or any other place the East Surrey Regiment found itself.

The waiter set down two brandy snifters, and Harry leaned forward to sign the chit, noting that the tray bore the crest of Dulwich College. The school did not have the prestige of Eton or Harrow, but it was all his parents had been able to afford for him, and it had served him well. In its three hundred years of history, it had produced a number of great men, and one of them was sitting beside him now.

Although he wore a plain dark suit and was ensconced in a comfortable club chair, Sir Ernest Shackleton, polar explorer, exuded energy. It was the same energy that had made him a leader among the boys in Harry's dormitory at Dulwich, and the same energy that he

41

was now using to prepare for another polar expedition. Harry, who had no interest in trekking across the Antarctic, was nonetheless envious. It was his own fault, of course. He had been robbed of his life's purpose by his own carelessness.

His army life was gone forever, stolen by the charge of a wild boar in an Indian jungle. For him, there would be no more snowcapped mountains or burning plains. No more casual camaraderie in the officers' mess. No more bugles, or drums, or warmth from a foreign sun. The doctors had pronounced him medically unfit and sent him home. All he could do now was lick his wounds and replay over and over the moment when the boar had charged from the thicket. If he allowed himself time to listen, he could still hear the sharp discharge of Lieutenant Cardrew Worthington's pistol as he put the horse out of its misery and the rapidly retreating voices of the bearers as they pursued the boar in pointless revenge.

Why had he wanted to kill the creature? Why had he wanted to kill anything? He had seen enough killing among the Boers at Mafeking and Ladysmith and been glad to leave South Africa. His mission in India should not have involved killing anything. He had been there to use his brain, not his rifle.

"Congratulations on your knighthood," Harry said, raising his glass in a toast to his companion. "I'm glad I ran into you here. I intended to write, but I'm afraid there were some circumstances that—"

"I know a little about your circumstances," Shackleton said. Despite the rigorous standards of Dulwich College, Shackleton had not lost his Irish accent. "It's hard to keep a secret in this club. Word has it that you were undertaking some confidential work up on the North-West Frontier. Peshawar, was it?"

Harry remained silent. He would never be allowed to speak of the months he had spent in disguise. He had been blessed with dark hair and dark eyes, and when he dressed in a shalwar kameez and a pakol cap, he could easily pass as a visiting Afghan. "You have it wrong," he said. "My regiment was in Lucknow." He tapped his leg. "That's where I got this."

Shackleton grinned. "If you say so, old man."

"I don't share your love of adventure," Harry said, hoping to change the subject. "I hear you're planning another expedition."

"If I can raise the funds," Shackleton said, "I plan to lead an expedition from one side of the continent of Antarctica to the other. It's never been done before, and we need a victory in the polar race. Peary has the North Pole, and Amundsen has beaten Scott to the South Pole."

He paused for a moment, and his tone changed. "I can't imagine how Scott must feel having dragged himself all the way across the Antarctic Plateau only to find Amundsen's Norwegian flag already there. Scott is not a patient man. I wouldn't want to be in his retreating party."

"Do we know where they are?" Harry asked.

Shackleton shook his head. "It will be months before we hear from them, and then only to confirm what we already know—Amundsen was first to the pole. We are going to need a British triumph to take away the taste of defeat, and I'm the one to do it. I planned to give a series of fundraising lectures to equip my expedition, but I'm afraid this *Titanic* business is going to delay things somewhat."

"Terrible business," Harry agreed. "Fifteen hundred people dead, or so they say, and just a handful of survivors."

"Twenty lifeboats launched and thirteen recovered," Shackleton said. "That's all. Just thirteen, and mainly women and children."

"Rule of the sea," Harry said. He wondered if the rule of the sea had truly been followed. The *Titanic* had had passengers from all walks of life, not all of them British, and not all of them accustomed to behaving like British officers and gentlemen. Had all the men agreed to step aside and let the women into the lifeboats? Only time would tell. The rescue ship was only now arriving in New York, and the newspapers were filled with speculation but very few facts.

"It's going to affect my fundraising," Shackleton said.

"Why?"

Shackleton sipped his brandy thoughtfully. "Several reasons," he said at last. "Some of the wealthiest men in the world went down with that ship. Apparently, the American stock market has taken a steep dive, and those who have money will want to hold on to it and won't want to invest it in Antarctic exploration." He sipped again. "That's just one reason. The second reason is that every Tom, Dick, and Harry or Harriet who managed to survive will be giving lectures and stealing my audiences."

"You think so?" Harry asked.

"I know so. This is my bread and butter, old man. I understand what the public will pay to hear. 'Sir Ernest Shackleton, polar explorer' has worked well for me up to now, but I can't compete with a firsthand account of the sinking of the *Titanic*." He leaned forward. "I'm in a better position than most to know about ice, and I must admit that even I would go to a lecture from a survivor. Watch the newspapers, Hazelton, and you'll soon see advertisements for lectures."

"In America, maybe," Harry said, "but not here."

"Not yet," Shackleton amended, "but not all the survivors will remain in America. They'll be here soon enough." He set down his glass. "Well, no point in dwelling on the inevitable. How about you? Now that you've been invalided out of your regiment, what do you plan to do to earn your daily crust?"

Harry subdued a surge of resentment at the intrusive question. Shackleton had been outspoken about his own need for money, and Harry had nothing to hide. Dulwich College was not a school for the independently wealthy. Dulwich students went into the army, into the church, or into industry; they did not live off trust funds or inherited wealth.

"I'm meeting the Bishop of Fordingbridge. He's one of ours but long before our time. Class of 1860," Harry said. "He is also a friend of one of my aunts."

Shackleton raised his eyebrows. "Are you thinking of going into the church?"

Harry shook his head. "No, nothing like that. I've been thinking of …"

"Of what?"

"Well, I thought I might open an investigative agency."

"Ha!" Shackleton's exclamation was loud enough to make heads turn in the dusty recesses of the club lounge. "I knew it."

"You were right," Harry admitted. "I know a thing or two about investigating. I've had some experience, which I will not speak of."

"And how would your experience assist the Bishop of Fordingbridge?" Shackleton asked. "I doubt that he runs into many Peshawari rebels in Fordingbridge."

"I told you that I will not speak of my experience, not even to say where I was," Harry reminded him. "The bishop is apparently looking for a missing relative. I feared that I would have to start my agency by following unfaithful husbands and office clerks stealing from the petty cash, so I'm glad that this is something a little less repugnant."

"If it's so repugnant, why would you—"

"Because my army pension is small and because I'm going crazy sitting here with nothing to think of but this accursed leg injury."

Shackleton nodded. "I understand. I can't wait to get moving again."

Harry sat back in his chair, nursing the snifter of brandy and feeling no need to speak. His friendship with Shackleton had been formed in childhood. They understood each other. No doubt Shackleton's memories were now taking him to the wind-scoured rocky shores of Antarctica, while Harry's mind still lingered on a British outpost and a pale woman in a white muslin dress. Shackleton had new memories to make, but Harry wondered if he would ever cast aside the weight of the memories he had already made.

The sociable silence was broken by the noisy arrival of a newcomer. Paying no attention to club etiquette, the rosy-cheeked young man inquired noisily for Sir Ernest Shackleton, *the explorer.*

"I hate when someone calls me that," Shackleton said. "Makes it sound like I'm going up the Nile in a dugout canoe."

"Who is he?" Harry asked.

"I imagine he's a very junior assistant in the offices of Hill Dickinson, specialists in maritime law. They've been retained as counsel to International Mercantile Marine—in other words, the White Star Line—in the matter of the *Titanic* disaster." He pulled a watch from his waistcoat pocket, consulted it thoughtfully, and returned it to his pocket. "He's early. He can wait."

"The White Star Line? If you don't mind me asking, how are you involved with the White Star Line? Do you use them to transport your team to Antarctica?"

"Heavens, no! I doubt that anyone would trust them near an iceberg ever again. Besides, we usually depart from New Zealand, and White Star has nothing going in that direction. That young whippersnapper is here to advise me on how I am to conduct myself as an expert witness in the Wreck Commissioner's inquiry into the sinking of the pride of the White Star fleet, the unsinkable *Titanic.* Ironic, isn't it, considering the way they have stolen my thunder?"

Harry shook his head. "From what I've read in the newspapers, the Americans are holding an inquiry, and they've already started. Why would we have another inquiry here?"

Shackleton sighed. "A US senator by the name of Smith is holding the chairman of the White Star Line and a number of the crew under a subpoena and asking all kinds of damfool questions, but I wouldn't call that an inquiry. It's just political posturing. Smith has his eye on the White House. We don't need an American kangaroo court to sort this out. It'll take a panel of experts to get to the bottom of what really happened." He gave Harry a wry grin. "I've been in the navy, and I know a thing or two about ice."

Harry tried to recall what he had read in the newspapers. The front pages of every paper in Britain had carried screaming headlines, and the interior pages had carried lists of those who had been lost, but none of them had so far suggested anything other than a collision with an iceberg as the initial cause of the disaster. "Surely it was an act of God," he said.

Shackleton sniffed scornfully. "I doubt that. I would say that running into an iceberg is an act of extreme carelessness. We'll know soon enough. The inquiry starts in a couple of days, when the survivors of the crew arrive back in England." He bounced to his feet, full of suppressed energy. "Well, I think I've kept the messenger waiting long enough." He extended his hand and gave Harry a firm handshake. As he started toward the exit, he turned as though he'd had a last-minute thought. "I assume you're staying here tonight."

"I am," Harry admitted. "I've made this my home for the moment. My family has property in Devon, but I haven't been down there yet." He tried to blot out the image of the ramshackle old house bequeathed to him by his parents. He was not yet ready to bury himself in the countryside and live the life of a wounded soldier. There had to be something better.

"Perhaps you could come with me tomorrow," Shackleton said. "I'll be going to St. Paul's Cathedral for the *Titanic* memorial service. As one of the White Star's favored witnesses, I'm supposed to have a reserved seat. We can go in together. I don't think this is something you'll want to miss. When you're an old man, you'll be able to tell your grandchildren about it."

Grandchildren? The word echoed through the mind space where Harry had once kept his hopes and dreams. The room where he had hung hazy portraits of a woman who could never be his, and children who would never be born, was empty now. There would be no children and no grandchildren to hear the story of how the nation had mourned for the victims of the *Titanic*. He imagined the great cathedral crowded with mourners and suddenly decided that it was somewhere he wanted to be. In such a place, his own mourning would go unremarked. He could allow his stiff upper lip to tremble, and he could embrace his own grief.

"I'll come," he said.

Shackleton clapped him on the shoulder. "Good chap. I'll see you at breakfast. We'll go together."

As Harry nodded his agreement, he looked toward the entrance of the club and caught sight of the ancient waiter practically prostrating himself before a man in frock coat and gaiters. The Right Reverend the Bishop of Fordingbridge had arrived.

Pier 54,
New York Harbor
Poppy Melville

Although Poppy, Daisy, and the remaining members of the *Titanic*'s crew were aboard the harbor tender, the sturdy craft was not moving.

The police sergeant, who had lost none of his Irish brogue in his time in New York, warned Daisy again.

"I want to know what's going on. What call do you have to be jumping into the harbor? Are you touched in the head, or are you up to something?"

"She's very upset. We've all had a terrible time," Poppy said. She had taken off her coat and wrapped it around her sister's shoulders, but Daisy was still shivering.

"Maybe you have," the sergeant agreed, "but that's no call to be jumping into the river. If you wanted to drown, you could have done that right off the *Titanic* and saved a place for someone else in the lifeboat."

Poppy was relieved to see Mr. Williams, the White Star representative, making his way toward them.

"What's the hold up here?" he asked. "These people should be on board the *Lapland* already. What's the problem, Sergeant?"

The sergeant, who was a head shorter but a good deal wider than

Williams, puffed out his chest. "I'm interrogating this young woman, the one we fished out of the harbor. I've a good mind to take her ashore."

"Go ahead," said Daisy. "Take me ashore. I'm not going back to England."

She attempted to make her point by stamping her foot, but her wet shoe and stocking made little sound. Poppy was afraid that Daisy had now exhausted her arsenal of feminine charms and might actually be arrested. Her bright, curly hair had been reduced to wet rat tails. The sparkle in her blue eyes had dulled and been replaced with something that looked very much like fear, and her curvaceous figure was huddled under Poppy's coat. The big police sergeant seemed totally impervious to any charms that still remained.

"Where are your papers, young lady?"

"Gone," said Daisy tragically, "along with everything else I owned. I've nothing but what I stand up in."

Mr. Williams added his agreement. "They've nothing, Sergeant. The crew was too busy helping the passengers to spend time searching for their papers. In fact, I've been told that most of their paperwork was kept by the purser. It probably went down with the ship."

Poppy glanced at the White Star representative and wondered why he was lying. The crew members were responsible for their own paperwork. Granted, she and Daisy didn't have any documentation with them, but that was not the fault of the White Star Line. They really had been too occupied with settling the passengers into lifeboats to spend time in fetching papers from their cabins. In the chaos that had accompanied the launching of the boats, Poppy had given no thought to what she had been leaving behind. By the time Poppy's lifeboat had been lowered from its davits to inch its way down the side of the ship, the cabins had already been filling with water.

"You can search me if you wish," Daisy said. She shrugged off Poppy's dry coat and then her own wet coat. Now she stood shivering with her dark woolen dress clinging to every curve of her body. She spread her arms. "Go ahead. Search me."

Williams stepped in. "That won't be necessary, will it, Sergeant? I'm sure plenty of passengers will go ashore without papers tonight."

"They'll go down the gangplank," the sergeant said darkly. "They won't hurl themselves into the harbor. If it wasn't for that fine, strong man who fished you out, young lady, you'd have gone under and never come up again."

Daisy shook her head. "I'm a strong swimmer," she declared.

Sullivan, still dripping water on the deck, shook his head. "You would never have made it. There's a powerful current out there."

Daisy flashed him a dark look. "I didn't need your help."

Poppy picked up her dry coat and tried once again to put it around her sister's shoulders.

Daisy pushed her away. "You wear it. I don't need it." She spread her arms again and turned to face the sergeant. "Go ahead. Arrest me if you want to."

"Daisy," Poppy implored, "put this coat on. You'll catch your death of cold."

Daisy reached up on tiptoe and spoke into Poppy's ear. "You keep it," she hissed. "There's something in the pocket."

"There's nothing in the—"

"Be quiet. Don't say anything."

"Daisy?"

"Shh."

The sergeant turned to Williams. "I should take her into custody."

Williams shook his head. "She's just a young girl. You have to make allowances for what they've been through, adrift in the ice with no hope of rescue and people dying all around them. I'm sure she didn't intend anything. We could all see that she fell; she didn't jump."

The sergeant was still hesitating when a great cacophony of sound swept over them, and all heads turned toward the shore.

"Well, that's that," the sergeant muttered in disgust. "They're letting the third-class survivors go ashore. I warned my captain. I told him it was a mistake to let the families come so close. There'll be no holding them back now." He shrugged his shoulders. "I know my own people," he said. "There'll be weeping and wailing and gnashing of teeth for every Irish man, woman, or child with any bit of news." He looked at Williams. "They're mostly dead, aren't they?"

"Well ..."

"Don't be playing games. We've heard what happened to the immigrant passengers. Locked down below, so they say. Not even given a chance."

"We don't know that," Williams insisted. "I'm sure there'll be an inquiry and—"

The Irishman would not allow him to finish. "You're not going to tell the truth. None of you will tell the truth." He flicked a dismissing hand at Daisy. "This little girlie hasn't spoken a word of truth, and I know it." He shook his head. "You can go with the rest of the crew," he said. "You were up to something, but I don't have time to bother myself with one little girl." He looked at Sullivan and then back at Daisy. "You should thank that big fellow. He saved your life."

Williams followed the sergeant to the gangplank that still connected the tender to the *Carpathia*. As the two men disappeared from sight, Poppy felt the deck move beneath her feet. This was it. They were pulling away from the shore. Instead of taking the train to California, they were heading back across the Atlantic.

She held her coat out to Daisy. "Put it on, please."

Daisy shrugged. "Fine, I'll put it on."

Poppy, a good head taller than Daisy, bent down so she could speak softly to her sister. "Why were you talking about something being in the pocket? I didn't have anything in the pocket."

"No," said Daisy airily, "I don't suppose you did."

"Did you put something in my pocket?"

"Why would you say that?"

"Because you said—"

"I didn't say anything. You're imagining things, Poppy. You shouldn't get so excited."

"Excited! I'm not the one who fell into the harbor."

"I didn't fall; I jumped," Daisy said.

"I think you fell."

"Well, whatever you think, at least I didn't just stand there like a silly goose while all our plans were being destroyed."

"They're not destroyed. We can try again."

Daisy gave her a secretive smile. "We'll do better next time."

Poppy looked over at Sullivan, who was leaning on the rail and looking back at the *Carpathia*. No one had even given him a blanket. She walked across to him, staggering slightly as the tender pushed through the choppy waters of the harbor in the wake of a flotilla of private boats.

He spoke without turning around. "At least they're safe," he said.

She stood beside him and followed his gaze. The immigrant survivors from the *Titanic* were moving along the dock toward the reporters, the photographers, and the anxious New York crowd. They moved slowly, as though they knew and dreaded what lay ahead. How many times would they be forced to relive the tragedy?

"Did you see my brother?"

"How could you leave your husband?"

"How many seats were in the lifeboat?"

"Why did you leave so many behind?"

Sullivan uttered a strange grunting sound as a passenger in a wheelchair appeared on the dock, pushed by a nurse and huddled in a blanket.

"So she lives," Sullivan said softly.

"Who is she?" Poppy asked.

Sullivan didn't respond. The harbor tender was picking up speed now. Sullivan leaned over the railing, still watching the dock. "And so does he," he said. He turned and looked at Poppy. "You will need to be careful," he said.

"Why?"

"You will need to take care of your sister."

Daisy again! Even now! "I always take care of her," Poppy said, "and I want to thank you for saving her."

His tone was grim. "She's the one who should be doing the thanking."

"I know," Poppy said. "I'm afraid she doesn't …"

She met his gray-eyed gaze and fell silent as she saw the shadows that lurked there.

"None of us will ever be the same again," Sullivan said quietly. "When I hit the water, it all came back. The cold, the dark …"

"I know what happened to you," Poppy said. "I was in lifeboat fourteen. We pulled you from the staircase. You sat next to me."

The shadow lingered in his eyes even as he finally flashed her a look of recognition. "Yes, it was you," he said. "You were the only one who stopped."

"It wasn't up to me," Poppy explained.

"I watched the lifeboats rowing away, one after another, and none of them stopping for the people in the water," Sullivan said.

Poppy lowered her eyes. She should not feel shame, and yet she did. "There were too many."

Sullivan nodded. "I know, and it was the right decision. Those who still had the strength to swim would have swamped the boats."

"But we saw you," Poppy said, "and …"

"You don't have to explain," Sullivan said, "but I'm grateful, so that makes us even, doesn't it?"

In the silence that followed, she could hear his teeth chattering. She spoke without thinking. "I saw you change your mind."

His eyes were sharp now. "I don't know what you mean."

She had not meant to say it. She had only meant to thank him, not to challenge him, but now she had started, she could not silence herself. "You went overboard for your own purposes. You took advantage of Daisy's diversion."

"No. You've got it wrong."

"You were trying to escape."

Sullivan scowled. "Just because I'm Australian doesn't mean I'm a criminal. We're no longer a penal colony."

She could not take back her words, but she did what she could to lighten them. "I'm sorry you didn't get away."

Sullivan shrugged. "So am I."

The Dulwich Club
Harry Hazelton

Hugh Gradstove, Bishop of Fordingbridge, greeted Harry with a firm handshake. He was a short, rotund man whose episcopal frock coat strained across his generous stomach. His face, topped by an unruly mop of white hair, was as soft and round as a cherub's. His cheeks were bright pink, and only his eyes betrayed the fact that he was no cherub and he had seen much of the unpleasantness that even Christians could inflict on each other.

He took charge immediately, acting as though he were the host. Well, Harry thought, the bishop had been a member of the Dulwich Club for many, many years. No doubt he thought of it as his London home.

Gradstove's voice was rich and mellifluous and somehow comforting. "Sit down, Captain. Let's not stand on ceremony. I'm told you had a nasty wound. How is it now?"

Harry returned to his seat and stretched out his left leg. "It's healing as well as can be expected, or so I'm told. I can't bend the knee, but at least they didn't amputate it."

Gradstove took the chair that had been vacated by Shackleton. "So you've been invalided out?"

Harry nodded gloomily. "They don't want an officer who can't stay on his horse."

The bishop pursed his lips thoughtfully. "I understand that your duties required you to do more than just stay on your horse and charge blindly at the enemy."

Harry remained silent. Perhaps the bishop was referring to the general duties of an army officer, or perhaps he had something else in mind. He wondered how many more people knew about his supposedly secret activities in India.

"I was dining with your aunt Cynthia two days ago," the bishop said. "She's very active in church circles."

Harry nodded. If the church were to allow female clergy, he was quite certain that Cynthia Hazelton would be a bishop by now.

"I shared with her some family concerns I have and my need for a private investigator, and she suggested you. She said you have experience."

When Harry tried to speak, the bishop held up his hand. "I am aware that you are not permitted to speak of your experiences, and she did not give me details. She only said that she had a nephew who was considering taking on private investigative work. When she told me that you were also a Dulwich College boy, I knew you were the man for the job." He sat back in his chair. "I am not going to ask you for references, and I am not going to ask about your work on behalf of our imperial interests in India."

The bishop clicked his fingers to summon the waiter and ordered two brandy and sodas. The waiter made an appropriate obeisance and tottered away. Silence settled on the room, broken only by the ticking of the carriage clock on the mantelshelf.

Harry considered his options. He had not yet opened an office or placed an advertisement in *The Times*, but here was his first client. He suspected that his aunt Cynthia had been badgering God in her daily prayers: *Find something to keep Harry's mind off his troubles. Help him accept that his old life is over. Amen.*

He flexed his left leg, deliberately exploring his torn and

cramped muscles and the pain of his shattered kneecap. He could not fool himself even for a moment. He was back in England, and he needed to make a living.

He studied the bishop's face, seeing a restless anxiety that lurked behind his prominent gray eyes. "What do you need me to do?"

The bishop smiled. "I have two nieces, who seem to have disappeared."

Harry's heart sank. He had no connections in England to help him find missing children. If they had gone missing in India, he would know where to look, but not in England, not in London's great network of vice and greed.

"They're not children," the bishop said, as if he could read Harry's mind. "They're young ladies. They are twenty-two and eighteen. I am certain that they have not been kidnapped. I think they have simply run away, and I can't say that I blame them."

"How long have they been missing?"

The bishop thought for a moment. "Two weeks or maybe three. I can't be certain."

"Have you called the police?"

The bishop shook his head. "No. I don't suspect foul play. As I say, they are not children, but they are both quite headstrong. I believe they've taken it into their heads to just run away from home. Unfortunately, they have led a sheltered life, and they've no experience of the world beyond their own family. It would be very easy for someone to take advantage of them."

Harry looked at the bishop's worried face. He was right, of course. They weren't children, but they might as well have been. Two young girls with no experience of the world could very easily find themselves in trouble, especially if they had gone to London.

The bishop sat forward. His knuckles turned white as he gripped the pectoral cross that hung from a heavy chain around his neck. "I blame myself," he said in a voice that had lost its comforting mellifluousness. "I should have stopped this before it even started."

"Were they living in your house?" Harry asked.

The bishop shook his head. "They were not, but maybe I should have taken them in," he said. "I failed in my duty to my sister."

The waiter approached and set two glasses on the table. Gradstove lifted his glass and took a long swallow. When he set the glass down again, he seemed to have recovered his equilibrium. "I blame myself. I should never have allowed my sister to marry that man."

"You are referring to the father of the missing girls?" Harry asked.

"Yes, I am. Horace Melville, Earl of Riddlesdown."

Harry made a mental adjustment. The missing girls were the daughters of an aristocrat. The thought was not comforting. He imagined they'd been raised by a series of governesses, that they'd never done a hard day's work in their lives, and that they had no skills that would earn them any money. He agreed with the bishop. They had to be found before they got into real trouble.

"It all started twenty-five years ago, when the Earl of Riddlesdown proposed marriage to Evadne, my youngest sister. My family was thrilled that Evadne had snagged herself an earl, and we thought he was to be the stepping stone for all of us to prosper. In those days, I was very ambitious. I was confident that having an earl in our family would surely result in a bishopric for me, and as you can see, I was correct. I am now the Bishop of Fordingbridge. I have a seat in the House of Lords. The rest of my family has achieved dizzying heights of social respectability. With a bishop and a countess attached to the family tree, the doors of society have been opened to us. We have all achieved more than we ever expected, except, of course, poor Evadne. She paid the price for all of us."

Harry waited as the bishop fought to control a powerful emotion.

When he finally spoke, his voice was shaky. "I should never have let the marriage happen, but I was blinded by ambition. The decision, of course, was taken by my parents, but I allowed my own ambition to blind me to reality when I spoke in favor of the match."

"But in the end, this was surely your sister's decision," Harry said.

The bishop shook his head. "Evadne was a very sweet girl. She would not have dreamed of arguing with my father. If he wanted her to marry the earl, then that was good enough for her. She had no idea, of course, what that would involve. She was quite innocent of … well … let me just say that she was unaware of what marriage entails. She dreamed of being a mother, but she knew very little of the way that children come into the world."

Gradstove stared down into his glass. "I find it hard to forgive myself."

"But it was not your decision. Surely it was your father's permission that was needed," Harry said. He was not sure how a conversation about his proposed investigation had turned into an opportunity for the Bishop of Fordingbridge to confess his sins.

"I am not so easily absolved," Gradstove said. "As an ordained priest, I was the marriage officiant. I had it in my power to stop the service. I looked at Evadne standing in front of me, waiting to be united in matrimony with a scowling stranger, a man she hardly knew. Her face was veiled, but I could see her shoulders trembling. I think perhaps she was crying, but even that didn't stop me. I spoke the words required of me. 'If any of you know cause or just impediment why these two persons should not be joined together in holy Matrimony, ye are to declare it.' I waited—one always waits. No one spoke. No one said that poor little Evadne was going like a lamb to the slaughter."

Harry settled into his seat and allowed a little time for Gradstove to compose himself before he brought the bishop back to the matter in hand. "Tell me about the missing girls. How do you know they are missing?"

"I received a telephone call from Nanny Catchpole. She was Evadne's nanny, who went with her to Riddlesdown to care for the next generation. When Evadne died, she remained."

Harry waited. He was not surprised to hear that the bishop's little sister had died. He had sensed her death in every guilty word the bishop had uttered.

"Evadne died in attempting to give my brother-in-law a son and heir," Gradstove said. "She had given him a daughter, but he wanted a son. My sister was not strong. She gave birth to another daughter and died two days later. Nanny Catchpole was left to raise Evadne's girls while my brother-in-law fretted and fumed at his lack of a male heir and set out to find another woman to bear his children. So far he has killed two women and is about to kill his third."

Harry rocked forward in his seat. "Surely not."

"Not literally," Gradstove admitted. "He hasn't strangled any of his wives or pitched them down the stairs, but nonetheless, I hold him responsible." He shifted in his chair and cleared his throat, obviously uncomfortable with the conversation. "I know we men don't speak much of women's business and the, shall we say, technicalities of childbirth, but you've been in India and South Africa, where I believe the native people are more comfortable with discussions such as this."

Harry felt a slight tug of inappropriate amusement. Although the Church of England had no rules to the contrary, he suspected that the bishop was not a married man. Of course, neither was Harry, but he was a soldier, and soldiers did not mince words.

Having ascertained that Harry was not uncomfortable with the subject, the bishop continued his story. "Matilda, the earl's second wife, after a very long interval, gave birth to a girl who would be about twelve years old by now. Poor Matilda died two years later. I'm not sure of the cause, but I will say that the earl did not seem to mourn her passing. She was scarcely in the ground before he married again and fathered another child."

Harry read the bishop's expression, something between sorrow and wry amusement. "A daughter?" he asked.

"Yes, another daughter. He now has four daughters."

"I assume the estate is entailed," Harry said. "It can only go to a son?"

Gradstove shook his curly head. "No, not at all. The oldest daughter can inherit if there is no son."

"Then why—"

"My brother-in-law holds women in very low esteem. He will not rest, or allow his wife to rest, until he has a son. He fancies himself descended from the Tudors and thus sets himself the same standard as Henry the Eighth. According to Nanny Catchpole, the current Lady Riddlesdown, Agnes Melville, the third wife, is due to give birth very soon, and for everyone's sake, I pray God that it's a boy. If it is another girl, I am not sure I can vouch for the safety of Lady Riddlesdown."

Harry shook his head. "Surely not. King Henry's wives were—"

"I know what happened to King Henry's wives," Gradstove said sharply. He pulled a gold watch and chain from the pocket of his frock coat. "Look at the time," he said. "I do apologize, Captain Hazelton, for taking so long to come to the point, but I thought you should know the background, because I think it explains why the Earl of Riddlesdown doesn't give a twopenny damn about my nieces, and it's left to old Nanny Catchpole to phone me. Poor old soul thinks the telephone is the devil's instrument, but she managed to reach me and tell me that Lady Penelope and Lady Marguerite had gone to London to buy clothes for the new baby, that they had not returned, and that no one seemed to care."

"You are saying that neither of the girls returned home and no one has inquired where they are?"

"Yes, that's exactly what I'm saying. When you meet my brother-in-law, you will understand what I mean."

"Have you arranged for me to meet him?" Harry asked in surprise. He had not yet accepted the commission. Why was the bishop so sure of himself?

Gradstove shook his head ferociously. "Oh, no, not at all. Any meeting will have to appear accidental and on the spur of the moment. A neighbor dropping by."

"But I'm not a neighbor."

"He doesn't know that." The bishop sighed wearily. "Look here, old chap. I have no one else to turn to. If I send the police, Horace will shut them out with his aristocratic bluster. This will require subtlety and, well, deception. You'll need to get into the house and speak to Horace, and his new wife, and see what you can ferret out without them realizing that you have any suspicion that the girls are missing. Nanny Catchpole will help you."

Harry thought of the level of deception he had achieved on the North-West Frontier. At times he had dyed his skin and grown a long beard and ferocious whiskers. For the sake of the empire, he had risked his life in snowy mountain passes, enemy camps, and crowded bazaars. He had been a dark shadow of a man, able to appear and disappear at will. His true name had not been known, and yet, even unnamed, he had been a legend. Now he was reduced to "dropping by" the country estate of a blustering descendant of the Tudors and holding secret meetings with someone named Nanny Catchpole.

"Just a few hours of your time, that's all I ask," Gradstove said. "I really am very concerned. I did nothing to help my sister, but I cannot abandon her children."

Staring down into his brandy glass, Harry conjured up a vision of his aunt Cynthia's face, and he knew he was beaten. He could say no to the bishop, but not to Aunt Cynthia. He set down the glass and extended his hand. "Just a few hours," he said.

"Good man."

"I try to be."

CHAPTER FOUR

**On Board the *Lapland*
New York Harbor
Ernie Sullivan**

Sullivan peered through the cabin porthole at the lights of New York City, so near and yet so far. The harbor tender had delivered them directly to the *Lapland* two days ago, but the liner had not sailed immediately and was still at the dock. He had explored every possible way of escaping the ship, but every effort had been thwarted. Any attempt to even go up on deck had been met with resistance from the burly guards, who seemed to watch his every movement.

The men who had been hired to guard the remnants of the *Titanic* crew were no larger or stronger than Sullivan, and on a good day, he would have taken them on, but today was not a good day. His blistered hands still throbbed beneath their soiled bandages, and he burned with fever. The other crew members grumbled constantly about feeling chilled to the bone, as though icy water had replaced the blood in their veins. They had been given clothing by a New York charity, but still they complained of needing woolen scarves and gloves. Their feet, in hand-me-down shoes, felt like blocks of ice, or so they said. Sullivan had felt the same way at first, but not tonight. Tonight he was bathed in sweat.

Although he desperately wanted to go ashore, and even more desperately wanted to avoid being returned to England, he knew he was in no shape to attempt an escape. He was weak and sick, and his fever would not break. His fellow firemen could do nothing for him as he tossed and turned on his bunk in the cabin he shared with three other survivors.

He flinched as a calloused hand touched his forehead. He looked up and recognized George Beauchamp, another of the stokers.

"You've still got a fever, mate," Beauchamp said. "You need a nurse."

Sullivan groaned. "Brandy," he said. "I need brandy."

"Well, there's none of that on board for the likes of us," Beauchamp said, "but some of the stewardesses are nurses, and maybe they can fix you up. Come on. Get out of that bunk and come with me."

Sullivan, too sick to argue, staggered to his feet. His head was spinning, and Beauchamp's voice came from far away. "Hey, Dillon, get over here and give me a hand with this big lummox. We'll take him down to the dining room and see what we can find."

Paddy Dillon swam into view. "Don't you think you should bring the nurse here to him?"

Beauchamp laughed mirthlessly. "They'll not allow a woman in here with us." He lifted Sullivan's arm and draped it across his shoulders. "Take the other side."

Dillon grunted as he took Sullivan's weight, and his Irish voice sounded mildly irritated. "Can you not take some of your own weight?"

Sullivan straightened up and made an effort to clear his head and concentrate. "I can stand," he said, disgusted with the tremor in his voice. He shrugged off his helpers. "Lead the way. I'll follow."

With an effort of will, he walked unassisted into the cavernous third-class dining room and was dimly aware of the crew members gathered around the tables. They had this part of the ship to themselves. The *Lapland* had not yet taken on any passengers. It was, in effect, a prison for the *Titanic* crew.

Beauchamp pushed him down into a chair. "Miss Stap, the senior stewardess, won't help you," he said. "I've tried talking to her before, just friendly words here and there because we're all in this soup together, but she'll have none of it. She brushes me away like I'm a fly. I'll get Miss Jessop. I've heard tell she has some nursing experience, and she's a friendly sort."

Sullivan slumped forward with his head on the table, devoid of any thought until eventually some inner instinct sensed a feminine presence beside him. He looked up, and focusing his eyes with a great effort, he saw a woman's face framed in dark hair. She seemed young but stern. Presumably, this was Miss Jessop.

"Are you the great fool who jumped into the harbor?" she asked. "I suppose I am."

Another woman pushed her way forward. "What's going on here?"

Miss Jessop rested her hand on Sullivan's forehead as she spoke to the newcomer. "It's all right, Miss Stap. I can take care of this. This is the man who jumped into the harbor. Some people would call him a hero."

Miss Stap assessed him sourly. "He's no hero."

Sullivan made an attempt to sit up and managed only to lift his head from the table and mumble. "There was a girl in the water."

"It was Daisy," Miss Jessop said, "one of our own stewardesses."

"I know who it was," Miss Stap snapped. "That girl will never work for us again if I have my way."

Miss Jessop sat down beside Sullivan and began to unwrap the bandages on his hands. "Don't you know enough to know that harbor water is filthy, little better than sewage? Now your hands are infected." She tutted to herself as she removed the last of the bandages and examined the palms of his hands. "The infection's in your system by now, but maybe it won't be too bad if I can get this cleaned up."

"If there were any justice in this world," Miss Stap said, "it would be young Daisy lying in her bunk with a fever and not you."

Sullivan, having recovered slightly from his lurching walk to the dining room, was able to focus on the group of people surrounding him. He saw the frowning face of Miss Stap and behind her the friendlier faces of a cluster of women. Apparently, now that they no longer had passengers to care for, his condition had attracted the attention of all the stewardesses. His head was pounding, and his eyes would not stay focused.

A voice spoke from the back of the group. "Daisy is my sister, and I'll thank you not to talk that way about her, Miss Stap."

The speaker swam into view. He saw a tall young woman with light blue eyes. Her sandy hair was pulled back severely from a long, pale face. He fought against the fever, struggling to remember. She was the one who had been in the lifeboat, and she had ... what had she done? Oh yes. She had spoken to him after he had pulled the girl from the water, and she'd accused him of not wanting to rescue the silly little thing, and now she was angry—not with him but with the other stewardesses. She was giving the chief stewardess a piece of her mind.

"My sister is somewhat impetuous," she said, "but that's no excuse for making such disparaging remarks."

Miss Stap rounded on her. "She's an employee of the White Star Line, and I'll talk about her any way I want. I've had enough complaints about her to last me a lifetime. It's time she got out of her bunk and came along here to answer a few questions."

The tall woman took a step forward, and her voice was icy. "My sister is unwell, and she will not be answering any questions."

Sullivan had spent only a few weeks in Britain before boarding the *Titanic*, but he'd dealt with jumped-up Pommies all his life, even in Australia. This woman's voice held all the aristocratic disdain of every Englishwoman who had ever been driven out from Government House in Sydney to see the descendants of transported criminals sweating under the blazing outback sun. It made no difference to him that the woman's scorn was directed at Miss Stap and not at him. He had known and disliked her type all his life.

Miss Jessop ignored the voices behind her and turned to speak to another stewardess. "We need clean bandages and disinfectant, and we will have to find a way to bring down his fever."

"Aspirin," said the tall Pommy girl. "It works wonders. I have some if you would like to use it."

Sullivan looked at her in surprise. Her expression had changed from icy disdain to sympathetic interest.

She edged Miss Jessop aside and leaned forward to look at his hands. "You should never have gone into the water with open wounds like that." She stooped low to examine his burns. "You must have been desperate to escape," she whispered.

"How did this happen?" Miss Jessop asked, taking control once again. "How were you burned?"

"I'm a fireman," Sullivan said.

Sullivan saw Dillon pushing his way forward, grinning mischievously at the stewardesses. Obviously, his bunkmates had no intention of returning to their cabin while they had a good excuse for being with a bevy of attractive young women.

"He's one of the black gang brought on board in Southampton to fight the fire in bunker six," Dillon said. "Them poor devils shoveled hot coal for days. It was no picnic down there. Does anyone want to see my burns? I'm sure I need tender loving care."

"I'm sure you need to go back to your cabin," Miss Stap snapped.

The tall girl placed a hand on Dillon's shoulder and turned him to face her. "Are you saying that there was a fire in a coal bunker?"

"Coal does that," Dillon said. "It smolders, you know."

"Yes," the girl snapped, "I know that coal smolders, but are you saying that there was a smoldering coal fire in one of the bunkers and—"

"It was doing a lot more than smoldering," Dillon said.

The stewardess gasped. "So the boat was actually on fire when we sailed?"

Dillon's reply was nonchalant. "Not the boat itself," he said, "just one bunker. It happens sometimes. You get used to it."

Sullivan thought of the hours and days he had spent belowdecks, shoveling smoldering coal into the massive boilers. Dillon was being dismissive now, but no one had been dismissive when White Star recruiters had scoured the dock in Southampton, looking for workers to fight the fire.

Miss Stap glowered at Dillon. "That's enough," she said. "We shouldn't be speaking about this. Careless remarks like that will bring trouble down on all of us. That's why we're locked up here and unable to go ashore. White Star doesn't trust us to talk to reporters."

Despite the pain in his head and the fuzzy feeling of fever, Sullivan wasn't willing to let Miss Stap have the last word. "If fire is an everyday event," Sullivan said, "like Dillon says, and if everyone knows it happens, why shouldn't we—"

Miss Stap interrupted abruptly. "Be quiet, Mr. Sullivan."

Sullivan looked around for support from his crewmates, but they were all looking elsewhere, refusing to meet his eyes.

"We hit an iceberg and we sank," Miss Stap said icily. "There's no call for any of us to say anything else. If you can't speak well of the White Star Line, go and work for some other company. You won't find me saying a word against my employers. Careless talk about fires in bunkers will damage the line, and if we're not careful, we'll all lose our positions. I am not going to let that happen."

Beauchamp laid a hand on Sullivan's shoulder. "She's right, mate. Let it go."

"What good will that do?" Sullivan asked. Frustration momentarily overcame his fever and chills. "Locking us up won't stop other people from talking. The Americans are already holding an inquiry. They have all our officers and some of the firemen. They'll find out eventually. They have Fred Barrett. He knows about the bunker. He knows why we were hired."

"Keep still," Miss Jessop said as she set about washing the suppurating blisters on Sullivan's hands.

Sullivan saw that Miss Stap was still glaring at him. "I'm sure Mr. Barrett knows that it would be best if he says nothing," she said. "The passengers don't know anything about what was going on belowdecks, and the deck officers won't talk, so the Americans are not going to know about the fire, if it ever existed, unless you or one of the other belowdecks crewmen decides to speak."

Miss Jessop looked up from her task, and her young face was set in an expression of overwhelming sadness. "Not very many of those men made it as far as the lifeboats," she said. "None of the engineering officers survived, and there are just a handful of you and …"

A wave of anger lent strength to Sullivan's voice. "So we should just forget it?" he asked.

"It's irrelevant," Miss Stap said. "You and your gang of stokers are irrelevant to the inquiry."

"Irrelevant," Sullivan repeated. "That's a good epitaph, isn't it? You ladies all stepped into the lifeboats and rowed away. Do you have any idea what we did for you? Brave men died just to keep the lights burning. It was hell down there, hell with the lid off, and people should bloody well hear about it."

Miss Stap tutted loudly. "There's no need for such language, Mr. Sullivan."

"Oh yes there is," Sullivan growled. He looked at her hawk-nosed, disapproving face. It was obvious that she knew nothing. She was a senior stewardess, but she had never been down into the bowels of a ship, where the immense boilers turned the segmented boiler rooms into virtual ovens. She didn't know that a man could shovel for only a few minutes, holding his breath to avoid scalding his lungs, before retreating to the vent pipe to fill his lungs with fresh air. She had not been there when the scalding steam of the boilers had suddenly been replaced by icy water gushing up around their feet and rising inexorably.

"I was in number six, along with Fred Barrett and Dillon and Beauchamp, when we heard the warning bell," Sullivan said. "We saw the red light come on above the watertight door, and we had seconds to make up our minds. We threw ourselves into number five just as the door came crashing down. Another second, and we'd have been goners."

"Things weren't so much better in number five," Dillon added. He had lost his troublemaking grin, and his face was dark. "Water was coming in, but it seemed like maybe the pumps could control it. Some of the stokers had gone up, but Mr. Hesketh called us back to box up the boilers."

"He means they had to shut down the boilers to keep the steam under control but still have enough power to keep the lights on," Sullivan said. "That's what we did for you. We kept the lights on so you and your pampered passengers could see your way to safety."

"I don't need your explanations of what happens in the engine room," Miss Stap said. "I was born at sea on a White Star liner commanded by my own father. I've been at sea all my life. I know exactly what goes on in every part of the ship. I also know that speaking of the fire will not change anything. I am sure that the company has already decided what information will be shared, and we will do well to let them handle things. All we need to do is keep quiet and say as little as possible."

Sullivan felt the sudden pressure of Miss Jessop grasping his hand. He looked up and saw tears in her eyes. "Thank you," she said softly. "I don't suppose anyone else will thank you, but you were all heroes. If the lights had gone out, I don't know what we would have done, but they stayed on until the very last minute, and we could see to load the lifeboats. When we rowed away, they were still on. I think she was all under before they went out."

Sullivan nodded. "Yes, that's what I thought."

"How could you tell from belowdecks?" Miss Stap asked sharply.

Sullivan hesitated, knowing that he had spoken carelessly.

"You didn't have to be above decks to know that she was listing and down by the head," Dillon said. "Water was just pouring in, flooding everything. There was no way to stop it."

Miss Stap shook her head vigorously. "Don't say another word.

Your minds will never settle if you keep reliving your experiences."

Sullivan freed his hand from Miss Jessop's grasp. "We don't answer to you," he said, "and none of our officers survived, so we can make up our own minds about what we choose to remember. You may think you know what's best for us, but you don't. Every man in those boiler rooms was a hero. We stayed below to keep the pumps running so the poor old ship would stay afloat even a few minutes longer. It's a miracle any of us are alive, and I'm not going to forget it."

He closed his eyes, blocking out the faces surrounding him and the feel of Miss Jessop bandaging his hands and allowed memory to take hold. .

It was obvious that the pumps could no longer slow the rising water. With his view restricted by the watertight doors and the great bulk of the boilers, Sullivan had no clear idea of the extent of the damage to the hull. All any of them knew was what they could see for themselves and what they had been told by their officers— they would have to keep the pumps running until rescue arrived, and the nearest ship was four hours away.

Later, when Engineer Harvey arrived to take stock of their situation, Sullivan could tell from the young officer's face in the flickering light of the boiler room that Harvey was only going through the motions. They did not have four hours.

"Lift the manhole cover, and let me get a look at the pumps."

Knowing it was a pointless task, Sullivan lifted the cover and waited as Harvey lay on his stomach, looking down at the lift pumps laboring under their impossible load. It did not take an engineer to tell Sullivan that all the pumps in the world could not keep the ship afloat while the entire Atlantic Ocean reached up to claim its prize.

Squatting beside the engineer, Sullivan buried his head in his hands, accepting the inevitable. When he looked up, Engineer Shepherd was racing toward them, shouting that the bulkheads were failing. Sullivan stood, forgetting that he had removed the manhole cover. Although Shepherd managed to avoid falling down the hole, he stumbled over the cover and fell onto the deck with one leg crumpled beneath him.

"Well," Shepherd said, "I suppose I won't be climbing any

ladders."

Sullivan, stricken with guilt, looked down at the young officer. "I'll come back for you. When it's time to take to the ladders, I'll give you a hand."

Shepherd looked up at him. "We won't have much warning. She's going fast."

Shepherd was wrong. When the time came, there was in fact no warning and no chance to do anything for Shepherd. The bulkhead between five and six burst open, and a great wave of water engulfed the remaining stokers. Beauchamp and Dillon fled up the ladder. Sullivan hesitated, remembering his promise to Shepherd, but he was too late. Shepherd had already been washed away by a torrent of icy water. With water lapping at his heels all the way, Sullivan scrambled up a maze of ladders and stairs and out into the night, where the air was alive with the groaning of the great ship and the screams of her passengers.

The Pommy girl's voice came from a distance. "I'll go and get the Aspirin powder. It will help with the pain and bring down your temperature."

Sullivan looked at her blankly for a moment. His mind had been so far away from New York City and his berth on the *Lapland*. He studied the concerned faces closing in around him: Miss Stap with her company loyalty, the tall English stewardess fighting against her natural disdain of the working classes, Dillon and Beauchamp, who would live with terrible memories all their lives. Nothing he did now would change the past. Nothing would bring back the frozen dead who had drifted in the water as he clung to the shattered remains of the staircase: men, women, and little children with frost forming on their faces and in their hair.

The *Titanic* and the survivors were not his responsibility. He could not allow his rage for justice to bring about his own ruin. He had no choice but to return to England on the *Lapland*, but he had no intention of staying there. When the *Lapland* put in at Southampton, he would buy passage on the first ship heading back to New York. With any luck, he would be back at sea before anyone realized who or what he was. Justice would have to be meted out by someone other than Ernest Sullivan. He had his own mission. He was bent on a different justice. As for Daisy and her sister, he owed them nothing.

Whatever Daisy had done, it was nothing to do with him.

London
Harry Hazelton

Harry honored the victims of the *Titanic* disaster by wearing his full-dress uniform for the memorial service. When he removed the red tunic from its paper wrappings, a lingering scent of jasmine brought a rush of uncontrolled memories. Only nine months had passed since his batman had packed the tunic in Harry's trunk and helped him to put on unfamiliar civilian clothes. With Harry out of uniform, the batman had eschewed his normal salute and offered a handshake instead.

Good luck, sir. We'll miss you.

Nine months in storage had not neutralized the subtle odors of India, redolent of flowers and spices, but Harry hoped that a bracing walk across London to St. Paul's Cathedral would clear the air. The tunic, the sash, and the medal ribbons would soon carry only the scent of London's coal fires and damp fogs, and Harry would be able once again to turn his back on the past.

He found Ernest Shackleton waiting in the Dulwich Club's breakfast room, and they set out together toward the cathedral. The city bustled, as always, but Harry sensed a pattern in the pedestrian traffic. At this time of day, the streets would usually be clogged with people coming and going on their daily business, and alive with the clatter of horse-drawn vehicles and the newer motorcars with their aggressive klaxons. Today a strange hush seemed to have settled like a blanket over the city. As they started along the Strand, Harry realized that he was walking in unison with a great crowd of ordinary, everyday people all traveling in the same direction.

He could not explain how it happened, but somehow the sense of unity with the crowd and the fact that he was in uniform eased the pain in his leg, and he walked easily with little use for his cane.

Shackleton kept up a good pace. "Come on, old chap, or we'll be trapped in the crowd."

Harry imagined that Shackleton had been no different on the trek across Antarctica that had won him his knighthood. Even now Shackleton pressed ahead with his head lowered as though he were being buffeted by a polar blizzard instead of merely making an attempt to be in time to get a seat in the cathedral.

Soon they were climbing Ludgate Hill, and they could see the statue of Queen Anne and the broad steps of the cathedral under the shadow of the dome. Although they were still almost an hour away from the start of the service, the streets surrounding the cathedral were jammed with people. Many of the women wore black, and many of the men wore mourning bands around their arms. Harry wished he had taken time to do the same thing. He felt out of place in his colorful red uniform. He had thought to honor the dead, but instead, he had made himself conspicuous.

"Come on," Shackleton said. He pushed Harry forward, and although Harry could have sworn that there was no way they could reach the steps, somehow the crowd parted.

It began as a few murmured words of recognition, but soon it was taken up by the police on crowd duty. "It's Sir Ernest Shackleton. Let him through."

Harry felt a sense of guilt as he climbed the broad steps toward the open doors of the cathedral. Was this how it had been on the *Titanic*? he wondered. Did the ordinary, everyday people stand back as the famous and wealthy were ushered to the lifeboats? He could feel no ill will as the crowd parted. Shackleton was a popular figure, and Harry, now leaning on his cane, was a wounded soldier. Although they were being given preferential treatment in being admitted to the cathedral, the people left behind were not under a death sentence. He could not compare this experience to the sinking of the *Titanic*. No one here was going to die.

A police officer ushered them into the crowded cathedral, where the organ was already playing. Only hushed whispers came from the people in the pews, punctuated by an occasional sob.

Harry surveyed the crowd as he followed Shackleton to the front of the church. This congregation was not made up of survivors—they were still in America. Even those who longed to return home would not be back for several more days. Perhaps some of the mourners were relatives of the victims. A list of survivors had been sent by radio from the *Carpathia*, and the reporters had made their own assessments. They had the passenger list. They had the list of survivors. Therefore, they could make their own lists of victims. Even when the *Carpathia* arrived in New York to give firsthand information, the list had changed only slightly.

The altar had been stripped of all ornamentation and draped in simple black and white. How strange, Harry thought, that the *Titanic*, the last word in luxury and adornment, should be celebrated in such simplicity. He looked down at the printed service sheet that had been thrust into his hands as he entered, and recognized the archaic language of formal prayers drawn from the Book of Common Prayer. It seemed that Thomas Cranmer's prayer book, written nearly four hundred years before the *Titanic* had been built, had a prayer for every eventuality, even such a tragedy as the sinking of a great ship.

He stopped reading when Shackleton nudged his elbow. "Look behind the altar."

"Look at what?"

"The men in front of the choir."

Harry focused on a figure in ornate black-and-gold robes. "The Lord Mayor, I assume."

"Not him. Look at the other men."

"Who are they?"

"Members of Parliament and company bureaucrats of the White Star Line. Hypocrites all of them."

"You think?"

"I do indeed. They're sitting there in their black ties and mourning bands and pretending that what happened was an act of God."

"Wasn't it?"

Shackleton turned to face Harry. "How could it be?"

Before Harry could respond, the organ music swelled to a crescendo and settled into the familiar melody of "Rock of Ages." The congregation took up the tune, and Harry gave himself over to the dreadful solemnity of the moment.

The service drew to a close with a full-throated rendition of "For Those in Peril on the Sea." When the Dean of St. Paul's offered a benediction and a prayer for "those who go down to the sea in ships and occupy their business in great waters," Harry was reminded that the *Titanic* was just one ship among many. Even as a thousand people were offering prayers for those who had died at sea, ships were still setting out to carry people and trade to the far corners of the world.

The life of his island nation was totally dependent on the lives of those who sailed the ocean liners, cargo ships, fishing vessels, and tramp steamers setting out daily from great harbors and small ports all along the coast. However dangerous the seas may be, they had to be endured.

After the enforced silence during the service, Harry had expected Shackleton to be talkative. As a boy, he had always been full of ideas and plans, and as a man, he was a noted public speaker. Now he was silent. They stood together on the steps of the cathedral, two men who had seen their own share of conflict and death, unable to put their feelings into words.

"I think a brisk walk will do us good," Shackleton said eventually.

Harry spared a thought for the nagging ache in his left leg but fell in beside Shackleton as they set out. Shackleton had not set a destination, but as they passed Mansion House, home of the Lord Mayor, their destination became obvious. They were being drawn toward the Thames, whose rising tides brought ocean waters into the heart of London. It was the closest they could come, at that moment, to the waters that had swallowed the *Titanic*.

At Tower Hill they encountered a great throng of people gathered around a man haranguing them from the height of a temporary platform, his voice both amplified and distorted by a loudhailer. Beside him a photographer stood even higher, perched on a stepladder. It seemed that an effort was underway to take a photograph of the rapidly growing crowd.

With some effort, Harry managed to understand the shouted directions.

"One thousand five hundred and twenty three."

Shackleton tapped the shoulder of a man at the outer edge of the crowd. "What's going on?"

The man, a laborer in a tweed cap, assessed Harry and Shackleton for a moment before he spoke. "That there is Ben Tillett."

Harry and Shackleton looked at each other.

Harry spoke first. "We don't know who he is." Seeing a resentful look on the laborer's face, Harry added words of explanation. "We've been out of the country."

The laborer twitched his mustache as he gathered his words together. "Ben Tillett," he repeated. "He's the one what took us out on strike and formed our union. Champion of the working class, that's what he is."

"And what is he doing here?"

"Taking a picture," the laborer said. "He's getting one thousand five hundred and twenty three people 'cause that's what went down on the *Titanic*, and most of them were third class and crew. It's all very well singing and carrying on up at St. Paul's, but this is the real picture. This is what we lost. They saved all them first-class toffs, but who saved the immigrants and the working men? That's what he wants to know."

"There weren't sufficient lifeboats," Harry said.

"Right," said the laborer triumphantly. "There weren't sufficient lifeboats, so who gets left behind? I'll tell you who. The working man, that's who gets left behind."

"Well," said Harry, "thank you for the information. We'll get out of your way."

The laborer laughed harshly. "You ain't going nowhere, mate."

Harry turned his head to see that even in the few minutes he had been speaking, the crowd had grown. They were hemmed in on all sides.

Ben Tillett's voice reached him through the megaphone. "You in the back, the officer in uniform. Come down to the front. Come and be counted."

"No, really," Harry protested.

The laborer sniffed at him. "Thought so," he said. "Too good to care about the working man, ain't you?"

It didn't matter, Harry thought. It really wouldn't make any difference to say that he had been invalided out and he would not wear the uniform again. He was, in fact, a common man just as the laborer was a common man.

"All right," he said. "I'll be in your picture."

"And him," said another man, who was tugging at Shackleton's sleeve. "Put him in the picture. People know who he is. That's Sir Ernest Shackleton, the explorer. I've seen his picture in the paper."

Very much against their wills, Harry and Shackleton found themselves manhandled to the front of the crowd, directly below the speaker's platform. As they stood obediently waiting for the photographer to make his interminable adjustments, Ben Tillett leaned down to speak to them. They exchanged names and handshakes. Close up and without the loudhailer, Tillett was a soft-spoken man with a strong Bristol accent. Although he was small in stature, with the calloused hands of a man accustomed to physical labor, his eyes burned with the kind of fervor and self-confidence that would always mark a leader of men. Harry had seen it often enough among the ranks. He knew that certain men, even if they had no stripes, could lead where others would follow, and Tillett was such a man.

At long last the photographer declared himself satisfied with the composition. Runners in the crowd completed the count, and 1,523 Londoners stood in for the 1,523 men and women who would never be seen again.

When the crowd dispersed, Shackleton departed for a meeting of the Royal Geographic Society. Harry walked down to the Thames embankment and stared down into the river's murky depths. Ben Tillett was wrong, he thought. It was not just the poor and needy who had died on the *Titanic*. Men who were rich and famous had handed their wives into lifeboats and waited behind to die alongside the immigrants. The captain had gone down with his ship.

He tore his thoughts away from the labor leader's fiery words and turned them to his current problem. Where would he find the nieces of the Bishop of Fordingbridge?

New York City
Alvin Towson

Towson collected his new travel papers. He was now Kenneth Rotherhithe, a manufacturer's representative from Detroit, dealing in automobile parts. His letters of introduction included meetings with the Rolls Royce company in Manchester – and the GWK Motor company in Maidenhead. Inky Rockman had done a fine job of forging the papers, and Towson had done a fine job of inserting himself into a high-stakes poker game and winning enough money for a first-class ticket on the *Lapland*.

The location of the *Titanic*'s crew was no secret. It was, in fact, the talk of New York. The officers and a handful of significant crew members were presenting themselves daily at the Waldorf Astoria to be questioned by Senator William Smith. The remaining survivors were being held under guard on board the *Lapland*.

Towson had made several attempts to board the ship and had been firmly rebuffed. No one was permitted to talk to the crew, not even the reporters who lined the dock, waiting for at least a glimpse of a crew member taking the air on the third-class deck. Towson soon realized that the only way to follow the thieving stewardess would be to actually sail on the *Lapland*. She could not possibly escape him once they were at sea.

He joined the procession of first- and second-class passengers waiting to board the ship. He was amused by the complaining tone of the travelers as they boarded. These were people who had expected to travel to Southampton on board the *Titanic*, and now the White Star had given them accommodation on the only ship available—a small ship that was not up to the standard of luxury or comfort they had expected. Towson wondered what they would have made of his accommodations on the *Carpathia*, where he had slept on the floor of the dining salon.

Inky Rockman had offered to make him one of the newfangled standard passport documents, but Towson had refused.

"Just one piece of paper," Inky said. "Think of that. No letters of introduction. No having to prove who you are. Just one piece of paper and a photograph. It's going to save me a lot of work."

"Maybe next time," Towson said.

Inky studied him through thick lenses. "Word is that Alvin Towson went down on the Titanic. His name was on the list of survivors, but he was not among those who went ashore when the Carpathia *docked." He shrugged. "Some would say that the record is inaccurate and Towson must be dead, but not everyone is so easily dismissed. I, of course, offer complete confidentiality, but I would advise Mr. Rotherhithe to stay in Europe, where he may find the climate more to his liking."*

Towson dismissed Inky's advice. The forger knew nothing about the Matryoshka. The presence of the Russian courier on board the *Titanic* had been a closely guarded secret, and anyone who did know of it would assume the jewel and its courier were at the bottom of the Atlantic. Towson intended to discard his false identity and return to the United States as soon as the jewel was in his possession. He would pay his debts; the men in black overcoats would leave him alone; and he could return to working his trade on the luxury liners of the world. The only thing standing in his way was a slip of a girl. He did not know her name, but he knew where she was. She was here, on board the *Lapland*.

He sniffed impatiently and shuffled his feet while he waited for the purser to placate a New York dowager who wanted to be assured that her Pekinese would be allowed in the first-class dining room. The purser's suggestions about kennels and dog food had been met with horror, and the line of passengers was forced to wait while the dog's owner was soothed and reassured as to the safety of her lapdog. The heavyset woman dabbed at her eyes. "Those poor dogs on the *Titanic*. Only three were rescued, you know. Only three! Imagine that! So uncaring!"

Towson bit his tongue. More than fifteen hundred people had died, and dogs had been the last thing on anyone's mind as the ship buried her bow in the water and waves rolled across the deck.

When the woman had departed with her dog tucked under her arm, Towson presented his papers. "I hear you have members of the *Titanic* crew on board," he said as the purser sorted through Inky's finest work. Towson knew that Inky's work was impeccable, but even so, a little distraction wouldn't hurt.

The officer nodded. "Yes, we have some of the firemen and restaurant staff, several of the stewards, and all of the stewardesses."

"Is it possible to speak with the crew?" Towson asked.

The officer was already looking past Towson to the next passenger approaching along the gangplank. "Sorry, sir," he said abstractedly. "The *Titanic* crew is confined to third class and not allowed to make contact with anyone."

"Why would that be?"

"I don't know, sir. I assume it would be to keep the press at bay."

"But I'm not a reporter."

"Of course not, sir. But there have been problems, and so guards have been posted. There will be no mingling."

"I see."

"Will you require assistance in finding your cabin?"

Towson thought of his arrival on the *Titanic*. In Southampton no one had expected him to find his own cabin. The gangplank had been teeming with porters and stewards to smooth his way along carpeted corridors to his first-class cabin. The *Lapland* was an entirely different story. He knew that there would be slim pickings at the card table on the aging Red Star liner. He should probably keep to himself and avoid games of chance. He had sufficient money for the time being, and he should concentrate on a way to reach the stewardesses. Perhaps the sentries would be stood down after the ship had sailed. If not, well, it would have to wait until they reached Southampton. He forced himself to relax. The girl was a prisoner on the ship. He would find her in due course.

On Board the *Lapland*
Poppy Melville

The first- and second-class passengers had arrived, and at last the *Lapland* was on its way. The choppy harbor waters soon gave way to rolling waves as the ship left the Statue of Liberty behind and set its course for England. Poppy stood at the porthole, watching the skyline of New York slowly diminishing into nothing but a dark smudge against the morning sky. Despite the fact that she had missed her chance to view the statue on her way into New York, Daisy had angrily insisted that she would not now come up on deck to watch it disappear behind them, and so Poppy remained with her in the cabin, viewing the statue through the porthole.

"I'm not leaving the cabin, and you can't make me."

Poppy shrugged. "Do as you please."

"You're still angry with me," Daisy accused.

"Of course I'm angry," Poppy responded. "If Mr. Sullivan hadn't rescued you, you would be dead."

Daisy shook her head. "No, I wouldn't. I would have swum to the shore, and by now I would be on my way to California instead of on my way back to England. I didn't need to be rescued by that Australian oaf."

"What you did was stupid and dangerous," Poppy said. "I know you didn't mean it."

"I did," Daisy insisted. "I meant to jump into the water."

"No, you didn't," Poppy said. "You were making a very foolish display of yourself, and because he had to rescue you, Mr. Sullivan is now quite ill. You know he risked his life to save you."

"Why did it take him so long?" Daisy asked.

Poppy bit her tongue. She was not going to tell Daisy of her suspicion that Sullivan had never intended to save Daisy and had only used the distraction of Daisy's escapade as an opportunity to get off the ship. Perhaps she was wrong. The rest of the crew thought he was a hero. She was the only one who doubted his intentions, and now was not the time to speak.

She pushed her suspicions aside. Whatever his original motive for going into the water, there was no doubt that he had saved Daisy's life.

"You're lucky to be alive," she said. "The way you were thrashing about, it's a wonder you didn't drown Mr. Sullivan. You should get out of bed and go and thank him."

Daisy pulled the blanket up around her shoulders. "If you're so grateful, you go and thank him. I'm staying here."

"You are very fortunate to have that choice," Poppy said, wishing that her sister would just for once think of others before herself.

"What do you mean?"

"We're no longer crew. Miss Stap can't come and drag you out of bed and set you to work. This time we're passengers, and our time is our own."

"Third-class passengers," Daisy sniffed, looking around at the cramped cabin.

"Oh, for goodness' sake," Poppy snapped. "Stop feeling sorry for yourself. Come up on deck and see the rest of the crew. Look at it from their point of view. Most of them have been at sea since they were fourteen or fifteen years old, but they've never been passengers on a ship; they've always been workers. After what we've all been through, they deserve this. They deserve some time to heal. I don't care what you think of the White Star Line and the way they've treated us, at least they've done one good thing. They've chartered this whole ship just to get us home."

Daisy shook her head. "You don't really believe that, do you? They chartered this ship so that the passengers booked on the *Titanic's* return trip from New York to England would still be able to travel. They didn't do it just for us. We're nothing."

No, Poppy thought, *we're not nothing. We're the White Star Line's worst nightmare.* Daisy was right in saying that the White Star Line had had to make arrangements for the paying passengers who had been waiting to make the *Titanic's* return trip to England, but that wasn't the reason why the lowliest members of the *Titanic's* crew were now getting a free ride across the Atlantic. They were on this ship because the White Star Line wanted to be quite sure they would not find a way to go ashore in New York. They would do anything to prevent the surviving crew from talking to the newspapers.

Poppy sat at the foot of Daisy's bunk and looked into her sister's sullen face. "Some of those men are still in a bad way, Daisy. We stewardesses just stepped from the deck of the *Titanic* and into a lifeboat, and we never even got wet, but they—"

"I didn't," Daisy said. "I didn't just step into a lifeboat. I got wet."

"Yes, I know," Poppy said, studying her sister closely. "Why did that happen? Why did you get wet? Why weren't you in your assigned lifeboat?"

Daisy's face turned from sullen to secretive. "Stop asking questions. Leave me alone."

Poppy rose to her feet. "All right, I'll leave you alone. I'm going up on deck. We'll talk about this later."

Poppy's mind was fully occupied as she threaded her way through the maze of corridors and stairs that led from the third-class cabins to the allotted third-class deck space. Unlike Daisy, who had spent the past twenty-four hours sulking, Poppy had been making a plan. In nine days' time, the *Lapland* would be in Southampton. The White Star Line would pay their wages, and there was nothing to stop them signing on to another ship and earning even more money. The harbor at Southampton was always filled with transatlantic liners, and they always needed crew members.

Poppy knew that Miss Stap and the other stewardesses would help her to get a good reference, and there would be nothing to stop her from walking off one ship and onto another. The dream wasn't over; it was just postponed. Of course, she would have to think of a way to get a good reference for Daisy, and that would certainly not come from Miss Stap, but maybe it would not have to. When she stopped sulking, Daisy would have no trouble getting her own reference from one of the officers. All she had to do was shake her curls and cry a few tears.

Poppy climbed the last set of narrow stairs and walked out onto the third-class promenade deck, relishing the idea of sitting in a deck chair. She realized how very tired she was—tired of working, tired of being cold, and tired of worrying about Daisy. She found a corner where the towering bridge deck provided shelter from the wind, and pulled a deck chair into a patch of sunlight. With a sigh of relief, she lowered herself into the chair and propped her feet on the footstool. She had never sat like this on the *Titanic* or even on the *Carpathia*. *So this is what it means to be a passenger.*

She allowed her thoughts to drift. Just this once she would not worry about Daisy, or California, or the possibility that her father would somehow discover where she was. Her waking thoughts fractured and dissolved into a dreamscape of the woods and fields of her childhood.

She was startled awake by an abrupt change in the steady thrum of the engines and the motion of the waves. Panic took hold, catapulting her from the deck chair to stand shaking and clutching for an explanation. The ship had stopped. Was it happening again? Were they sinking? Her mind would not allow her to stay safely aboard the *Lapland*. Her eyes refused to see daylight. Memories crowded in, replacing the sunshine and blue sky with a bone-chilling, moonless night.

The cry of seagulls became the cry of a thousand people struggling in the water.

Arms reached up to cling to the sides of the lifeboat.

"Let them in. We have room."

"There are too many. They'll sink us. Pull on your oars."

Poppy stretched out her arm. "Just this one. Just this woman."

"I said to leave them alone."

A hand on her shoulder pulled her back to reality. The night faded, and the sunlight returned as she looked into Ernie Sullivan's scarred face. He held her with a steady gray-eyed gaze.

"You're all right. Nothing to worry about." It seemed as though a shadow passed across his eyes. "The memories will fade with time."

She still teetered on the edge of panic. "What's happened? Why have we stopped?"

"Nothing's happened," he said. "Well, not so far as we're concerned. We've instructions to heave to and wait for a tugboat coming out from New York."

Poppy blinked her eyes into focus and looked around. The *Lapland* was wallowing in the troughs between waves with only minimal forward movement. A spit of land crowned with a white lighthouse lay to their starboard, and beyond that she could see the rise and fall of deep ocean waves. Why would they stop here?

"Is the tug bringing someone?" she asked. "Another crew

member?"

Sullivan shook his head. "Taking some people off."

He turned away from her and hooked his foot under a deck chair, dragging it forward so that he could sit beside her. His hands were swathed in clean bandages, and the white slash of scar faded into his pale face. At least he was no longer flushed with fever. Apparently, the Aspirin powder Poppy had offered had succeeded in breaking his fever.

He settled into the deck chair. "Mind if I sit next to you? I'm not up to standing at the moment."

"My sister is very grateful," Poppy said as she returned to her own deck chair.

"Perhaps she could tell me that herself," Sullivan suggested.

Poppy lowered her eyes, embarrassed that she could not make Daisy leave her bunk and at least thank the man who had saved her life.

"So who is being taken off?" Poppy asked. "They don't want Daisy, do they?"

Sullivan raised his eyebrows in an expression that spoke louder than words. *No one wants Daisy.*

"The American senators, in their wisdom, have decided they want to speak to Quartermaster Hichens and a few other crew members, so they're being taken off."

"Why? What have they all done?"

"Hichens was at the helm when we hit the berg. They want to ask him some questions. As for the others, I don't know what they did or didn't do, but the rumors are already starting. A whole lot of people died, and someone has to take the blame. Things are going to become very unpleasant for all of us unless we are careful." He grinned. "I disagreed with Miss Stap at the time, but now I am not so sure. I see the value of silence. Don't volunteer information."

"I don't have any information," Poppy said.

Sullivan grinned again. "Make sure your sister keeps quiet. She may know too much."

"She doesn't know anything."

Sullivan shook his head. "She knows something." He glanced over his shoulder. "Here come the lambs for the slaughter."

Five men appeared on deck, each carrying a kit bag. They were dressed in ill-fitting civilian clothes donated by the citizens of New

York. Perhaps those suits had once been smart and eye-catching, but now they could not draw the eye away from the grim, haunted faces of the men who wore them.

As the five men assembled, other members of the *Titanic* crew appeared on the deck. Even Miss Stap and her coterie of stewardesses emerged to find out what was happening.

One of the five crewmen, a small man with a receding hairline, set his kit bag on the deck and stared moodily back toward the city. "It wasn't up to me," he said. When no one responded, he repeated his declaration. "It wasn't up to me. I done what I was told. I ain't the lookout. They should be taking Lee, not me."

A voice rose from among the assembled huddle of crewmen. "They have Fleet. He's the one who saw the bloody thing."

"But Hichens is the one who hit it."

Poppy looked at Sullivan. He was the only man paying attention to her. The attention of everyone else was on Hichens. If Daisy had been on deck, it would have been a very different story.

"Is it true?" she asked. "Is he the one who hit the berg?"

Sullivan shook his head. "I suppose you could say that, but it's not the way it sounds. Steering an ocean liner is not like steering a little motorboat. There is a man at the helm with his hands on the wheel, but he's not making decisions. He's given a compass heading to keep, and that's what he does. He spends his watch staring at the binnacle. The watch officer is there to make sure he stays on course, and the lookout is aloft, watching out for trouble. I don't know why anyone would blame Hichens."

"Because it's easy," Poppy said thoughtfully. "He was steering. He's an obvious target."

"Quite right, young lady."

Poppy looked up to see Joughin, the *Titanic*'s chief baker, studying the other crew members with obvious disdain.

"Our troubles are not yet over," Joughin declared. "Let us hope to God that these few men are all that will be taken off the ship and that this is the last time we're forced to stop. The Americans have gone wild. If they keep this up, there will be diplomatic repercussions. It's obvious they have no real plan to make a proper inquiry. They're posturing for the newspapers. Their Senator Smith is not a seaman. He hears that Hichens was at the helm, so he calls for him to be brought ashore. He understands nothing. He's just an ambitious politician grasping at straws."

"You haven't been ashore," Poppy said. "How do you know all this?"

"I have my own common sense," Joughin replied, "and I have also spoken to the *Lapland*'s officers. We have none of our own officers on here, so they speak to me, recognizing that I am an educated man and it is better to speak to me than to try to talk with a crew of deck monkeys."

"Hey," said Sullivan. "You might want to think twice about talking like that, mate."

Joughin inclined his head. "I take it back. Some are more like apes than monkeys, but you, Mr. Sullivan, are neither an ape nor a monkey. I have not decided what you are."

No, Poppy thought, *neither have I.*

"It's all about compensation," Joughin said. "If the inquiry led by Senator Smith can prove that the *Titanic* was being driven at an irresponsible speed, or was manned by an irresponsible crew, or that the ship itself was unfit to sail and falsely certified, the White Star will be liable for massive compensation claims."

Poppy could not help glancing at Sullivan for confirmation. Something about the Australian marked him as a leader, a man who would know what others did not know.

He nodded his head. "We're all on that hook," he said. "The Americans are only just beginning to ask questions, but Britain won't be far behind. We'll all be giving evidence before this is over."

"Surely not the cabin staff," Poppy protested with a sinking heart. "They won't want to talk to the stewardesses."

"Why not?" Sullivan asked.

"Because we don't know anything."

"You may know more than you think," Sullivan said. "In fact, we may all know too much."

Riddlesdown Court
Harry Hazelton

Harry's first impression was that time had been kind to Riddlesdown Court, seat of the 9th Earl of Riddlesdown. The sprawling redbrick house was comfortably at one with the landscape, with ivy climbing the walls and ancient oak trees providing it with shade. The wrought-iron gates stood open as if to welcome him as he walked up from the train station.

He leaned on his Malacca cane and made no attempt to disguise his limp. Before setting out for Riddlesdown, he had dressed in a suit of rough tweed and used a toothbrush dipped in Blanco to add streaks of white to the flecks of gray in his hair and mustache. He regarded the cane as part of his disguise. He was not Captain Harry Hazelton of the East Surrey Regiment; he was Samuel Lloyd, an elderly man possessed of a slight Welsh accent who was interested in finding a retirement cottage. Having stumbled across the Riddlesdown Estate, he thought he would inquire whether the earl had anything he would like to sell or lease. With the white hair of age and the obvious limp, he would be hard to turn away from the door. Perhaps he would be invited in for at least a drink of water.

He felt a familiar thrill as he stood by the side of the road and made ready to inhabit another persona and become someone he was not. Admittedly, this was a far cry from impersonating an Afghan warlord or an Indian beggar, but he still needed to remind himself of the challenge involved. The Earl of Riddlesdown had no reason to be suspicious of him, but Harry was a naturally cautious man, and now, studying his surroundings, he revised his first impression of Riddlesdown Court. The gates, standing open as if in welcome, had been standing open for a very long time. Weeds had grown up around their bases, and woodbine vines were tangled in the ornate metalwork and were well on their way to obliterating the Riddlesdown family crest that sat atop the gates.

Having taken note of the neglected entryway, Harry studied Riddlesdown Court itself with a more jaundiced eye. He could see now that it was not careful landscaping that gave the impression that the old house was at one with nature. It was in fact in grave danger of being completely overtaken by nature. Ivy straddled up and over the latticed windows, crept across the roof, and threatened to pull down the ornate Tudor chimneys. Dead leaves from the oak trees lay in thick drifts across the neglected lawns and terraces, and the trees themselves were scarred and split by lightning strikes.

Harry mounted the shallow steps leading to the massive oak front door and hunted in vain for a bellpull. Apparently, visitors arriving at the front door had no way to announce themselves. Perhaps all visitors were expected to arrive at the back door or the kitchen door. He shook his head. He would enter by the front door or not at all. He had been too long in India, where a white man was treated like a lord, and too long in the army, where an officer commanded respect. Of course, he was no longer in India, and no longer in the army, but he decided that Samuel Lloyd was a man who would not use a tradesman's entrance. Samuel Lloyd would want to enter by the front door. He briefly rehearsed his Welsh accent and then lifted the Malacca cane and rapped on the door ... again and again.

Persistent rapping finally paid off, and the door slowly cracked open. Harry peered through the crack and caught a glimpse of a small child. "It's a man," the child declared before disappearing from view and leaving Harry to his own devices.

Taking the cracked door as an invitation, Harry pushed it open and stepped inside. The entrance hall of Riddlesdown Court was unmistakably Tudor, from black and white tiles on the floor to the hammer-beam ceiling and the tall arched windows. The child, a girl in a smocked dress, fled at his approach, stirring up dust motes that floated in the beams of light filtering through the windows. As she ran on bare feet toward the rear of the house, she repeated her warning. "It's a man."

Before Harry could follow the little girl, an interior door opened, and an older girl appeared, followed by a sour-faced woman in a loose house dress. The little girl addressed her in a high-pitched, excited voice.

"It's a man, Mama. It's a man." She began to skip in small, excited circles, repeating the information in a high singsong voice. "A man, a man, there's a man at the door. A man, a man ..."

Harry was not sure how long he could listen to this chant without receiving damage to his eardrums, but fortunately, a thundering voice from the top of the stairs brought the child to an abrupt halt.

"Be quiet! Stop that damnable screeching. Go away."

The two girls fled in terror. When the woman turned to follow them, the voice from the stairs thundered again. "Not you, Agnes. You stay until we see what the fellow wants."

The Earl of Riddlesdown was a tall man with stooped shoulders. His long face was adorned with a drooping mustache that matched the unfortunate carroty-orange hair spread thinly across his head. His pale blue eyes stared at Harry with a look of habitual disapproval.

Harry quickly reviewed the information he had received from the bishop. The sour-faced woman must be Lady Riddlesdown, the earl's third wife. He noted that she quivered nervously as her husband descended the stairs.

The earl turned his attention to Harry. "Who the devil are you?" he demanded.

"Samuel Lloyd," Harry said. Although the man on the stairs was nowhere near as powerful or dangerous as even the most ill-equipped Peshwari rebel, Harry allowed himself to sound intimidated. "I'm hoping to become a neighbor," he said.

"A neighbor," the earl expostulated. "We don't need neighbors."

"I am hoping to find a retirement cottage or perhaps buy a small plot of land ..." Harry allowed Samuel Lloyd's voice to waver into uncomfortable silence.

A sour expression crossed the earl's face, but it could not hide a flicker of interest.

"I won't sell so much as a square inch of my land."

No, Harry thought, *you won't sell your land, but you obviously need money.* From the corner of his eye, he caught a look of something approaching desperate greed on Lady Riddlesdown's tired face.

"I understand," Harry said. "I'm sure the land has been in your family for many years."

"Five hundred years," the earl snapped.

Harry took a halting step forward, leaning heavily on his cane. "Five hundred years," he said breathlessly. "How very wonderful. If I cannot persuade you to part with a small corner—"

"You cannot."

Harry pasted an unctuous smile on his face and continued. "Perhaps a lease," he suggested, "of one of your workers' cottages. I would, of course, undertake all necessary renovations at my own expense."

"At your own expense," the earl repeated.

Harry felt the thrill of the fish taking his bait. "Of course."

The earl descended to the bottom step and thrust out his hand. "Lord Riddlesdown," he said. He gestured to his wife. "Lady Agnes Riddlesdown."

Harry shook hands with the earl and inclined his head to Lady Riddlesdown, taking in the fact that Lady Riddlesdown's dress was draped across an extended pregnant belly. For a moment, he forgot where he was and what manners required of him. It would be ungentlemanly to even notice Lady Riddlesdown's condition, and he certainly should not stare or wonder if the woman was about to bear twins, but he had been too long out of England. He had served in the Boer War. The tribal women of South Africa wore almost no clothes, and a pregnancy could not be concealed. Even the Boer women his regiment had captured and placed in concentration camps had been proud of their condition, proud to be bearing new Voortrekkers for their *vaderland*. As for India … He swallowed hard. No, he would not think about that.

Lady Riddlesdown, whose sallow face seemed to have swollen to match her belly, looked warily at her husband. "Shepherdsfold Cottage," she said tentatively.

The earl scratched fiercely at his thin hair. "I suppose I could consider it." He glared at Harry. "I will not part with my son's inheritance," he said, "but a lifetime lease with you paying for the renovations …"

"So you have a son," Harry said, knowing full well that was not the case. He decided on impulse that Samuel Lloyd also had a son, maybe even two or three sons. "I have sons," he said. "How old is your boy?"

"He is not yet born," the earl said between gritted teeth, "but my wife tells me it will be very soon. All I have now is an unfortunate gaggle of girls."

Harry hastily added a daughter to his family. "I have a daughter," he said. "She's just turned twenty-one. I'm sure she'd be delighted to have the companionship of your daughters if you have any her age."

"I have two who are about that age," the earl growled, "but I haven't seen them today. I assume they're around here somewhere and can be summoned to speak with you."

"They went to London," Lady Riddlesdown said.

The earl scowled at her. "I know that. They went shopping for clothes for their brother. That was days ago. I remember giving Penelope money for their expedition. Are you telling me they haven't come back?"

Lady Riddlesdown looked down at the floor. "Not yet," she said.

The earl scratched at his hair again. "Why not? Where the devil are they?"

"I suppose they were delayed," Lady Riddlesdown said vaguely.

Lord Riddlesdown dismissed the question of his daughters with a sudden wave of his hand. "Let's not worry about that now." He turned back to Harry. "I'll have a word with my estate manager about the cottage, and we'll talk again. Where can I reach you?"

Where indeed? Harry asked himself. As there had not been time to complete his disguise with a printed calling card, he settled for giving the earl the phone number of his aunt Cynthia and hoping that he could contact her in time to tell her that she was now the relative of an elderly Welshman.

The earl turned back toward the stairs. "Lady Riddlesdown will see you out," he said.

Harry watched the earl disappearing into the dusty upper reaches of the house. His task was only partially accomplished. He had confirmed that the bishop's nieces were not at home, and that their father and stepmother neither knew nor cared where they were. Now he needed to talk to Nanny Catchpole.

He looked at Lady Riddlesdown standing uncomfortably with her hands resting on her belly. "Perhaps," he said, "I could sit down for a few minutes." He tapped his leg with is cane. "Boer War," he grunted. "Got this at Ladysmith. Plays up every now and then. Just need a short breather, and then I'll be on my way."

"Yes, of course," Lady Riddlesdown said. "Come into the parlor, and I'll arrange for some tea."

Harry followed her into a dusty sitting room and sank onto a spindly sofa as Lady Riddlesdown tugged on a tasseled bellpull. While they waited for whoever had been summoned, the little girl who had opened the door for him tiptoed into the room and plonked herself down on the hearthrug before the empty grate. She had her father's sparse hair and her mother's olive complexion. "They're gone," she said in a small, spiteful voice, "and they're not coming back."

"What are you talking about?" Lady Riddlesdown asked wearily.

"Penelope and Marguerite. They're not coming back."

"Don't be ridiculous, Olivia."

The door opened, and the older child entered. Although he knew them to be half sisters, Harry could see little resemblance between the two girls. While Olivia had her father's hair and, unfortunately, his nose, this older child had a mop of brown curls and petite features.

"They've taken all their clothes, and they're not coming back," she said.

Before she was able to control it, an expression of pure relief flashed across Lady Riddlesdown's face. She masked her initial reaction by resorting to irritation. "Don't be absurd, Dianna. You have no business to say such things."

Dianna placed her hands on her hips. "If they're not coming back, and if your baby isn't a boy ..."

A look of terror crossed Lady Riddlesdown's face. "It is a boy."

"But if it isn't," Dianna persisted, "and if they don't come back, then I'm the oldest, and I can be the countess."

Lady Riddlesdown shook her head. "You are going to have a brother. Your father has decided."

"Nanny says that only God decides."

Lady Riddlesdown staggered to her feet and pointed to the door. "Your father decides," she hissed, "and he will not have it any other way. Leave this room at once. Take Olivia with you."

Dianna leaned down and dragged Olivia to her feet. Olivia's screams of protest shook the rafters. The earl's voice thundered from somewhere beyond the doorway, and Lady Riddlesdown hurried after the two children.

Harry was suddenly alone with only the distant shrieking of the child and the roaring of the earl for company. He could not help thinking of Henry VIII as he stared up at the hammer-beam ceiling. The Tudor architecture of Riddlesdown Court, the carroty color of the earl's hair, the death of two previous wives, and the insistence that the current wife should produce a son dragged him from his own world and back into the blood-soaked world of the Tudors. King Henry VIII had had two daughters he didn't want, but they had both lived to become queens. Perhaps the earl's daughters would have the same good fortune.

He was still shaking his head at the absurdity of his thoughts when the door opened and a plump woman in an apron entered with a tea tray.

"Nanny Catchpole?" he asked.

PART TWO

HOMEWARD

BOUND

To my poor fellow-sufferers: My heart overflows with grief for you all and is laden with sorrow that you are weighed down with this terrible burden that has been thrust upon us. May God be with us and comfort us all.

Eleanor Smith, wife of the late Captain Smith

Eileen Enwright Hodgetts

CHAPTER FIVE

On Board the *Lapland*
Poppy Melville

Daisy was strong, but Poppy was stronger—she had always been stronger, and she had always known what was best for Daisy. She had kept quiet for three days and allowed Daisy to remain in bed and wallow in self-pity, but enough was enough. The time had come for Daisy to show some backbone. She could almost feel Nanny Catchpole cheering her on as she stripped the blankets from Daisy's bunk.

"I'm not getting up," Daisy said sullenly. "You can't make me."

Poppy flung Daisy's hat and coat onto the bunk. "Put them on, or I'll do it for you."

"I don't want to go outside," Daisy wailed. "It's cold out there, and it's not even morning. It's the middle of the night."

Poppy spoke through gritted teeth as she wrestled her sister's arms into the sleeves of her coat. "That's why we're going outside now. I don't want anyone else to see you like this. You've gone three days without even washing your face and combing your hair. You're a disgrace."

"I don't care," Daisy said. "It doesn't matter what I look like. No one's looking at me—at least no one who matters."

"I'm looking at you," Poppy said, "and I don't like what I see." She softened her voice. "What's this all about, Daisy? Why are you behaving like this? Are you embarrassed about falling into the harbor?"

"Embarrassed?" Daisy snorted. "Why should I be embarrassed? I didn't fall; I jumped. I took decisive action. Father would be proud of me."

Poppy shook her head. "Father doesn't care, but I do. We're

going up on deck so you can get some fresh air, and then you're going to take a bath. We're only a couple of days from port, and you are not going to arrive looking like a derelict gutter girl and smelling like a tramp."

Daisy gave Poppy a sideways glance. Her expression was hard to read. She looked as though she was about to cry. Poppy wondered if they would be real tears or just the crocodile tears that Daisy could produce on demand. Because Daisy and the truth were so often at odds with each other, Poppy was always on her guard.

Tears began to trickle down Daisy's face as she meekly allowed Poppy to button her into her coat. "I'll go outside if you want me to," she said, "but I'm really, really, really afraid."

"Afraid of what?"

"Of being outside. Of ... of ... of remembering."

The last words were uttered with a choking sob accompanied by a flood of tears. Poppy sighed in confusion. She remembered the words of Nanny Catchpole, the only woman who was a constant in their lives. *Sometimes you have to be cruel to be kind.* This felt cruel. There was a chance that Daisy was telling the truth and she really was terrified to go outside. It was entirely possible that she was suffering from delayed shock. Miss Stap had kept her staff very busy on board the *Carpathia*, and there had been no time to really think about all that had happened. Now that they were passengers on the *Lapland*, they had all the time in the world to remember, and their memories were the stuff of nightmares.

Poppy was sorely tempted to leave Daisy where she was. For the three days that Daisy had been huddled beneath blankets and refusing to move, Poppy had experienced a new level of freedom. For once in her life, she was not looking over her shoulder to see what Daisy was doing. For three days, she had shared in the company of the surviving *Titanic* crew, sitting with them in the dining room or walking on the decks.

Miss Stap had remained sour and disapproving, but she had no authority over them. Poppy was not even sure that they were still White Star employees. If the pay had stopped, then so had the company's ability to control them. She was well aware that their passage on the *Lapland* had been purchased in order to keep them away from American reporters. She wondered what would happen when they reached Southampton. Surely the British reporters would be waiting for them.

Poppy stiffened her resolve. She could not be certain that Daisy was telling her the truth about her fears, but it made no difference. It was time for Daisy to wash her face, comb her hair, and rejoin the crew.

Poppy reached into her pocket for a handkerchief. Just as she had done when Daisy was a small child, she wiped her sister's eyes and held the handkerchief to her nose. "Blow."

Daisy blew her nose like an obedient three-year-old.

"That's better," Poppy said. "Now, let's talk about what's really the matter."

"I don't feel well. Probably the harbor water."

"If that were the case, you would be as sick as poor Mr. Sullivan, who has not yet recovered from his infected wounds. You're not sick, Daisy. What is really the matter?"

Daisy's glance slid away from her. "It was all so horrible," she said.

"Yes, it was," Poppy agreed, "but we survived. Now we have to pick ourselves up, dust ourselves off, and—"

"You sound like Nanny Catchpole," Daisy complained.

"And you sound like a whiny child," Poppy snapped. "Come on. If you won't walk, I'll carry you."

"You wouldn't."

"Oh yes I would." Poppy leaned down and scooped up her startled sister. Although Poppy was tall and strong and Daisy was quite petite, Poppy had a struggle to heave her onto her shoulder and hold her there one-handed as she opened the door and stepped out into the corridor.

"You're hurting me," Daisy complained.

Poppy set her down. "Are you going to walk?"

"Oh, all right. I'll walk."

Poppy kept a firm grasp on Daisy's hand as they climbed the stairs to the open deck. She had chosen this moment in the dead of night to drag her sister from her bed because she knew the deck would be deserted. Daisy liked to play to an audience, but Poppy knew she would find no audience this time of night. She pulled open the outer door and stepped out onto the third-class promenade deck.

The air was cold, frighteningly reminiscent of the night the *Titanic* had foundered. Poppy staggered a little at her own rush of memory. The moon peeked from beneath a bank of clouds, but the sky directly overhead was alive with stars, just as it had been on the night when an iceberg had ripped her world apart. She shivered in the cold night air, imagining that the wind was carrying the chill of icebergs somewhere perilously close by. She tipped her head back, trying to glimpse the crow's nest. Someone was on watch. After what had happened to the *Titanic*, surely every ship would have doubled its watch.

She fought down her memories and took a few deep breaths. When she was certain that she had herself under control, she pulled Daisy out into the open air.

Daisy took several steps forward, stumbled, and then fell dramatically to her knees. "I hate you," she gasped.

"I know you do. Try to stand up."

"I can't."

Perhaps that was the truth. Perhaps at that moment Daisy could not stand. On the other hand, Daisy was quite capable of this level of pretense. *One thing at a time.* Poppy decided that she would choose to believe this emotion was real. She squatted down beside Daisy, who was still on her knees.

"We have to do this, Daisy," she whispered. "If you can't face up to an ocean crossing, you'll never achieve your dream. Hollywood is on the other side of the ocean. There's no other way to get there. I'm here to help you. Tell me what happened."

"I can't."

"Yes, you can."

Poppy slid down into a sitting position and pulled Daisy's head onto her lap. Stroking her sister's tangled hair, she asked again. "What happened?"

April 15, 1912
On Board the Titanic 1:00 a.m. (Ship's Time)
Daisy Melville

When Mr. Crawford knocked on the cabin door and told Daisy and Poppy that they should put on their life jackets and rouse the women under their care, Daisy had been quietly thrilled. Obviously, nothing was seriously wrong with the Titanic—that would be impossible—but the call to put on life jackets was at least an interruption in the dreariness of working her passage across the Atlantic. Who would have thought that serving a handful of wealthy women would be such hard work?

She knew that it was because she was well spoken and well groomed that she had been assigned to the first-class cabins along with Poppy. Despite her complete lack of attention to their governess, Daisy had managed to become fluent in French. Apparently, she had a gift for languages, and the ability to speak fluent French and some elementary German had been seen as an asset. She had assumed, wrongly as it happened, that the wealthy women would be traveling with their own maids. Some were, but some were not, and Daisy found herself taking on the typical tasks of a lady's maid. She helped with hairdressing; she laid out clothes; and she even filled bathtubs. She was extremely impatient to arrive in New York and be rid of the spoiled old dowagers and hatchet-faced maiden ladies who had been taking up all her time.

She peeked out into the corridor. The ship was still quiet with most of the passengers asleep. She suspected that there would be some gentlemen lingering in the smoking room, but the ladies, at least, were all abed. Obeying Mr. Crawford's command, she and Poppy helped each other into their life jackets and exited the cabin, closing the door quietly behind them.

"What do you think is happening?" Daisy asked.

Poppy shrugged. "Lifeboat drill, perhaps. I'm sure there'll be some very angry passengers by the time we arrive at our lifeboat stations. Still, I suppose we had better get on with it. Do you know your lifeboat number and station? Did you study the list?"

"Of course I did," Daisy lied. "I'll go and wake up all my miserable old ladies and see you on the boat deck. It's really cold outside, and they are going to be very unhappy." She stopped to think. "You don't suppose this is a real emergency, do you?"

Poppy shook her head. "Of course not. We all know the Titanic *is the safest ship afloat. Besides, if we were really sinking, don't you think the crew would look a little more worried?" She gestured to a group of stewards who were proceeding very quietly along the corridor and knocking gently on cabin doors. They were all wearing life jackets, but they didn't seem serious about awaking the passengers. "If this were an emergency," Poppy said, "they'd be hammering on the doors. I don't know what's going on, but it's nothing serious."*

Daisy parted from her sister and proceeded to the cabin occupied by Miss Helena Bonelli and her niece Augustine, two ladies who were nothing but trouble. They had first-class tickets, but Daisy knew they were not accustomed to being among society ladies. Miss Bonelli had only two evening gowns, and Miss Augustine's clothes looked as though she had borrowed them from a considerably larger lady. They fussed over Daisy's mismanagement of their hairstyles and her inability to properly steam the creases out of their fusty old dresses. They were on their way to visit Miss Bonelli's brother in Youngstown, Ohio, where he was, so they said, a successful jeweler.

At least that part of the story was true, Daisy thought. Miss Bonelli had several very nice necklaces, and her niece had insisted on wearing a rather splendid comb in her hair every night. Every night! Daisy sniffed disgustedly. When they reached California and she became a star, she would have a different diamond comb for every night of the week. She would never wear the same one twice.

As Daisy lifted her hand to knock on the cabin door, she heard the voices of two men talking together as they came along the corridor. She lowered her hand and waited for them to pass and was surprised to see that one of the men was Captain Smith, who she recognized immediately. Although she had never dined in the first-class dining room or visited the bridge, she had seen the captain numerous times making his own patrols around the vessel. He was a commanding figure with a neat white beard, a jacket ornamented with a dazzling amount of gold braid, and a stern but not unfriendly face. She took a moment to recognize the other man, who wore no uniform and looked as though he had dressed in a hurry. Thomas Andrews, she thought, chief designer and architect of the Titanic.

The two men were both frowning and speaking in worried tones, although she could only catch a word or two. They were talking about the mail room. "Water in the mail room. Water in the squash court."

Daisy tugged at her life jacket. Were they serious? Was water coming into the ship? Poppy had said this was only a lifeboat drill; nothing had happened to the ship.

Captain Smith focused his eyes on her, and his frown

deepened. *"What are you doing?"*

"I'm a stewardess, sir. I was told to wake my ladies and have them put on their life jackets, sir." She was surprised that she had twice addressed the captain as *"sir."* She was not in the habit of being respectful and obedient, but the word had come from some deep instinct created not only by his obvious rank but by the aura of urgent command that seemed to crackle in the air around him.

Mr. Andrews placed a hand on her shoulder. *"Do it now,"* he said. *"Try not to alarm them, but make sure they go to their lifeboat stations."*

Daisy's heart seemed to have left its moorings and was bouncing around in her chest. *"Why? What's happened."*

"We've struck an iceberg," Mr. Andrews said. *"It was not a violent collision. In fact, I felt no more than a small bump, but our hull is damaged, and we are taking on water."* He fixed her with a stern brown-eyed gaze. *"We will need to put the women and children into the lifeboats."*

"Are we going to sink?"

Mr. Andrews said nothing and turned his head toward Captain Smith. *"What should we tell the passengers?"*

"We'll tell them the truth," Captain Smith said with a hearty air that did not sit well with Daisy. *"We'll tell them we're putting them into the boats so we can effect repairs."*

"But why do they have to go into the lifeboats?" Daisy asked. The captain's suggestion made no sense. Why would he want to put all the women and children into small boats? How would that help them to repair the ship?

Captain Smith did not raise his voice; he merely narrowed his eyes. *"That, young lady, is what you will tell them. You may also say that there is another ship nearby. We can see her lights, and we are raising her on the Marconi. Our sailors will row the ladies to this other ship, where they will be safe while we deal with ..."* His voice died away for a moment. He shook his head. *"It is enough for them to know that they will be safe. Now get on with it. We do not have much time."*

Captain Smith and Mr. Andrews walked away along the corridor, and Daisy stood still for a moment. Her heart was still hammering against her ribs. If everything was under control, if the damage could be repaired, and if another ship was close by, why *did the captain look so very worried? More to the point, why did Mr. Andrews look so very sad?*

Well, she'd been told what to do, and she supposed she should do it. Until she had arrived on the Titanic, *she had taken orders from no one. In the past few days, she had been forced to bite her lip several times to avoid telling her "ladies" exactly what she thought of them. If only they knew who she really was, they would ... She reined in her angry thoughts and concentrated on what the captain and Mr. Andrews had said to each other. Water in the mail room. Water on the squash court. The Titanic had struck an iceberg, not with a loud bang, but very gently, and yet nothing could hide the despair in Mr. Andrews's eyes.*

She made up her mind to go up on deck and make sure that Poppy knew what was happening. Fortune had smiled on her, and she knew what no one else knew. Surely Poppy must be her priority, not Miss Bonelli and her whining, demanding niece.

Before Daisy could turn to leave, the cabin door was flung open, and Miss Bonelli herself stood in the doorway. She was clad in a quilted robe, and her hair was wrapped in a satin scarf to preserve her hairstyle, a frivolous array of ringlets that Daisy thought totally unsuitable for a woman of Miss Bonelli's advanced years. Well, what could she expect? Miss Bonelli was an old Italian lady, and her ticket had been purchased by her nouveau-riche brother. The only first-class thing about her was her jewelry.

"What is this? What is happening?" Miss Bonelli demanded to know.

" You are to put on your life jacket and go up to your lifeboat station."

"Eh? What do you say?"

Daisy sighed. Miss Bonelli was hard of hearing, and even when she did hear, she didn't understand. Her English was only very rudimentary.

The niece, Augustine, appeared behind her aunt. "What is it, Zietta?"

"She say life jacket."

"Life jacket," Augustine repeated. She looked at Daisy, and her dark eyes flashed. "Why life jacket?"

"Because we've hit an iceberg and we're going to sink," Daisy said impatiently. "Put on your life jackets, and go up to your

boat station."

When she turned away, Augustine caught hold of her arm. "Sink? You say we sink?"

Daisy belatedly remembered the captain's instructions—she was to be reassuring and say nothing about the possibility of sinking. She waved away her previous remark. "No, we're not going to sink. I never said that we are going to sink."

"You said—"

"Never mind about that. Try to understand me. You will be put in a lifeboat and be rowed across to another ship. You'll be perfectly safe. Now put on your life jackets. They are on top of the wardrobe."

"You stay here and you help," Augustine insisted. "Is your job."

"No, no. I have to tell the other passengers."

"No. You help me," Augustine insisted. She snatched the life jackets from their place on top of the wardrobe. "How do we do this? You show me."

Daisy spread her arms and turned in a circle. "Look, see what I've done. Now you do the same."

Instead of looking at Daisy, Augustine's aunt was rummaging through the chest of drawers.

"Life jacket," Daisy repeated impatiently.

"Corsetto," said Miss Bonelli. "Il mio corsetto."

Augustine shook her head. "Not now, Zietta." She held out the life jacket. "This. We put on this."

Daisy nodded. "So you're fine? You understand? Good. Tell your aunt she won't need her corset, not that it ever made any difference. Now I have to get on and tell other people. You go to your lifeboat station, and I will see you there."

When she stepped out of the cabin, Daisy found that the corridor was no longer deserted. Instead, it was crowded with bemused passengers, some wearing evening clothes and some wearing nightclothes. Stewards were pressing in among them, forcing reluctant ladies to put on life jackets.

"I shall look ridiculous in this thing."

Daisy tried to ignore the chatter of the overprivileged passengers. This woman wanted her fur coat; another wanted to bring her lapdog; another had a maid struggling behind her, dragging a *trunk.*

"The whole thing is absurd."

"Mr. Andrews himself told me at dinner that he has designed watertight bulkheads. If the ship has a little tiny leak, it's not going to sink."

"You will come in the lifeboat with me, won't you, darling?"

" *Oh, I couldn't. It's women and children only."*

"But I can't go without you."

"It won't be for long. They'll soon have the problem fixed, and you can come back on board. We'll have breakfast together."

Daisy struggled through the crowd. Hands reached out to her.

"Stewardess, stewardess, what's happening? Are we going to sink?"

Eventually, Daisy found herself pressed up against Mr. Crawford, who was attempting, with infinite patience, to direct the slow-moving, reluctant passengers toward the exit. Studying the smile on his face and his calm, methodical instructions to the passengers, she concluded that Mr. Crawford did not think the Titanic would sink. If sinking were a real possibility, he would not be standing still and directing traffic. If he had a brain in his head, he would be up on deck, making sure he had a seat in a lifeboat.

Perhaps she had misunderstood Mr. Andrews and Captain Smith. They were troubled, of course, because the mail room was wet. The Titanic was a Royal Mail Ship, and there would be the devil to pay if she arrived in New York with bundles of soggy, ruined mail. As for the squash court, well, men did like to play squash, and the Titanic was supposed to have all the amenities. The lack of a squash court would be a black mark against the Titanic.

Daisy considered what she should do next. Perhaps the ship was sinking and perhaps it was not, but a decision had been made, and that was all she needed to know. The captain had given his orders, and the ladies, some of them very wealthy, were to be put into lifeboats. The only remaining question was how she could turn this situation to her own advantage.

She had gathered from the other stewardesses that gratuities would be offered at the end of the voyage. Even little favors would reap financial rewards. Now Daisy could see the possibility of big rewards. She should immediately put herself in a position where she could be caring and solicitous. She could be the brave little heroine who would make sure her first-class ladies were safely installed in a lifeboat and rowed to the safety of the ship whose lights were nearby. If the Titanic did not sink, they would be rowed back again. At all times, Daisy would offer comfort and courage. At the end of the voyage, when her ladies were safely ashore, they would show their gratitude. She nodded her head in agreement with her own plan and set about putting it into practice. When her ladies arrived on deck, they would find her standing beside her assigned lifeboat and ready to do whatever was required.

She decided that she should avoid the crowd of bemused, slow-moving first-class passengers by taking the service stairs to the deck below. From there she could make her way to less crowded stairways and up to the boat deck, where she would stand beside her assigned lifeboat, offering comfort and reassurance as the ladies came on deck.

As Daisy turned in the direction of the service stairs, she found herself face-to-face with Miss Bonelli, who was being hustled along the corridor by Augustine.

"You," Miss Bonelli shouted, wagging an arthritic finger. "You go to my cabin."

Daisy shook her head.

"You go and get my jewels." She flicked her teeth with her thumbnail in an unmistakably rude gesture and glared at Augustine. "She forgot."

Daisy looked at Augustine. "Does she really want me to go back for her jewels?"

"Sì, yes."

"I can't. I have to go to my lifeboat station."

Miss Bonelli overwhelmed Daisy with a torrent of Italian invective. As Daisy stood unmoved, Miss Bonelli turned to pleading. "Per favore. Look, I give you reward."

Daisy widened her eyes. "Reward?"

"You fetch my jewels; I give you reward."

"What kind of reward?"

"Jewels. I give you jewels."

Daisy considered the old lady's offer. Perhaps she could reap a double reward. It would only take a moment to retrieve Miss Bonelli's jewels, and she could still be at her lifeboat station ahead of the shuffling, complaining passengers.

"Where are your jewels?" she asked.

"They are in the top drawer of the chest of drawers," Augustine said. "Very good jewels. In a red box."

"You bring my jewels and my corset," Miss Bonelli said, "and I give you good reward. One piece nice jewelry."

Daisy pursed her lips as if resisting temptation. "I have a duty to my passengers. I must be beside the lifeboat."

"Diamonds," said Miss Bonelli.

Daisy forgot about the lifeboat. "You wish to reward me with diamonds?"

"Sì, I give you diamonds."

Nanny Catchpole's face was so clear in Daisy's memory. A bird in the hand is worth two in the bush.

"Per favore," said Miss Bonelli.

"Oh, very well. I'll go. I will see you up on the boat deck. Keep moving, and don't take off your life jacket."

"Il mio corsetto?"

"Oh, all right, I'll get your damned corset."

Nanny Catchpole reappeared in Daisy's mind. Such language. I should wash your mouth out with soap.

Daisy turned back toward Miss Bonelli's cabin, pushing through a throng of passengers who were moving in the opposite direction. She had only taken a couple of steps when suddenly everything changed. A terrible shrieking sound pierced the air and blotted out all other sensations. The crowd of passengers, who had been milling around, reluctant to go outside and annoyed to be disturbed, was galvanized into action. Pushing, shoving, and screaming so as to be heard above the earsplitting din, they moved as one toward the exit. Daisy clung to a handrail and held her place. Whatever was happening outside, she still had time to earn her reward.

On Board the *Lapland*
Poppy Melville

Poppy continued to stroke Daisy's hair as she tried to calm her. "It was the boilers venting steam," she said. "It was a terrifying noise. Everyone on the boat deck was shouting to be heard. It was chaos, but at least it convinced the passengers to get into the lifeboats. It was hard to argue when you couldn't make yourself heard."

"Suddenly everyone was gone," Daisy said. "I was on my own, and so I thought I would still have time to get to Miss Bonelli's cabin."

"You should have come up on deck," Poppy said. "Our lives are more important than money."

Daisy was no longer sobbing, and her voice had settled into an accusatory whimper. "You can say that now because you know what happened, but at the time, I thought it was worth a try. It was a chance for us to get the money we really need."

"But, Daisy," Poppy said, "you could have drowned."

"I very nearly did," Daisy replied. "I started along the corridor. There was no one around. The lights were flickering, and that noise kept screaming and screaming, and the carpet was wet, and I started sliding downhill."

Poppy's breath caught in her throat at the thought of Daisy alone belowdecks, terrified but determined to earn her reward and have money for her California dream—the dream that Poppy had impulsively embraced.

On that day three weeks before, when Daisy had whispered to her that she was going to run away to Hollywood and become a movie star, Poppy had seen a door opening to a new future for herself. She had lived for years under her father's oppression and disappointment and his almost daily complaint that she should have been a boy.

"If you were a boy, I would send you to Eton ... If you were my son, you could have a commission in my old regiment ...

There has always been a Riddlesdown in the House of Lords, but no one is going to let you take that seat."

As the years passed and two stepmothers proved incapable of giving him a son, the earl's complaints took on a grudging and insulting acceptance that Poppy could possibly become his heir.

"The least you can do is give me grandsons ...

Your looks will never get you a husband. Can't you do something about yourself?"

With Agnes pregnant again, the tension in the house was unbearable. The earl would not even consider the possibility that his wife would give birth to another daughter. This one, he decreed, was a boy. Agnes tiptoed around the house. Her face bore a haunted expression, and her hands constantly cradled her belly.

"It's a boy. I can tell by the way I'm carrying and craving nettle tea."

Nanny Catchpole served the nettle tea, took care of the unwanted girls, and confided her doubts to no one except Poppy.

"Wishing won't make it a boy, and drinking nettle tea don't mean nothing. It is whatever it is, but heaven help us all if it's another girl. You should tell your stepmother to keep away from the stairs."

"Are you suggesting ...?"

"If this one don't give him a boy, then he'll want another one."

Nanny Catchpole placed a consoling hand on Poppy's shoulder. "You'll never be enough for him, but it's not your fault."

The earl decreed that his two oldest daughters should go to London and buy clothes for the imminent birth of his son.

"He will not wear hand-me-down clothes from his sisters. He will have everything befitting the next Earl of Riddlesdown. Go to Harrods."

Daisy had not spoken until the night before their trip to London.

"I'm going to America. Will you come with me?"

Poppy resumed her gentle stroking of Daisy's hair, suddenly glad to have the opportunity to talk about her own experience. She still did not trust the authenticity of Daisy's current emotional breakdown, but it gave her the chance to speak, and she needed to speak. "Up on deck, we could see what was happening," she said, "and that's why everyone was in a panic. It was obvious that we were going into the water nose-first. They called it sinking by the bow, and it was clear that it would not take long before the whole ship went under. Everything was beginning to slide downwards towards the water, and we could see for ourselves that there were nowhere near enough lifeboats."

Poppy felt the prickle of tears that always threatened to fall whenever she thought of the terrifying minutes on the deck.

For a while, it had seemed that everything was under control, with men standing back and allowing the women and children into the boats, but soon it became obvious that their time was running out. The Titanic could not be saved. She was going under, and hundreds, maybe even thousands of passengers would not find a seat in a lifeboat.

Poppy could not see Daisy, but surely she was at her lifeboat station. Lifeboats were being launched from both sides of the ship, and it was impossible to see from one side to the other. Knowing Daisy, Poppy assumed her sister would be first into the lifeboat. She would see her again when they reached the other ship, the one whose lights winked at them in the far distance. The screech of the boilers venting steam drowned out any possibility of asking questions, and who could she even ask? Discipline was breaking down. The crew and a small number of gentlemen were fighting a losing battle of the good manners of the few against the survival instincts of the many.

Desperate hands pulled her into lifeboat fourteen, which was hanging precariously in the davits, waiting to be launched. She was already seated in the boat with a crying child on her lap when fighting broke out on the deck. The screech of the boilers had stopped abruptly, and now Poppy could hear the voices of chaos from all around the ship, pleading, cursing, and threatening. Officer Lowe appeared on the deck with a pistol. She heard the crack as he fired three times and then leaped into the boat and ordered the boat to be lowered.

The descent was slow and precarious. Stranded passengers on the lower decks watched with hungry eyes as they inched down toward the water, and Lowe held them off with the threat of his pistol.

Slowly, almost imperceptibly at first, the lifeboat began to tilt. The bow was touching the water, but the stern was hung up on its ropes. The passengers screamed, and for a moment, Poppy thought they would all be pitched forward into the water.

"Cut the falls," Lowe ordered.

A sailor with a knife slashed at the ropes, and the boat dropped suddenly nose-first, with the stern crashing down and sending a wave of water across the passengers. Then they were free and rowing away from the sinking ship. Voices, both angry and imploring, carried across the water. The Titanic was down by the bow, and Poppy could make out figures scrambling up toward the stern as it rose higher and higher. She could not bear to watch. Instead, she looked out across the water, hoping to see the other lifeboats.

She had been sure that Daisy had taken her place in one of them. If she had known that Daisy had still been belowdecks ... Even now she could not complete that thought.

Daisy sat up. "I kept sliding on the wet carpet," she said, "and I could see water creeping towards me along the corridor. I couldn't do it. I know we needed the money, but I just couldn't ..."

She swiped a hand across her eyes. "I'm sorry, Poppy. I wasn't brave enough. I'd left it too late. The lights started to flicker, and I thought they'd go out at any minute, so I just started to run until I found the service stairs, and I went up. I was thinking about you all the time. I knew you'd be worried. I just kept going up every time I found a stairway, and every time I looked back, the water was rising behind me. I lost track of where I was. I passed some cabins and a big room. I think it may have been second class. Everything was deserted, so I thought I had best find a way up to the deck and get to my lifeboat station. I didn't think they'd leave without me, but they did, didn't they?"

Poppy nodded. "The lifeboats weren't waiting for anyone."

"I tried to find my way out," Daisy said. "I caught up with some people who seemed to know where they were going, and started to follow them."

"Did they help you?"

"Help me?" Daisy laughed scornfully. "No, they didn't help me. They were all scrambling and fighting among themselves. They were mostly men, some passengers, some crew—I'm not sure. They were all trying to get to the boat deck, but everything was uphill, and they wouldn't get out of my way."

Poppy took in a long, calming breath. She had spent a lifetime rescuing Daisy from one scrape after another. She was well accustomed to Daisy's breathless recitation of her adventures, but this was something different. Although Daisy was now telling a coherent tale, she could not forget that this was the same Daisy who, just a few minutes ago, had been on her knees, screaming in terror— real or pretend, Poppy did not know. However, she did know one thing: as usual, there was something Daisy was not telling her. Something had happened to terrify her.

"Daisy," Poppy said, "how long were you belowdecks?"

Daisy shook her head vigorously. "I don't know. I wasn't

looking for a clock." She took a shuddering breath. "The furniture was sliding. Big pieces of furniture were sliding across the floor and crashing into people."

Poppy massaged her temples as Daisy continued with a recitation of the dreadful things she had seen. The *Titanic* had taken just over two hours to sink. What had Daisy been doing on board for so long? How could she have seen all the things that had only happened in the last few minutes before the *Titanic* had slid under the water?

"I don't understand," Poppy said. "Even if you were caught up in the crowd, why couldn't you find your way to the boat deck? The other people didn't know their way around the ship, but you did."

Daisy's expression turned in an instant from tearful to angry as she sprang to her feet. "I don't know what you want from me," she said. "I'm telling you the truth. It was horrible, and I couldn't find my way to the lifeboats. Stop asking me questions."

"I just wanted to help you overcome your fear," Poppy said mildly. "I thought that if you talked about it—"

"I've talked about it," Daisy said. "I've told you everything, and you don't even believe me. Well, that's enough. I don't want to be out here, and I'm going inside."

Poppy watched her sister retreat across the deck and through the door to the warmth and light of the interior. Alone on the deck, she could not help shaking her head helplessly. She wondered if she would ever be free of her intense need to protect her sister. Daisy was her own worst enemy. How much longer could Poppy go on protecting Daisy from herself?

As Poppy rose to go back inside, a light flared in the shadows. Someone had struck a match. The scent of strong tobacco drifted across the deck toward her. She saw the glow of a cigarette and the shape of a tall figure stepping out from the darkness into the starlight. The light caught the white slash of scar across his cheek— Sullivan the fireman.

The tip of his cigarette glowed brightly as he took a long drag. "Well," he said eventually, "she's lying."

"No, she's not."

The Australian said nothing. He took another drag on his cigarette and then tossed it over the rail.

"You shouldn't be listening to other people's conversations,"

Poppy said.

He came closer, and his voice was just a breath in her ear. "Someone has been watching you."

"Where?"

"I'll take you inside. Don't look up."

Alvin Towson

After three days at sea, Towson still had not found a way to reach the *Titanic*'s crew in the third-class section of the *Lapland*. He had a vast experience of ocean liners, having spent a number of years persuading gullible passengers to open their wallets and wager far more than they could afford on the turn of the cards. He was unaccustomed to lying low and refraining from forcing friendships and joining in the bonhomie of the card tables.

Instead of trying his luck at cards, although luck was not really an issue for him, he had spent hours trekking through the *Lapland*'s maze of corridors and stairs in the hope of finding an unlocked door that would lead down to the third-class cabins. He met with defeat at every turn until it occurred to him that maybe he could find a way to his destination by staying above deck. Even third-class passengers would have a promenade deck, not as lavish or as sheltered as the first- and second-class promenade decks, but third-class passengers were not usually cut off completely from the open air.

He waited until the hustle and bustle of the ship had stilled for the night and the cabin stewards had taken to their beds. He knew that the ship would post a night watch, but in light of recent events, the watch would be too busy looking out for icebergs to notice one lone passenger roaming the corridors.

He stayed away from the lift and climbed the several flights of stairs leading to the deck where the lifeboats stood waiting to be swung out on their davits. Some people would see the sturdy wooden crafts as reassurance, but he knew better. There were so few of them, not enough for even half the passengers.

He repressed a shudder and told himself that he would never again think of his night on the water. He would put all memory behind him and concentrate on the future. If he could recover the Matryoshka and return with it to America, there would be no more talk of breaking legs and fingers, and injuring other body parts. He could pay his debts and, so it was rumored, have enough money to last him a lifetime.

"A diamond is being carried from Siberia. They call it the Matryoshka."

"I have never heard of it. How many carats?"

His informant laughed. "Its value is not measured in carats. It is unique. It is the only one ever found."

"I don't understand."

"No one does. No one knows how such a thing can happen. You know the meaning of this word matryoshka?"

"No."

"It is the word for Russian dolls, the ones that nest one inside the other. This diamond is like a Russian doll, one diamond nestled inside another."

Towson's heart sank. He had paid for this information, but the information made no sense. "One inside another?" he repeated.

"Yes. It is a diamond that is hollow inside, and inside the hollow is another diamond. It can be seen to move. You can look through the diamond and see the other diamond inside."

Towson edged past the lifeboats, still making his way toward the stern of the ship. He saw a railing ahead. Had he come to yet another dead end? He approached cautiously, keeping to the shadows. Despite the thrumming of the engines, he could hear the sound of women's voices raised in anger.

He glanced up at the crow's nest. The lookout was invisible. He assumed that if he could not see the lookout, the lookout couldn't see him. He reached the railing. It did not seem to be a substantial barrier. He could climb over it with no trouble. He set his hand on the upper rail and looked down. He could see the third-class promenade, a desolate and windy space about forty feet below him. Two women were kneeling on the deck. One was screaming angrily, and the other seemed to be trying to soothe her. The noisy one stood up, and Towson recognized her immediately. The thief who had snatched the Matryoshka was right there, so near and yet so far.

He looked for a ladder. Surely there had to be a way down. As he moved along the rail, he saw a figure taking shape in the shadows below. The faint spill of the navigation lights fell across an upturned face marked with a white scar. The man made no other movement and stood completely still, but the brooding quality of the figure below was enough to make Towson take one step back, and then another, and another, until he was in full retreat.

He retraced his footsteps across the boat deck, telling himself that he had seen enough. He knew where she was. She would not escape him in Southampton.

CHAPTER SIX

The Dulwich Club
Harry Hazelton

The promise of spring had given way to a cold drizzle, and Harry was chilled from his walk across London from the Cunard offices. As he entered the Dulwich Club, he was pleased to see one of the club's geriatric waiters bringing in a scuttle of coal to add to the dying embers of the fire. Sir Ernest Shackleton, who was seated in a wing chair beside the grate, looked up from the paper he was reading as Harry approached.

"Hello there, Hazelton. Have you seen today's headlines?"

Harry shook his head. "I've been busy. I've called in at three shipping offices today."

"Still looking for the missing girls? Do you suspect they've been sent overseas?"

Harry gave a bitter laugh. "If they had been kidnapped anywhere east of Suez, I would be the man for the job, and I'd have a half dozen guttersnipes out looking for them. Unfortunately, all I have is a garrulous servant named Betsy Catchpole, who suspects them of being on a ship."

Harry waited for the waiter to restore life to the fire before he took the wing chair on the other side of the grate from Shackleton.

The waiter stooped deferentially. "Will you be wanting something, Captain?"

"Tea," said Harry.

Shackleton frowned. "Tea? The sun's over the yardarm, old man. It's time for a gin and tonic."

Harry fought against a stab of memory.

Gin and tonic was being served by turbaned waiters in the officers' mess at Lucknow. Outside, the tropical sun was finally losing its searing heat. In the gathering dusk, a nightjar tried out its first tentative notes. A murmur of voices announced the arrival of the general, returning from a long leave in England. Tomorrow he would inspect his troops. Tonight his troops would inspect the general's bride.

She entered on her husband's arm, bringing with her the fresh remembrance of everything that Harry had left behind among the green fields and walled gardens of home. The nightjar became a nightingale, and her white muslin dress glowed as brightly as a moonflower, but it was the expression on her face that held him back as others moved forward. This bride, this English rose, was terrified.

Harry forced his mind back to the present. "Just tea," he said.

Shackleton rattled the newspaper as he refolded its pages. "News from America," he said. "Apparently, they won't be letting the *Titanic's* officers come home anytime soon. They're moving the inquiry from New York to Washington, and they're bringing out the big guns with a whole raft of senators poking and prodding and revealing their total ignorance of maritime regulations. What does a cattleman politician from Texas know about ice in the North Atlantic?" He slapped the newspaper angrily onto the table beside his chair. "They seem to have settled on a scapegoat. They're going to blame Ismay for the speed the ship was making."

"Ismay?" Harry queried. Having decided in his own mind that the Americans had no business inquiring into the loss of a British ship, he had stopped reading reports of their inquiry. Although he could not avoid the headlines screamed out by newspaper boys, he had not been keeping up with what was happening in New York. For the moment, the name Ismay had slipped his mind.

"Bruce Ismay, the chairman of the White Star Line," Shackleton said impatiently. "He made a severe misjudgment when he took a seat in one of the lifeboats."

Harry thought of the crowd who had assembled on Tower Hill, each member representing a victim of the disaster. So many had died. What did it really matter if one man had lived? How would Ismay's death change anything? "I'm not sure what I would have done in the circumstances," he said. "If the seat was empty and the choice was a dry seat in a lifeboat or taking a chance by plunging into the sea and finding something that floats ..."

"Choosing the sea would be an instant death sentence," Shackleton said. "I heard tell that they threw deck chairs overboard, thinking people could float on them, but there was never a chance. No one can last more than a few minutes in water that cold. On our way to the pole, we had a fellow fall through the ice, and the cold cracked his teeth. With water that cold, it's impossible to even draw breath. If there's no one to pull you out, you'll be dead in minutes. It's a miracle anyone who went into the water from the *Titanic* has survived to tell the tale. Of course, they had life jackets, so they didn't go all the way under, but it's still a miracle."

"So perhaps Ismay was wise to take a seat in a lifeboat," Harry ventured. "Better than being dead."

Shackleton shook his head. "He may as well have died. He's dead to society already. He was chairman of the line, virtually the owner of the *Titanic*. He had an unwritten duty to go down with the ship. I guarantee there'll be no word said against Captain Smith, because he did the right thing, but Ismay will be a social pariah. With no one else to blame, the Americans are going to blame him. I can see it coming. The Yanks are going to give us trouble. Just you wait and see."

Harry stretched his leg to ease his cramped muscles. "Speaking of America ..."

"What about it?"

"My informant, Nanny Catchpole, who insisted on meeting me behind the stable block after dark—"

"Really, old man."

"She's an old lady," Harry said. "If Madame Tussaud's made a waxwork of the standard British nanny, Nanny Catchpole could be the model—all apron and pillowy bosom."

Shackleton smiled in remembrance. "I had Nanny O'Connell."

"I had Nanny Mulligan," Harry said, "and the daughters of the Earl of Riddlesdown have Nanny Catchpole. Thank goodness they have someone to care about them, because Riddlesdown Court is a Tudor madhouse with a would-be Henry VIII ruling the roost. The earl is so desperate for a son that he's already killed off two wives, and I doubt that the third wife will live much longer. He has daughters, and the estate is not entailed. The oldest daughter can inherit, but the earl can't abide the thought."

"And what does this have to do with America?"

"Nanny Catchpole thinks that is where the girls have gone. She said that she overheard them talking and planning."

"Will their uncle, the bishop, pay for a ticket to New York for you? You could find guttersnipes for hire when you get there, or you could disguise yourself as a cowboy."

Harry scowled. "I'm serious, Shackleton. I'm going to find these girls."

Shackleton nodded. "Yes, of course you are. Sorry, old man. Carry on. What are you thinking?"

"I'm thinking that Nanny Catchpole is wrong. Whatever they may have planned, they did not, in fact, sail off to America. They've been missing for three weeks, and I've studied the passenger lists for every ship leaving England for the United States in that period of time, and I see no record of them."

"Well," said Shackleton, "they may be the daughters of an earl, but they probably didn't have money for first class, so did you look at second class, or third class?"

Harry scowled at his old classmate. "I'm not an idiot, Shackleton. I admit I'm used to a very different kind of investigating, but I'm not completely at a loss. I studied every passenger on every ship. I even looked at the *Titanic*. It is possible they were on there—the timing is right—but their names are not on any passenger list, living or dead. Maybe they changed their minds and took the boat train to Paris. They could be anywhere by now."

Shackleton picked up the folded newspaper. "Don't give up on America just yet. The *Titanic* list is not yet final. They're still identifying victims and sorting out survivors. White Star is reluctant to call it a final list, because apparently the American president, the fat one—"

"Taft," said Harry.

"Yes, that's the one. President Taft has been clinging to the hope that there are still survivors. He's suggesting they could be floating around on an iceberg or trapped underwater in one of the watertight compartments, or may have been picked up by a passing trawler. If White Star says this is the final list, he's going to be less than pleased, and that will rub off on the presidential hopes of the senator in charge of the inquiry."

Harry shook his head in bewilderment. "But that's plain nonsense. Facts are facts."

"Not where American politicians are involved," Shackleton said. "Facts can be whatever will get you the most votes."

"It's been ten days," Harry said. "It's absurd to think that there are any more survivors. I know that some of the world's most rich and famous went down with the ship, but that's just the way it is, and wishing won't change it. They're gone."

"Taft isn't willing to admit that. He's refusing to come out of his office or take care of business. He's waiting for word on one man in particular," Shackleton said. "There's a fellow by the name of Major Archibald Butt ..." He paused and grinned, looking very much like the boy Harry remembered from his school days. "Butt," he said, "is a very unfortunate name, don't you think? Imagine what we could have done with that in the fourth form at Dulwich."

Harry nodded. A new boy still wet behind the ears and carrying the name of Butt would have been put through the wringer, no doubt about it.

"Despite his unfortunate name," Shackleton continued, "Major Butt was a trusted confidant of the president and could possibly have been carrying an important document either from the Pope or the kaiser—no one seems to be sure which. That is why President Taft is unwilling to have him declared dead, or to have the list declared final. It makes no sense to us, but that's the cause of the delay."

Harry picked up the newspaper. "Is the new list in here?"

"It is," Shackleton confirmed. "Unfortunately, they've found no new survivors, but they add names to the list of the deceased as they identify the bodies. Because most of the victims were wearing life jackets, they're still on the surface, and they're drifting into the shipping lanes. The *MacKay-Bennett* has gone out from Nova Scotia to round them up and identify them when they can. They've found Astor. Poor fellow is very mangled. Looks like something heavy crushed him. Maybe the smokestack. The survivors report that it fell among the people on the deck."

"Golden lads and girls all must, as chimney sweepers, come to dust," Harry said thoughtfully. "In the end, his fortune meant nothing, and the poor fellow ended up as an obstruction to shipping." He shook his head and turned to call the waiter. *Forget about the tea. I need a drink.*

115

Shackleton held out the newspaper. "The new list includes crew members," he said.

"The girls wouldn't—"

"The *Titanic* had female crew members," Shackleton said, "stewardesses and cashiers for the restaurant. Two young ladies with not enough money for a ticket might well apply for a position."

Harry opened the newspaper and ruffled the pages impatiently until he found the crew list. Shackleton was wrong, of course. The girls were probably in Paris, having the time of their lives. He scanned the surprisingly long list of surviving crew members, thinking that their survival rate was something that should be investigated.

The family name of the Earl of Riddlesdown was Melville. Unless they had managed to obtain forged papers, they would have to use their own names. He ran his finger down the page.

Thomas Mayzes, Fireman
James McGann, Trimmer
William McIntyre, Trimmer
Daisy Melville, Stewardess
Poppy Melville, Stewardess
John Moore, Fireman

He remained still for a moment, his finger resting on the two names. There they were. It had to be them. Daisy and Poppy Melville. Lady Marguerite Melville and Lady Penelope Melville— Daisy being Marguerite in French, and Poppy being a short form of Penelope. They had signed on as stewardesses, and they had been among the survivors.

Shackleton grinned. "You found them," he declared.

Harry nodded. "I've not only found them; I know where they are. They're on board the SS *Lapland*, due into Southampton on the twenty-ninth of April. I have to phone the bishop."

Shackleton leaned back and stretched his feet toward the fire. "Perhaps we should go into partnership," he said. "My brains and your ... What exactly was your contribution to the solving of your case?"

"My willingness to buy you a slap-up dinner," Harry said. "Simpson's in the Strand. Roast beef and all the trimmings."

On Board the *Lapland*
Approaching the Scilly Isles
Daisy Melville

Daisy leaned over her sister, listening to her breathing. She wanted to make certain that Poppy was indeed asleep and not watching her in her usual suspicious fashion. Even Poppy had to sleep sometimes, and the *Lapland*'s steady motion as it rode the long Atlantic rollers had finally sent her off to the land of Nod, as Nanny Catchpole used to say.

Daisy breathed a sigh of relief. She had begun to fear that she would never have a moment alone to put her plan in place. Their journey was coming to an end. Tomorrow the coast of Cornwall would be in sight. By tomorrow night they would be in Southampton, and Daisy had something to do before they arrived.

She had spent several days observing the actions of Ernie Sullivan, the Australian who had forcibly prevented her from going ashore in New York. Far from feeling that she owed him her life, she felt that he owed her a debt. She had not needed to be rescued just so he could play the hero. He had spoiled everything, and it was up to him to put it right.

Two nights ago on her way to the women's lavatory in the small hours of the night, Daisy had observed Sullivan making his way up the stairs to the open deck. Last night, using the same excuse, she had observed him again. She could not imagine what he did up there all alone, if he was in fact alone, but she needed to speak to him, and now she knew where to find him.

She slipped out of the cabin and crept quietly along the corridor. She had not been up on deck since the night that Poppy had forced her from the cabin. On that occasion, Daisy had found it necessary to produce fear where no fear existed, because Poppy would not approve of the truth. It was not fear that had kept Daisy in her bunk since they had left New York; it was just a matter of preference. If they had been traveling first-class, she would have joined in every activity, from dining to dancing to deck quoits. However, not only were they traveling third-class, but they were alone in third class, with no one for company except the surviving crew. It made sense to her that she should enjoy lying snugly in her bed with Poppy to bring her food. By the time they reached England, she would be well rested and ready to make another attempt at reaching the legendary streets of Hollywood.

She reached the door to the third-class promenade deck and hesitated with her hand on the door handle. Her heart was beating very fast. She took a deep, steadying breath, suddenly uncertain as to how she would react to whatever lay beyond that door. She was alone now, without Poppy to hold her up or become her audience. She told herself that her heart was pounding with excitement and not fear, but still she hesitated.

Beyond the door lay the endless night sky and the dark, heedless ocean, and she did not know if she could control her memories. If she mistakenly looked down into the depths, would her memory show her the lights of the *Titanic* shining up from beneath the surface? Would she hear the cries of the people in the water? Would she imagine that even now four frozen dead men floated alongside the *Lapland*? Would she see their angry eyes staring up at her and their frozen hands clawing at the hull?

Daisy willed courage into herself. She would not fear the dead, and surely they were all dead. Three of them had been too drunk to move. They had not even bothered with life jackets. In fact, she was not certain they had even been aware that the ship had been sinking. The other one, the fourth man, had been well aware. She had seen him snatch a life jacket from the arms of a steward as he had pursued her through the flooded corridors, but he was a man, and men had not been allowed in the lifeboats. She could still see his face, flushed red despite the cold, staring down at her as the last collapsible inched its way down toward the water, and then came the crash of the funnel and the great wave of water.

He was dead. They were all dead. She had nothing to fear and everything to gain. She opened the door. The small promenade deck was bathed in moonlight. This was another night on another ship, and she would not allow herself to be afraid of ghosts.

Sullivan was immediately visible, leaning against the rail with the wind ruffling his blond hair and snatching the smoke from his cigarette. Although she had not made a sound, he was instantly aware of her presence. He turned to face her as she stepped out into the open. The slash of a scar across his face shone white in the moonlight. She hoped that it was only the scar pulling at the corner of his mouth that gave him a sardonic and dangerous expression.

In the last few years, as her body had ripened and filled out, she had found no reason to be afraid of any man except her father. Most men could be controlled by a dimpled smile and a toss of her curls, but if anything more were required of her, she would do whatever was necessary … So far nothing more had been necessary, but it was possible Sullivan would demand a higher price.

His first words gave her no encouragement. "Go back inside. You shouldn't be out here."

"I can be anywhere I want to be."

Sullivan tossed his cigarette over the rail. "All right, then. You stay out here. I'll go inside."

"But I wanted to talk to you."

"Why?"

"You owe me."

Sullivan raised his eyebrows. "I owe you? How do you work that out?"

"You stopped me from going ashore."

"I saved your bloody life."

"I wasn't going to drown."

Sullivan folded his arms and leaned back against the rail, a move that made Daisy nervous. What if the railing gave way? It should be impossible, but it could happen. Everything on a ship should be completely safe and reliable, but if the *Titanic* had been able to sink, anything could happen. She pushed the thought to the back of her mind. She would not spend the rest of her life as a slave to her memory of the *Titanic*.

"Listen to me, little girl," Sullivan said. "If I hadn't grabbed you, the tide would have taken you. You didn't stand a chance."

"I didn't ask to be rescued."

Sullivan shook his head. "You didn't jump on purpose. What happened?"

Daisy remembered the moment on the *Carpathia* when the Cunard officer had reached out to grab her and pull her from the rail. He had been about to call her bluff, and she hadn't been ready. She hadn't yet achieved her purpose. She had tried to move away. Her hands had slipped. She would never forget the surge of fear as she felt herself tipping backward, her hand reaching for something, anything, then the long drop and the momentary loss of consciousness as she had struck the water in an ungainly sprawl.

"Of course I jumped," Daisy said. "I needed to go ashore, and they weren't going to let me. I would have made it if you hadn't interfered."

Sullivan's face still registered nothing but disapproval, and so Daisy stamped her foot, a weapon of last resort. "You owe me."

He smiled the indulgent smile of an adult to a child. "What is it that you want?"

"Tomorrow we'll be in Southampton, and we'll have to leave the ship."

He nodded.

"I don't want to go home."

Sullivan's eyes flicked away from her into a distant stare. "Be glad that you can."

"You don't understand."

He was grinning again. "Poor little rich girl wants an adventure."

She stamped her foot again. "I'm going to Hollywood to become a movie star. That's all you need to know."

Sullivan eyed her thoughtfully. "You may have what the movie producers are looking for. They seem to like silly, pretty faces. As for your sister—"

"My sister is very smart."

"Your sister is a good woman," Sullivan said. "You don't deserve her."

"I suppose she is," Daisy said unenthusiastically. The conversation was moving in the wrong direction. Why were they talking about Poppy? This had nothing to do with Poppy. She settled her mouth into a slight pout. "I didn't come here to talk about Poppy."

Sullivan shrugged. "What did you come to talk about?"

"Us," Daisy said, "and what we can do for each other."

"I doubt that you can do anything for me," Sullivan said, "and I doubt I can do anything for you, but go ahead and tell me."

"I want to get on the next ship out of Southampton," Daisy said. "I'm not going back home. I'm going to America. I don't believe you wanted to save me. I think you were trying to swim ashore in New York, so that makes us both the same, doesn't it? When we get to Southampton, I want you to help me get onto another ship. I know you'll be looking for a ship, so I want you to take me with you. We don't have to work. I have money."

He raised his eyebrows. "Does your sister know about this money?"

"She wouldn't understand, but I think you would."

"So you intend to leave her behind?"

Daisy shook her head, surprised by a sudden pang of fear or maybe guilt. She had never been without Poppy, but she was not sure Poppy could be persuaded. *We'll cross that bridge when we come to it.*

"She'll come with us," she said aloud, "but she doesn't know I'm asking you for help. I knew you would need to be persuaded, and I thought I'd do a better job of persuading you."

He raised his eyebrows. Daisy swallowed hard. She needed this. She really needed this. "I don't think she'd be as persuasive as I am willing to be."

She took a bold step toward him and looked up at him from beneath lowered lashes. He had said she was pretty. She would show him just how pretty she could be. She was close enough now to touch him. She had not realized how big and how very masculine he was. He towered over her, exuding a powerful scent of cigarette smoke, liquor, and something else she could not identify. Its allure was overwhelming, but compelling. She wanted to know more—to experience more.

He turned away from her. "Don't do that."

"Why not?"

"Because you have no idea what you're doing."

"Of course I do. I know exactly what I'm doing." She licked her lips and fixed her wide-eyed gaze on his back. He would turn around. Surely he would turn around, and she would be ready … for anything.

At long last he turned and shook his head. "That's twice I've saved you from yourself," he said as he pushed past her and disappeared through the door that led to the cabins.

Southampton, England
Harry Hazelton

The train from Paddington announced its arrival in Southampton with a hiss of steam and a screech of brakes. Harry lifted his overnight bag from the overhead rack and stepped from the first-class carriage onto the platform. He paused to get his bearings and to breathe in the salty sea air carried on a light afternoon breeze.

He caught a glimpse of a flag flying at half-mast and reminded himself that he was not here to board a ship or relax at a seaside resort. Southampton was a city in mourning. Almost all of the *Titanic*'s crew had come from the small homes that huddled around the dockyard, a tight-knit community now mourning the loss of fathers, sons, husbands, and brothers. Strange as it seemed, however, he knew that two members of the crew did not come from this community but instead came from a magnificent Tudor estate where their aristocratic father had not even noticed their absence.

A porter with a handcart hurried toward him, intent on handling whatever luggage Harry might have in the goods van. He waved the man away. Normally, the majority of the passengers arriving on this train would require a porter, or maybe several porters. Harry had only one bag and no steamer trunks to be taken to the docks.

The dockyard, clearly visible no more than a few hundred yards away, seemed eerily deserted. The vacant White Star dock dominated his view, a ghostly reminder that the pride of the White Star fleet would never find a home in Southampton again. Farther along the docks, but not in pride of place, another dock was being prepared for the arrival of the *Lapland*. The *Titanic* would not be returning, but the *Lapland* would bring what remained of her crew, along with the Royal Mail and American newspapers.

Harry, having been told that the *Lapland* would arrive on the morning tide, had reserved a room at the South Western Hotel, where he would be in sight of the docks and prepared to meet the two girls as they stepped off the ship. The Bishop of Fordingbridge had been generous with his praise and his payment, and Harry was looking forward to the luxury of the Great Western, a hotel that had hosted innumerable first-class guests arriving and departing from the far corners of the globe.

Ignoring the pain in his left leg and fighting the melancholy that had enveloped him as he looked at the flag flying at half-mast, Harry picked up his bag and strode out of the station. The South Western Hotel was immediately visible, a magnificent redbrick edifice built to house the most discerning guests. The walk should not have taken more than a couple of minutes, but he found his way barred by a crowd of people, men in work clothes and women in headscarves. They were gathered around a speaker, who was haranguing the crowd from a precarious perch on a pile of beer crates.

"Plymouth," he shouted. "They're not coming here. They're coming to Plymouth, and you know what that means."

Harry, who did not know what that meant, pushed himself forward. He thought he recognized the voice. Ben Tillett did not have a loudhailer this time, but the union leader he had met on Tower Hill had a voice that carried easily to the agitated people who surrounded him.

"They're going to blame the crew," Tillett declared. "The officers and the nobs will get off scot-free, and it's the working man who'll get the blame."

Harry felt someone tugging at his arm. He looked down and saw a ragged boy who appeared to be no more than ten years old. "Do you want to see them?" he asked, his expression sly but hopeful.

"See what?"

"The rooms where they stayed," the boy said. He pointed up at the towering walls of the South Western Hotel. "I can show you where Mr. Ismay stayed, but he's not one of the dead ones. Mr. Astor's dead, and he had a room here, and Mr. Guggenheim, and—"

"Wait a minute," Harry said. "Are you trying to make money by showing me rooms where *Titanic* victims slept?"

"I can't show you inside the rooms," the boy said bitterly, "because the bellboys at the hotel are doing that, but I can show you the windows." He studied Harry's face. "For sixpence," he said hopefully.

Harry shook his head in disbelief. Didn't this boy understand what had happened? Didn't he care that more than a thousand people were dead? How could he just ...?

"Threepence," the boy offered.

"No, not a penny."

"Hey, you, boy!" Ben Tillett's voice thundered above the voices of the agitated crowd. "I told you not to do that. Leave that gentleman alone."

Harry looked up and met Tillett's fevered gaze. Tillett jumped down from his impromptu platform and made his way through the crowd. He caught the boy by the scruff of the neck. "I won't have it. I won't have little guttersnipes making money out of this tragedy."

He won't let the child make money, Harry thought, *but he'll make political capital. What's the difference?*

123

"My dad's gone," the boy said. "He's not on the crew list, and my ma has nothing." Showing no fear, he glared at Tillett. "What are we supposed to do? My ma says the union won't do nothing for us."

"The union will do everything it can." Tillett's voice lost its loud, hectoring tone and became soft and friendly. "We'll get everything we can from White Star. Tell your mother that the union is going to bring a case for damages. What did your dad do on board?"

"Fireman," the boy said. "They say the firemen didn't have a chance. They kept the lights on, but they weren't allowed in the boats. That's what I heard."

"That's what we've all heard," Tillett said. He ruffled the boy's hair. "I'm sorry, lad, but you'll have to rely on charity for a while. This won't be sorted out overnight."

"My ma says I'll have to go to sea. They'll take me if I say I'm twelve."

Tillett shrugged. "You don't look like you're twelve, but I'm thinking the White Star is going to be desperate for a crew."

Harry dug into his pockets and pulled out a handful of coins. He saw the silver glint of several half crowns and florins, along with the brass of a threepenny bit. He placed the coins in the boy's eager hands. "Don't go to sea. Take this to your mother. Don't tell her what you've been doing." He placed his hands on the boy's shoulders. "We do not make money out of tragedy."

The boy skittered away, and Harry and Tillett were left staring at each other.

"Hazelton," Tillett said at last. "I try not to forget a name. You are Captain Hazelton of the East Surrey. You were with Shackleton."

Harry nodded, surprised that Tillett had remembered him from their very brief encounter on Tower Hill.

"Are you leaving?" Tillett asked. "Going back to your regiment? When are you sailing?"

Harry thought for the moment of the voyage he so longed to make—out through the Solent, across the rough waters of the Bay of Biscay, and down the African coast to Cape Town. After a brief respite in the shelter of Table Mountain, the journey would take him ever eastward, following the scent of spice and jasmine until Calcutta appeared as a smudge on the horizon, and he would be back in a land where his life had meaning.

"Your regiment is in India, isn't it?" Tillett asked.

Harry raised his eyebrows. "I'm surprised you would know that."

"I make it my business to know. I met you when you were with Shackleton, and that means something. He's a good man to know. Politics are all about who you know. So, I am assuming that if you know Shackleton, you, too, have connections."

Harry shook his head. "Shackleton and I were at school together. That is the extent of my connection. I'm not here to take a ship to India. I'm here to meet the *Lapland*."

"May I ask why?"

"No, you may not."

"Yes, of course. Forgive the intrusion. Whatever your reason for meeting her, I have to tell you that the *Lapland* won't be here in the morning. She's putting in at Plymouth."

"I didn't know that."

"Change of plan," Tillett said. "She's carrying the *Titanic* crew and —"

"I know that."

"And she's putting in at Plymouth."

"Yes, I heard you say that."

Tillett glanced around and then laid his finger alongside his nose in a sly and unmistakable gesture—he was about to impart information that was not generally known. "They're all to be taken ashore in Plymouth. White Star is sending lawyers to take depositions from them. It's my guess that only those crew members who are willing to tell the story the White Star wants them to tell will be allowed to keep their jobs. Poor devils haven't been paid yet, and White Star will hold them for ransom."

"Are you sure?"

"Haven't you read what's been happening in the United States?"

"No, not really."

"A whitewash," Tillett declared. "White Star takes no responsibility for the disaster. They say it was an act of God."

"I suppose it was," Harry said mildly. "Only God can make an iceberg."

"And only a fool would drive his ship into one," Tillett said. "There's a lot at stake here. It's not just ramming into an iceberg and sinking an unsinkable ship; it's the whole bloody nightmare of the lifeboats."

"Women and children first," Harry said.

"Women and children first," Tillett parroted. "That's not what happened. Shots fired, men tossed overboard, immigrants locked belowdecks, and boats launched half-empty. Sir Cosmo Duff-Gordon and his lady had a lifeboat to themselves, just rowed away. Oh, there's a lot to be told, and the crew are the people who can tell it given half a chance."

"And you think they won't be given a chance," Harry said.

"Yes, that's what I think. I've not been permitted to wire them on the *Lapland*, so I have to reach them somehow and warn them of what lies ahead. They've been at sea for seven days without a word from anyone ashore. They don't know what's about to happen. I should be going up north to organize the coal miners' strike, but I'll have to change my plans. I'll have to drive to Plymouth and be there in the morning to represent the unions. The White Star Line and their political allies will have me to deal with. I won't allow the working man to take the blame."

"What about the female members of the crew?" Harry asked. He knew that such a specific question would reveal his personal interest in the crew, but he needed to know. Was it possible that the earl's daughters would be detained?

Tillett nodded sagely. "Ah, I see. So you've heard. I thought you didn't follow the newspapers."

"Heard what?"

"A first-class passenger has laid a charge against one of the stewardesses. She's accused of stealing a quantity of diamond jewelry. I'm not sure that the union will be able to do anything for her."

CHAPTER SEVEN

Plymouth Sound, England
Poppy Melville

Poppy was awake at once, sitting up in her bunk and trying to still the trembling in her hands. Something had happened. The motion of the ship had changed.

It's nothing. Probably changing course.

But what if we're sinking?

We're not sinking. It happened once; it will never happen again.

Why not? Ships sink all the time.

Pull yourself together. Look out the porthole.

We'll be trapped. We have to go up on deck. I have to wake Daisy.

You have to stop making a fool of yourself. Do you hear anyone running? Do you hear any alarms?

She took a deep breath to calm herself and peered out of the window at the very limited view that a third-class porthole was able to offer. A cool early-morning light showed her a distant headland and a lighthouse. She studied them for a moment and satisfied herself that the *Lapland* was not moving. They had arrived. They were back in England.

She climbed from her bunk and reached over to shake Daisy. "We're here."

Daisy rubbed sleep from her eyes and joined Poppy at the porthole. "No, we're not," she said. "I remember what Southampton looks like, with all the cranes and ships. This is not Southampton. I don't know where we are, but we're not there yet. I'm going back to sleep. We're not supposed to arrive until lunchtime, and I don't think it's even breakfast time."

Poppy stepped away from the porthole. "This makes no sense. If this isn't Southampton, why have we stopped?"

Daisy shrugged her shoulders. "Maybe someone is going ashore. What does it matter? Oh, wait, I have an idea." Her eyes were alight with determination, and she clutched Poppy's arm excitedly. "If we're going to dock here, wherever here is, maybe we could … you know."

"No, I don't know. What are you suggesting?"

"We could go ashore. We could sneak away. That way, no one will even know where we are, and we'll avoid trouble."

"But we're not in trouble."

"Speak for yourself," Daisy muttered.

Poppy studied her sister's face. "What are you talking about? What have you done, Daisy?"

Daisy waved the question away. "I haven't done anything. I just mean that if we can go ashore without anyone knowing, there'll be no way that Father will be able to find us. We can get on board another ship and sail away, and he'll be none the wiser."

"I wouldn't worry about Father," Poppy said. She felt the familiar tug of isolation as she spoke, knowing that whatever she did, her father could not love her. She was not the boy he wanted. She was just a girl who counted for nothing. "I don't suppose he's even missed us," she said. "He won't care where we've gone."

"Well, someone might care," Daisy said fiercely. "Someone could be looking for me … us."

"If we don't go ashore with the crew," Poppy protested, "we won't be paid."

Daisy was wide awake now and sorting through her small collection of donated clothing. She picked up a dark skirt and flicked away specks of dust. Her voice was casual. "We don't need to be paid."

Poppy yanked the skirt from her sister's hands. "Why not? Why wouldn't we need to be paid? You've been dropping hints for days now, so it's time you told me the truth. What have you done, Daisy?"

"Ask me no questions, and I'll tell you no lies," Daisy said darkly. "You wait here, and I'll go up on deck and see what's happening."

She pulled the skirt from Poppy's hands and began to dress. She grinned as she ran a comb through her hair. As usual, her hair fell into perfect ringlets framing her excited face. She shrugged into her coat and turned as she reached the door. "I'll come back for you."

No, you won't. If you get ashore, you won't bother coming back for me.

Poppy fumed with anger as she rummaged through the pile of discarded clothes, looking for something to wear. She could not go up on deck in her nightgown, and she certainly couldn't follow her sister ashore without packing bags for both of them. As usual, Daisy was running ahead, leaving Poppy to pick up the pieces and prepare for her next escapade.

Poppy was still stuffing clothes into a bag when Daisy stomped in through the door, her bottom lip set in an offended pout.

"Well," she declared, "that's not going to work. We're nowhere near land."

"Of course we are. I can see it from the porthole."

"That's not what I mean. We're close to land, but we've stopped. They've dropped the anchor in the middle of the harbor or bay or whatever this is. No one is going anywhere."

"So where are we?"

"Miss Stap says we're in Plymouth."

"Plymouth," Poppy repeated. "That's in Devon. Why are we stopping here when we could be in Southampton in a couple of hours?"

"I don't know," Daisy said. "No one will tell me anything. Miss Stap says we're to report to the dining room. She says she'll explain when we get there, and we're to go at once." Daisy wrinkled her nose in annoyance. "We're not her crew anymore. I'm not reporting anywhere just so she can give orders."

"We should find out what's happening," Poppy said firmly. "I know Miss Stap is annoying, but I want to be paid even if you apparently don't."

Daisy arched her eyebrows and said nothing.

Poppy shrugged. "I'll go and find out what she wants. Do you want to come with me?"

Daisy eyed her bunk, with its inviting bundle of blankets. "I don't know why you woke me up so early. I could have stayed in bed for another hour."

"I thought you'd be glad to know we've arrived. At least we're close to land again. At least we're safe."

"Oh, pooh," Daisy said. "Why are you always worried about being safe? What are you so afraid of?"

"Sinking."

Daisy's face was suddenly serious. "You shouldn't have said that," she whispered. "How could you be so cruel? Now you've made me remember everything."

Poppy put her arm around her sister's shoulders. "I don't think we'll ever forget," she said, "but it will get better with time. I remember how I felt when Mama died, and I thought I would never be happy ever again, but I'm all right now."

"I don't remember Mama," Daisy said.

Poppy watched as Daisy's expression changed. Perhaps Daisy had, for just a fleeting moment, considered the loss of their mother, but that moment was gone, dismissed with a toss of Daisy's curls.

"Nothing is going to stop me from going to California," Daisy said, "so I'm going to put all this behind me and find another ship as soon as I can." She caught hold of Poppy's hand and dragged her toward the door. "As I can't go ashore yet, I suppose I'll come with you and see what Miss Stap has to say for herself."

They could hear a chorus of raised voices before they even entered the dining room. While the other crew members milled around uncertainly, Joughin, the chief baker, was standing on a chair and speaking loudly enough to be heard above the babble of complaining voices.

"This," he declared, "is not acceptable. We were told we would return to Southampton. Now they want to put us off here, in the middle of nowhere."

"It's just for processing," Miss Stap said, attempting to draw attention away from the visibly angry baker. "We will go ashore here and fill in some paperwork, and then we'll go on to Southampton. I can assure you, Mr. Joughin, that it's nothing to worry about."

Poppy heard a sudden bark of laughter, and all eyes turned toward Sullivan, who was sitting at a table with a cup of coffee in one bandaged hand and a cigarette in the other. "Nothing to worry about?" he queried. "I think we have plenty to worry about."

"I'm sure the company has our best interests at heart," Miss Stap insisted.

"The company has no heart," Sullivan said. He ground out his cigarette on his saucer and rose languidly. "Look where we are," he said. "We're out in Plymouth Sound. We're not even going into the harbor."

Joughin looked up at Sullivan. Although the baker was standing on a chair, Sullivan was still taller. "You are not experienced in management, Mr. Sullivan," Joughin said. "Down belowdecks you do not hear what I hear. I have seen this before many times. We are simply waiting for the tide to rise, and then we will proceed into the harbor."

Beauchamp, who had been sitting beside Sullivan, stood up to contradict Joughin. "You don't know what you're talking about. You can't see nothing from inside your kitchen. Take it from me, this ship isn't waiting for high tide. Plymouth's harbor is deep water at any point of the tide, and the *Lapland* is small. I've put in here many times in ships this size and never waited for the tide. Something's going on. We're being held here for some reason. I don't like it."

Beauchamp was shouted down by a number of disputing voices. With no officers in charge, and with Joughin unable to reassert his authority on the basis of being the chief baker, the arguing continued until the sudden appearance of a deck officer from the *Lapland*'s crew, blowing on a whistle and demanding silence.

"This is Plymouth," he declared.

"We know that," Beauchamp responded.

"And this is where you're going ashore."

Daisy pushed herself forward and looked up at the young officer. "If we're going ashore, why are we at anchor out here?"

Miss Stap tutted loudly and scowled, but the officer summoned a smile as Daisy gave him the benefit of her blue-eyed gaze.

"Nothing to worry about, miss," he said. "The harbor tender will come for you and take you ashore, and then the *Lapland* can be on her way."

"But why?" Daisy asked. She looked around at the crewmen. "We were told we would go to Southampton." She turned an accusatory stare on Miss Stap and Joughin. "Were we misinformed?"

Poppy tugged on the back of Daisy's coat. "Be quiet. Stop making trouble."

"Well, miss," the officer said, apparently mesmerized by Daisy's eyes and quite unwilling to look at anyone else, "we have been asked to disembark you here in order to avoid the crowds and the sort of trouble they had in New York."

Poppy thought back to their arrival in New York on board the *Carpathia*: the flashing cameras, the demanding reporters, and the crowd, some grief-stricken and some merely ghoulish. Surely nothing like that would await these last few survivors.

"We're nobodies," Poppy said. "We're not even officers. Why would anybody want to see us?"

The officer smiled at her, although not with the warmth he had bestowed on Daisy, which was no surprise for Poppy. "While you've been at sea, a lot has happened," he said. "The US Senate is conducting an inquiry, and I'm afraid a good deal of information and maybe misinformation is being bandied about. The general public, of course, want to know about the rich and famous passengers, alive or dead, but it doesn't end there. The world's gone mad with rumors and people, as far away as Australia, clamoring for details. You would think there had never before been a shipwreck."

"There hasn't been one like this," Sullivan said. "*Titanic* sent out Marconi messages, and that is how we managed to be picked up by the *Carpathia*, but Rostron was not the only captain listening in. For the first time ever, a ship went down while the world watched."

The officer looked at Sullivan with renewed respect. "That's it exactly. The *New York Times* was reporting the sinking the very morning it happened. People are fascinated."

"There is nothing fascinating about us," Miss Stap said coldly. "We know nothing that would interest reporters."

"You may know nothing about what caused the collision," the officer said, "but—"

Dillon, seated beside Beauchamp, interrupted him before he could finish his thought. "Someone knows something," he said slyly. "They may have kept Frederick Fleet in America, but there were two lookouts that night, and the other one is here with us." He turned to point at an inconspicuous man with a receding hairline, who stared down at the floor and refused to look up at him.

"Leave Lee out of it," Sullivan growled. "If you start pointing fingers, the blame will go where it doesn't belong."

Poppy saw the other men nodding their heads. It seemed that they all respected Sullivan. He was only a fireman, a man who was almost never seen above deck, but they saw something in him. Poppy had seen the same thing—a dangerous intelligence.

Joughin managed to make his way past Sullivan and attract the attention of the officer. "We will say nothing to the press," he announced. "We are union men. We will say nothing to anyone, not even management, until we talk to our various union representatives."

His announcement was greeted with a low murmur of agreement. The officer shrugged and raised his hands. "I'm just telling you what I know," he said. "Don't be surprised at what you see when the tender takes you ashore. There's already a large crowd, and there'll be even more when word reaches Southampton that you've been put ashore here."

With another smile at Daisy, the officer departed, and his mild voice was replaced by Miss Stap's commanding alto. "Go to your quarters and pack up your possessions." She clapped her hands like a teacher on a playground. "All of you. Off you go."

To Poppy's surprise, the whole contingent of crew, strong men who had worked in the most dangerous places on the ship, shuffled away without any complaint. Poppy made her way over to Miss Stap. She knew the stewardesses would have nothing to say to any inquiry or any newspaper about why the *Titanic* had struck an iceberg, but sinking was not the end of the story. Someone would want to know what had happened in the lifeboats. Lowe had fired his gun; hands had reached up to them from the water; they had rowed through floating bodies. How would they justify their actions?

"Miss Stap," Poppy asked, "do we have a union representative?"

"I am sure the National Union of Ship's Stewards, Cooks, Butchers and Bakers will represent us," Miss Stap said. "You will have nothing to worry about."

Sullivan loomed behind Miss Stap with a grim expression on his face and beckoned Poppy to join him out of earshot of Miss Stap.

"What is it?"

"The union rep."

"What about him?"

"I think you will be fine. You appear to be a very law-abiding young woman, and your union rep will keep you out of trouble. It's your sister I worry about."

Daisy again. It is always Daisy. Poppy hid her disappointment. She could hardly admit, even to herself, that she found the Australian inappropriately attractive. She would never act on the attraction, but she had spent time thinking about him, wondering how he had come by the scar. Was it a sword cut? He was obviously educated, so why was he working as a stoker? Was he fleeing from an illegal dueling incident? Now, as usual, she had to face the fact that his attention was not on her, but on Daisy.

"You have no need to worry about my sister. We can take care of ourselves."

"I think she's in more trouble than you realize, and a union rep is not going to help. She needs to get off this ship. I'll help if I can."

Poppy drew herself up to her full height, put aside her jealousy, and summoned righteous anger. *How dare he? Daisy is not some trollop to be spirited away by any Tom, Dick, or Harry.* For a moment, Poppy Melville, stewardess, was replaced by Lady Penelope, the future Countess of Riddlesdown—*if Agnes cannot produce a son.*

"We will have no need of your assistance, thank you very much."

Sullivan shrugged. "Don't say I didn't warn you."

Plymouth
Harry Hazelton

Harry was already approaching Plymouth when the *Lapland* steamed into the sound. Ben Tillett had driven through the night to reach the port ahead of the expected throng of reporters and sightseers. By the time Harry, Tillett, and two of Tillett's union men had left Southampton, word had already been spreading that the White Star Line was attempting to outsmart the reporters and smuggle the *Titanic*'s crew ashore. This had been followed by a rush to secure train tickets and any available transportation headed west to Plymouth. Harry had been surprised and relieved when Tillett had offered him a ride, and even more surprised to find that Tillett owned a sleek new Vauxhall motorcar.

The Vauxhall ate up the hundred fifty miles between Southampton and Plymouth with ease. They stopped only once in the sleeping town of Exeter, where Tillett replenished the water in the radiator from the horse trough in the market square. They returned to the road in the predawn darkness and headed out across the uninhabited wilderness of Dartmoor. Dawn was showing its first light by the time they crested the moor and looked down on the city of Plymouth and its busy dockyard. As they watched, the *Lapland* came into sight with her navigation lights blazing brightly against a background of gray, threatening clouds.

Tillett drove with a quiet intensity that was at odds with his usual hectoring manner. This fact, along with the union man's unexpected ownership of a brand-new motorcar, told Harry that Tillett was not the run-of-the-mill working man he had appeared to be. As for the two union men, Willets and Cannon, they had very little to say. They had been introduced to him as officers of the British Seafarers' Union as they climbed into the back seat, and they had remained silent for the remainder of the journey.

By the time they had argued their way past the guards at the dockyard gates, the *Lapland* was clearly visible within the sheltering arms of the sound, but she was no longer moving.

"They're not going to dock," Harry said, watching the activity on deck that accompanied the dropping of the ship's anchor. The *Lapland* swung on her anchor chain, turning her bow to the incoming tide. The funnels emitted small puffs of smoke, indicating that she had not quenched her boilers and she was ready to depart again as soon as possible.

After a brief, muffled conversation between the three union men, Harry found himself left alone in nominal charge of the Vauxhall while Tillett and his companions went into the harbormaster's office. They were gone long enough for Harry, waiting restlessly beside the Vauxhall, to witness the arrival of a passenger train, which disgorged a sea of excited reporters along with a handful of women, some carrying children. The reporters and families who had been waiting in Southampton had now reached Plymouth. The arrival of the train was followed immediately by the arrival of a strong contingent of police armed with truncheons, whistles, and a determination to keep the crowd in order and away from the docks.

The two union men, Willets and Cannon, reappeared with thunderous expressions on their faces.

"They're up to something," Cannon declared. "There's a harbor tender raising steam at the Great Western dock to go out and fetch the crew, and we've been refused permission to go aboard as official representatives of their union."

Willets leaned against the car and studied the activity taking place around the train station. "What do they want with that many policemen?" he asked. "Someone's expecting trouble."

Cannon lit a cigarette and joined Willets in studying the crowd, which was now being chivied and threatened into place behind a fenced area of the dock. "They're afraid of what the crew will say," he declared. "Someone has to answer for all those lives. It'll be the working man who takes the blame." He looked at Harry suspiciously. "What's your part in all this? Why did Mr. Tillett bring you along?"

"I don't know," Harry said. "I've met him a few times, but I'm not one of his union men. My only function here is to find two runaway girls and return them to their home."

Cannon squinted at him, doubt written on every line of his face. "The police have moved everyone away from the dockside, but they haven't come near you, have they?"

"Probably because of the car," Harry said. "It's quite a splendid vehicle. No doubt the police believe it belongs to someone of importance."

"Mr. Tillett is important," Willet said. "No one is going to ride roughshod over the trade unions."

"Did the harbormaster give you a reason why you couldn't go out to the ship?" Harry asked.

Cannon drew on his cigarette before replying. "He says it's nothing to do with him. His hands are tied. The Board of Trade is in control now, along with the White Star lawyers, and of course, they have the police in their pockets. They say they'll be taking depositions from the crew, right here and right now, and no one is to talk to them before that's done."

Harry was puzzled. It was obvious the two union officers were angry and suspicious, but so far he could see nothing suspect in the morning's activities. The harbor authorities had a plan to avoid the kind of chaos that had occurred in New York, and the British Board of Trade wanted to take depositions from the *Titanic*'s crew before they dispersed to their homes.

He studied the two impatient union men, realizing that nothing in his own life had given him a perspective on why they were so suspicious. He had gone from Cambridge into the army. From the moment he had been commissioned, he had been a man set aside from the ordinary, everyday soldier. He had given orders. He had eaten in the officers' mess. He had traveled first-class. Granted, he had fought and bled just like any other soldier and borne the burden of command, but he had never been at the bottom of the barrel, forced to work for a pittance to maintain a family that had no other source of income. He had never needed a union to protect his rights.

Tillett came from the harbormaster's office at a run and

impatiently instructed Cannon to hand him the loudhailer he had stored in the car's boot. "I've hired a boat," he declared. "If we can't go on the tender, we'll take ourselves out there independently, and I'll try to get their attention. They must be stopped from speaking."

"Why?" Harry asked.

"Because Senator Smith in America is looking for a scapegoat, and he hasn't found one yet, so now it's the turn of Lord Mersey, our Wreck Commissioner, to do what the Americans couldn't do. These inquiries, the American and the British, are about as unbiased as the Spanish Inquisition, and I intend to defend our union members with everything at my disposal. The poor devils on the *Lapland* are fresh bait for Mersey's fishing expedition. He'll twist and turn them until they don't know what to say. They weren't allowed to land in New York, and they've had no communication for all the time they've been at sea. They have no idea what to say and what not to say."

"If they speak the truth ..." Harry suggested.

Willets laughed. "They don't know the truth."

"Of course they do," Harry protested. "They were there."

"They were on a ship with two thousand two hundred other people," Willets said. "It was dark, and they were sinking. How much truth does anyone really know?"

Harry considered Willets's response. He was correct, of course. No one would ever be able to know everything that had happened.

Tillett strode away in the direction of a modest sailing craft snugged up against a small finger dock. A young boy was attending to a rust-red sail that flapped impatiently in the morning breeze, and a gray-bearded man in a heavy Aran sweater sat with his hand on the tiller.

Harry followed Tillett, who stepped easily into the boat, but there was nothing easy or sure-footed about Harry's arrival in the boat. He cursed his stiff leg and winced at the pain in his knee as he landed heavily beside Tillett.

The union man gave him a sympathetic grin. "Not as easy as it looks," he said. "I served time before the mast when I was a lad. Once you learn, you never forget."

Harry stared out at the harbor, unwilling to accept sympathy.

"I can't ride a horse," Tillett said, as if to somehow equalize their disadvantages. "Never learned."

Harry concentrated on the *Lapland* swinging on her anchor in the center of the sound. He did not need sympathy.

Cannon and Willets arrived with a heavy thudding of boots that set the small craft rocking. The skipper shouted to the boy in the bow, and moments later they were skimming across the water, the sail straining in the wind and the boat heeling in a way that Harry found quite alarming. He said nothing, of course. Tillett would no doubt have something else sympathetic to say. Harry hated being so far out of his element. *Drop Tillett into a Peshawari market, and see how well he does.*

Tillett leaned forward and poked Harry's leg. "What do you suggest?"

Harry looked up questioningly.

"You're a soldier, aren't you? You know how to plan a campaign. What's our best means of attack?"

Harry studied the *Lapland*. The harbor tender had already steamed across the short span of water and was snugged up against the ship's side. In any other element, the tender would be a ridiculous craft. She was short and stubby, with a high funnel and an elevated platform that would allow passengers to step aboard without descending to the level of the water. The sound was far from calm, but she held her position, and Harry could see the *Lapland*'s crew shepherding the *Titanic* survivors across the deck.

Were they nervous? he wondered. They were the same people who had clung to the gunwales of the *Titanic*'s lifeboats as they had inched their way down the hull of the sinking ship. Of course, some of them had not been so fortunate. Some of them had been left behind on the sinking ship and had leaped overboard at the last minute in the desperate hope that they could swim to safety. Others, so he had heard, had even gone under with the ship and been forced back to the surface by the violent venting of the boilers. Now they were ordered to make yet another transfer at sea. Of course, they were in sight of land, and help was at hand, but Harry knew that fear was not always conquered by rational thought. He had his own irrational fears, but fortunately, there was nothing in England's green and pleasant land to reawaken memories formed in the heat and dust of Britain's far-flung empire.

Drawing closer to the *Lapland*, he could see a handful of neatly dressed women intermingled with the shabby crew. He was not close enough to see faces or hairstyles. The bishop had said that one of his nieces took after her father, tall and lean, with the ginger hair the earl ascribed to his Tudor forebears. The other one was apparently petite and very lively—a real handful and not at all like her mother.

"Well?" Tillett asked.

Harry dragged his mind away from the two girls and set to studying the tender. It would be impossible to jump from this small boat onto the elevated deck, but … While he was thinking, the tender pulled away from the *Lapland*. When she presented her stern view, he could read her name: *Sir Richard Grenville*. He wondered if Sir Richard was flattered at having such an ugly craft named after him. He watched the *Sir Richard Grenville* start her progress toward the shore and saw a platform on the stern just a few feet above sea level. He shook his head. The platform was set directly above the propeller—one slip, and he'd be cut to pieces. Once upon a time, before his injury, he would have taken the leap in his stride. In those days, he had been able to land with silent, catlike grace, but those days were gone.

If forcing themselves aboard like a pirate raiding party was impossible, how were they to get aboard? He reviewed the options.

"I would suggest harrying them," he said eventually.

"Do what?"

"Impede their progress. Become a nuisance, a danger to shipping. You shout at them with your loudhailer and tell them who you are and what you want, and I'll have our skipper set up a course that will prevent them heading straight for the dock. If we put ourselves between the tender and the land, the passengers will run over to see what's happening and who is doing the shouting. The weight of all the passengers on one side will make the tender unstable, and our skipper, if he's willing, can make it impossible for them to safely change course. They'll have to take you on board rather than risk running us down."

He gestured toward the shore where a crowd of spectators milled about. "He won't want to drown us in front of all those people."

Tillett picked up the loudhailer and prepared to address the crew of the *Titanic*.

Eileen Enwright Hodgetts

PART THREE

GOING ASHORE

"My dad hardly ever spoke about the Titanic. It upset him too much. I only heard about what happened through my mum. Mum told us Dad had lost his father when he was nine and it hit him hard. My grandmother didn't work so had no money when my grandfather died and times were tough."
John Veal, Southampton

The dead crew members were the unsung heroes of the disaster— the "black gang" of workers who continued to toil deep in the bowels of the vessel as it sank. Southampton Echo

CHAPTER EIGHT

Plymouth
Poppy Melville

Poppy watched from the top deck as four men from the little sailboat were taken aboard the tender. The boat that had brought them out from the harbor darted away toward the shore where a great throng of people waited.

The tender resumed its course, no longer heading toward the crowded docks but turning to take a course parallel to the shore. A swell of anger erupted from the crewmen, who had lined the rail to watch the antics of the little boat with red sails. It was not hard to understand the cause of their anger. The shore was just here. Within minutes, they would have their feet on dry land, and some at least would have their arms around their loved ones. No doubt the crowd waiting on the shore consisted mainly of reporters, but there were women and children among them. Word of their arrival in Plymouth must have reached Southampton, and at least some of the anxious relatives had found a way to be in Plymouth. After all this time and everything they had suffered, the White Star Line was still controlling them and keeping them confined.

"It's New York all over again," Daisy said miserably. "They're not going to let us go ashore."

Poppy put her arm around Daisy's shoulders. "Don't be silly, Daisy. They can't keep us out here forever. This is a harbor tender, not the *Flying Dutchman* circling the globe and never finding land."

Miss Stap appeared suddenly at Poppy's elbow. "This is most irregular," she said, "but we should do as they suggest."

"As who suggests?"

"The trade union representatives. The four men who just came

143

aboard. Were you not listening to their instructions as they came alongside?"

"I knew they were shouting something," Poppy said, "but I couldn't make out the words."

"They were telling us to be silent and not to speak to anyone without a union representative being present. Our unions stand ready to protect our interests."

Poppy's heart sank. After all they had been through, were they now going to somehow be blamed for the loss of the *Titanic*? Had some new information come to light while they had been at sea? Had the Americans decided that the crew was at fault?

"Are we all in trouble?" Daisy asked.

Miss Stap's usual self-control seemed to have deserted her. Her face was slack with disappointment. "I've trusted the White Star Line all my life," she said. "I was born on board a White Star liner. They have never let me down, but now this ..."

"This what?" Poppy asked.

"The White Star Line has issued orders that are completely at odds with the advice of our union representatives. The White Star insists that we do not speak to reporters. In fact, we are forbidden to speak to our families who have come here to meet us. We are not to be paid until we have done what they ask and given our depositions."

"I thought the White Star was your family," Daisy said petulantly. "I don't know what you're worried about."

Poppy tightened her grip on Daisy's shoulders. *Not now. Don't make trouble now.*

"I have family," Miss Stap said stiffly. She waved her hand toward the other crew members. "These men have families, who want to touch them and hold them and ..." Her voice stumbled to a halt.

Poppy realized that despite her life spent at sea and her devotion to the White Star Line, even Miss Stap had someone ashore who wanted to touch her and hold her. Perhaps, Poppy thought, she and Daisy were the only crew members who could not expect anyone to be waiting for them—certainly not their father. She saw Sullivan's blond head among the crewmen who stood at the top of the ladder to greet the union representatives. Would Sullivan, obviously very far from home, have someone waiting to meet him?

Daisy put her hands on her hips and looked up at Miss Stap. "They think we know something," she said.

"Well, we don't," Miss Stap replied.

Daisy cocked her head to one side in exaggerated thoughtfulness. "Maybe we don't know what we know."

"I have no idea what you mean."

"Perhaps we saw and heard things that mean nothing to us, but if it is all put together in one place, it will tell a story."

Poppy smiled. Daisy rarely thought of anything but her own comfort, but when she could drag her mind away from her own problems, she had a quick intelligence. That intelligence was working now. She was right, of course. Every survivor had a piece of the story. When all the evidence was gathered in one place, surely someone would link the pieces together. What would emerge? she wondered. Would it be a noble story of self-sacrifice in the face of terrible tragedy, or would it be a story of incompetence and panic?

Poppy left Miss Stap and walked across the deck to stand at the back of the crowd of survivors who were listening to what their union representatives had to say. Three of the men spoke. Although their speeches were passionately reassuring, Poppy did not feel reassured. They promised that the crew could be represented at all times. They already had lawyers preparing to defend them at the British Wreck Commissioner's Inquiry.

Dillon, always aggressive, spoke up on behalf of everyone else. "Protect us from what? We've done nothing. Why would we need protection?"

The most senior of the union representatives was a self-assured man who introduced himself as Ben Tillett. He was well groomed, with a captivating voice and intense dark eyes, and he was flanked on either side by two men who spoke reassuringly but who lacked Tillett's charisma. As the argument went back and forth between the trade unionists and the crew, Poppy studied the fourth man who had come aboard from the small boat. Military, she thought, observing his upright posture and the set of his shoulders. Although he wore a tweed suit, she could not help but replace the suit with a red tunic and gold braid. His hair and eyes were dark. His face, as handsome as she had seen on any man, fell into lines that revealed an ongoing pain. She had seen such lines on her mother's face. Her mother had tried to hide them behind a determined smile, but to Poppy, they had always been visible.

As Poppy watched, the stranger stepped back from the group and limped to the rail. Although he remained rigidly upright, she saw how tightly he grasped the rail. He had an injury, and he needed the rail to balance himself against the motion of the tender. They were turning toward the shore now, approaching an isolated dock. He would not have to stand for long.

She pulled herself up short. Why did she care how long he had to stand? He was none of her business. No doubt he was here on some military matter. Maybe there were deserters among the crew. No, not deserters. Military police in uniform would come for deserters. This military man was after something else. A spy, maybe, or a saboteur. She shook her head at her own foolishness. She had been too long at sea with no one to talk to except her traumatized shipmates and her highly imaginative sister. She needed to get her feet on dry land, collect her pay, and form a new plan.

She glanced back at the soldier, and their eyes locked. She saw something impossible in his face—recognition. She had never met him before. She would surely remember such a man. She did not know him, but he knew her. He looked away, and his eyes searched the assembled crew before returning to look at her again. He was puzzled.

The tender was close to shore now. A couple of dockworkers appeared at the tip of a small dock set apart from other docks and guarded by a tall iron railing. From her elevated position on the top deck, Poppy could see the mass of reporters and relatives running along the road connected to the docks. Police whistles sounded, and a phalanx of uniformed officers waded into the crowd, which was rapidly becoming a mob.

As the tender was made fast, the crowd shouted and called out names and questions.

"Henry. Henry Bailey!"

"Is my Albert on there?"

"The *Daily Mail* will pay for an interview!"

"What about the lookout? Is he on there?"

"Why can't we see them? I've brought the children!"

Poppy and Daisy picked up their bags and followed the crewmen as they shuffled toward the ladder that would take them to the lower deck. The line moved slowly as many of the men took advantage of their elevated position to look over the crowd, searching for familiar faces. For ten days, Poppy had seen these men as only isolated units, not family men, not fathers, brothers, or sons, but just crewmen of the *Titanic* who were lucky to be alive. Now, as they waved and shouted names, she saw them for what they truly were: men earning a living. Excitement riffled through the crowd at each recognized face, but Poppy knew that for every reunited family, there would be two or even three families who would forever have an empty place at the table.

Poppy felt someone pressing against her as she waited at the top of the ladder. She turned and saw Sullivan. He was not looking out at the crowd; he was looking down at Daisy's bag of clothing. He reached out a long arm and plucked it from her hand. "Let me carry that. Don't want you to trip and break your neck now that you're almost home."

Daisy looked up at him with an expression Poppy could not read. Her face was red, and she could not meet his eyes. Obviously, something had happened between them, but Poppy could not say what it was.

Sullivan reached out his other hand and took Poppy's bag. "Don't worry. I'll give it back to you," he said. He grinned at Daisy. "Everything will be all right."

The crowd, its anger growing, threatened to bring down the fencing separating them from the survivors. The police responded by forming a cordon and creating a narrow pathway for the crew to pass through. As Poppy and Daisy prepared to run the gauntlet of the sweating police officers and the semihysterical crowd, the wounded military man suddenly appeared beside them.

"Allow me to escort you," he said softly.

Daisy instinctively dimpled up at him. "Oh my. Who are you?" she asked.

"Captain Harry Hazelton," he said. "I can't prevent what's happening now, but I'll do my best to get you released."

Poppy, who had never known how to react to a handsome man offering her his arm, stood still, resisting the press of the crew members shuffling along behind her.

"I don't understand what's happening."

"I believe the White Star Line is protecting its interests," the soldier said. "You should keep moving and keep your head down. You don't want your picture in the papers."

Poppy and Daisy moved forward with the captain limping

between them.

"We should be able to get away," Daisy said, not bothering to lower her voice. She smiled up at the officer. "If we could just duck out ..."

"You won't have a chance," their escort replied. "These premises are heavily guarded."

The animation in Daisy's face was replaced by fear. "Are we under arrest?"

"I don't think so."

Poppy, with the advantage of being taller than the average woman, could see that they were being channeled, or maybe herded, into the railway waiting rooms. She hoped this meant they would be taking a train to Southampton.

"May I help you find your luggage?" the captain asked suddenly.

Poppy could not restrain a smile. "We have nothing," she said. "It all went down with the ship."

"But," Daisy interrupted, "we were given clothing in New York. Sullivan has our bags."

"Sullivan?"

Daisy pointed to the blond head of the fireman towering over the crowd. "He's a fireman from Australia." She lowered her voice. "I think he may be a criminal."

Poppy could not help springing to Sullivan's defense. "I keep telling you, Daisy, not all Australians are criminals."

"Would you like me to retrieve them from him?" the captain asked.

"I'm sure he'll return them to us in due course," Poppy said. "I'm sure he's not a criminal. Besides, there's nothing in there he could possibly want."

"Speak for yourself," Daisy muttered darkly.

They shuffled along, carried forward by the press of people behind until they arrived at the entrance to the first building, and Poppy could see that instead of the usual waiting-room benches, the space was now furnished with trestle tables and chairs. Glancing through an open door, she was alarmed at catching a glimpse of a room where army camp beds had been set out in rows. Perhaps they were not officially under arrest, but she could not help feeling that they were prisoners.

A uniformed police officer stood at the door, officiously checking names against a list. Poppy's escort stopped beside him, heedless of the fact that he was holding up the line. "What's going on here?" he asked.

The policeman glanced up at the captain's face and seemed to recognize that he was speaking to someone in command, although Poppy was not certain what the captain commanded.

"I'm told the crew are to be served lunch, sir," he said.

"I don't see any lunch."

"No, neither do I."

"So what else have you been told?"

"We're to keep the crew here until further notice."

"Anything else?"

The policeman gestured with his thumb. "There's a room back there with tables. I don't see any food, but I see lawyers. They're here to take depositions."

"And suppose these ladies do not wish anyone to depose them?"

"Well …"

"Well what?"

"I would have to prevent them from leaving." The policeman assessed the captain once again. "I am authorized to call for reinforcements."

The captain nodded. "I see." Ignoring Daisy, who was giving him her best blue-eyed gaze, he turned to Poppy. "I think it best that you do what you are asked, and in the meantime, I will explain the position to your uncle."

Suddenly Poppy understood. "My uncle sent you?"

"Yes. I was engaged by the Bishop of Fordingbridge to locate his nieces. He had spoken to Nanny Catchpole, who said you had not returned home from London."

Poppy interrupted the explanation. "You were not sent by my father?"

"No. I spoke to him, of course, but he was not aware of your absence."

The information lay like a cold stone in Poppy's heart. Unless Agnes produced a son, Poppy was her father's heir, and yet she was so unimportant to him that he had not even realized that she and her sister were missing.

"These ladies have to go inside," the policeman said. "They're holding up the line, and there'll be trouble if they don't move along."

"Yes, of course."

The captain took a step forward, and the policeman thrust out an arm. "Not you, sir. You're not crew."

The captain took the rebuke in his stride. He gave Poppy a reassuring smile. "I will make arrangements," he said, "and return as soon as possible." He inclined his head in a slight bow and turned away.

Daisy clutched at Poppy's arm as they stepped away from the door and found Miss Stap beckoning them to her side.

"Who was that man?" Miss Stap asked.

"You'd like to know, wouldn't you?" Daisy taunted. "He's someone special. He was sent just for us."

Miss Stap gave her a puzzled smile. "Someone else has been sent just for you," she replied. "He's waiting over there. He's a detective from Scotland Yard, and the woman with him is a police matron. I'm sorry to say that someone has accused you of theft."

Daisy's voice was little more than a squeak. "Who? Who has accused me?"

Miss Stap shook her head. "I don't know, but the White Star is taking the accusation very seriously. Our reputation is at stake."

"Your ship sank," Daisy said accusingly. "I don't suppose that was good for the White Star's reputation."

Miss Stap ignored Daisy and turned to Poppy. "I'm afraid you are also implicated, as you are sisters and you have been sharing a cabin. The police would like to search your bags and the clothing you are currently wearing. They believe that you may still be carrying the stolen items."

Poppy glanced at Daisy and saw that her sister's face had lost all color and she looked ready to faint.

"What items?" Daisy asked weakly.

"Jewels," Miss Stap said. "Specifically, jewels belonging to Miss Bonelli and her niece. She says that she sent you to fetch them before the lifeboats were launched."

Daisy's color and energy were miraculously restored. "Yes, she sent me," Daisy said, "and I nearly drowned trying to get them."

"Miss Bonelli has made a formal accusation," Miss Stap said, "and we will have to get to the bottom of this. Where are your bags?"

Poppy suddenly realized that she had forgotten all about their bags of secondhand clothes. Sullivan had been ahead, carrying her bags, when she had been swept away by the man her uncle had sent. Where were the bags now?

Sullivan was a sudden presence beside her, dropping both bags at Miss Stap's feet. "Here you are, Miss Stap. I've been carrying them for the two ladies."

Poppy noticed his emphasis on the word *ladies*. However, Miss Stap seemed unaware of Sullivan's words and gave him a suspicious stare. The Scotland Yard detective approached, accompanied by a uniformed police officer and a police matron. The matron, a large woman in a belted black coat with official-looking epaulets, took hold of Daisy's arm with one hand and closed her other hand around Poppy's arm. Her grip was tight and inexorable. Poppy had no choice but to go with her. The policeman followed behind, carrying the two bags, and Miss Stap brought up the rear.

The matron glared at her. "There's no need for you to come," she announced.

"They are my stewardesses," Miss Stap said, "and my responsibility."

"That's what you say now," Daisy declared, "but where were you when I was nearly drowning?"

Poppy kicked her sister's ankle. *Not now. Please not now.*

"I demand you release me," Daisy said, "and give me back my bag."

"The police officer will inspect your bags, and I will inspect you," the matron said. "Miss Stap may be present if she wishes."

Poppy could not decide what would be the greater humiliation—being subjected to the matron's inspection without Miss Stap to protect them, or having Miss Stap witness the indignity of the whole thing.

The matron conducted them into the small, dark ladies' room, adjacent to the waiting room. The air in the cramped room was redolent of Jeyes Fluid, and Poppy shivered in disgust.

The police matron eyed Daisy malevolently. "Strip," she said.

"I will not."

"Then I will have to do it for you."

The matron was a muscular woman who looked perfectly capable of carrying out her threat, but she was no match for Miss Stap. The chief stewardess took up a position in front of Daisy.

"You will treat my staff with respect," she said. "There is

absolutely no need for either one of these young ladies to remove their clothing."

"That's right," Daisy said angrily. "I haven't got Miss Bonelli's diamonds. I nearly killed myself trying to rescue them for her, and this is all the thanks she shows me. You'd do better asking her niece about them."

Miss Stap looked at Daisy. "Are you implying that Miss Bonelli's traveling companion took the jewels?"

"I wouldn't put it past her," Daisy said eagerly. "She hated the old witch."

Poppy made a gesture to try to get Daisy's attention. Daisy had managed to plant a seed of doubt, and she would be wise to let it grow in peace. Daisy ignored her and continued heedlessly. "You can search me if you like, but you won't find anything. In fact, it would be a better idea to search the niece's bags and leave ours alone."

"Miss Bonelli's niece is in New York," the matron replied. She considered Daisy for a moment. "You have a point. Perhaps the niece should also be investigated. I shall suggest it to my superiors. Meantime, I have my orders. You will both strip."

"No, we will not." Poppy was surprised to hear the words coming so strongly from her own mouth. "If we were thieves, do you really think we would arrive here with stolen jewelry in our possession? We've had two weeks since the *Titanic* sank, and that's all the time in the world to find an accomplice. We could have given them to someone on the *Carpathia*, or someone going ashore in New York."

The matron gestured to Daisy. "I'm told this one tried to go ashore."

"But she didn't succeed," Poppy argued.

"And so she could still have the jewels," the matron replied triumphantly.

"Or maybe not," Daisy said. "Maybe I gave them to someone on the crew of the *Lapland.*"

Poppy almost laughed. At the rate Daisy was going, the police would be forced to search every *Titanic* crewman and maybe every member of the *Lapland*'s crew.

Miss Stap seemed to have arrived at the same conclusion and stepped in impatiently. "If your orders are that you should search these two young women, you may search their pockets, but you will not remove their clothing." She leaned in toward the matron, and her expression was suddenly fierce. "Do you know what we have all been through? Have you any idea what happened on the *Titanic?* Whatever you may have read in the newspapers does not do it justice. It was inhumane of Miss Bonelli to order my stewardess to return for the jewels, and yet I believe this young woman risked her life trying to do so."

Miss Stap's face was flushed, and she was obviously angry. Poppy wondered how long she had allowed that anger to simmer. Was it just the fact that Miss Bonelli had sent Daisy back to the flooded cabin, or was it a sudden reaction to a lifetime of coddling and cosseting spoiled wealthy women? Throughout their ordeal, the chief stewardess had held herself and her staff together by sheer force of will, and she probably expected that she would be rewarded for her efforts. They were back in England now, and still the White Star had not released them. In fact, they were being held to ransom with their pay withheld until they had been deposed. Would it still be withheld if they did not say what the White Star wanted them to say? Would there be any reward for any of them?

Daisy's shoulders slumped, and tears glittered in her eyes. "Miss Stap is right," she said weakly. "Miss Bonelli made me turn back. Instead of going to the lifeboats, I had to go back to the cabin, but I couldn't … I couldn't …"

Poppy stared at her sister, who seemed to have run out of invention. *Couldn't what? Come on, Daisy, say something they can believe.*

Daisy straightened and looked at the matron fiercely. "I don't have to explain myself to you. Go ahead and search me. Search my sister if you want. I don't care."

Poppy studied her sister's face. She could see worry hiding behind Daisy's sudden capitulation. Daisy was willing to be searched—she was even willing to allow Poppy to be searched—and yet she was obviously anxious.

For a moment, Poppy recalled standing on the deck of the harbor tender in New York while Daisy, who had just been pulled from the harbor, whispered in her ear: *There's something in the pocket.* Daisy had put something in the pocket of Poppy's coat! Could it possibly have been the stolen diamonds? Was there some truth in Miss Bonelli's accusations?

Poppy took a deep breath to hide her alarm. Daisy really didn't care if the matron searched her pockets, but it seemed she cared very much about anyone searching her bag. She was making a good impression now, playing a good game, but it was too late. The bags were small and contained very little clothing. The police detective would be finished by now. If so, why wasn't he knocking on the door and telling the matron he'd found what he wanted?

As if in answer to her unspoken question, someone knocked on the door, softly at first and then, failing to receive a reply, loudly and angrily. The matron turned on her heel and flung open the door. She took a step back as Sullivan crowded the doorway. She was surprised to see that Brown, the first-class cabin steward who had bewailed the loss of his boar-bristle clothes brushes, was standing just behind him.

"You can let the ladies go," Sullivan said.

The matron was not easily intimidated, not even by Sullivan. "I will do no such thing," she said. "Go away."

"She didn't steal nothing," Brown said—apparently, he had forgotten his gentlemanly grammar in his excitement. "No one didn't steal nothing from the first-class cabins."

"How can you possibly know that?" the matron demanded.

"It's all right, Matron," said a voice from behind Sullivan. "I think the ladies can come out now."

Sullivan stepped aside to give them a view of the police detective who was standing with his hands in his pockets and a look of studied nonchalance on his face.

Poppy looked at Miss Stap. The senior stewardess nodded her head. "Yes, I think we should all step out of here. This is really a very unpleasant little room. I don't know what they use for disinfectant, but it is most pungent."

The matron led the way out into the main waiting room. Poppy could see that a police officer was in the process of closing the bags they had brought from New York. Had they found something, or nothing? She had no idea what to think.

Sullivan folded his arms and leaned against one of the tables. "Mr. Brown has something to say. Go ahead, Brown."

Poppy could not fail to notice that Sullivan had taken on an air of command that was completely at odds with his ragged appearance.

"We locked the cabins," Brown said. "Me and Mr. Crawford locked the first-class cabins while the people were leaving." He shrugged. "We were told they'd be coming back and they'd want their possessions to be safe, so we locked the doors." He shook his head ruefully. "No one took it seriously. No one thought we'd sink, and we didn't want no trouble or thieving."

"And you can prove this, can't you?" Sullivan prompted.

"I can," said Brown proudly. "All you have to do is ask Victorine, Mrs. Ryerson's maid. You see, Mrs. Ryerson was just like that Miss Bonelli. She sent her back to fetch her jewel case and her traveling rug."

Poppy shivered. How many fine ladies had sent their maids back to fetch trinkets?

"So," said Brown, "Victorine was in the cabin, fetching the things, and Crawford locked the door with her inside and went on his merry way locking doors. She's lucky I heard her screaming and I let her out. She'll swear to it. I know she will. So even if this stewardess did as she was told and went back, she couldn't have entered the cabin. All the first-class cabins were locked."

Poppy looked at her sister. Daisy had said nothing about the door being locked. Sullivan's intervention had saved them so far, but they had not yet reached the end of the story. One way or another, Poppy was going to get the truth out of Daisy, but not here and not now.

The Scotland Yard man approached holding the two small bags containing Poppy's and Daisy's possessions. He shook his head. "Nothing in there."

Poppy caught the look of startled relief on Daisy's face. This was not what she had expected. So there had been something.

"It appears that Miss Bonelli was mistaken," Miss Stap said.

The matron nodded. "Perhaps she was."

"We should demand an apology," Daisy said. She grinned at Poppy. "Shall we do that? Shall we insist?"

"No," Poppy whispered as she dragged her away from the detective. "For once in your life, will you please be quiet?"

"But you don't understand."

"I understand perfectly well," Poppy hissed. "You had something you shouldn't have. Maybe it wasn't Miss Bonelli's jewels—"

"It wasn't. I swear it wasn't."

"Well, whatever it was, it's not here now, and you should be very glad it isn't. Someone helped you out of a very tight corner."

"It was Mr. Brown."

"Mr. Brown is only half the story," Poppy said. "Someone else helped with whatever you had in your bag."

"Who?" Daisy asked, suddenly angry. "Who has been looking in my bag?"

Poppy looked across the room and saw Sullivan leaning against the wall. "I can think of only one person," she said.

Ernie Sullivan

Sullivan lounged against the wall of the waiting room. While his crewmates milled around, complaining to each other, to the union representatives, and to anyone else who would listen, he kept his eyes on the two stewardesses and the police officers. He allowed himself a moment of satisfaction. The British police had not been kind to his family in the past, and he was pleased to see them lose out on what should have been a sure thing. He looked down at his hands, still wrapped in bandages. The task of surreptitiously removing an item from one of the bags had been considerably more difficult than he had expected. The burns on his hands were beginning to scab over, pulling the skin tight, making his fingers stiff. Miss Jessop's salve had protected him from a serious infection, but he thought his hands would never be the same again.

He glanced around at his fellow firemen. No doubt they all had burns and scars on their hands. Of course, they had no need of fine motor skills. Even scarred hands could hold a shovel.

Miss Stap was now in deep conversation with the matron and the detective. She was, he thought, a dried-up stick of a woman, but she was a tiger when it came to protecting her staff. She'd loosened the reins a little after the rescue, when the crew had been passengers on the *Lapland*, but now they were back on land, she was ready to reinstate her rules. The handful of stewardesses and restaurant staff had already been ushered out of the room, with the door closed firmly behind them.

While Miss Stap talked to the detective, the two sisters started to repack their bags. Like every other member of the crew, they had come empty-handed to the lifeboats, and their personal possessions had gone to the bottom of the sea along with the ship. However, the people of New York City had been generous in donating clothing, and Sullivan's eye caught a glimpse of lace-edged underwear as the smaller of the sisters stuffed the clothing back into her bag. The puzzled expression on her face was almost enough to make up for what had happened in New York. He shook his head. No, it wasn't enough. It was not nearly enough. *Daisy!* Her name was Daisy, and she had just about as much intelligence as the lawn weed she was named for. Her plunge into New York Harbor had destroyed everything he had planned, and now he was back in England, while the person he had been sent to find was in New York.

He remembered standing on the doorstep of Joanna Sharpe's London house. He had been well dressed then, with his grandfather's letters of credit to ensure he would have everything he needed to represent the family in style.

The manservant who opened the door studied his appearance and treated him with appropriate respect. "I'm sorry, sir, but she is not here."

Joanna Sharpe was trying to give him the slip, but surely she knew that he would follow. The revenge of the Sullivans was not something she could avoid.

"When will she be back?"

"Not for some time, sir. She's taken passage on the Titanic *to New York."*

He remembered his anger and frustration as he had endured the train journey to Southampton.

Did she think he was a fool? Did she really think she could escape him by sailing away to America? He would not only follow her; he would follow on the same ship.

By the time the train reached Southampton, his anger had cooled, and he was thinking clearly. If he purchased a ticket as a passenger on the Titanic, *his name would appear on the passenger list, and she would know that Richard Sullivan's grandson was still following her. She would be on her guard. He could not sail under his own name, and he had no time to find a forger to create a new identity for him. He made his decision as he stepped off the train.*

Joanna Sharpe would read the passenger list all the way down to the last name in third class, but she would never read the crew list.

He went aboard as the last man recruited. Fireman, they said, last-minute emergency. He had not known that his grandfather's need for justice would take him deep into the bowels of the ship, where the heat was so great and the air so scarce that a man was forced to suck cool air through a tube every few minutes or pass out with heat stroke or lack of oxygen. He had thought himself strong enough for anything until he worked his first shift, laboring with urgent intensity to feed four furnaces at a time with coal that was already burning.

The collision was almost a relief. At first the order to quench the furnaces had come as a welcome respite. Obviously, something had happened, but it couldn't be anything serious, not on the Titanic. For a few blissful moments, he ceased his backbreaking work and then ... and then the bulkhead gave way, and the problem of the bunker fire was solved—permanently.

They did not need an officer to tell them it was time to make for the ladders. He knew he should try to get himself into a lifeboat, but he could not save himself, not yet. He had not forgotten his quest. Joanna Sharpe had to live.

He could still see the shock on her face as he heaved her into the lifeboat.

"You!" she whispered.

"Yes, me," he agreed. He watched until the lifeboat was lowered inch by inch down the hull and into the water. Then he turned away and joined the men who were left behind. Some of them were already drunk. Most of them had given up. He would not give up.

He shook away the memory of that long, cold night. He was back in England now, and he would have to make a new plan. In the meantime, he watched the two stewardesses as they recovered from their encounter with the police.

He was sorry that the older sister had been drawn in. She had a natural quiet dignity, and he was quite certain that she had no idea what her sister had really done or why they were both being searched. He studied the younger one, who was obviously puzzled—relieved, of course, but very puzzled. She had expected to be arrested, but the police had found no evidence. He waited for her to put two and two together, but she seemed too dazed to realize that he was the one who had saved her from arrest. She did not even look at him. Well, she was not the smartest girl he'd ever met. She was one of the prettiest, no doubt about that. She was like a little firecracker. Her corkscrew curls seemed to be a physical embodiment of her personality, as though her pent-up energy bubbled up through her hair as it released itself in wild thoughts.

He had no regrets about rejecting her advances that last night on the deck. He was not sure she even knew what she had really been offering. She may have seen him as a big, ugly, ill-bred fireman, but he knew what he was. He knew he was not the kind of man to take advantage; another man may have seen things very differently.

His hands closed over the bundle in his pocket. It was time to return Daisy's property. He corrected himself. He knew full well that the property did not really belong to Daisy, but it was quite possible that it now belonged to no one. The owners of these items were probably at the bottom of the ocean. They didn't need these things, but apparently, she did.

He pushed himself away from the wall and sauntered across to the sisters. "I'll carry your bags," he said.

The tall, quiet sister looked at him, and he knew that she suspected him. She wasn't sure what had happened, but she knew he was involved.

Daisy glared at him. "I can carry my own bag, thank you very much."

Poppy shook her head. "Let him carry the bags, Daisy."

"No."

Poppy's voice was quiet but firm. "Let him carry the bags."

Daisy pouted and dropped the bag at Sullivan's feet. "Carry it if you want to," she said, flouncing away to follow Miss Stap.

"I'm not sure what you did or why," Poppy said, "but thank you."

Relieved that he would not have to fumble with the fastenings on Daisy's bag, Sullivan dipped his hand into his pocket and retrieved the bundle. "You'd better decide what to do with this," he said, slipping it into Poppy's hand.

Tears formed in Poppy's pale blue eyes. "What is this? What has she done?"

Sullivan shook his head. "You should ask her yourself."

Poppy nodded wearily, swiped at her eyes, and gave him a half smile, although her face still registered a deep sadness. Someone had hurt her very badly, he thought.

He watched as she opened her sister's bag and dropped the bundle inside. He waited until she had closed the bag, and then he picked up both bags and followed Poppy through a door that led to the outside courtyard, where an omnibus waited with its engine running and a police escort standing by.

Miss Stap stood on the platform, looking almost jaunty as she gripped the conductor's pole. "Come along, ladies. We are going to the Duke of Cornwall Hotel. I have refused to allow you to stay here any longer. We will be given rooms at the Duke of Cornwall, and we will proceed to Southampton tomorrow. Come along. Hurry up."

Sullivan stood in the courtyard until the omnibus disappeared from sight, passing through a crowd of relatives and reporters who lined the road beyond the security fence. He thrust his hands into his pocket and considered the advisability of going for a walk. He would take a stroll, just to get his land legs back, and if the stroll became a walk, and the walk became a hike … The thought was barely hatched before he was approached by two police officers.

He was a prisoner. They were all prisoners. The courtyard swarmed with police, and the waiting room swarmed with lawyers. He thought about the three union men who had forced their way aboard the harbor tender. Did they really think they could do something to change the situation?

He had no idea what was happening at the inquiry in New York, but he knew what was happening here in Plymouth. White Star was frantically trying to save its reputation. He wondered what reward they would give to the crewmen who were willing to say whatever was wanted, and what the penalty would be for those who would only say what they had seen with their own eyes.

When Sullivan turned toward the waiting room, he found the three union men huddled together at the doorway, whispering furiously to each other. They stared at him as he approached.

"Where have you been?"

"Nowhere. It seems we're prisoners. If you're our union representatives, I'd like to know what you are going to do about it."

Tillett scowled. "There's not much we can do at the moment. The lawyers in there have warrants from the Board of Trade, which is to say they are under the direction of Lord Mersey, the Wreck Commissioner."

"That's a big title," Sullivan said, "but what does it mean to us? You represent us men, don't you?"

Tillett indicated his companions. "Mr. Willets and Mr. Cannon represent the British Seafarers' Union. I am here to watch and advise."

"And what do you advise?" Sullivan asked.

"Our hands are tied," Tillett said. "The White Star will not pay any of you until you've given your depositions, and I don't have the power to force the issue. Unfortunately, the White Star's lawyers are hand in glove with the Board of Trade's lawyers, and these depositions are a joke. I can guarantee you that anyone who tells a tale different from the one the White Star wants to be told will not be summoned to the inquiry."

"But we can talk to the press," Sullivan said. "They'll have to let us go free eventually, and they can't stop us from talking."

"It won't matter what you say to the press," Tillett replied. "The newspaper reports on both sides of the Atlantic are nothing but wild rumors and speculation. None of it will count when it comes to apportioning blame or claiming compensation. Anyone can say whatever they like to a reporter, but only a selected few will speak at the inquiry, and it will all depend on what you tell the lawyers today. Say the right thing, and you'll be called. Say the wrong thing, and your deposition will disappear. Insist on talking, and maybe *you* will disappear."

Sullivan shook his head as he pushed past the three men and into the waiting room. Britain's legal system had been carried to every country of the British Empire. Australian justice, and he had some experience with Australian justice, had grown out of the British system, as had the justice systems of India, Canada, New Zealand, and so many other nations. Now Tillett was telling him that the White Star Line and the Board of Trade had every intention of perverting justice, and there was nothing he could do about it.

Confusion reigned in the waiting room. Lawyers were now seated at the long tables, facing crew members who were being asked to tell their stories. Sullivan walked among them, listening to what was being said. The lawyers asked no questions and allowed the crewmen to speak freely. They wrote down every word, and most of it, Sullivan thought, was nonsense. He had been there. He knew what he had seen and heard, but apparently, his crewmates had been on some other ship. They had been on a ship where the captain had been a hero and the officers had been noble, and there had been no panic, no chaos, and exposure to the water had not been almost instant death.

He listened to snatches of speech.

"I saw Captain Smith swimming with a baby in his arms. 'Take her,' he said. 'I'm going to follow the ship.'"

"The ship was near sinking, and the captain shouted, 'Each man for himself.' Before that he was on the bridge, pacing up and down and sending up rockets. It's a dirty lie to say that such a man as he would shoot himself."

Sullivan paused. He had never heard anyone say that the captain had shot himself. The lawyer continued to scribble, taking down every untruthful word.

"I saw an Italian woman holding two babies. I took one and made the woman jump overboard with one while I did the same with the other one. When I came to the surface, the baby in my arms was dead."

"I saw the first boat lowered. Thirteen people were on board, eleven men and two women. Three were millionaires. One of them was Ismay."

"I saw the first officer fire at two or three men who were trying to rush the boats."

"I swam around for about half an hour and was swimming on my back when the *Titanic* went down."

Sullivan listened in amazement. He knew that the only reason he was still alive was because he had managed to climb out of the water onto the floating remains of a staircase. Anyone who had been fully immersed in that water for half an hour would be dead. They would not be here in Plymouth telling lies.

"I tried to get aboard a boat, but some chap hit me over the head with an oar."

Sullivan grimaced at his own memories—a thousand or more people in the water and just a handful of lifeboats. The captain had given the order: every man for himself. Who could blame a man for lashing out with an oar when he was safe and dry in a boat and another man in the boat would be one man too many?

"Sir Cosmo asked me if I wanted to smoke, and he gave me a cigar. We kept rowing. We didn't go back for the people in the water."

Sullivan saw the lawyer hesitate. His pencil was poised. He looked to an older man, who had been prowling the room, overseeing the junior lawyers. The senior man nodded, and the junior began to write.

Interesting! Apparently, even the aristocracy are not to be granted protection.

He stepped away from the table, mingling with the men who had already given their depositions. He had no need of the money, and so he had no need to tell the lawyers what he knew. *Let them find out for themselves.*

CHAPTER NINE

Duke of Cornwall Hotel
Plymouth
Poppy Melville

When the omnibus passed through the police cordon and out of the dockyard, Poppy sighed in relief. The journey was not yet over, but at long last they were truly on dry land and leaving the waterfront behind.

The other stewardesses, even Miss Stap, exclaimed in wonder as they approached the Gothic splendor of the Duke of Cornwall Hotel. It was a magnificent gray stone edifice ornamented with numerous turrets and one tall tower. A phalanx of police officers awaited them on the forecourt as if prepared to repel relatives and reporters, but it seemed that their destination had been kept secret from any possible spectators. The twenty-five surviving women stepped warily down from the bus, each wearing the coats and hats given by the White Star in New York.

Miss Jessop summed up their reaction. "First class at last," she said.

"I'm sure our rooms will be in the attic," Miss Stap snapped, "but it will be better than sleeping on an army cot in the waiting room." She grasped her bag and proceeded to the elegant front entrance. The other women, even Daisy, followed behind her like chicks behind a mother hen.

Poppy kept hold of her temper until she and Daisy were alone. Despite Miss Stap's predictions, they were not in the attic. They had been given a spacious room with wide windows that did not provide a view of the harbor but overlooked the rooftops of the town. Poppy stared out of the window for several minutes, trying to find comfort in the presence of trees, streets, and good, solid buildings. The dark and dangerous ocean could not be seen from this viewpoint, but she knew it was there. She knew she would have to see it again, just as she knew she would have to confront Daisy.

"I'm going to take a bath," Daisy declared. "I smell like lavatory cleaner. A hotel like this will have good soap, maybe Yardley's lavender. I'm going to scrub myself, and then I'm going to soak."

Poppy positioned herself in front of the door. "You're not going anywhere."

"Just to the bath," Daisy said, reaching past her to open the door. "I won't be long."

Poppy grabbed the doorknob and slammed the door. "Stay where you are."

Daisy pouted. "What on earth's the matter with you?"

Poppy held out her hand. "Show it to me."

"Show what?"

"You know what."

Now that Poppy had acknowledged her anger, she found it building to a force that was almost beyond her control. It wasn't just today's anger; it was the anger of almost every day since Daisy had learned to walk and talk and had converted those skills into physically running away and verbally defying instructions. Poppy, trying desperately to replace the mother who had died so soon after Daisy's birth, had made every attempt to mother her willful little sister, and somewhere along the way, she had lost her own childhood. Life for her had always been about giving in to Daisy's whims.

"You are not the only one who needs a bath," Poppy hissed. "I smell like the gardener's lavatory at Riddlesdown."

Daisy shrugged. "You can go first if you want to."

Poppy released the door handle, put her hands on Daisy's shoulders, and shoved her. "Don't play games with me."

Daisy stumbled backward and landed on the bed. Her eyes were wide with surprise. "Hey, that hurt."

"And it's going to hurt some more if you don't tell me what you've done."

Daisy looked up at her. Her bottom lip quivered, and tears formed in her eyes.

"No," Poppy said, "don't try to get around me with tears. It won't work. You've stolen something, and I want to know what it is."

Daisy sat up and straightened her skirt. "I did not steal Miss Bonelli's jewels," she declared.

"So what did you steal?"

Daisy looked down, refusing to meet Poppy's eyes. "Nothing."

Poppy raised her hand. "If you don't tell me ..."

Daisy scooted backward on the bed with an alarmed and disbelieving expression on her face. "You wouldn't."

Poppy's hand itched to make contact with some part of Daisy. She wanted so badly to slap some sense into her. She was taller and stronger than her sister, and she could hold her down if she had to. This was all Daisy's fault. She could blame Daisy for everything that had happened. If Daisy had not wanted to go to America, they could have been at Riddlesdown now, awaiting the birth of the brother who would finally put an end to the earl's discontent.

Poppy took a deep breath and tried to control herself. "You had something in your bag, and Mr. Sullivan removed it."

Daisy bounced to her feet. "It was him. I knew he was a criminal. Australians are all criminals, aren't they? I should go and find him and—"

"We put it back in your bag."

"We? You mean you helped him? Why would you do that?" Daisy asked.

"I didn't help *him*; I helped *you*," Poppy replied. "He removed an item from your bag so that the police wouldn't find it. I don't know how you got him involved in this, but—"

"I didn't," Daisy interrupted. "I didn't involve him. I don't want anything to do with him."

"Why should I believe a word you say?"

"Because I'm your sister."

"That's not a good enough reason. Now listen to me, Daisy. I am going to get to the bottom of this. You are not going to take a bath. You are going to stay right there while I look in your bag and see what you have."

Daisy's defiance suddenly melted away, replaced by a wide-eyed pleading. "It wasn't stealing. They didn't care, and they were going to die anyway."

Poppy opened Daisy's bag and tipped the contents onto the bed. She turned over the pile of secondhand clothing until she found the bundle that Sullivan had been holding. It was, in fact, a knotted gentleman's handkerchief. It was heavy, and the contents were lumpy.

She picked at the knot. "What is this, Daisy?"

"It's our ticket to Hollywood."

The knot came free, and Poppy spread out the contents of the handkerchief on the bed. She stared in disbelief at two gold pocket watches, three money clips with folded paper money, a little pile of diamond studs and cuff links, a small black velvet pouch, and several gold signet rings. Without speaking, she picked up one of the money clips and studied the crinkled paper, a thick wad of Bank of England five-pound notes. She looked up at Daisy.

"These are gentlemen's possessions. Where did you get them?"

Daisy ignored the question and picked up another of the money clips and held it out. "American dollars," she said happily.

"But where did you get them? Did you steal them?"

"No, not really."

"Not really? What does that mean? Did someone give them to you?"

"Not exactly." Daisy shrugged. "It doesn't matter anymore. I'm sure they're all dead."

"Who?" Poppy demanded. "Who is dead?"

Daisy leaned back against the pillows on the bed, relaxed now. "All of them," she said, picking up a diamond cuff link. "Oh, do stop scowling, Poppy. You know I'm right. Hardly any of the men survived, and something like this shouldn't just be left at the bottom of the sea." She smiled slyly. "I had a heck of a time trying to get the paper money dry, because it was in my pocket when I went into the water. It's still a bit damp, isn't it? The good thing is that you know about it now, so I can spread the notes out and dry them properly."

Poppy shook her head. "We have to return them. We can't just keep them. This money could belong to some poor immigrant family. They may have been saving all their lives for—"

"You're wrong," Daisy interrupted impatiently. "Immigrants don't have money clips and gold watches and diamond cuff links." She looked up at the ceiling for a moment and chewed on her bottom lip thoughtfully. "I'll tell you what I think."

"No," Poppy said. "Don't tell me what you think; tell me what you did, and be quick about it, because I have to return these to a White Star official before you get arrested for theft."

Daisy continued to stare at the ceiling, no longer impatient or worried, merely thoughtful. "I think," she said eventually, "that there was a thief on board the *Titanic.*"

Poppy's anger bubbled back to the surface. "Of course there was a thief. You are a thief."

Daisy shook her head. "No, I'm not. You heard what Mr. Brown said. I could not have stolen Miss Bonelli's jewels, because the cabins were locked."

"I'm not talking about Miss Bonelli's jewels," Poppy snapped. "I'm talking about these things."

Daisy sprang from the bed, grasped Poppy around the waist, and rested her head against Poppy's breasts. She looked up at her with wide, innocent eyes. "Someone is feeling very grouchy," she said. "Why don't you go and have a lovely long bath? You'll feel better."

"A bath is not going to solve this problem," Poppy said, standing still and making no attempt to unwind herself from Daisy's embrace. How long had it been since anyone had touched her with affection? How long since anyone had cared about her welfare? She faced the fact that Daisy, with all her annoyances and selfish little tricks, was the only person who actually loved her, or at least needed her.

"Just tell me," she said wearily. "Where did you find these?"

Daisy released her with a smile. "I knew it," she said. "I knew you would understand. As you say, I found them. I think someone had got into the first-class cabins before they were locked. The women's jewels would not be easy to find, either in a drawer or locked in a trunk, but the gentlemen would leave their wallets and rings on the dressing table for the night. I've tidied enough cabins to know that's the case. They would be easy for a thief to find. I think the thief ran through the cabins, picking up whatever he could find, tied it all up in a handkerchief, and tried to get to the lifeboats. Something happened. Someone stopped him, or maybe he panicked. I found this just lying on the floor, so I picked it up. I wasn't sure what it was at first, not until we were on the *Carpathia* and I had time to look." She held out her hands, palms up. "What do you want me to do? I don't know who they belong to."

Poppy sighed. She wanted to believe that Daisy was telling the truth, but there was something about the story that did not ring true. Had there been time for a thief to run through the cabins, gathering up any items left out in plain sight? If that same thief had taken the time to tie them all up in a neat bundle, wouldn't he or she have made sure to keep hold of the bundle instead of dropping it on the floor?

She shook her head. The truth of Daisy's story was not important. It was obvious that Daisy had no right to keep these treasures, and they would have to be turned over to the White Star representatives first thing in the morning. She hesitated. Would the White Star officials believe Daisy, or would she again be accused of theft?

A thought flashed through Poppy's mind. Perhaps Sullivan would know what to do. He seemed to be very resourceful. She dismissed the thought immediately. She knew nothing about the Australian. How could she possibly trust him?

If not Sullivan, what about Captain Hazelton? The wounded soldier had been extremely courteous and solicitous for their safety, and the bishop had trusted him enough to employ him. Apparently, he offered his services as a professional investigator, so he would be the best person to give her confidential advice. Perhaps he would know how to locate the owners of the stolen items, or if not the owners, the surviving relatives.

She found herself warming to the thought. She would find Captain Hazelton and have a quiet tête-à-tête. He would know what to do.

She smiled at Daisy and snatched up one of the fluffy white towels folded at the foot of the bed.

"I'm going to have a bath," she announced, "and a long soak."

Daisy Melville

Daisy sat on the bed after her sister had departed. Her hand reached out automatically, and her fingers explored the little heap of valuables. The paper money was still slightly damp. She would have to remove it from the money clip and spread it out. Now that Poppy knew the secret, there was no need to keep it hidden. The gold watches, although quite distinctive, were not engraved. They could not be traced back to an owner, so they would be easy to sell. The money could just be spent. No one could lay claim to anonymous paper money that could have come from anywhere. On the other hand, the item in the little velvet bag presented a problem. It must be valuable, but she could not see why. She had watched one man attempt to shoot another man in order to acquire it, but what was it? She wondered if Sullivan would know. She suspected that he knew many things. He had spurned her once, but she had not told him everything. She had not told him that she had money.

She leaned back against the pillows. If Miss Bonelli had not sent her back for the jewels, none of this would now be happening. She really should be grateful to the old bat.

April 15, 1912
1:40 a.m.
On Board the Titanic
1:40 a.m. (Ship's Time)

She was too late, and she would never reach Miss Bonelli's cabin. Fighting her way back against the tide of increasingly alarmed passengers had taken too long, and now the water was rising in the corridor outside the cabin and lapping at the door. She took a bold step forward and waded determinedly into the icy cold water. It was no use. The water had a life of its own, an unrelenting current that tried to sweep her off her feet. She clung to the railing set in the wall and watched the water swirling around her knees.

It's going to happen, she thought. This ship really is going to sink.

She turned away from the promise of Miss Bonelli's jewels. She had to find a way to climb upward onto the open deck. She had to find a lifeboat. Her wet skirts tangled around her ankles as she pulled herself free of the water and opened the service door that would take her up to the next deck. As she climbed, she turned to look over her shoulder. The water was still rising—creeping up the stairs behind her. She could not even imagine what was happening on the lower decks. What had happened to the people who had dismissed the warnings of their cabin stewards—the ladies who would not wear a life jacket because it was unbecoming and the gentlemen who had told their wives to go ahead and they would see them in the morning?

She imagined that the grand staircase, where the first-class passengers paraded every evening in their finery, was now underwater. The deck was at an acute angle, with everything pitched forward. She struggled up the last of the stairs, still fighting against the entanglement of her wet skirts and petticoats. Perhaps she should not have accepted Miss Bonelli's offer of a reward for retrieving the jewelry from her cabin. She could be in a lifeboat now if she had ignored the old woman's demands, but the offer of diamonds had been impossible to resist.

Daisy had big plans for herself. She was glad to have coolheaded Poppy with her, but she would never rely on Poppy to assist in her quest for fame and fortune. Poppy had already suggested that marriage was the best route for Daisy to obtain security.

Find a rich husband, Daisy. You could charm the birds out of the trees with your smile. You don't have to go to America. There are plenty of rich men in England.

Poppy didn't understand that Daisy had no interest in domestic security. Even now, with the water rising behind her and the lights beginning to flicker, Daisy felt more alive than ever before.

She reached the top of the stairs and stumbled into a wide wood-paneled room. She recognized it immediately. The service stairs had brought her to the first-class smoking room, a place where gentlemen drank and played cards out of sight of their wives.

She stood for a moment, shocked into immobility. They were still here. The room was filled with men, some in evening dress and some with coats thrown over their nightclothes. A few of the men wore life jackets, but most had removed them. She was filled with dread as she sensed the atmosphere in the room. This was the place of last resort, and if she lingered here, her hopes would die. These were men who were too noble to save themselves. They had gathered here to await the inevitable. Their acquiescence was contagious.

They were drinking. The smell of liquor fought with the musky scent of their fear. For a moment, she thought that the gentlemen's scruples had abandoned them and they had raided the bar, but then she saw the barman. With a life jacket over his uniform, he was still at work. Although he clung to the bar to prevent himself from sliding forward, he still opened bottles and sloshed liquor into glasses held out before him.

In this room, the tables had been affixed to the floor, and so they remained in place while the chairs followed the tilting of the deck. Four men were still seated precariously at a table and were still attempting to play a game of cards. She suspected that they were now so inebriated that they could not reason. One man seemed to be the winner of their noisy, drunken game, and he had gathered not just money but valuable items that the other men had at hand.

She looked at them in disgust. These were the kind of men Poppy expected her to marry—men so foolish that they would drink themselves into a stupor rather than go outside and see if they could find a place in a lifeboat. They were men whose honor was worth more than their lives, filling their last moments by trying to outsmart each other at a ridiculous card game.

She eyed the man who was gathering the winnings into a handkerchief. He was an unremarkable man with sparse hair and rounded shoulders, but his fingers were quick and nimble. He did not seem to be as drunk as his companions. He extended his hand to pick up one final item, a small velvet bag. One of the men attempted to rise, shouting drunkenly and attempting to retrieve the velvet bag.

"No, not that!"

The winner ignored him and scooped the bag onto the handkerchief. The loser was on his feet now. He pointed a wavering finger and shouted incomprehensible words in a guttural accent in which Daisy only understood two words. "Cheat! You cheat!"

Daisy shook her head in disgust. They were all going to die, so what did it matter if someone was cheating?

The charge that one of their number had been cheating brought the other men out of their stupor. They were all standing now and making threatening noises. The cheater produced a pistol and waved it carelessly around. How ridiculous, *she thought.* What were they going to do? Were they going to report him to the captain and have him thrown off the ship? Was the man with the pistol going to shoot someone? That would be murder, but who *would care?*

The winner, the man who had been cheating, tied a hasty knot in his handkerchief while the other players watched with their drunken mouths hanging open. The gunman's ill-gotten gains were now hidden from view, but Daisy could see them in her own mind. The bundled handkerchief contained two or maybe three money clips. She imagined what she could do with that money. Her earnings as a stewardess were a mere pittance, but this was real money, and it was there for the taking. These men were going to drown, but why should their money go to the bottom of the sea, where it would do no good to anyone?

She glanced around the room at the men who waited, some stoically and some with fear on their faces. No one was looking at her, and no one was looking at the card-playing drunks. Every man prepared for death in his own way, and for once in her life, Daisy's presence had no effect on them. The ship lurched as a great crash and rending sound came from somewhere far below. The card players stumbled into each other, grappling and throwing wild punches. Daisy sprang forward and snatched up the handkerchief. For a brief moment, she met the eyes of the man with the pistol. She realized with alarm that he was stone-cold sober and he had registered her presence.

Grasping the handkerchief in one hand, she picked up her skirts and ran out onto the open deck, where chaos reigned.

She heard a gentleman's voice call out as she approached. "Here's a woman. She can go in lifeboat four with Mrs. Astor."

Rough hands pushed her from behind. "Follow these people down to the promenade deck."

She stuffed the handkerchief into her pocket and followed the fleeing passengers, almost tripping over a boy who was dragging a dog on a leash. When they reached the deck below, the group stopped in horror at finding the promenade deck enclosed by windows. She felt her frustration rising as reality began to take hold. She had waited too long. She was quite certain that quiet, law-abiding Poppy was already safely ensconced in a lifeboat and probably wrapped in a warm, dry blanket. She felt unreasoning anger. If it were left to Poppy, they would have nothing but their pitiful earnings from the White Star Line, and that would never be enough to get them to California in style. Why did Poppy always play it safe? Why was it always left to Daisy to take all the risks?

The crew had finally managed to open the windows, but the boat was listing badly, and the lifeboat, swinging on its ropes, was too far out to be reached. An officer took command, ordering the crew to start piling deck chairs to make a bridge to cross over to the lifeboat. The boy wanted to take the dog, and Mr. Astor wanted to go with his wife because she was in the family way. He didn't use those words, but Daisy knew what he meant. Were they going to stand there all night arguing while the ship sank? She saw tears in the boy's eyes as he dropped the dog's leash, and heard Mrs. Astor's plaintive mewling when she was told her husband could not accompany her.

At long last the first person ventured out onto the deck-chair bridge. Daisy was elbowing her way forward when she became aware of someone else trying to push into the group. She caught a glimpse of a man. Well, he wouldn't be allowed. It was all very silly and chivalrous—women and children only—but it worked to her advantage. The newcomer poked her in the ribs. She made up her mind to report him. She turned her head and looked him in the face. Her scream died before it was born. The man she had robbed was no longer in the smoking room. He was here, and he was most definitely sober. Their eyes met in a flash of recognition. Daisy turned and ran.

Leaning against the pillows in the comfort of the Duke of Cornwall Hotel, Daisy was finally able to relax. The secret was out now. Poppy knew what Daisy had been concealing, although she had no idea how Daisy had come by her bundle of treasures. Of course, being Poppy, she would try to do the "right thing," whatever that might mean, but it would come to nothing. She could not return the money to the drunken men who had been playing cards instead of trying to find a way off the sinking ship.

Daisy could find nothing but contempt for the losers. Maybe they had been impelled by some ridiculous sense of noblesse oblige, but there was nothing noble about spending their last few minutes in a drunken brawl with a card sharp

She reached forward and picked up the velvet bag. This had been the final straw. The thought of parting with this had brought the loser to his feet in protest. She opened the bag and stared down at a rather ugly necklace with a diamond pendant and wondered why anyone should care so much about this particular stone. Even the Riddlesdown family jewels contained diamonds of greater size and in far more elaborate settings. She picked up the jewel and held it to the light from the window. Whoever had cut and polished the stone had done a very poor job, or perhaps they had given up upon discovering that the stone had a flaw: a dull smear at its very heart. She dropped it back into the bag. Perhaps it had sentimental value. Perhaps the gambler had realized, at the very last moment, that he was about to lose something more important than money.

She smiled at her own thoughts. The gambler no longer mattered. He had gambled with his life and lost. By now he was nothing more than a hazard to shipping, a frozen corpse held on the surface by a *Titanic* life jacket.

On Board the *Lapland*
Alvin Towson

Towson stood on the deck of the *Lapland* and stared at the white cliffs and green hillsides of the English countryside slipping by as the *Lapland* sailed away from Plymouth. He had been awakened early by the rattling of the anchor chain and the sudden change in motion. He forced down a moment of panic. This was not the *Titanic*, and they were not sinking. He knew he would have to conquer that panic now, or it would remain with him for the rest of his life.

He took the stairs to the first-class promenade deck and saw that a harbor tender had snugged up against the *Lapland* and was taking on passengers. Panic rose again, and cold sweat prickled at his hairline. The *Titanic*'s crew was boarding the tender. They were leaving. He could see the women, in their thick coats and sensible hats, standing on the raised deck of the tender. He could even pick out the girl who had the Matryoshka. Where was she going? How could he follow her?

His panic gave way to fear when he saw a small boat with red sails scurrying back and forth and harrying the harbor tender as if determined to sink the ungainly craft and put the whole crew in the water. Surely the girl could not drown now. She could not tumble into the water and take the jewel to the bottom of the harbor.

He breathed a sigh of relief as the tender finally reached the shore and the *Titanic* crew disembarked. At least the Matryoshka was safe for the time being, but how was he to find the girl again? He should go ashore now!

No amount of pleading, cajoling, or outrage would persuade the purser of the *Lapland* to have a boat lowered to take him ashore. Eventually, he realized that his near-hysterical insistence was attracting too much attention from the other passengers, and he forced himself to be quiet. He had done nothing to attract attention to himself during the voyage. He had not played cards or joined the gentlemen in the bar. He had taken his meals in his cabin. He had done his best to make himself invisible. He should not now make himself memorable.

Most of his fellow passengers were people who had been booked to travel from New York to London on the *Titanic's* return journey. Throughout the voyage, he had overheard only two topics of conversation: the lack of luxury on the *Lapland*, and the fate of the *Titanic*.

"Such a shock! When I heard the news, I could hardly believe it."

"It could have been us. They say the captain was mad for speed."

"Trying to set a record."

"Risking the lives of the passengers."

"Greed, nothing but greed."

"All those people in the water."

"I can't imagine. It must have been dreadful."

Towson had remained silent. He could, if he wished, have told them just how dreadful it had been, but it was Towson, the notorious and desperate gambler, who had been on the *Titanic*, not Kenneth Rotherhithe, the man he had now become. Rotherhithe was a boring man. No one cared what he thought. No one asked what he knew.

The purser returned to his duties; the crew pulled up the anchor; and the *Lapland* steamed away from Plymouth. Towson tried to tame his seething impatience by telling himself that he would find the girl again in Southampton. The crew would not remain in Plymouth. Whatever the reason for the diversion, they would eventually have to return to Southampton to collect their pay. He would just have to wait.

Harry Hazelton
Duke of Cornwall Hotel
Harry Hazelton

"She was supposed to sink. It was all planned."

Harry looked up from his breakfast plate and studied the two men seated at a table in the breakfast room of the Duke of Cornwall Hotel.

The man who had just spoken, a sandy-haired man with an impressive walrus mustache, shot a challenging glance at his companion.

"Are you really going to submit that story?" his companion asked.

"Yes, I am."

"You'll be laughed out of the editor's office. They'll never print it."

The two men ate in silence for a moment. Harry waited, suddenly feeling very much at home. This was what he knew how to do. He had spent many years on the fringes of the empire, lurking in cafés and taverns, listening to the quiet conversations of dangerous men and women. Sometimes he heard nothing but nonsense, but it was not all nonsense. Over the years, he had learned to sift and sort and separate the wheat from the chaff. He was not sure about this particular conversation, but he had heard enough to catch his attention. He looked down at his plate and continued to listen.

He assumed the two men were reporters. If so, they were far more enterprising than the horde of reporters who were still waiting at the Plymouth railway station for a glimpse of the *Titanic* crew. Very few people knew or even cared that the surviving women had been taken to the Duke of Cornwall Hotel to spend the night. Perhaps they assumed that the women would have very little to say. They were stewardesses and restaurant cashiers, so what did they know about the operation of the ship? As for the sinking, they had been given priority in boarding the lifeboats, and they had arrived dry and safe on board the *Carpathia*. Harry checked himself. They had not all been dry and safe. Daisy had, apparently, been very wet. How that had happened was none of his business, but it was a loose thread in the story, and he didn't like loose threads.

The sandy-haired man selected a piece of toast from the silver rack. "I don't need an editor's approval. I'll submit it to Interrogantum. He'll know what to do with it."

His companion shook his head. "That's not journalism, Dan. You're putting two and two together and making five."

Harry dropped the information into the file folder that he was creating in his mind. The sandy-haired man was Dan. Who was the other man? More importantly, who was Interrogantum, and which newspaper did he represent?

"No, Charlie," said Dan. "I'm putting two and two together and making money." His mustache twitched eagerly. "This is the story of the century. If we can prove that she was deliberately scuttled—"

Charlie, who was the owner of an impressive stomach, interrupted immediately. "How are you going to prove that? It's not enough to say that you have a hunch."

"It's more than a hunch," Dan insisted.

Charlie nodded. "Maybe so. I agree that there are a lot of things here that seem highly suspicious, but it's a big stretch to say that she was sunk deliberately. She hit an iceberg, and most people would see that as an act of God. How are you going to prove it wasn't?"

"If she hadn't hit an iceberg, she would have hit something else," Dan said. "It was all planned."

The chair creaked ominously as Charlie leaned back and folded his hands across his belly. "Even Interrogantum requires some element of proof."

"No, he doesn't. I tell him; he tells selected newspapers; and they print whatever he tells them in the form of provocative questions."

"I wonder why," Charlie said. "How does he have that much power?"

"I don't know," Dan said, "and I don't care to find out. He pays cash, and he takes everything I bring him. Here's something else I've heard. Do you know that J. P. Morgan had a reservation on the *Titanic*, and he canceled at the last minute?"

"So what?" Charlie asked. "The man's a millionaire. He can afford to cancel a ticket. Apparently, he's holed up in France with a little French tart. That's not news, Dan."

"Canceled at the last minute," Dan repeated. "I'm telling you, he knew something. And what about the US ambassador to France? Same thing. Canceled at the last minute. In fact, so many people canceled or failed to book that the ship sailed half-empty. She was a thousand passengers short of a full load, and she had a last-minute scratch crew. Why?"

"You're suggesting a huge conspiracy," Charlie said. "It's not possible for so many people to keep a secret."

"It's possible for that many people to believe a rumor," Dan insisted. "That's all it takes."

"Well," Charlie said, "I have to admit some things don't add up. There could be a kernel of truth in all the speculation."

Dan's wide grin sent shivers through his prolific mustache. "That's all we need, isn't it? Just a kernel of truth. Interrogantum will do the rest."

"Even if he doesn't believe you?" Charlie asked.

"He doesn't have to believe me. That's not the point. I don't have to prove anything. He said to bring him everything I can find, so that's what I'm going to do. There's more. You're going to like this. I heard something else."

"Go ahead," said Charlie. "What did you hear?"

"Officers," Dan replied. "There's something really fishy going on there."

"Like what?"

"Well, Captain Haddock of the *Olympic*—"

Charlie interrupted with a bark of laughter. "Something fishy. I should say so."

Harry kept a straight face as he stared down at the scrambled eggs and bacon on his plate. Charlie's interruption had been inappropriate and in tremendously poor taste, and yet he understood the impulse to laugh. The newspaper reporters and their readers had been stewing in bad news for days on end. The stories emerging from the US inquiry were uniformly horrific. They seemed to reflect ineptitude and complacency on the part of the crew and outstanding bravery or foolishness on the part of the many wealthy gentlemen who meekly agreed to be left behind to drown. If Charlie had found something to laugh at, Harry could only envy him. It had been a long time since he had laughed.

"Try to take this seriously," Dan said stiffly. "Haddock is captain of the *Olympic*, the *Titanic*'s sister ship. He sailed on the third of April without his chief officer because Wilde was suddenly transferred to the *Titanic*."

"And you find that suspicious?"

"Transferring him to the *Titanic* as chief officer meant moving all the officers down a notch, which is something I'm sure they didn't appreciate. Then they threw out the junior officers and brought in new ones."

"I don't see—"

Dan's expression was smug. "Why would White Star suddenly throw the crew into confusion? Why would they take men who had been working together to prepare the ship, and move them down the chain of command?"

Charlie shook his head. "I don't know, but I'm sure you're going to tell me."

Dan nodded and licked his lips. "Because they wanted things to go badly," he said. "They knew Smith was incompetent. He'd been through a series of avoidable accidents. When he took the *Olympic* out of Southampton, he ran her into another ship, and he grounded her a couple of times. Why would they give him the *Titanic*, the pride of their fleet, to command? He should have been retired, but he wasn't."

Charlie cocked his head to one side, looking suspiciously at his companion. "Even Interrogantum will have a hard time printing that. Where's the proof?"

"I don't need proof," Dan said. "Truth doesn't sell newspapers, but speculation does. I am willing to speculate that White Star gave Smith the command because they could afford to lose him. They knew this would be his last voyage."

Charlie shook his head fiercely. "It was his last voyage because he went down with his ship, but no one could have planned for that to happen."

Dan leaned forward and lowered his voice. "Don't be so sure about that. If everything went as planned and the *Titanic* went down without a trace, it could all be blamed on Smith's incompetence. He'd been making mistakes all along, and he was more than ready to retire. He hit an iceberg. Case closed."

"It won't wash," Charlie said. "Even if what you say is true about the reshuffling of officers and the people who canceled at the last minute, what would be the purpose? Why would White Star want to sink the *Titanic*?"

"Why would White Star have a ship waiting just over the horizon?" Dan asked.

"What ship?"

"There was a ship. The survivors saw its lights. It didn't approach. It just waited."

"I don't like this," Charlie said. "I don't care what this Interrogantum fellow pays, our job is to report news and not rumors. I don't want any part of it."

"You're missing out on a good thing," Dan warned. "I'll be making a name for myself while you'll be hanging around the pubs on Fleet Street just pretending to be a reporter."

"I'd rather be warming a seat in the Cheshire Cheese than peddling lies," Charlie declared. "I have standards, and I won't stoop to outright lies."

Dan leaned forward to pour tea into his cup. "Suit yourself," he said.

Harry, who was allowing his breakfast to grow cold, mimicked Dan's gestures and poured himself a fresh cup of tea. He was more or less certain that Charlie was right and Dan was talking nonsense, but a career of overhearing conversations that were not intended for his ears had given him an ability to listen without judgment. Later, when he was alone, he could analyze what he had heard. All he had to do now was listen.

Unfortunately, his opportunity to overhear any more of the conversation was interrupted by the arrival of Ben Tillett. The trade unionist's voice carried from the reception desk into the dining room, and the two reporters fell silent.

"I'm here to protect the interests of the ladies," Tillett said loudly.

Harry was not certain who was being addressed, but whoever he was addressing was getting an earful. "I won't have it," Tillett declared. "They may be women, but they are still members of the union, and no one, absolutely no one, will speak to them without a union representative present."

Harry thought he detected a faint voice answering Tillett's bellicose announcement. The reply, whatever it was, drove Tillett to new heights of defensiveness.

"It's all very well for the White Star Line and the Board of Trade to come in here and try to make scapegoats of my union members, but they cry foul when we want to bring in our own lawyers. Well, it's not good enough. I will instruct the ladies to remain silent unless I am in the room. Show me where they are, and be quick about it. I have a lot to do today. Problems everywhere."

Harry hastily abandoned his breakfast. He had been awake since dawn, waiting for the two sisters to appear so that he could escort them away from the Duke of Cornwall Hotel and deliver them to their uncle. He had expected the stewardesses to arrive en masse in the breakfast room, but it seemed they had been taken elsewhere in the hotel.

He dropped his linen napkin onto the table, swallowed a last mouthful of tea, and hurried out to the lobby. He was in time to see Ben Tillett being escorted to the double doors of the ballroom.

Tillett turned to dismiss the desk clerk and caught sight of Harry. His face lit up with delight. "Captain Hazelton, good morning. Are you still waiting for your two runaway girls?"

Harry racked is brain, trying to recall everything he had said to Tillett. He had told him he was looking for two crew members, but he had never said they were girls, and he had never said they were runaways.

"How did you …?"

Tillett dismissed the hovering desk clerk with a flick of his wrist. "We'll take care of ourselves," he said. "No need to wait." The clerk shuffled away, and Tillett grinned at Harry. "It was very obvious what you were doing," he said. "I assume that you were far more secretive when you were employed in the king's service."

"What I did on behalf of the king is none of your business," Harry said through clenched teeth.

"No, of course not," Tillett said. "I am simply observing that it was not difficult to find out what you were doing. I saw you escorting the two young ladies from the tender to the shore, and I observed the way they walked and the way they looked at other people, and I knew at once that they were the daughters of an aristocratic family. I've seen it before. I've seen young gentlemen who thought it would be fun to get out from under the parental gaze and run away to sea. One voyage as a stoker puts an end to that idea, and they're sending home for money for a first-class ticket back. I must admit I've never seen girls try it." He shrugged his shoulders. "They got more than they bargained for, didn't they? I'm sure they are ready to go home."

Harry shook his head. "I'm escorting them to their uncle in Fordingbridge." He looked at the closed doors of the ballroom. "I thought they were not to speak until you were present."

Tillett glowered. "The unions will have a day of reckoning," he said, "but at this moment, our hands are tied. The White Star is withholding pay, and there's not a person on the crew who doesn't need money." He paused. "Except maybe your young ladies," he added.

Harry thought about the moldering splendor of Riddlesdown Court. "They need the money," he said.

"And so they, too, are telling their stories," Tillett said. "Well, let's go and see what they're saying."

When they entered the ballroom, Harry's eyes immediately searched for his two charges. Lady Penelope—or Poppy, as she seemed to be called—sat quietly in one of the gilded chairs set against the wall. Daisy was holding center stage with a dramatic recitation of her experiences. A young law clerk scribbled as fast as he could, but he had little hope of keeping up with Daisy's flow of words.

"It was all wrong," Daisy said. "We were on the boat deck, where Mr. Lightoller said we should be, but then the captain came and—"

"You saw the captain himself?" the clerk asked.

Daisy was impatient. "Of course I did. Why wouldn't I? So he, the captain, said that we shouldn't launch from the boat deck; we should launch from the promenade deck. I mean, the boat was right there, and we couldn't get into it. Something about there being so many people the rope might break or something like that, so anyway—"

"And this was boat number four?" the clerk asked.

"Yes. I already told you that. So we all went down the stairs as fast as we could, which was not very fast, because Mrs. Astor was leaning on her husband, and he was saying that she was in a delicate condition—I'm sure you know what that means."

The clerk nodded and continued to write.

"So," said Daisy, "there was Mrs. Astor and her maid and her nurse, and there was a boy who had an Airedale terrier with him, and there was a big fuss when he was told he had to leave it behind." Daisy paused, and her voice was suddenly soft. "That was actually quite sad," she said.

The clerk continued to write.

"So," Daisy continued, "we got down to the promenade deck,

and we had to wait a long time because the place where the captain had sent us was closed in with windows. You'd think he'd know that, wouldn't you? You'd think he would know we would have to climb out the windows, and I don't think they'd ever been opened before, and it was a big struggle. Then the boat was lowered, and that wasn't easy, because it was too far out, and they used a bridge of deck chairs that we had to crawl across, and the boy was still crying about his dog, and Mrs. Astor was still crying for her husband, and he was being very polite and gentlemanly, but he really wanted to go with her."

Daisy paused for breath, but the clerk continued to write. Harry thought that he was writing maybe one word in every five that spilled out of Daisy's mouth.

"So when we got down to the water," Daisy said, "our crew started to row along the side of the ship to see if anyone else wanted to get on board from down on the lower deck. No one came on board that way, but one man swam over to us, and we pulled him in."

"How many were in the boat?" the clerk asked.

Daisy shrugged. "I don't know. About forty or so."

Harry noticed that Poppy was leaning forward in her seat and looking at her sister with undisguised confusion on her face. Apparently, something that Daisy was now saying was at odds with something Daisy had previously told her sister. Harry reluctantly squelched his curiosity. He was not here to find out what had happened on the *Titanic*. He was here to take the girls home.

A middle-aged man whose clothing and air of authority marked him as a senior lawyer came to stand behind the law clerk. He looked down at the notes and then up at Daisy.

"You say you had to crawl across a bridge of deck chairs?" he said.

Daisy nodded. "Yes, that's what I said."

"Do you know anything about a sounding spar?"

Daisy shook her head. "I don't know what you're talking about."

" Other witnesses have said that lifeboat number four was delayed while the crew went down several more decks to chop off a sounding spar that would have prevented the boat from reaching the water."

"It was all delay," Daisy said peevishly. "If you weren't there, you wouldn't understand."

The older man folded his hands together and pursed his lips.

"No," he said, "I don't understand. My clerk has taken your deposition, and I will read it in due course. I'm sure we can clear up any discrepancies if we find any."

So far as Harry was concerned, the lawyer's tone indicated that he would, without a doubt, find discrepancies.

"One more thing," the lawyer said.

Daisy's tone was impatient. "What?"

"Some people have reported lights of another ship," the lawyer said. "Did you see any lights?"

Daisy considered the question. "I'm not sure," she said cautiously.

The lawyer shook his head. "Either you did or you didn't."

"I heard about lights," Daisy said, "but I don't see how there could have been another ship, because it would have launched lifeboats, wouldn't it? If there had been another ship, we wouldn't have been left all alone."

The law clerk scribbled for a moment and then looked up at the lawyer and then at Daisy. "Anything else?"

"I was sorry about the dog," Daisy said wistfully. "The boy had to let go of the lead, and the dog just stood there looking at him. He didn't understand." She rose abruptly. "I don't want to talk about this any longer."

Tillett took a step forward and laid a hand on her shoulder. "You don't have to say another word. I think we've all heard enough."

Harry studied Daisy for a moment. The clerk had captured most of her words on paper, but he doubted that he had captured the truth. He suspected that it was only when she had spoken of the dog that Daisy had truly said what she had felt and what she had seen.

CHAPTER TEN

Southampton
Harry Hazelton

Harry was allowed aboard the special train that carried the surviving members of the *Titanic* from Plymouth to Southampton. Sitting with the Melville girls on the train should have given him his first chance for real conversation with them, but he soon realized that they had no wish to talk. The other survivors crowded into the carriage were equally reluctant to speak, even to each other. Their silence had a quality he had experienced in all ranks after a hard-fought battle. Eight days on board the *Lapland* had not been long enough to recover from their ordeal.

Poppy's silence had a quality of quiet serenity, as though she had said all that needed to be said. Daisy, on the other hand, gave the impression that she had plenty to say, and it was only her sister's disapproving glances that kept her quiet.

Harry had expected a raucous welcome when the train reached Southampton, but the crowd on the platform was as silent as the survivors on the train. It took him a moment to realize that no reporters were present. Someone had finally done the right thing, he thought, and kept the reporters outside. This was the place where the final act of the *Titanic* tragedy would be played out and where many of the waiting families would be relieved of their last faint hopes.

The public already knew who had been lost. The lists had been printed in newspapers all around the world, but it was only human for the families to hold on to the hope that mistakes had been made and a name or two had been added in error. One last confirmation was required. The surviving crew would have to look the widows and orphans in the eyes and confirm what everyone already knew—there were no other survivors. The list held by White Star was a final list. There would be no miracles.

Harry had wanted his two charges to go immediately to Fordingbridge, where he could deliver them to their uncle, but Poppy had been insistent.

"I'm going with the rest of the crew to collect my pay."

He observed Daisy's reaction as Poppy spoke. Daisy was full of nervous impatience and not at all interested in collecting her pay. He wondered why. He thought he had judged the situation correctly and that Daisy had not stolen the old lady's jewels, but it was difficult to understand why the girl didn't want to be paid. Perhaps she had given up her plan to run off to America.

"We don't need the money," Daisy said.

Poppy's position was immovable. "I earned that money, and I am going to have it."

With no conversation to distract him, Harry studied Poppy as the train rattled along the track from Plymouth to Southampton. On first sight, he had thought her rather plain. Certainly, she did not have the fiery allure of her sister. However, he was beginning to see new depths in her. Despite her willowy height, or maybe because of it, her movements were graceful, and her face had a serene charm. Her appearance stirred images he could not afford to examine. Nothing could be gained by remembering the slight figure in a white muslin dress who had taken tiffin with him and confessed her loneliness and fear.

When the train halted at the station with a loud hiss and an accompanying belch of steam, Harry observed the crew's reaction. The stewards and deckhands remained impassive, but several of the stokers visibly flinched. Even Sullivan, the big blond Australian, grimaced. He could only guess at the hell they had experienced in the *Titanic's* engine room and the memories stirred by the sound of venting steam.

In order to avoid staring at Poppy and renewing old memories, Harry had spent some time studying Sullivan. He realized that the Australian did not fit the mold that had produced the other firemen. The firemen were mostly small, wiry men whose build allowed them to fit easily into the cramped engineering spaces of the *Titanic,* but Sullivan was tall and broad shouldered. The other men had scarred hands, and their faces were pitted with burns inflicted by sparks from burning coal. Sullivan's hands were bandaged, but his face was free from scars apart from the one long slash across his cheek. That slash was not caused by anything that could have happened on the *Titanic*. To Harry's experienced eye, it was a sword slash inflicted some time ago. If he had been working the case of the *Titanic*, which he was not, he would have pegged Sullivan as a person of interest.

Harry was only momentarily surprised to see Ben Tillett at the very front of the crowd of waiting relatives. Of course, Tillett had a motorcar, and so he was bound to arrive before the train. He watched as Tillett made a hopeless attempt to control the crew members as they flung open the carriage doors, but the authority of his union was helpless against the raw emotions of the families.

Daisy made to rise, but Poppy held her back. "We'll wait," she said firmly. "Let them have their time. We haven't lost anyone, but some of them have lost everything."

Even Daisy was patient as they watched the scene unfold. Harry saw reunions, men kissing their wives, children hugging their fathers, but along with joy came inevitable sorrow. No mistakes had been made. The record of names was correct.

"Your father died when the funnel fell."

"I lost sight of your brother."

"I saw your son go into the water."

Harry looked up as Sullivan dropped suddenly into the seat beside Daisy. To Harry's mind, he was sitting far too close to the daughter of the Earl of Riddlesdown. On the other hand, Sullivan would not know Daisy's position in society. He was simply taking the opportunity to sit next to a pretty young stewardess.

The big Australian smiled at Daisy, and she responded with an uncharacteristic look of fear. Harry wondered if he should intervene. This was hardly the right time to start a brawl, and Sullivan looked like someone who would not stand back if there were any fighting to be done.

He schooled himself to be patient. In a few minutes, they would leave the train, and whatever was causing the problem between Sullivan and Daisy would be of no consequence. They would not have to see each other ever again.

Poppy was looking at Sullivan with surprising sympathy. Harry couldn't help thinking that Sullivan would have been wiser to sit next to her and leave Daisy alone.

"How are the burns, Mr. Sullivan?" Poppy asked.

Sullivan wriggled his fingers experimentally. "Much better. You

and Miss Jessop did good work. Perhaps you should be a nurse."
Poppy shook her head. "I'm afraid that would not be possible."

Sullivan shrugged. "Anything's possible if you want it badly enough and if you're prepared to pay the price." He looked at Daisy. "Your sister knows all about that."

Harry tensed. Something was happening here. The tension in the air could almost be cut with a knife. He knew he would come off poorly if he challenged Sullivan, but he could not let this continue. These girls were daughters of the aristocracy, and this man was ... well, he didn't know what this man was.

He cursed the pain in his knee as he considered how to expel the fireman from the carriage. If it came to a physical fight, the stiff knee would slow him down. He assessed the scar on Sullivan's cheek and wondered who had won that bout. He looked at Daisy, and she flashed a dimpled smile. He thought the smile contained a challenge. The little ... He settled on the word *minx*. The little minx would love to see two men fighting over her.

The carriage door opened abruptly, and Ben Tillett pulled himself up the step. He closed the door behind him and took a seat next to Poppy.

"Heartbreaking," he said.

Harry nodded. "I assume there were no surprises. No unexpected last-minute revelations."

Tillett shook his head. "No. The list of those who were lost is accurate. Apart from the men left behind in the States, the surviving crew members are all here, one hundred and sixty-five men and women."

"I'm so sorry," Poppy whispered. "It would have been lovely if even one woman had discovered that her husband was still alive."
Tillett nodded. "The flags in Southampton will remain at half-mast until the White Star Line has done its penance."

"You blame the company and not God?" Poppy asked.

Tillett shrugged. "I don't know who is to blame, but I'll tell you one thing."

"What's that?" Sullivan asked laconically.

"We're not going to allow the Americans to make the final decision," Tillett said. "I never have been and never will be on the side of management, but I agree with them on one thing—the Americans don't know what they're doing. They're asking the wrong questions, and they're stirring up a hornet's nest on both sides of the Atlantic. I wouldn't want to see the White Star go under and have all these fine fellows lose their employment just so one American senator can make a name for himself."

"Could that happen?" Harry asked.

Tillett shrugged. "Times are hard, and competition is fierce, and now we have a coal strike. If it's not ended soon, our ships won't be able to find enough coal to keep up the schedule, and the Germans will move in and take over the Atlantic routes."

Although he had no wish to provoke an argument, Harry knew he had to make his point. "Mr. Tillett, you're the trade union leader. Don't you support the coal strike?"

"I support organized unions," Tillett said, "not wildcat, unauthorized strikes. Our unions must learn to work together instead of against each other. The coal strike is disastrous for the shipping industry."

Poppy, who had been looking out of the window, interrupted abruptly. "Mr. Sullivan, shouldn't you be getting off the train already to collect your pay? Isn't this where we are supposed to be paid?"

"She's right," said Tillett. "In order to avoid confusion, they've sent the paymaster to the station to keep you clear of the crowds at the office. You'll receive your pay from the paymaster here, just so long as you gave them your deposition."

"I don't see why that has to be a condition of paying us," Poppy said angrily. "We worked for our money. In fact, we nearly died for it."

Harry could see that Poppy's gibe had hit home, as the trade union leader took a step backward.

"We shouldn't be held to ransom for our depositions," Poppy said fiercely. "The White Star Line is taking advantage of the fact that the crewmen need that money for their families. Why isn't your trade union stepping in to do something about this?"

Harry saw the way Poppy's chin lifted as she met Tillett's gaze, and he was unexpectedly pleased to find fire behind her cool exterior.

"It's not right," Poppy said. "They know that beggars can't be choosers, and so they offer them no choice."

"There's a choice," Tillett said, "if they dare to make it. The trade union has no power unless the members are willing to sacrifice."

"About seven hundred of them made the ultimate sacrifice," Poppy said.

Tillett shook his head. "I'm sorry. I didn't mean it quite like that. I mean that the workers have to be willing to risk losing their pay if they take a stand against their employers, and not all of them are willing to do that. For example, I assume you want to be paid, and so I assume that you gave your deposition."

When Poppy failed to reply, Sullivan leaned back in his seat, smiling lazily. "Maybe she doesn't choose to answer you," he said, "but I'll give you my answer. No, I didn't give a deposition."

Daisy, who had also been looking out of the window and had been showing no interest in the conversation, turned to look at Sullivan. "So what will you do now?" she asked. "You won't have any money, and White Star won't want to employ you again."

Sullivan winked at her. "I'll think of something. I have to find a ship. I don't know any other way to get to America, unless you can think of something."

When Daisy glowered at him, he turned his attention to Tillett. "If the coal miners are on strike, I doubt there'll be much traffic leaving Southampton. I may have to go over to France to find a ship."

"It's not just the coal strike," Tillett said. He looked at Poppy. "You may think that the unions don't do enough, but we have made a start, and we intend to continue. In fact, we already have the White Star Line on the ropes."

Poppy was obviously puzzled by the boxing metaphor, but Harry understood perfectly. "The men aren't even home yet," he said, "and they've had no chance to take action. Has something else happened?"

Tillett could not keep the pride out of his voice. "Oh, yes, I would definitely say that something has happened. The *Titanic*'s sister ship, the *Olympic*, has been trying to sail for the past five days, and she hasn't got past Portsmouth yet."

"Because of the coal strike?" Poppy asked.

"No, no. She had enough coal. The shipping companies have been scrounging coal wherever they can. I hear that some of the ships coming from America have been carrying sacks of coal in the hold. No, it's not the coal; it's the lifeboats. The men won't sail again with just a handful of lifeboats."

Poppy shuddered, and Harry fought a sudden urge to put his arm around her shoulders. Despite the heated air of the train carriage, Poppy suddenly looked half-frozen. He restrained himself immediately. Lady Penelope Melville was not the kind of girl who would welcome a man's arm, even if it were only offered in sympathy.

"The crew of the *Olympic* heard what happened on the *Titanic*, and they're refusing to sail under the same conditions," Tillett said. "She should have sailed three days ago, but they came out on strike— not an authorized strike, but nonetheless a strike."

"Just talking about the number of lifeboats is not enough," Poppy said. "People may have read the newspapers, but they don't know everything. They don't know how badly people behaved and how everything was chaos. It wasn't just a matter of not having enough lifeboats. Some of the boats were only half-full. It's a wonder that anyone was saved. It's only by the grace of God that the *Carpathia* arrived before we were all lost."

Harry thought of the two reporters he'd overheard at breakfast. According to them, God had not been involved.

Daisy fluttered her lashes at Tillett, who seemed unmoved by her charms. "Did they get the lifeboats they wanted?" she asked. She looked at Harry and then at Poppy. "It was awful," she said in what sounded like an afterthought.

Tillett gave her a wry grin, and Harry thought that the union man had now taken the measure of Miss Daisy.

"Well," Tillett said, "White Star rounded up forty collapsible military lifeboats. The only trouble is that although they'd been passed by the Board of Trade, the men insisted on inspecting them for themselves. When they found that half of them were rotten, they went on strike. They all collected their kit and left the ship. They are now picketing in the dockyard, raising hell and obstructing traffic. The Board of Trade is threatening to charge them with mutiny."

"How can that be?" Harry asked. "It's the White Star Line, not the Royal Navy."

"Merchant navy is subject to the same rules," Tillett said. "A ship is not a democracy."

"But now that they know the lifeboats are rotten," Poppy said tentatively, "will the White Star try to find more lifeboats? Don't they care at all about the safety of the men?"

Tillett shrugged. "Apparently not."

"But they care about the passengers," Harry said. "They'll want the passengers to be safe."

Even as he spoke, he remembered the numerous times he'd embarked either on a troop ship or a regular passenger liner. Had he ever counted the lifeboats or worried about lifeboat drill? He had a sense that this new, highly visible loss of the *Titanic* was going to change everything.

"The North Atlantic is crawling with ships," Tillett said. "America is the new promised land. The shipping companies are gambling on the odds that what happened to the *Titanic* won't happen again."

"Are you sure we know what happened to the *Titanic?*" Harry asked.

Tillett responded to the question with a very small shake of his head and a look that seemed to say, "Not here. Not now."

Tillett continued as though Harry had not spoken. "White Star brought a hundred strikebreakers up from Portsmouth. The passengers went on board, and the *Olympic* steamed out of Southampton. Unfortunately, she only got as far as Spithead before she stopped yet again. Seems the passengers got wind of the problem with the lifeboats, and they are insisting that they see for themselves whether or not the boats will float. They are demanding they be tested again. Meantime, the deck crew has downed their tools and refused to sail with a crew of strikebreakers."

Tillett gave a satisfied smile. "Management should stop underestimating the power of the unions. We're growing daily. I'm very proud of our lads. It's about time they stood up for their rights even if it does mean cancelling the voyage. I'm afraid that's bad news for you, Mr. Sullivan. I'm not sure how you got a berth the first time, but—"

"I suppose you could call it luck," Sullivan said. His lips twisted, and the scar across his cheek tugged his face into an enigmatic smile. "Twelve of us were taken on at the last minute to deal with a problem."

Harry was suddenly alert. "What kind of problem?"

Sullivan shook his head and held out his bandaged hands. "They called us a black gang. Ask any sailor, and they'll tell you what it means."

"I'm asking you."

Sullivan's look was sharp and challenging. "I don't know who you are. I know you came to meet these two young ladies, but I don't know why. If you're a company man, you will know what the black gang was about, but I'll tell you nothing, because I'm not looking for trouble. Whatever I know, I'll keep to myself for the time being."

Harry was tempted to respond to Sullivan's challenge, but engaging the Australian would mean revealing more than he wished to reveal. It was unlikely that the fireman would ever meet Daisy or Poppy again. He did not need to know that they were the daughters of the Earl of Riddlesdown.

Sullivan was on his feet now. He reached into his pocket and pulled out a slip of paper, which he handed to Poppy. "If you should need me, I can be reached through this address."

"Why would we ever need you?" Daisy said irritably. "Good riddance, that's what I say."

Sullivan nodded. "Of course you do." He turned to Harry. "Keep an eye on that one. She's trouble."

He sketched a salute, opened the carriage door, and stepped down onto the platform.

Poppy unfolded the paper, looked at it in obvious surprise, and then slipped it into her pocket.

"So what is it?" Daisy asked. "Is it the number of his jail cell?"

Poppy shook her head. "It's the address of his bank."

Southampton
Ernie Sullivan

Sullivan walked the harbor wall, studying the ships that lay alongside the docks. Only one of them appeared to be making ready to depart. According to Tillett, lack of coal had sidelined the luxury liners. He could see only one small, somewhat shabby liner taking on cargo. Of course, if all else failed, he could take the ferry over to France and try from there. The French were not embroiled in a coal strike. He shook his head. That would take too much time. The trail was already going cold, and he had no time to waste.

He took a note of the steamer's name, the *Philadelphia*. She wasn't much of a ship when set against the magnificence of the *Olympic* or the lost *Titanic*, but apparently, she had coal, and she planned to depart.

He turned away from the harbor view and set off toward the offices that lined the streets adjacent to the harbor, where he could read an updated bulletin. Although, under normal circumstances most passengers would plan in advance and buy their tickets in London, Sullivan was well aware that chaos had overtaken the port. The coal strike and the mutiny of the *Olympic*'s crew had played havoc with the schedule. Anyone with an urgent need to reach the United States would have to take whatever accommodation they could find, and he had an urgent need.

He imagined his grandfather, now confined to a wheelchair, sitting on the wide veranda of the old house and looking out over the sun-parched acres of Goolagong Sheep Station. He knew that the old man would expect that the long-awaited confrontation had happened by now. Newspapers very rarely traveled as far as Goolagong, and even if his grandfather had learned of the *Titanic* disaster, he would not know that his grandson had been involved. He could not know that Sullivan had been forced to chase the woman all the way to New York and that he had still failed in his quest for justice.

He had been little more than eight years old and mourning the loss of his father when his grandfather had told him that the family quest now lay on his young shoulders.

1882
Goolagong Sheep Station
New South Wales, Australia

The old man pushed back his sleeves and held out his wrists.

"Do you see this, Ernie? Do you know how these scars were made? Take a good look."

Ernie obediently focused on the deep scars encircling his grandfather's wrists.

"Do you know what these are?" the old man asked.

"No, sir."

"These are the marks of the manacles I wore when I was transported. Five months at sea. Fifteen men died on the voyage. Fifteen good men, who'd done nothing but try to feed their families, died at sea, with their bodies thrown overboard for the sharks."

Ernie tried to look away, but his grandfather was not finished. He scrabbled at his shirt. "I can show you the marks of the lash. This is what they do to people like us. Convicts."

"But I'm not a convict," Ernie said.

A dark cloud settled over his grandfather's weathered face. "I'm a convict, and that makes all of you convicts," he said. He waved his hand to indicate the vast acreage of the sheep station. "None of this matters. We're still convict stock. Why do you think we never go into the city? I don't know if I'll ever be able to send you to boarding school. Do you know why?"

Ernie shook his head. He had no concept of a city and no thought that he would ever be sent away to boarding school. "I don't know."

"Because I'm a convict."

"What did you do?"

His grandfather spluttered furiously. "Nothing. I did nothing. It was a lie. Even the magistrate knew it was a lie. He knew she had made it up to save her reputation. If he'd really believed her, it would have been the rope, not transportation. Her family had the money to buy the guilty verdict but not enough to buy a hanging."

Sullivan studied the posters on the walls of the shipping offices, realizing that they all told the same story of cancellations and postponements. The coal strike was rapidly bringing a halt to all transatlantic shipping. Eventually he found a poster advertising the SS *Philadelphia*, the ship he had seen taking on cargo. She was a ship of the American Line, and she would sail for New York at noon on May 1.

He would have to wait three days for her to sail, but taking the ferry to France and searching for another ship would be just as time-consuming. He was here now, and the only sensible thing to do was to wait for the SS *Philadelphia*.

He was glad that his grandfather had no way of knowing that the mission was not yet accomplished. Sometimes he imagined that Richard Sullivan was with him in spirit, watching him with faded, bloodshot eyes and holding out his hands to show the scars of the manacles.

He looked across the harbor, seeing sheep grazing on the green hills. English sheep were fat and lazy and bore no resemblance to the thousands of sheep that grazed on Goolagong's parched acres. Nothing here was familiar. He felt cramped by the encircling hills and the lack of horizon. He didn't belong here. Everything was wrong; he was wrong. He was too big for this tiny, colorful jewel of a country. He wanted very much to go home, but that wasn't possible.

Why not? You almost died. Isn't that enough? When will you be free of him?

He hesitated. He heard his grandfather's voice, still carrying the soft Devon accent of his childhood.

"It will never be over. We served hard time, and they said we would be free, but we're not free. We'll always be convicts. It's up to you to put it right. Find that woman and clear my name. Clear the family's name. The Sullivans are not convicts. Make her admit it was a lie. I am not a rapist, and I did not father her child."

"You signing on?"

Sullivan turned to see a stooped old man in a grimy tweed coat who studied him with faded eyes set in weather-beaten features.

"No. I think this time I'll buy a ticket."

"Better be quick about it," the old man remarked. "She's going to take the second- and third-class passengers from the *Olympic*, because the *Olympic* ain't going to sail. The *Philadelphia* will be sold out as soon as White Star gets their numbers straight." He eyed Sullivan's burned hands and ill-fitting clothes. "You don't look like a man who would buy a ticket. You look like a crewman to me." He studied Sullivan's face. "You didn't get that scar down in the boiler room, but those burned hands tell a different story."

"*Titanic*," Sullivan said, and he was surprised to find a note of pride in his voice.

The old man sniffed. "Smith," he said. "Captain blooming Smith. How could he hit an iceberg? I've been sailing sixty years, man and boy, sail and steam, and never came close to hitting an iceberg."

"Well, he did," Sullivan said as he turned away in search of the American Line's office. He recalled coming this way on April 10, when he'd searched out the White Star office and signed onto the crew. He had been in a hurry that time as well, determined not to lose track of the woman who had ruined his family. She knew he was on her trail, but she'd had no idea that he had followed her onto the *Titanic*.

She knows now, he thought. He remembered the expression on her face as he had heaved her into the lifeboat. She would be hoping that he had gone down with the ship. She had no idea that a thirst for vengeance stretching across three generations was enough to keep Sullivan alive in the icy sea and give him the strength to climb on top of a splintered staircase. He was coming for her. It was only a matter of time.

His mind was jerked away from thoughts of his grandfather's vengeance as he slowly became aware of raised voices. He rounded a corner and found himself drawn into a loud, chanting crowd. For a moment, he assumed that he was among the surviving *Titanic* crew. They'd received their pay and their bonus when they had left the train, so now were they willing to protest what had happened to them? He felt sorry for them, sorry for any man who had to compromise his principles for the sake of money. He felt glad and even a little self-righteous that he had not fallen into line and given the lawyers the deposition they wanted. He didn't need whatever money the White Star had been willing to dispense. He could go to the bank. He had kept his letters of credit on him at all times. Even in the panic of the sinking ship and the rapidly rising water, the letters had been safely strapped to his body in their waterproof pouch— slightly scorched, but not as scorched as his hands and his hair.

Hands reached out to him as he tried to turn away. "Come on, mate. Let's hear you. More lifeboats! No strikebreakers! You're with us, ain't you?"

Oh, yes, I'm with you, but not now.

He tried to back away, realizing that he had become entangled in the mutinous crew of the *Olympic*. On any other day, he would have joined in their protest. They had every reason to strike. No one should have to endure what he had endured. No one should die as the men in the *Titanic*'s boiler rooms had died.

He fought against the pull of the crowd, wincing in pain as he pushed and shoved with his burned hands. He felt a groundswell of movement. The crowd was changing direction. Something was happening. He heard raucous cries of protest and the shrilling of police whistles.

No, this couldn't be allowed to happen. He was not going to be swept up and jailed along with the roistering crew of the *Olympic*. He had to sail on the *Philadelphia*.

A hand closed over his wrist and pulled. "This way. Hurry up."

Sullivan looked down at the slightly built man who had a death grip on his wrist. He saw a flourishing brown mustache, soulful brown eyes above a sharp nose, and an aggressively determined chin. Ben Tillett.

"Leave me alone."

"I can get you out of here," Tillett said.

"Don't worry, mate. I can get myself out."

"You won't get aboard the *Philadelphia*."

Sullivan stood still and allowed the crowd to wash around him like waves around a rock. "What do you know about it?"

"I know they're watching for you."

"Who?"

"White Star."

Sullivan resisted Tillett's renewed tugging. "Leave me alone. I'm not one of your union men. I don't need protecting. I'm taking the next ship to America."

"The *Philadelphia* is the only ship leaving for America, and White Star has guards posted. You won't get aboard."

"Of course I will. I intend to buy a first-class ticket."

Tillett released his arm. "Try it and see. Go on over to the ticket office, and see what happens."

The police whistles were closing in, their piercing blasts competing with the belligerent responses of the mutineers. As Sullivan fought to free himself from the melee on the dock, he was annoyed to find that Tillett was still at his side. When he was finally clear of the struggle, he headed for the office of the American Line. Tillett was forced to trot to keep up with his fierce, long-legged stride, but he stayed with him and did not stop until the American Line office came into sight and Sullivan halted abruptly.

"I warned you," Tillett said.

Sullivan studied the two big men who lounged against the doorway of the ticket office. He assessed the situation. He could take them both on, and even with burned hands, he stood a good chance of beating them, but what then? The booking agent would not sell a ticket to a passenger who left two unconscious men on the doorstep as he entered. He beat a hasty retreat. The two men had not seen him, but without Tillett's warning, he would have run right into them.

He looked at Tillett. "What do they want with me?"

Tillett shrugged. "Two possibilities: either they want you to talk, or they don't want you to talk."

"Is that the best you can come up with?" Sullivan growled.

"At the moment, yes. Give me a few hours, and I hope I can do better."

"I don't have a few hours."

"Yes, you do," Tillett said. "The *Philadelphia* is going to sail without you, and I know that there's not another ship leaving Southampton this week. You need to come with me."

"Why?"

Tillett looked up at him, and his eyes were no longer soulful. "I'll tell you why," he said. "Because the White Star's newest and safest ship sank and the company is facing bankruptcy. Because men of vast wealth and influence died, and their death has thrown the stock market into chaos. Because fifteen hundred lives were lost, and someone has to be blamed."

He paused, and Sullivan felt the force of his piercing gaze and the certainty of his words. "And because, Mr. Sullivan, they think you know why it happened."

The Grapes
Southampton
Alvin Towson

Yesterday the *Lapland* had entered Southampton Water on the afternoon tide, and Towson had hurried ashore to find a room for the night at The Grapes, an old public house set close to the docks. He ordered a plate of sandwiches at the bar, and when they were delivered by a friendly barmaid, he began to ask questions. The barmaid was eager to supply information. She began by informing him that he would be a fool to go near the docks tonight, because the strikers were raising a ruckus—this was said with a nod of approval. The barmaid was in favor of the seamen's strike.

"There's not a house on the waterfront that's not lost someone—family, friend, or neighbor—on the *Titanic*. It's criminal. That's what it is."

Towson bit into his ham sandwich. "Do you know what's happened to the *Titanic*'s surviving crew?"

The barmaid knew, and she had an opinion on the subject.

"Taken off the ship in Plymouth like they were criminals. They didn't commit no crime. The crime was White Star taking that ship to sea. Not that anyone will say it. We all know what side our bread is buttered, don't we?"

Towson nodded sagely and ventured another question. "When will they come back to Southampton?"

"Not until tomorrow," the barmaid said angrily. "It's not right to keep the families waiting. All they want is one final word. They want to know how their menfolk died. Is it too much to ask? Nothing will bring them back, but the families should be told."

Several additional questions provided Towson with the information that the scheduled train from Plymouth would arrive at three thirty tomorrow.

"And let's hope the paymaster is ready for them. There's families here hurting for money."

Towson spent the night in the room above the bar. For a brief period of time, he lay awake, listening to the shouting of the strikers on the dock. He had to agree with the barmaid that they had plenty of good reasons for their strike, but they were none of his concern. His only concern was the stewardess who had stolen from him, and now she would soon be within reach. He settled himself to sleep.

In the small hours of the morning, he struggled awake from a dream of big men in dark coats, but it was only a dream. He lay back in the bed. The threat would soon be a thing of the past, and his life could return to normal.

He slept late and ate a hearty breakfast before strolling along to the train station to meet the three-thirty train from Plymouth. He was overcome with a sinking feeling as he approached the station. He was half an hour early, but the station was deserted. If the *Titanic*'s crew was about to arrive in Southampton, surely there should be newspaper reporters waiting. They were not here. Where were they? Where were the families, the pathetic children and the weeping widows? Where was the curly-headed stewardess with his stolen treasure?

The train unleashed a great hiss of steam and settled down onto the tracks like a dragon settling down for a long nap. The railway guard folded his flags and tucked them under his arm as he walked the length of the train, slamming doors on empty carriages.

"You," Towson said. "You there."

"Sir?"

"This is the three thirty from Plymouth?"

"Oh, yes, sir, she is. Was you expecting someone?" The guard's voice rolled lazily over the syllables, his accent unfamiliar to Towson. "There won't be another train until tomorrow."

"What about the *Titanic* crew?" Towson asked. "I was told they'd be coming in from Plymouth today."

"Aye, sir, that they did."

"No, they didn't. I watched everyone who stepped down, and there was no one from the *Titanic*."

The softness was gone from the guard's syllables. "And you'd know that, would you?"

"Of course I would."

"Was you expecting to talk to someone?"

"Yes, I was."

"American, are you?"

"Yes, I am—not that it's any of your damned business."

The guard nodded. "No, sir. As you say, none of my damned business. Reporter, are you?"

"No, I am not."

The guard looked him up and down, raised his bushy gray eyebrows a fraction of an inch, and shrugged. "She's been and gone."

For one wild moment, Towson thought that the guard was referring to his quarry, the stewardess. He clenched his teeth and bit back the words, reminding himself that the guard had already applied female pronouns to the train. Apparently, in England both ships and trains were women.

"Are you saying that the train with the *Titanic* crew has already arrived?"

"Been and gone," the guard repeated. "Special train, on account of us folks in Southampton wanted to give the families a bit of privacy, keep them away from prying eyes."

"I'm not prying," Towson growled. "I was expecting to meet someone. I wanted to speak to one of the women, a stewardess."

The guard nodded. "Took a fancy to her, did you?"

"None of your damned business."

"No, sir, none of my damned business. Why don't you move along? There's nothing to see here."

"I should report you for impertinence."

The guard nodded slowly. "Well, sir, the way I see it, if you was

201

really a friend or relative of this stewardess, she would have told you that White Star laid on a special train for them this morning. They're all gone—collected their pay and gone home."

For a brief moment, Towson was unable to think. Not for the first time, he wondered if this increasing mental fog was a result of the night spent balancing on the hull of an upturned lifeboat with freezing water washing around his knees. Two weeks had passed since he'd been taken on board the *Carpathia* with frostbitten toes and fingers and only his anger to keep him warm, and he was still feeling the effects.

He studied the guard. Would it be foolish to ask him if he had noticed a stewardess with bright, curly hair and blue eyes? The guard was a man, and that stewardess was someone every man would notice. The guard glared. Something had upset him. Perhaps it wasn't personal. Perhaps it was just the sight of the grieving widows and orphaned children. Towson was no longer sensitive. He'd had plenty of time on board the *Carpathia* and the *Lapland* to ponder the vagaries of fate and wonder why some people were saved and some were not.

Well, he had no more time to waste. If the girl had reached Southampton, she would probably be working out how to get the best price for her stolen treasures, and she was no doubt too stupid to realize what she had. He needed to find out her name. He needed a list of White Star crew survivors. He would waste no more time here. His next stop must be the White Star office.

CHAPTER ELEVEN

The Dulwich Club
Harry Hazelton

Ignoring the tragedy of the *Titanic* and the ongoing stress of the coal strike, the month of May positively frolicked into London. Harry opened the window of his small room at the Dulwich Club and breathed in the floral-scented breeze. In his years of fighting the Boers on the dry, dusty Highveld and drilling his troops on the burning plains of India, he had longed for mornings like this. His English soul had yearned for the scent of the sea and the ever-underlying promise of gentle rain—not a lashing monsoon but a short shower that fell lightly on roses and daffodils and brought forth scattered daisies on green lawns.

He turned away from the window. *Sentimental claptrap.* He straightened his tie, buttoned his jacket, and went down the stairs to the club's breakfast room. This morning the usual scrambled eggs and bacon had been replaced by a dish of kedgeree. The odor of fish and curry transported him to the officers' mess at Lucknow and the sight of the general's bride walking across the parade ground in the cool early morning. He remembered the way her white muslin dress strained against her increasingly obvious pregnancy. *Now she's pregnant, he'll leave her alone. She'll be safe for a while.*

Harry turned away from the breakfast buffet. The kedgeree had destroyed his appetite. All he wanted now was a cup of coffee, and then he would ... What would he do? His first investigative case had gone well. He had returned the two runaway girls to their uncle and received his payment. Where would he find his next case? He should probably place an advertisement in *The Times*.

He was deep in thought, mentally wording his advertisement, when the aging waiter appeared at his elbow. He seemed more tired and more doddery than usual. Harry wondered why the man had not been pensioned off.

"Captain Hazelton, are you going to eat breakfast? Was the kedgeree not to your liking?"

Harry looked back at the offending dish on the sideboard and shook his head.

The waiter stooped to refill Harry's coffee cup. "The chef thought you would enjoy an Indian dish."

"Thank him for the thought," Harry said, "but I'm not hungry."

"In that case," said the waiter, "I am to inform you that you have a visitor waiting for you in the lounge. Should I bring him in here?"

Harry felt a spark of optimism. The day had been a yawning chasm of boredom, and now it held the possibility of change. He had slept late, and the breakfast room was deserted. The waiter would not have suggested bringing the visitor into the room unless he was obviously a gentleman. Perhaps a client had once again fallen into his lap.

"Bring him in," Harry said. "See if he would like coffee."

Moments later Harry rose to greet his guest. He knew immediately that the man who strode purposefully into the room had been a soldier. He did not even need the regimental tie to tell him that his visitor was a product of the Grenadier Guards. His training and status revealed itself in the set of his shoulders, the straightness of his back, and the lofty way he assessed the Dulwich Club's somewhat shabby premises.

The waiter stood straighter than usual and announced the visitor with a flourish. "Captain the Honorable Clive Bigham."

Having made his announcement, the waiter scuttled away to fetch the coffee pot from the sideboard.

Harry eyed his visitor. They were of similar height, and Bigham was as light as Harry was dark, with close-cropped sandy hair and flourishing mustache. When they exchanged a handshake, Harry felt that he was in a competition, with Bigham's grip threatening to crush his fingers. Determined that he would not be dominated, not even by an officer in the Guards, Harry gave as good as he got.

Having completed an initial test of strength, Harry gestured to a seat. "What can I do for you, Captain?"

Bigham sat down and stretched out his legs. With every gesture, he seemed to gain increasing control over the space around him. He oozed confidence.

"I've heard good things about you," Bigham said.

"I do my best," Harry said nonchalantly. *Good things? What kind of good things?*

Bigham waited for the waiter to pour coffee before he spoke again. "We've been in the same business," he said.

"And what business is that?"

Bigham looked around the room and then gestured to the waiter, who hovered near the sideboard. "Be a good fellow and leave us alone," Bigham said. "We don't want to be disturbed."

The waiter gave Harry an inquiring glance. Despite Captain Bigham's authoritative air, the waiter was not about to take orders from a nonmember. Harry allowed himself a small smile. Bigham was no doubt a product of Eton or Harrow, and he was probably a member of one of the prestigious clubs that would delight in having a Grenadier Guard on their rolls. Nonetheless, this was the Dulwich Club, and Harry gave the orders.

"You can leave us," Harry said. "We'll let you know if we need anything."

When the waiter had vanished through the green baize door that led to the kitchens, Harry leaned back, mirroring Bigham's positioning, and stretched out his equally long legs. "What business?" he asked again.

Bigham leaned forward. "We have both shed our uniforms at times to protect His Majesty's imperial interests." He lowered his voice. "People speak well of your performance along the North-West Frontier. I have concentrated on Persia, the Balkans, and the Ottoman Empire. I also heard that you have been in touch with some survivors of the *Titanic*."

Harry nodded but said nothing. He knew better than to confirm Bigham's statements.

Bigham was silent for a moment.

If he's waiting for an answer, he won't get one.

"My father," said Bigham, "is Lord Mersey, who has been appointed Wreck Commissioner for the purpose of finding out what happened to the *Titanic*. We will convene the full panel for the first time tomorrow."

"We?" Harry queried.

"Yes. I have the honor of being secretary to the commission, and I can assure the world that we are fully prepared to get to the truth."

Harry could not find an appropriate response to Bigham's bombastic statement. From what he had seen for himself in Plymouth, he imagined that no one, not even a Guards officer, could be prepared for what the survivors of the *Titanic* would say about the disaster and their treatment. He had also begun to believe that no one would ever be able to find a path through the chaotic memories of the survivors and arrive at the truth of what happened.

"I'd like to show you what we have in place," Bigham said, "and I would … value your opinion."

Harry was mystified. Why was Bigham here, and what did it matter that they shared a background in the murky world of spies and informants? Their paths had never crossed. Bigham had worked on the fringes of Europe, far from Harry's tropical world. Now, out of the blue, Bigham wanted Harry's opinion on a totally unrelated subject.

Bigham sprang to his feet. Every gesture he made was filled with energy and competence. "Walk with me," he urged. "It will be worth your while."

Harry considered the empty hours that yawned ahead of him. He really had nowhere else to be, and he was intrigued. Suspicious but intrigued.

Bigham was still for a moment, waiting for Harry to speak, and then he slapped his own leg. "Sorry, old man. I forgot. I heard about your run-in with a wild boar. Slows you down a bit, I suppose. I have my fair share of scars. I've always found it best to keep moving. It's only a short walk. Won't take long."

Harry swallowed his anger and rose silently to his feet. He had no need to compare wounds and take advice from the obnoxiously dashing captain. Now he was determined to walk all the way across London if necessary, even if he could find no reason for the journey.

As it turned out, the walk along Pall Mall was as short as Bigham had promised. Within a few minutes, and long before the pain in Harry's leg became unbearable, they entered the London Scottish Drill Hall on Buckingham Gate.

The hall was vast.

"This is where we'll hold the inquiry," Bigham said. "The damned place is large enough to parade troops indoors, though I don't know why anyone would want to do that. You'd never catch the Grenadiers parading indoors."

Bigham looked around with pride as he gestured to the long burgundy drapes that covered the brick walls. "Acoustics are terrible, but I think the drapes will solve the problem."

Harry glanced at the drapes. He had no opinion on their ability to improve the acoustics, and no real interest. He still didn't know why Bigham had brought him here.

"I have it configured like a courtroom," Bigham said, "but there'll be no wigs or robes. We'll keep it informal."

Harry eyed the arrangements, from the long judicial bench to seating for hundreds of spectators. Bigham could say that he had no plan to intimidate witnesses, but the arrangement of the room belied his words.

Harry's eye was drawn to a massive model of the *Titanic* that stood on display in front of the bench. It was at twenty feet long.

Bigham approached it with pride. "Built to scale," he said. "Just the starboard side, but it will give the commission a sense of where everything was situated, and of course, we have the blueprints. This will be nothing like the American debacle, with Smith grandstanding for his own political gain. No one will gain from this trial."

Harry waited to see if Bigham would correct himself.

"Not a trial," Bigham said eventually. "No, we don't call it a trial. It is an inquiry. We have limited ourselves to just twenty-six questions. They will suffice to tell us what occurred. The witnesses will be questioned under controlled conditions by the Solicitor General, Sir John Simon, and the Attorney General, Sir Rufus Isaac, on behalf of the Board of Trade. White Star will be represented, of course, and we will permit an additional but limited number of other legal representatives."

Harry was still very mindful of Ben Tillett's determination to do right by his union members. "What about the trade unions?" he asked.

Bigham waved a dismissive hand. "They have someone to speak for them," he said. "He's an Irishman, Thomas Scanlan, MP for North Sligo. Not up to the standard of the others, but quite feisty, so

I'm told."

Harry looked around at the vast, echoing expanse of the Drill Hall and the rows of empty seats. Tomorrow those seats would no doubt all be filled. According to the newspapers, every member of society was on tenterhooks waiting for the formal opening of the British inquiry. On the other side of the Atlantic, Senator Smith was still harassing the *Titanic*'s officers and asking leading questions of the first-class survivors, but in London things would be done differently. He assumed that nothing definitive could really be decided until Smith released the officers he was holding under subpoena, and no one knew when that would be. Nonetheless, it was obvious that the Board of Trade could not wait to start flexing its muscles and asserting its control over the investigation.

Harry could not help himself. The room was overwhelming and intimidating, and the model was impressive, but where were the witnesses? "Who will you question?" he asked. "Most of the officers are dead, and none of them are here."

"But we have the crew," Bigham said.

Harry shook his head. "Smith subpoenaed anyone who would know anything. He has the helmsman and the lookout—"

"One of the lookouts," Bigham amended. He clapped Harry on the shoulder. "Have faith, old man. My father knows what he's doing. I studied for the bar myself, you know, and Pater taught me my most useful lesson. When in court, never ask a question to which you do not already know the answer. That's where you come in."

"I was beginning to wonder," Harry admitted.

"All in good time," Bigham said. "While it is true that the star players are still in Washington, we still have the chorus."

Harry shook his head, unable to follow Bigham's logic.

"The crew," Bigham said. "We have the crew. I agree that they will have no opinion as to whether the *Titanic* was going too fast for conditions, or whether the deck officers were adequately prepared, but they were not mere bystanders. Every single one of the surviving seamen took a place in a lifeboat and had a front-row seat for whatever happened next, and some of them will also know what happened before the collision. None of the engineers survived, but a few of the firemen made it to the surface. They'll be able to tell us what was going on down below."

"I met a few of them," Harry said. "I had the impression they were still stunned."

"Yes, of course they were, and that's why we took their depositions before they could recover their wits or decide what side they want their bread to be buttered. We have it all on paper. Best thing all round."

"Best for whom?" Harry asked. "From what I could see, the crew members were coerced into giving their depositions, with their pay withheld until they had complied."

Bigham waved away Harry's correction. "We didn't want to lose track of them. Some are from Ireland, some from Scotland. We couldn't go chasing all over the British Isles in search of them."

Bigham smiled broadly as he assessed his completed arrangements. "You," he said, "are the final piece in the puzzle. When I heard about your connection to the Earl of Riddlesdown's daughters—"

"I'm not really connected. The Bishop of Fordingbridge asked me, and—"

Bigham interrupted hastily. "It was a bit of a comedown, wasn't it? After the work you did in India, finding missing girls must seem very tame."

Harry shrugged. "It became more interesting after I found out that they were on the *Titanic*."

Bigham draped an arm around Harry's shoulder and guided him toward the rear of the hall. "I heard about what you did in Lucknow," he said as they walked.

Harry remained silent. So much had happened in Lucknow. He could not guess what rumors would have reached the Guards officer.

"The general's wife," Bigham said. "Damned plucky of you to take that situation in hand. Sorry it ended so badly. It's a terrible mistake to take the memsahibs out there. The poor girl never stood a chance, although I would agree that finding an Indian midwife was a better idea than leaving her in the hands of the regimental surgeon. An army sawbones is no use at all when it comes to women's business. I heard the general had someone take the baby to England."

Harry was momentarily overwhelmed. After more than a year of trying to forget, the image was once again in the forefront of his mind.

The Indian women had already cleaned away the blood and wrapped the infant in swaddling clothes. The general's wife lay immobile in the bed, her face as white as the sheet, her hands folded across her breasts.

The midwife addressed him in Hindi. "Who will tell the sahib?"

"I suppose I will," Harry said. "He will be back next week."

"The baby is a boy. He is small but strong."

And that, *Harry thought,* is all the general will want to know.

The midwife cradled the baby. "I will find a wet nurse."

Harry wondered how the general would feel about his son being nursed at the breast of an Indian woman. He was still wondering when Cardrew Worthington came to tell him about the boar hunt, and he made the fateful decision to ride out with him.

Bigham, unaware of Harry's racing thoughts, led him to an office in the rear of the building and pointed to a stack of papers piled on a desk. "The depositions taken in Plymouth," he said.

"And what do you expect me to do with them?" Harry asked. He was impatient to leave and be alone with his memories.

"I expect you to resume your employment with His Majesty's Government," Bigham said. "You are exactly what we need."

Harry was silent. His mind was in India.

Bigham frowned. "Something wrong, old man?"

It was not Bigham's fault. No one had ever known of Harry's relationship with the general's wife. *No, it was never a relationship. She was lonely. We talked about books.* Harry shook his head. "No, no. Just … No, there's nothing wrong. I don't like to be reminded of India."

"Gets into the blood, doesn't it?" Bigham said. "I feel the same way. I miss the old cloak-and-dagger shenanigans, but I think you will find this to be an adequate replacement. There's all kinds of information squirreled away in these papers, some of it dangerous. The crew doesn't know what they know, if you get my meaning. Read what they had to say, and then get out among them. Present yourself any way you choose, and see if you can come back with some answers."

"So you would like me to find answers to questions you don't know you need to ask," Harry said irritably.

"No, not exactly."

Bigham gestured to a seat, and Harry sat, grateful to take the weight off his leg.

Bigham rifled through the pile of papers. "I've taken a quick look," he said, "and I have an inkling of what we're after." He gave Harry a comradely look. "You understand, don't you? You know how it is. Sometimes it's the facts, and sometimes it's the lack of facts, and sometimes it's too many facts."

Harry nodded. He was intrigued by the situation. Very few people would understand what Bigham was saying, but Harry knew exactly what he meant. *A feeling in the bones.* Bigham had found something, and he wanted to know if Harry would find the same thing.

"Our inquiry will be quite straightforward," Bigham said. "I'm sure that the newspapers will look for scandal, but that's not our intent. We already know that the tragedy brought out the best in some people and the worst in others. There's nothing we can do about that.

"Senator Smith in America is fixated on determining the speed of the ship through the ice field. As the captain is no longer with us, he would like to pin the blame for that on Bruce Ismay, chairman of the line. So far he's found no proof that Ismay urged the captain to greater speed, but he's ruined the man's reputation, not just because he could possibly be held responsible but because he took a seat in a lifeboat. Right or wrong, Ismay will be a social pariah. It won't matter what conclusion the Americans reach—the damage is done."

Harry tried to imagine how life would be for Bruce Ismay once he returned to England. For the moment, he was trapped in the United States at the mercy of the American press. Thanks to them, he would always be known as the man who had saved his own life while fifteen hundred people had drowned and frozen. Perhaps he was regretting the moment he stepped into a lifeboat. Perhaps he would be better off dead.

Harry looked up. Bigham was speaking again. "Agents of the Board of Trade inspected the ship before she sailed. She was certified after her trials in Belfast Lough, and she was certified again in Southampton." Bigham held up a hand before Harry could speak. "I know what you're going to say."

"Do you?"

"You're going to say that someone should have mentioned the lack of lifeboats. The answer is that she had the number of boats required by law. Of course it wasn't enough, but it was legal. The lifeboats are not pertinent."

Harry shook his head. He wasn't sure if he liked or trusted Bigham, but for the first time since Lucknow, his mind was fully engaged. He thought about the rumormongering reporters he'd overheard in Plymouth. He knew that if he spoke, he could not retreat. "I'm not even sure that the iceberg is pertinent."

"Good man," Bigham said softly.

Harry took a moment to organize his thoughts. If Bigham was looking for answers, he should start at the beginning, and for the *Titanic*, the voyage began with the agents who had certified her as seaworthy.

"You say she was certified in Belfast and again in Southampton. Do you have any reason to suspect that she was not seaworthy? Are you suggesting that something was covered up or passed over by the inspectors?"

Bigham shook his head and looked disappointed. "I don't think that's the right place to start."

"Why not?" Harry asked impatiently. "It seems a logical starting point."

"Because we don't have time for irrelevancies," Bigham said.

"It's hardly irrelevant," Harry protested.

Bigham lowered his voice as if to take Harry into his confidence. "We're playing a high-stakes game here, and I don't know how long we have. You should start with the crew's depositions. You may find that words have been spoken that should not have been spoken."

Harry's senses tingled. He was no longer sure what was being asked of him. He had a feeling that Bigham was looking for a specific result from his investigations—one that was not necessarily the truth.

He walked to the front of the room and studied the scaled-down replica of the *Titanic*. She had been the pride of the Belfast shipyards.

"White Star never advertised her as unsinkable," Bigham said. "She was the latest in safety technology, but no ship is ever completely unsinkable. The newspapers made up the myth that she was unsinkable. With four of her watertight compartments flooded, she had nowhere to go but down."

Harry ran a finger along the hull, feeling the pattern of simulated rivets beneath his fingers. "It's hard to imagine that merely scraping along the side of an iceberg would tear a hole so large that four compartments would flood," he said thoughtfully. "Are you certain we shouldn't begin by finding out if she was properly inspected?"

"Questioning the certificates is akin to questioning the White Star Line itself and suggesting that they were complicit."

"Maybe they were," Harry said.

Bigham once again draped his arm around Harry's shoulder. The gesture suggested comradeship. Bigham's voice was still low and confidential. "What you suggest would result in the passengers making a claim for compensation against the White Star Line."

Harry waited. His silence invited Bigham to explain himself.

Bigham sighed, removed his arm from Harry's shoulders, and stood tall. "It's a matter of national security," he said.

"I don't see how."

"A claim for compensation would bankrupt not only the White Star Line but also International Mercantile Marine. Britain cannot afford to lose its grip on the transatlantic ocean trade. We can't let Germany get the upper hand. King and country, old man. War clouds on the horizon, I'm afraid. Do I need to say more?"

Harry allowed the silence to continue while he analyzed his jumbled thoughts. He had started with a simple task: find the nieces of the Bishop of Fordingbridge. How could that task have turned into something of international significance? Why was Bigham turning this moment into a challenge of Harry's patriotism?

"We've both taken the king's shilling," Bigham said.

Harry understood the meaning and the challenge. He and Bigham were soldiers. They had pledged their loyalty to the Crown, and a career-ending injury did not wipe out that oath.

"Where are these war clouds gathering?" Harry asked.

Bigham's face was grim. "At the moment, they are gathering in the Balkans, but the next war we fight will not be isolated. The foreign possession of every country involved will no doubt go to the winners, and so far as Britain, Germany, and France are concerned, that is a hefty portion of the globe," he said. "It's going to be a war such as we've never seen before. A war to end all wars."

"And my contribution to the war effort would be to read the depositions of the *Titanic*'s crew?"

"It may seem like nothing, but I can assure you that it is important."

"What am I looking for?"

"I don't know, but I trust you will know it when you find it."

"And if I do find something?"

"Leave that to me."

Harry thought of the weary men and women he'd seen in Plymouth. He had no intention of leaving them to Bigham's tender mercies. He would do as Bigham asked and read the depositions, but what he did after that would be a matter for his own judgment.

He smiled at Bigham. "When would you like me to start?"

Bigham slid the pile of papers across the desk. "Now would be a good time."

The Bishop's Residence
Fordingbridge
Poppy Melville

The chaplain escorted Poppy into the bishop's office. Uncle Hugh sat behind a massive oak desk. He was attired in his formal purple cassock, and his bishop's crook leaned against the wall behind him. He gestured for Poppy to take a seat.

"Let me come straight to the point," he said. "Much as I would like to, I can find no excuse for keeping you here any longer. You and Daisy have both had a couple of days to recover, and I think it's time to go back to Riddlesdown and talk to your father."

"Has he asked to see us?"

"No."

"Does he know what we did?"

"I informed him on the telephone."

"And what did he say?"

"He said that he sent you to London to buy baby clothes for his son. He can't imagine how you ended up on the *Titanic*. He thinks it was very careless of you."

Poppy could not restrain a sudden hysterical laugh. "Careless! He thinks we were on the *Titanic* by mistake?"

The bishop shrugged his shoulders and smiled. "Yes. Apparently, that's what he thinks. He would not for one moment entertain the idea that you and your sister had run away to sea because you did not care to be at home."

"Uncle," Poppy said, "you have no idea …"

Her uncle leaned forward and looked into her eyes. "You're wrong. I know what your life is like and how he thinks of you, but bear in mind that you are his heir. If your stepmother does not produce a son—"

Poppy held up her hand to stop him. "If this one is not a boy, there will be another one. If this wife dies, there will be another wife."

"My father will never see me as his heir." Poppy felt a prickling of tears. "In fact, he doesn't see me at all." She reached into the pocket of her robe, pulled out a handkerchief, and told herself to stop sniveling. *More than fifteen hundred people died.. You saw them and you heard them, while you were safe and dry in a lifeboat. You have nothing to cry about.*

"Poppy! Poppy!"

Poppy put her handkerchief away as Daisy's voice called to her from outside the door.

"Come and see what I have."

The bishop waved a dismissive hand. "You'd better go and see what she's up to. You know what she's like." His smile was fond as he spoke of Daisy. Poppy knew that he, like almost every other man, could only see Daisy's charm and wit. They had no idea what devious thoughts were really going on behind that dimpled smile and those bright eyes.

Daisy stood in the hall, surrounded by shopping bags and hatboxes. "Come on," she said. "Help me carry these upstairs."

Poppy stared in amazement. "Where did you get all these things?"

"I've been up since the crack of dawn, and I went into Winchester. They really have some very nice shops. Not as good as London, and of course, nothing is made to measure, because there was no time, but I know all my clothes fit me, and I did my best to find something for you. You are such a beanpole, Poppy. It's not easy."

Poppy had trouble regaining her voice. "You went into Winchester?"

"Yes. It's not far. I told one of Uncle's flunkies, or acolytes or whatever they are, to call a taxi for me. You were still asleep."

"But how did you pay for all this?"

Daisy put her hands on her hips. "How do you think?"

"You spent that money?"

"Some of it. Not all of it. I couldn't spend the dollars, and I haven't had the courage to go into a jeweler's to try to sell the watches and rings, and the other money was mainly French. Which has given me an idea. Suppose—"

Poppy could hardly contain her anger, but she managed to speak quietly. "It's stolen money, Daisy. It's not ours."

"It's not anyone else's. I'm sure they're all dead. They weren't doing anything to save themselves, except for the one man who chased me, and he's probably dead too. If he'd been saved, he would have been on the *Carpathia*, and I didn't see him there."

"You didn't see anyone, because you were hiding from Miss Bonelli."

Daisy gathered up a handful of bags and started up the stairs. "When I'm finished with all these clothes, Miss Bonelli won't even recognize me, and neither will that horrible man if he happens to have survived. Anyway, he wouldn't look for me here. He will think I went ashore in New York."

"Does he know you were a stewardess?"

Daisy shrugged. "I don't know. Maybe. Either way, it doesn't matter."

Poppy gathered up the remaining bags and followed Daisy up the stairs. She set them on the bed in the guest room and watched as Daisy pulled out one garment after another. Soon the bed was piled high with ruffled blouses, sprigged muslin dresses, feathered hats, and satin shoes.

"These are all mine," Daisy declared. She opened another bag. "These are yours."

Poppy's eyes feasted on a periwinkle-blue blouse and navy walking skirt, an ivory tea gown, and a royal-blue woolen coat. "They're beautiful," she said softly.

Daisy held out a wide-brimmed blue hat crowned with a confection of marabou feathers. "I bought some pomade for your hair, just to bring it under control. I am going to make you beautiful."

Poppy shook her head and dropped the clothes back onto the bed. "It's stolen money, Daisy."

"We didn't steal it. He did."

"Two wrongs don't make a right."

Daisy picked up the beautiful hat. "Just try it on. Please."

Poppy could not say how it happened, but somehow the hat made its way onto her head, and her feet turned her toward the mirror on the dressing table. Daisy flitted around, tucking Poppy's hair neatly under the hat. For once Poppy could not object. She was stunned by what she saw in the mirror. With her troublesome hair tucked under the hat, and the blue of the hat bringing out the blue of her eyes, she saw someone she had not seen before. *I am not beautiful, but I am interesting.* She studied the woman in the mirror, seeing the shadow of tragedy in her haunted eyes. She would never be Daisy. She would never dazzle, but she was not ugly, and she was not plain. Daisy was pretty and could please every eye, but Poppy finally saw that she, too, had something to offer. She was not shallow. She had depths that were worth exploring.

Poppy continued to stare into the mirror, reluctant to remove the hat. She watched her lips framing the words. "Daisy, we have to go home."

"No, we don't."

"Uncle Hugh insists."

"He can insist we leave here, but he can't insist we go home," Daisy declared. "We have money, Poppy. We can go anywhere."

"It's not our money. Also, we have no identity papers. We can't travel outside the country."

Daisy gave her a teasing smile. "That's where you're wrong. I made cautious inquiries, and I found someone who can supply us with a letter from the Bishop of Fordingbridge to say that we are his nieces."

"What do you mean? Are you saying that someone is going to forge a letter from Uncle Hugh to identify us?"

"Unless you think he would write one himself."

Poppy thought of the expression on her uncle's face and the sadness with which he had urged Poppy to return home. She shook her head. "No, he wouldn't do it, and you're not going to do it either."

Daisy flung herself down on the bed, disrupting the careful display of new garments. "You don't understand," she said between clenched teeth. "This is really, really urgent. We have to go to America now."

"Why?"

"Because of Dorothy Gibson."

Poppy looked down at Daisy's angry face. "Who is Dorothy Gibson?"

"Who indeed?" Daisy asked, jumping to her feet again and beginning to pace the floor. "Dorothy Gibson is a Hollywood film star, and she was on the *Titanic*, and she didn't die, which is a great pity."

"Daisy!"

"Oh, it's all very well for you to sound shocked, but consider what she's done. She's made a movie. She's starring in her own story, wearing the same clothes she wore on the night she was rescued. Do you know that a film company actually came out to meet the *Carpathia* and film her arrival in New York?" Daisy's anger turned to pouting. "That's while I was stuck down belowdecks and didn't even see the Statue of Liberty, let alone a film crew. So Dorothy Gibson is starring in some made-up story, and I have a much better story. Can you imagine the scenes where I would wade through water up to my waist to rescue the old lady's jewels?"

"You didn't rescue them."

"I almost did. And then I was chased by a crazed card sharp. And then I had to break through a cordon of crewmen who were fighting to let the women get into the very last lifeboat, and the purser was firing his gun, and I only got a seat because one of the first-class ladies was too frightened to climb in, but I wasn't frightened."

Poppy stared at her sister. "I knew that story wasn't true."

"What story?"

"The one about the boy and his dog and opening the windows on the promenade deck."

Daisy shrugged. "It was partly true. I saw them, but then that man chased me. I couldn't tell that story to the lawyers, could I? They would want to know why I was being chased."

"So what boat were you in?"

"It was one of the collapsibles. The ship was almost all under, and people were in a panic, but they were still loading this one boat. It was much smaller than the other, with canvas sides, and it didn't look very safe. Some of the ladies were still refusing." She shrugged her shoulders helplessly. "Is it my fault that some women are stupid ninnies?" She shivered dramatically. "When we rowed away, there was water washing over the sides. We weren't like Dorothy Gibson. We were in real peril. I have a much more exciting story than she has. She left on the very first lifeboat. She didn't even get wet." She winked at Poppy. "Anyway, I'm much prettier than she is."

Poppy grasped her sister's shoulders. "Daisy, you gave a sworn deposition, and you didn't say anything about being in a collapsible."

"It doesn't matter."

"Of course it matters. What if we're summoned to appear in front of Lord Mersey in London? Everyone will know you lied."

"How?"

"Because the people in lifeboat four will say you weren't with them."

"Well, that's that, then," Daisy said with a grin. "That solves the problem. We can't give evidence if we can't be found. We'll just have to run away again. Only this time we'll go first-class. I'll have to go and see that forger again and get us some new names."

Poppy's attempt to express her outrage was interrupted by a knock at the bedroom door. She was grateful for the interruption, grateful for the opportunity to gather her thoughts after the barrage of Daisy's wild ideas.

She was surprised to find the bishop standing outside the door. He seemed equally surprised to see her.

"Oh, Poppy, my dear. How charming you look. I had no idea …"

Poppy was taken aback. She had forgotten that she was still wearing the blue hat . Apparently, she had not been mistaken when she had looked into the mirror. She really did look passingly attractive in her new clothes, or at least she looked much better than she had ever looked before.

Uncle Hugh peered into the bedroom and saw Daisy sitting amid a welter of new clothing and hatboxes. "I see you've been spending your earnings," he said.

Poppy compressed her lips. Uncle Hugh would have no idea how little they had actually been paid. The White Star Line had made a small concession and paid full wages and a bonus, but the final amount would not pay for any of the items on the bed.

"I couldn't resist," Daisy said cheerfully. "Hope you don't mind, Uncle. I asked one of your acolytes—"

"Chaplains."

"I asked one of your chaplains to summon a taxi for me. We had nothing but the clothes given to us in New York, and I had to do something."

The bishop nodded. "I understand completely, but I'm afraid that I've thought of a problem that will delay your return home."

"Oh, we're in no hurry," Daisy announced. "We like it here."

The bishop lowered his eyebrows in mock seriousness. "Be serious, Daisy. You know you have to go home, but—"

"No, really, Uncle."

"I mean it, Daisy. You will have to go home, but you can't go empty-handed. Your father gave you money to buy baby clothes, and despite the fact that you both nearly drowned, he is not going to welcome you with open arms unless you have the baby clothes."

Poppy's heart sank. Her uncle was correct. The Earl of Riddlesdown's mind was a train running on only one track. He could think of nothing but the anticipated arrival of a son and heir. The fact that his two oldest daughters had been cast adrift in the North Atlantic would not reduce his annoyance at finding they were returning empty-handed.

Of course, Daisy had enough money to take care of the problem, but Poppy could not bear to use stolen money. They would have to use their earnings from the White Star Line.

"You were supposed to go to Harrods," Uncle Hugh said.

Poppy nodded.

"Very well. We shall go to Harrods."

"I don't understand."

The bishop smiled happily. "I will escort you two lovely ladies to London. We will shop for infant clothing at Harrods. Then we will take tea at my club."

"Can't we have tea at The Savoy?" Daisy asked. "I don't want to take tea at your stuffy old men's club."

The bishop smiled fondly. "We have a beautiful ladies' lounge," he said, "and I am looking forward to taking you there and showing you off to all the young men."

"Dulwich College men," Daisy said under her breath.

"It's not Eton," said Uncle Hugh, who had surprisingly good hearing for a man of his age, "but we have some very fine young members. You may meet Sir Ernest Shackleton, the polar explorer. He's a Dulwich man."

"We would love to go to your club," Poppy said, "but you have to realize that we used the money for baby clothes to—"

"I know you don't have money," the bishop said. "I can see that you have been quite profligate in your spending. I was not aware that the White Star paid so well. Perhaps they gave you a bonus because of the fact that you almost drowned."

"Yes," said Daisy. "That's what they did."

The bishop smiled. "Don't worry. I will take care of the baby clothes, and you will go home tomorrow with everything you need." He pulled a watch from somewhere within the folds of his cassock. "It's getting quite late, so hurry up and put on your new dresses, and we will take the train."

PART FOUR

INQUIRY

No words can express the sympathy which everyone must feel for those who have suffered by this deplorable calamity. There is only one thing that gives some consolation ... that this disaster has given an opportunity for a display of discipline and of heroism which is worthy of all the best traditions of the marine in this country.

. Sir Robert Finlay, appearing for the White Star Line at the British Wreck Commissioner's Inquiry, day one, May 2, 1912

CHAPTER TWELVE

London Scottish Drill Hall
London
Harry Hazelton

Although Harry had a front-row seat, he had a hard time hearing what was being said. He imagined that reporters and members of society seated farther back in the great, echoing space would hardly understand one word in ten. Bigham's draperies had done very little to dampen the confusing echoes. Harry was certain that there were other suitable places in London with far better acoustics. Knowing what he knew about the international significance of the hearings, he suspected that Lord Mersey, Clive Bigham's father, was quite content for most of the testimony to be garbled and incomprehensible.

Harry did not plan to spend a long time listening to the witnesses. Their depositions were stacked up in the back office, where he had been reading them for the past two days. He had come out now in order to put a face to a name. Written words were hard to judge, but a face spoke volumes.

Lord Mersey was nominally in control of the proceedings on behalf of the British Board of Trade. Appearing without his usual wig and gown, he cut an unprepossessing figure, and his light, reedy voice barely carried as far as the witness box. It was not until Sir John Simon, the Solicitor General, took over the questioning that Harry was able to clearly understand the questions.

The "prisoner in the dock"—Harry knew that he should not think of the poor young man that way, but Bigham's arrangements certainly gave an illusion of a courtroom—lookout Archie Jewell, squirmed as uncomfortably as any true criminal. Despite the fact that he was not the lookout who had spotted, or failed to spot, the iceberg, his face was full of concern as he struggled to avoid incriminating himself in any way by providing answers to a barrage of essentially meaningless questions.

Because Harry had been present when the crew had come ashore from the *Lapland*, and had seen the haunted shadows behind their eyes, he had every sympathy for the man. He had to remind himself that Jewell was no younger than the men he had commanded in South Africa, and at least he was still alive. So many who had been under Harry's command were no longer alive.

"Mr. Jewell, were you one of the lookouts on the *Titanic*?"

"Yes, quite right."

"On the *Titanic*, did all the able seamen take their turns at the lookout, or had you a special set of lookouts?"

"There were just six of us on the lookout."

"And on the night of that Sunday, the fourteenth of April, which was your lookout? Which was your watch?"

"Eight until ten, sir."

"And where were you? Were you in the crow's nest or at the forecastle head or where?"

"In the crow's nest."

"Who was the man who was with you?"

"Symons. He is back in New York."

"And he was saved too, was he?"

"Yes."

Harry leaned forward, wondering if perhaps Sir John Simon was not listening to the answers to his own questions. Jewell had just said that his watchmate was back in New York, and he would not have said that if Symons was at the bottom of the Atlantic.

"So there were two of you in the crow's nest. Were there two of you on the bridge?"

"No."

"Or two of you forward?"

"No, not in clear weather."

"So just two of you. Was the weather clear?"

"Yes."

"Was there any moon?"

"No."

"Was it starry?"

"Yes."

Harry tried to avoid rolling his eyes. This slow, methodical questioning would take a lifetime. All these questions had been asked and answered in New York. Every newspaper had carried the report of the clear, starry night, the ocean so calm that you could see the stars reflected in the water.

The Solicitor General nodded sagely. "Now do you remember when you were on your watch, from eight to ten, any message coming to you about ice?"

"Yes, about nine thirty. The message came on the telephone in the crow's nest. We were to keep a sharp lookout for all ice, big and small."

"Up to that time, up to the time you got that message, had you seen any ice?"

"No."

"And when you were relieved at ten o'clock, did you hand on this message?"

"Yes."

"Who were the lookout men who relieved you at ten o'clock?"

"Fleet and Lee."

"And were they saved?"

"All the lookouts were saved. I think Fleet has given evidence in New York."

Harry shifted in his seat. The London papers had printed reports of Fleet's evidence, from which it was obvious that Fleet had given very slippery and unhelpful answers to the senator from Michigan. He had, of course, made one slip, which had been seized upon by the press. He had revealed the lack of binoculars in the crow's nest. His follow-up remark had been widely reprinted. Asked how much sooner he would have seen the iceberg if he had been using binoculars, he had simply said, "Soon enough to get out the way."

Harry rose impatiently. What was the point in questioning a man who had not seen the iceberg and had not even seen any ice?

He was acutely aware of the uneven step and drag of his footsteps echoing from the dusty rafters as he made his way to the door behind the judicial bench. As he left the room, he was approached by a police officer.

"Sir!"

"Yes? What is it? Do you require identification?"

The constable shook his head. "Of course not, sir. We all know who you are. I was wondering if you could give me your opinion."

"About what?"

"There's a man who turns up every day and sits in the back of the room, and every day he asks when the stewardesses will give evidence. Doesn't that strike you as a bit strange?"

Harry immediately thought of Poppy and Daisy Melville, the only two stewardesses he had met or for whom he felt any responsibility.

"Will the stewardesses be giving evidence?" the constable asked.

"I don't know," Harry replied, "but let's take a look at this fellow. Can you point him out to me?"

The constable eased open the door. Lord Mersey was addressing the witness in his usual reedy voice, and the burgundy drapes were proving as ineffectual as ever at preventing echoes from bouncing around the walls and obscuring his words.

"In the back row," the constable said. "Red-faced fellow."

Harry studied the man in question, noting his narrow shoulders, flushed cheeks, prominent pale eyes, and his sparse scattering of gray hair.

"Doesn't look like much of a threat," he commented. "What do you know about him?"

"Gave his name as Rotherhithe," the constable said. "He's an American."

"And he wants to see the stewardesses?"

"That's what he's asking. When will they give evidence?"

"He looks pretty harmless," Harry said, "and we have no grounds to remove him, unless he makes a nuisance of himself. I suggest that you tell him that it is unlikely that any of the stewardesses will be called, and that should see him off."

The constable nodded. "We see all sorts in this business," he said. "Begging your pardon for mentioning it, but some men have very strange … desires."

Harry once again thought of Daisy and Poppy. He assumed that they were safely ensconced at Riddlesdown, and he hoped that Bigham would not decide to call them. On the other hand, if they were not called, he would have no reason to see them again—no reason to see Poppy.

He clapped the constable on the shoulder. "Keep an eye on him, and let me know if he says anything else."

The constable saluted and stepped back, leaving Harry to continue on his way to his office.

When he reached the small room set aside for him, he found Clive Bigham ensconced in an armchair, puffing on a cigar and leafing through the pile of depositions.

Bigham looked up and nodded sympathetically. "Tedious, isn't it?"

"I don't understand the purpose," Harry said. "I know that your father is a distinguished—"

"Oh, forget about my father. This is the kind of thing that makes him happy. He's like a fishwife picking at a winkle. He'll pick and pick, and every witness he examines will provide food for the newspapers and throw them off the trail."

"What trail?"

Bigham leaned back and flourished his cigar, sending aromatic smoke wafting through the office. "The trail that I hope you are following."

Harry frowned and remained silent. He had spent the last few days leafing through the crew's depositions, looking for something that seemed to be just beyond his reach. Although he could not explain why, he was certain that the stories dictated by the crew added up to more than the sum of their parts. The hours of reading had given him a headache and a longing to be out in the fresh air and away from the smoke of London.

"It's as I feared," Bigham said. "The Americans are hoping to prove that the ship was going too fast and ignoring the ice warnings. They want us to believe that Bruce Ismay was really in control and not the captain. They would also like to prove that the crew was poorly trained, that no orders were given to abandon ship, that the *Californian*, another British ship, failed to come to the rescue, and that Sir Cosmo Duff-Gordon acted like a complete cad."

"Does all of that seem possible?" Harry asked.

Bigham examined the ash on his cigar for a moment, and then he sighed. "The whole of London knows that Duff-Gordon behaved appallingly and left the *Titanic* with only twelve people in his lifeboat. He'll never live it down. As for the rest, yes, it's all possible, and it paints a very poor picture of British shipping. If we are not careful, the loss of the *Titanic* will go down in history as a lesson in total incompetence alleviated only slightly by mindless gallantry.

Thousands of lives lost through sheer carelessness while gentlemen, who should have known better, allowed themselves to drown rather than step into half-empty lifeboats when there were no more women and children. If this impression is allowed to remain, it will be a bad day for British shipping, and it will lose us the transatlantic trade with disastrous consequences. If it comes to war, we will need those ships to transport our troops."

He looked at Harry impatiently. "How are you getting along with reading the crew's depositions? Is there anyone there who would benefit from a visit?"

"What kind of visit?"

Bigham said nothing. He did not need to say the words aloud. *Someone whose words should be ignored or changed. Someone who will be urged to remain silent unless ...*

Once again Harry remembered the two reporters at the Duke of Cornwall Hotel.

"Interrogantum will print any story we bring him."

Why? Why would anyone print a story that seemed so incredible? Who could possibly benefit from the deliberate murder of so many people? President Taft's special envoy had been on board, along with some of the richest men in the world. The loss of so many bankers, financiers, and railroad magnates had sent the stock market into a sudden dive.

Harry drew in a sharp breath. Was it possible that the mysterious Interrogantum was not just looking for wild rumors? Perhaps he was looking for truth to be discounted and lost among all the other rumors.

"If she hadn't hit an iceberg, she would have hit something else. It was all planned."

Bigham was leaning forward in his seat. "Well?"

"It may not have been an act of God," Harry said, "but—"

Bigham glared at him.

"But," Harry continued, "it could have been sabotage."

"Hmm," said Bigham. "Yes, I suppose that would do. Sabotage by foreign agents. What do you have?"

"The captain of the *Californian* is adamant that he did not see the *Titanic*," Harry said.

"He swears to it."

"And yet the people in the lifeboats saw the lights of a ship."

"That's what they say," Bigham confirmed.

Harry's mind was racing. As the *Titanic* had sunk, a ship had been hovering on the horizon, not making any move to rescue the passengers—just waiting and watching. He assembled the pieces. The president's envoy was lost. The deck officers had been replaced at the last minute. The command of the ship had been given to an incompetent captain. No binoculars in the crow's nest. J. P. Morgan had canceled at the last minute.

"If everything went as planned and the Titanic went down without a trace, it could all be blamed on Smith's incompetence …"

And thus on the White Star Line. International Mercantile Marine would be destroyed. As an added bonus, some of America's most prominent businessmen had been lost, and the stock market had tumbled. The United States had been destabilized; the British hold of the transatlantic trade had been weakened; and Senator Smith's ham-fisted inquiry had given rise to a diplomatic crisis.

How could such an ambitious plot be carried out, and by whom? Was it possible that the *Titanic* had had an inherent weakness that could have been exploited? She had received a certificate of seaworthiness before she had sailed. Had something been deliberately overlooked?

Harry stared down at the pile of crew depositions. Sullivan, the Australian, had not wanted to be paid and had not given his deposition. The answer was not on any of these papers; it was in Harry's memory of Sullivan's words.

"Twelve of us were taken on at the last minute to deal with a problem. They called us a black gang."

When Harry rose abruptly and headed for the door, Bigham followed him. "Where to?" he asked.

Harry shook off his headache. "Where are they keeping the crew members who are waiting to testify?"

Bigham pointed. "Over this way."

They found a lone witness in a small room just inside the entrance of the Drill Hall. He was a small man—it seemed to Harry that most members of the *Titanic*'s crew were small men. He wondered if this was because they were stunted in growth by a childhood of poverty. Poverty was what drove a man to make a living on the high seas, and service in the merchant navy was a tradition handed down from father to son. All they knew was the family necessity of leaving for months at a time and returning home with just enough money to last until the next voyage.

"Able Seaman Joseph Scarrott," Bigham said.

When Harry shook the seaman's hand, he felt the strength in his wiry fingers. Scarrott was small, but he was not weak. He was, however, extremely nervous.

"Are you our union man?" he asked.

Harry shook his head. "No, I'm afraid not."

"I wanted to talk to our union man. I don't know what to say when I get in there."

"Well," said Bigham, "there'll be no judges in wigs or anything like that, just a man in a suit who will ask you a few simple questions. Tell the truth, and you'll have no problems."

Scarrott's face twisted into a painful expression. "I had a bad feeling," he said, "when I went to sign up. I wasn't going to sign up on the big 'un, you know. I was after a job as quartermaster on a Union-Castle liner. I don't know what made me do it. But it was supposed to be a speed-up. I suppose that was it."

"Speed-up?" Harry asked.

"Southampton to New York, unload, and back again in sixteen days." Scarrott gave him a lopsided grin. "You're a military man, aren't you?" He looked at Bigham. "You're both military gents. You're not sailors."

"No," said Harry, "we're not sailors, but you are, and we have some questions for you."

"Mr. Lowe did the right thing," Scarrott said.

Harry and Bigham looked at each other and reached a silent understanding that they would let Scarrott say whatever was on his mind.

"I saw it," Scarrott said distractedly. "The iceberg. I saw it. Big as the Rock of Gibraltar and the same shape. I knew it was trouble, and it wasn't no surprise when they told us to go to our lifeboat stations. I had lifeboat fourteen."

Harry could not help thinking of Poppy Melville, Lady Penelope. She had been in lifeboat fourteen.

Scarrott was already racing ahead with his story. "I was the only sailorman there. Some men came and tried to rush the boat. They were foreigners, and they couldn't understand when I ordered them to keep away." He grinned at Harry. "I had to use some persuasion with the tiller. One man jumped in twice, and I had to throw him out. And then the passengers came, and three or four stewards, and I was that glad when Officer Lowe came along and said he was coming with us. We had fifty-four women and four children, and one of them a baby. And we had a stewardess, a nice young lady, very helpful."

Harry smiled. "I know who she was."

Scarrott grinned back. "She's a bit posh, but she's nice, ain't she?"

"Yes, very nice."

"I don't know if they'll ask me," Scarrott said, "but if they do, I'll tell them that I was glad Mr. Lowe had his revolver. I told him I'd had trouble with them foreign men, and he brought out his revolver and fired three shots, not at them, just along the side. That saw them off, and then we went down the falls and dropped into the water." He looked at them anxiously. "Is it all right if I say all them things?"

"So long as they are the truth," Bigham replied.

"And about Mr. Lowe?"

"Officer Lowe is still in New York," Bigham said, "but I'm sure he'll tell them that you did a good job of persuading the foreigners with the tiller."

Scarrott laughed. "I've knocked about a bit. I know how to look after myself. Are they going to call me soon? I've been waiting here for a long time. They're talking to Archie Jewell, ain't they?"

"Yes, they are," Harry confirmed.

"He don't know nothing. He didn't even see it. He wasn't on lookout when we hit. Don't know why they want to talk to him. We told the lawyers all this in Plymouth. They wrote it all down. Why do they want us again?"

"Well," Harry said, "as you so wisely observed, we are military men, not lawyers and unfortunately not sailors, and that's why we have a question for you."

"Fire away."

"What is a black gang?"

"Oh."

Harry waited.

Scarrott chewed on his mustache. "A black gang," he repeated.

"Yes. What is it?"

"It's a job I wouldn't give to my worst enemy. It's called a black gang on account of coal being so black and them being covered in it. It's a group of men—firemen, I suppose you'd call them—but most firemen wouldn't do it. Anyway, it's a group of men what comes on board to put out fires in the coal bunkers."

"Is this something that happens often?"

Scarrott nodded. "Often enough. You know the way coal is. Once it gets going, it ain't easy to put out, and so sometimes a bunker will be on fire, and if the ship's in a hurry to leave, you have to get a black gang to come on board and shovel it."

"Shovel it where? Over the side?"

"Lord love you, no! How would you do that? No, best thing to do is to shovel it into the furnaces."

"Did the *Titanic* take on such a gang?" Harry asked.

Scarrott shrugged. "I don't know. I'm deck crew. I can't say whether *Titanic* had a last-minute scratch-up, but if she did, it could mean she had a bunker fire."

"And presumably, this scratched-up gang would have put out such a fire if it had existed," Bigham said.

Scarrott looked at him with suddenly mournful eyes. "It's out now," he said.

The Ladies' Lounge
The Dulwich Club
Poppy Melville

The ladies' lounge at the Dulwich Club turned out to be an unexpected and very welcome surprise. Shopping at Harrods had been somewhat of a trial. While Poppy and Uncle Hugh concentrated on finding suitable clothing for the wished-for baby boy, Daisy darted from counter to counter, making greedy exclamations of delight. Poppy's attention was split between assessing the suitability of tiny sailor suits and knitted blue matinee jackets and making sure that Daisy did not attempt to spend any more of the stolen money.

Poppy had no idea what should be done with Daisy's ill-gotten gains. She only knew that it would be wrong for Daisy to continue to spend it. It was, in fact, wrong for Poppy herself to continue wearing the beautiful hat and coat that Daisy had purchased for her. She wrestled with her conscience every time she caught a glimpse of herself in a store mirror. She had not known she could look so elegant. She had not known that other women could look at her with envy and men would turn their heads. Guilt followed her wherever she went.

At long last Uncle Hugh signed for the purchase of the baby's layette, and Poppy was able to lead Daisy out of the store.

"It's just a short walk to my club," Uncle Hugh said, "and we have plenty of time for tea before you take the train home."

"Couldn't we go to The Savoy?" Daisy asked.

Uncle Hugh shook his head. "We're going to my club."

The Dulwich Club presented a dim exterior to the outside world. Its stone facade was begrimed by years of weathering London's notorious, sulfurous fogs. Its lobby was decorated with mahogany paneling and a full alphabet of trophy animal heads, from antelopes to zebras.

Several antiquated flunkies met them in the lobby and expressed obsequious delight at seeing the bishop and almost overwhelming shock at the sight of Daisy and Poppy in their bright new clothes. From the corner of her eye, Poppy saw heads turning in the dim recesses of the members' bar as the bishop led them proudly to the ladies' lounge, which had been constructed only a few years previously.

"Not all the members were in favor," Uncle Hugh said as they trailed behind him along a dim passageway, "but we must change with the times, and the ladies do like to come to London occasionally."

Poppy wondered if there would ever come a day when ladies, or girls, would be admitted to Dulwich College on their own merit, and what would the members think of that?

The ladies' lounge, built at the farthest possible remove from the members' bar, was housed in a wonderfully ornate conservatory. Rays of sunlight, admitted through the high-domed ceiling, glinted on spindly gilt chairs. The floor was black-and-white tile. Potted ferns were set against the walls, and hanging spider plants sent long trails of offspring into the airy space. They caught a kitchen boy in the act of spreading a starched linen tablecloth on a round central table. He looked up in alarm and scuttled away, only to return a few moments later with a vase of pink roses.

"This is lovely," Poppy said.

Even Daisy agreed. "Not what I expected."

Uncle Hugh beamed with pride. "We had some real fights in committee," he said, "but this is the result. Take a seat. We'll order tea, but there's no hurry. I suspect that the chef will have sent someone to Fortnum & Mason for petit fours and iced dainties."

As Poppy and Daisy settled into their seats, the bishop summoned the waiter, ordered tea, and asked him if Captain Hazelton was anywhere on the premises.

Poppy could not say why, but she felt a flush creeping across her cheeks. She was glad of the concealment of her wide-brimmed hat. On hearing that Captain Hazelton was in the bar, she blushed again. She realized that the hat did not provide sufficient concealment when Daisy kicked her ankle under the table. The sisters looked at each other. Daisy raised her eyebrows, and Poppy shook her head angrily.

Captain Hazelton arrived long before the kitchen had produced tea or any other kind of refreshments, and he was not alone. Poppy took note of the subtle way that Daisy adjusted the angle of her extravagant pink hat, and vowed that she would not do the same thing. She had no need to impress Captain Hazelton. Apart from anything else, he had already seen her at her worst on arrival in Plymouth. Daisy's eyes were on Hazelton's companions. One companion was as tall and as blond as Hazelton was dark. He walked with a swagger, and his eyes were bold. The other companion did not share their military bearing. He was of average height, broad shouldered, and dark haired. He could have been considered ordinary if it were not for the energy that seemed to radiate from him.

"Allow me to introduce my companions," Hazelton said. "This is Captain the Honorable Clive Bigham, and this other gentleman is Sir Ernest Shackleton."

Daisy kept her eyes on Captain Bigham, who seemed happy to return her bold stare. Poppy only had eyes for Shackleton. She had read every newspaper article she could find about Shackleton's popular expeditions, and it was hard to believe that she was actually meeting him. His appearance didn't disappoint. He was not tall, dark, and handsome like Captain Hazelton, or tall, blond, and handsome like Captain Bigham, but none of that mattered. His presence was magnetic. She knew of only one person who radiated that kind of confidence—Ernie Sullivan, the fireman from the *Titanic*.

She blushed again. *Stop it, Poppy. This is ridiculous.*

Hazelton introduced them as Lady Penelope and Lady

Marguerite. Daisy insisted that Marguerite was not a name she liked to use, and then spoke on behalf of her sister to say that Penelope would prefer to be called Poppy.

The gentlemen seated themselves at the table, with Uncle Hugh blithely sharing the fact that the gentlemen of the club rarely had a chance to enter the ladies' lounge, and wasn't it wonderful to have this opportunity?

Captain Bigham made an attempt to lean back in his chair, but his studied nonchalance lasted for only a couple of seconds, as the little gilt chair creaked in protest. He recovered his equilibrium and leaned forward to look at Daisy.

Of course Daisy. Why would he look at anyone else?

"Harry Hazelton tells me that you were both on the *Titanic*," he said.

"Yes, we were," Daisy replied with a flutter of her eyelashes.

"And that you were serving as stewardesses. That must have been quite a lark."

Poppy could not bite back her reply. "No, it was no lark, Captain Bigham. If I live to be a hundred, I will never forget that night, or the people who lost their lives. I assume that as soldiers, both you and Captain Hazelton are accustomed to death, but I am not."

Bigham raised his hands in surrender. "My apologies. I spoke without thinking, but I am surprised to hear that you were working your passage. Your father is the Earl of Riddlesdown, is he not?"

Poppy looked away. She did not owe this man an explanation. An uncomfortable silence settled on the tea table, and Poppy knew she was the cause. She had spoken out of turn. Of course Bigham was curious. Why wouldn't he be? She imagined that the whole of haute society would be curious to know why the earl's daughters had been working as domestic servants on the *Titanic*.

Hazelton cleared his throat. "I should explain that Captain Bigham is secretary to the Wreck Commissioner's Inquiry," he said. "He's responsible for all the arrangements and for calling the witnesses. He has a professional interest in your experience on the *Titanic*."

Poppy nodded. "I see." It was as close as she could come to an apology. She was tired of the interest that the tragedy had attracted. Despite the air of national mourning, the general tone of the newspapers was one of prurient sensationalism.

"If I could ask you both a couple of questions …" Bigham said.

Daisy fluttered her eyelids in reply. "Of course, Captain. Please ask anything you like. We're very interested in justice for the survivors, aren't we, Poppy?"

Poppy took a deep breath and tried to put aside her resentment. Bigham had spoken thoughtlessly, but apparently, he was entitled to ask questions. "What would you like to know?" she asked.

Poppy felt Hazelton's eyes on her as he cautioned Bigham. "Now is not the time," he said. "It's too soon to ask these young ladies to relive their experiences."

Poppy flashed him a grateful smile. *He's really very thoughtful and quite charming.*

Daisy shook her head vigorously as she leaned forward in her chair and fixed Bigham with her blue-eyed gaze.

"I'll be happy to answer your questions. It's our duty, isn't it?"

Bigham spread his hands in a conciliatory gesture. "I have no wish to revisit your perfectly dreadful experience in the lifeboats. I would like to take you back to several hours before the event. As you went about your … uh … duties, did you hear anyone speak of ice warnings?"

Daisy answered without a second thought. "Oh, yes. I overheard several people talking about how cold it was and how that meant ice and maybe icebergs."

"Are you speaking of crew members?"

"No. I'm speaking of passengers. They were complaining of the cold. It was quite sudden." Daisy shrugged. "I mean, the weather wasn't exactly tropical when we left Ireland, but it was bearable, and the ladies I cared for were happy to walk about outside, and then suddenly, on Sunday, poof, they were all freezing cold."

Sir Ernest Shackleton spoke for the first time, and Poppy noted his Irish accent. "That would be because you crossed from the Gulf Stream, which is relatively warm all year round, into the Labrador Current, which is extremely cold at this time of year. Captain Smith would be very well aware of the change in water temperature and what that would mean."

Bigham looked at him with interest. "You're on my witness list."

"Yes, I know."

"Have you any opinion to share now?"

Before Shackleton could reply, Daisy chimed in with another

observation. "I gave a deposition in Plymouth," she said, "but I didn't know what they wanted me to say, and so I said very little."

Bigham gave Shackleton an apologetic smile and turned back to Daisy. Poppy couldn't imagine what Daisy was going to say. She could not talk about why she had delayed getting into her assigned lifeboat, and she would be very unwise to mention Miss Bonelli's jewelry.

"Do you know Mrs. Ryerson?" Daisy asked.

Bigham shook his head. "I know of her, of course, but I have never met the lady."

"It was so sad," Daisy said. Her eyes were pools of sympathy, or so it seemed. "The Ryersons were returning to New York because their son had been killed in a motor accident, and so they weren't out and about socializing like some of the other passengers. She had a maid with her, a French girl called Victorine. I enjoyed talking to her, because I have excellent French and I like to keep in practice."

Poppy noted that Bigham was not impressed with Daisy's grasp of the French language, but he could not turn away from those blue eyes to continue his conversation with Shackleton.

"And did Victorine say something about the ice?" Bigham prompted.

"Oh, yes," Daisy said. "It was on the morning of the day we struck the iceberg. It was a Sunday, wasn't it? Not that it matters."

"It was a Sunday," Bigham agreed.

"Well, on Sunday morning Victorine persuaded Mrs. Ryerson to go outside and take the air. They were very surprised by how cold it was, and they had just commented on it to Mrs. Thayer when Mr. Ismay came along. As he was practically the owner of the ship, they asked him whether they should be worried about icebergs. He said they had ice warnings and they were starting up extra boilers. Victorine had the impression that he meant they were going to increase speed so they could get out of the ice field as soon as possible."

Shackleton interrupted in a firm voice. "That would be absurd. You decrease speed when ice is about; you don't go crashing through it at top speed. I think that either this woman Victorine misunderstood, or Ismay was talking nonsense."

Poppy glanced at the Irishman and saw real anger on his face.

"That's what Victorine heard," Daisy insisted. "Mrs. Ryerson told her that they would be arriving early in New York, either Tuesday evening or Wednesday morning, which was well ahead of what they expected. In fact, Mrs. Ryerson was worried because they had made arrangements to be met in New York, and now she would have to send a Marconigram to change everything."

Bigham shook his head and gave Hazelton a querying glance. "Did anyone else on the crew mention this in their depositions?" he asked.

"I'll look again," Hazelton said, "but I didn't see anything."

Poppy was puzzled by both the question and the answer. Why was Harry Hazelton involved in this? Why was he reading the crew's depositions?

Bigham's expression changed as he looked back at Daisy, and Poppy thought she could read a hint of a threat on his face and in his words. "Have you spoken to anyone about this?"

Daisy shrugged. "No, I don't think so."

"Are you certain?" Bigham asked.

Daisy, unaware that Bigham was no longer flirting and no longer sympathetic, placed one finger against her cheek and arranged her lips into a thoughtful pout.

"Did you tell anyone else?" Bigham repeated sternly.

This time, Daisy seemed to understand that the handsome officer was no longer flirting. "Yes, I'm certain," she said. "I've only just remembered it myself."

"What about this other woman," Bigham asked, "Mrs. Ryerson's maid, Victorine?"

"She's in America," Daisy said.

Bigham nodded. "It would be best if you didn't speak of this again," he said.

Daisy looked as though she planned to protest, but she was interrupted by the arrival of three of the ancient waiters. One was bearing a tray with a silver teapot and fine china teacups; one carried a cake stand; and another pushed a tea trolley. All conversation ceased as the waiters clattered about setting out silverware, napkins, a dish of tea sandwiches, and of course, petit fours and iced dainties.

The bishop pronounced a blessing over the whole ensemble and then steered the conversation toward trivial and unimportant social chatter. Wasn't it amazing that Harriet Quimby had piloted her plane across the Channel? What would she do next? Had they seen the splendid new statue of Peter Pan in Kensington Gardens? What did they think about the royal visit to India? Perhaps Captain Hazelton could give them an insider's view.

The tea party took on an air of unreality. Daisy fluttered her eyelashes, and Bigham's smile carried no evidence of his previous threatening glare. Poppy wondered if she had been mistaken. No one else seemed to have noticed Bigham's sudden change of mood, and now he was all smiles. She forced herself to relax and join in the conversation. Captain Hazelton recited some anecdotes about his time in India, and Shackleton joined in with stories of his polar travels. Poppy took in every word, realizing how isolated she had been at Riddlesdown and how much she wished that she did not have to return to her father's house. If she allowed Daisy to use the stolen money, they could ... She pushed the thought away and decided just to enjoy the moment.

When Uncle Hugh announced that it was time to leave, Poppy was reluctant to gather up their bags and boxes. For a few minutes, life had been almost normal, and the memory of the great ship sinking beneath the water had receded. It would always be there, of course, hovering at the edge of her thoughts. She didn't know how to make the shadow depart permanently.

Bigham and Hazelton escorted them as far as the lobby. For a few brief moments, they had all been enclosed in an illusory social bubble. Within the bubble, Captain Bigham and Captain Hazelton were just toy soldiers, gallant gentlemen with colorful uniforms and impeccable manners. Once they reached the lobby, the bubble burst. Bigham and Hazelton spoke in hushed undertones, and their eyes were hard, the eyes of men who had killed for a living, and those eyes were fixed on Daisy, who smiled obliviously when they took their leave.

Poppy watched as the two soldiers stepped out onto the street and were immediately surrounded by reporters and photographers.

Daisy clutched at Poppy's arm. "Look at that," she whispered. "Look at all the cameras."

The bishop looked down at Daisy. "It's the *Titanic,*" he said. "The public are obsessed with every detail. I suppose they think Captain Bigham will tell them something new."

"What about Captain Hazelton?" Poppy asked. She blushed as she said his name and was grateful for the broad brim of her hat.

"What can he tell them?"

"Nothing," said Daisy. "He wasn't on the *Titanic*. Neither of them knows anything. They should be talking to us, Poppy. They should be taking our pictures."

Poppy shook her head. "You heard what Captain Bigham said."

"Oh, pooh. I don't have to do what he says."

"He was serious," Poppy warned. "Please, Daisy, don't do anything silly."

"I want to talk to the reporters myself," Daisy said. She waved a despairing hand at the view through the glass outer doors. "Oh, look, they're all leaving. I'm going now before they all get away. They don't know we're in here, and they don't know we have a story."

Poppy's heart sank as she stretched out her hands. Nothing short of physical force could stop Daisy now.

Daisy danced away from Poppy's hands. "I'm going to be on the front page. 'Earl's Daughter Saved from the *Titanic*. Read Her Story.'"

"Father will find out what we did," Poppy protested.

"He doesn't care what we did," Daisy said. "It won't make any difference to him." Daisy flashed a dazzling smile. "This is even better than going to America. I can be famous here, and a movie producer will see my picture." Her voice rose triumphantly. "It's all going to work out."

The bishop looked at Daisy in disbelief. "You are not going to parade yourself around the street like a common—"

Daisy interrupted before her uncle could utter words that were unsuited to a man of the cloth. "Don't worry about me, Uncle. I know what I'm doing."

She adjusted her hat and pushed open the glass door to the street. Poppy could see that only one reporter and one photographer remained, and for a moment, she thought that they would ignore the new arrival. She was wrong, of course. Daisy fluttered out onto the sidewalk, and the photographer, no doubt weary of photographing lawyers and gentlemen of influence, lifted his camera. The reporter turned to look. The camera flashed.

Once again Daisy had taken her fate into her own hands, and all Poppy could do was follow behind her and try to pick up the pieces.

☐

CHAPTER THIRTEEN

London
Ernie Sullivan

The woman was singing again. Sullivan sat in the morning room and scowled at the closed parlor door. Eva Newton's operatic soprano voice, which had thrilled audiences throughout her native Australia, could not be blocked by a mere parlor door in a fashionable London house. He knew her morning routine by now. First, she would warm her vocal cords with a series of alarming and dissonant ejaculations. Then would come the scales, and then the arias. The fact that Miss Newton was an Australian did nothing to endear her to him. European opera might well appeal to the Sydney elite, with their desire to ape all things European, but the people of Goolagong preferred a harmonica or a fiddle and something with a bit of life.

He was over his first surprise at finding himself delivered into the hands of Ben Tillett's opera-singing mistress, who occupied a very fine London house and was the mother to four of Tillett's children, none of whom bore his name.

"My wife doesn't know," Tillett had said. "In fact, very few people know about Eva. No one will look for you here."

Sullivan blurted out a question before he could stop himself. "How can you afford all this?"

"I can't," Tillett said nonchalantly. "My wife and I live in a very modest establishment in Putney." He gestured at the spacious entrance hall and the maid in a white apron. "All this is paid for by Eva's family money. I'm surprised you don't know of her, you being from Australia."

"It's a big country," Sullivan said, and he was surprised by a sudden pang of homesickness for wide horizons and blue skies. He decided not to ask Tillett how or where, and definitely not why, he had obtained his wealthy Australian mistress. Tillett sold himself to the workers as a man of the people, a self-taught graduate of the "school of hard knocks." He wondered what the union members, lured into strikes by Tillett's rhetoric, would make of this comfortable house and Tillett's long-term infidelity.

Eva delivered the final piercing notes of an aria. Sullivan assumed that those in the know would admire her ability to reach a pitch that approached that of a dog whistle, but he was relieved that the final burst of sound marked the finale of her practice session. When silence fell, he turned back to the *Daily Inquirer* and continued to read the speculations of a reporter known only as Interrogantum. The *Daily Inquirer*, knowing that few of its readers would speak Latin, had obligingly provided a translation: "Questioner."

This reporter, who was apparently not worthy of a staff position or a byline with his own name, was careful to couch his most outrageous suggestions in the form of a question, but his questions pointed to facts and details, some of which were surprisingly close to Sullivan's own recollections. Interrogantum questioned the cause of the chaos surrounding the launching of the lifeboats. What about the rumors of gunshots, of third-class passengers locked belowdecks, or a man, or maybe men, dressed in women's clothes? Was it true that a baby had been tossed from the deck to a lifeboat far below? Had the band really played until the very last minute, and could anyone have heard them above the clamor? Had Captain Smith truly been in control of the *Titanic*, or had Bruce Ismay been standing behind him and ordering greater speed?

Sullivan frowned as he continued to read. The questions that Interrogantum asked were the same questions that Sullivan had asked himself.

And what of Captain Lord? the reporter asked. *Survivors state that they were directed to row towards a ship whose lights were clearly visible on the horizon. Crew members of the Leyland liner* Californian, *under the command of Captain Stanley Lord, state that they told their captain of rockets being fired in the night, and yet the* Californian *remained stationary. Is Captain Lord guilty of the death of the many people he could have rescued?*

Sullivan's anger flared. The reporter had not made an accusation;

he had merely posed a question, but what a question. Sullivan had not seen the lights himself, but he knew they had been seen, not just by the crew but by passengers who had no reason to lie. If Captain Lord's ship had been close, why hadn't he come? Sullivan had been in the water, swimming desperately, when the *Titanic* finally surrendered and slid beneath the waves, but he knew that she had gone down with her lights still blazing and her crew firing rockets. How could this Leyland captain say that he had not seen her?

Captain Lord has already left the United States, having failed to give a satisfactory answer to the U.S. Senate. When he arrives in England, will he give the British public a true account of his actions? Interrogantum inquired.

Sullivan could not help but admire the unknown reporter. He did not accuse; he merely questioned, but the questions themselves were accusations. It was masterfully done.

He was about to continue his reading when a commotion in the hall caught his attention. The children, two boys and two girls, all of whom had been formally introduced to him, were greeting their father in loud, excited voices. For a brief moment, Sullivan regretted that he had denied himself the chance to be a husband and a father— not that Tillett was the husband of Eva, but he was the father of these children. Unfortunately, Sullivan had known, even as a boy, that he had a purpose in life, and it did not include being led astray by marriage. He could not even think of marrying until he had taken care of his grandfather's mission. He brushed aside a distracting image of the two sisters on the *Titanic*: Poppy with her grave, thoughtful presence, and Daisy, full of fire and yearning to seize life with both hands. Either one of those women would be capable of changing his life.

Tillett entered the morning room and closed the door behind him. "Your clothes have been delivered from Harrods," he said. "I've had them sent to your room. In the meantime, you should read this." He tossed a newspaper onto Sullivan's lap and went to the sideboard to pour coffee for himself.

"Latest edition," he said over his shoulder. "More speculation from Interrogantum, and a picture of someone we both recognize. The cat is definitely out of the bag now."

Sullivan picked up the paper. The front page displayed a photograph of a massive White Star liner. For a moment, Sullivan thought it was yet another duplicate photograph of the *Titanic* published by newspapers who had very little new material to use. The iconic final pictures of the *Titanic* had been taken as she had left Queenstown and set out across the Atlantic on her first and final voyage. Those pictures were recycled in one newspaper or another almost every day.

Sullivan looked up at Tillett and shrugged. "I don't understand."

"Oh, you will," Tillett said. "That's not the *Titanic*; it's a picture of the White Star liner *Adriatic*. She's bringing Ismay and the surviving officers home. Note the headline: 'White Star Officers Flee ahead of Subpoena.'"

"Another subpoena?" Sullivan asked.

"It was bound to happen," Tillett replied. "Private citizens in the US are planning on bringing civil suits against the White Star Line. Ismay, Lightoller, and the other officers are running for their lives at the moment."

"Literally?" Sullivan asked.

"No, not literally," Tillett said. "I mean that whatever the verdict of the Senate inquiry, there will be civil suits, and the surviving officers will be called as witnesses. Their lives are not in danger, but their reputations will suffer."

Sullivan thought of his night on the water, of Lowe's steely determination to offload passengers and return to hunt for survivors among the floating wreckage, of Lightoller beating back men who would have rushed the lifeboats and killed everyone, of the engineering officers who did not even attempt to leave the devastation belowdecks and instead worked to keep the lights blazing. "They all deserve a medal," he said.

Tillett shook his head. "They won't get one. Captain Rostron is in line for all kinds of accolades for bringing the *Carpathia* through the ice and rescuing the survivors, but no one will give medals to the *Titanic*'s crew." He sighed. "All they will get is blame."

Sullivan tapped the newspaper. "Is this what you wanted to show me?"

"No," said Tillett. "Turn the page."

Sullivan turned the page and was confronted by a photograph of a face and figure he recognized immediately. "Daisy," he said.

Tillett shook his head. "No, not Daisy. Lady Marguerite Melville, daughter of the Earl of Riddlesdown."

"No. She's the …"

"One and the same," Tillett said. "Didn't you find it strange that the dashing Captain Hazelton turned up at Plymouth to retrieve the two girls?"

Sullivan frowned. Daisy was the daughter of an earl and surely not short of money. So why ...?

April 15, 1912
On Board the Titanic
1:40 a.m. (Ship's Time)

Sullivan stood in the doorway of the first-class smoking room. So this is the famous British stiff upper lip, *he thought as he studied the white-faced young man who steadied himself against the fireplace mantel. He had discarded his life jacket, and he stood very still, looking up at a portrait of an ocean liner steaming into harbor. Sullivan knew who this man was. He was Thomas Andrews, the chief architect of the* Titanic, *who had always accompanied the captain on his daily inspections of the ship, even coming down to the bunker where Sullivan shoveled burning coals. Whatever had happened to the* Titanic, *whatever flaw was now revealed, Andrews was carrying that weight on his shoulders as he quietly prepared to pay the ultimate price for the fact that his ship would never arrive in harbor.*

The smoking room was filled with men. Some still wore life jackets, and many were in formal evening dress, with just a few in their nightclothes. Sullivan imagined that the room contained some of the world's richest men—men who had put the women and children into boats and were now awaiting their fate. Some of them were passing the time drinking; some were gathered together with their heads bowed in prayer; some stood alone, staring into space. Four men were still gambling.

Sullivan hesitated. He was searching for a way to reach the upper deck, and he knew he was close. Possibly the door at the other end of the room would lead him out into the open, but if it did not, he would have to retrace his footsteps, and time was running out. He could feel the deck shifting beneath his feet. Any minute now, the Titanic *was going to take her final dive, and when that happened, he wanted to be out in the open and clinging to something that would float.*

He reached out to steady himself against the doorjamb as someone shoved him from behind. A curly-headed girl in a stewardess uniform rushed past him. Why was she still here? The stewardesses had all been sent to the lifeboats. He watched her as she dashed purposefully across the room. She was a crew member; she knew her way around the ship, and she would know how to reach the upper deck. He made up his mind to follow her.

The girl hesitated beside the table where the four gamblers had suddenly risen to their feet and were swinging wild, drunken punches at each other. For a moment, he thought the girl had somehow been caught up in their fight, but then he saw her dart forward and grab something from the table. He could not resist the sudden urge to laugh. She had stolen the winnings, and now she was running for the door at the other end of the smoking room.

One of the gamblers, obviously not as drunk as his companions, disentangled himself from the fight and set off in pursuit. Sullivan released his hold on the doorjamb. The slope of the deck carried him slipping and sliding downhill. The ship was groaning now, and the remaining gamblers tried and failed to regain their feet as the furniture began to shift. The men who had been playing fell in a heap. Sullivan stumbled forward, pushing aside the world's richest men as they staggered and grasped for handholds. He yanked open the door and found himself, at long last, in the frigid open air.

Sullivan stared down at the picture in the newspaper, resisting the memory of all that had followed. He would concentrate on this one thing. He knew who Daisy was, or so he had thought, and he knew what she had done. He had even tried to protect her from the consequences of her actions. Now he was discovering that she was the daughter of an earl. Why would an earl's daughter be working as a stewardess on the *Titanic*? Why would she steal money? He remembered the night she had sought him out on the *Lapland* and offered … Well, he was not really sure what she had offered, only that he had refused.

His mind was racing. If Daisy was an earl's daughter, then so was her sister. How could he have forgotten his first reaction on hearing Poppy's disdainful rebuke of Miss Stap, the senior stewardess? *My sister is unwell, and she will not be answering any questions.*

In the days that followed, as the *Lapland* had plowed slowly across the Atlantic, he had warmed to the tall girl and even felt sympathy for her. Now he knew her for what she was: the daughter of an earl, laughing behind his back and disdaining him as the descendant of criminals. Despite his disappointment, he could not bring himself to regret helping her when they had arrived in Plymouth. He knew what Daisy had done, but Poppy did not. Aristocrat or not, she did not deserve to be implicated in a crime she had not committed.

"I know a thing or two about that family," Tillett said. "Daisy is the second child, but Poppy, Lady Penelope Melville, is heir presumptive to the title. Unless the earl can produce a boy, Lady Penelope will inherit the title and a pile of Tudor bricks set deep in the Hampshire countryside."

"And yet she was on the *Titanic*, working as a stewardess," Sullivan said.

"Perhaps she shares her sister's ambition," Tillett suggested. "They were working their passage on the *Titanic* as the first step on their journey to California. Lady Daisy wants to be a film star, the next Mary Pickford."

Sullivan nodded. "I know what she wants," he said. He bit back his next remark. *And I know what she's prepared to pay.* "She's a pretty thing," he said aloud, "but mad as a wombat."

Tillett grinned. "Never having encountered a wombat, I'm not quite sure how mad that is."

Sullivan hesitated. "Maybe *mad* is the wrong word. She's cunning, and she will do whatever she can to get her own way."

"And the sister?"

Sullivan shrugged. "Daisy leads her around by the nose."

He set the newspaper down. "Look here, Tillett. I appreciate you putting me up, but I think you're making a mountain out of a molehill. It's possible White Star agents were looking for me when we first landed, but not now. The inquiry is already happening. Everything is out in the open. I have nothing to add."

Tillett shook his head. "I think that you saw something."

"I saw what everyone else saw."

"But you lived to tell of it."

"Tell of what?" Sullivan asked, raising his voice in frustration.

"It has to be something that happened in the engine room,"

Tillett said. "Hundreds of people survived to tell what happened above deck, but only a handful survived from the engine room."

Sullivan closed his eyes as he relived the horror: the icy water pouring into the bunker, the scalding steam, the alarm bell ringing as the watertight doors descended. Hesketh was dead. So was Shepherd.

"I wasn't the only survivor," he said. "The officers died, but Dillon and Barrett survived."

"We can assume that they've been silenced," Tillett said, "or told what to say. You're the problem. Someone is keeping you from leaving the country or speaking freely."

"I'll find a way to leave," Sullivan said defiantly. "I'm going to America."

"Why?"

It was a simple question, and yet Sullivan couldn't answer it. If he spoke the words aloud, Tillett wouldn't understand. Only another Australian would understand.

Tillett was needling him now. "What is so important that you can't stay here and tell the truth? The men who died deserve to be honored. Why can't you do it?"

Sullivan tried to shut out Tillett's words, but he was too late. *The men who died deserve to be honored.* The image of his grandfather, whose grudge had sent him on the long journey from Australia, began to recede and be replaced by the thought of the hell of the engine room, where brave men had suffered and died to buy time for the passengers. He saw them now: Engineer Hesketh reeling in shock as a jet of icy water knocked him off his feet, Engineer Shepherd lying helpless on the deck, and Engineer Harvey grimacing as he watched the laboring pumps. He drew in a sharp breath. He was forgetting something. He remembered the initial overwhelming force of the water, but there was something else.

"What about Hazelton?" Tillett asked.

Sullivan turned on him angrily. He had been on the very edge of remembering something vital. "What about him?" he growled.

"He's not what he seems." Tillett said.

Sullivan tried to return to the moment, but it was gone, replaced by Tillett, who was still talking about Captain Hazelton.

"I don't know why he's involved with the earl's daughters, but I've picked up hints that his time on the North-West Frontier was spent out of uniform."

"Meaning what?"

"I believe that he was working undercover. To put it plainly, he was a spy."

"What does this have to do with me?" Sullivan asked. "There's nothing for him to spy on here."

"I'm not so sure," Tillett said. "Hazelton is working with Clive Bigham, who is also known to listen in corners."

"So they're both spies," Sullivan said impatiently. "How does that help me?"

"Clive Bigham's father is Lord Mersey, who is heading up the *Titanic* inquiry. His son has been acting as secretary of the commission, and he's pulled Captain Hazelton in to work with him. Two spies. I find that interesting."

Sullivan growled impatiently. He had no interest in whatever game the British government was playing. He could see no reason why a man who had been a spy in India would be involved in the sinking of the *Titanic*. He could also see no reason why that same man would have gone to the trouble of meeting the *Lapland* and spiriting away the two daughters of the Earl of Riddlesdown. None of it made sense, but none of it mattered.

"I don't see how this helps me," Sullivan said. "It doesn't explain why I'm being detained here."

Tillett rubbed his hands together. "I think that this disaster is more than an act of God."

"Now you sound like that fool in the newspaper with his wild accusations."

"Well," Tillett said coldly, "I am not a fool, and I am not making accusations. I am trying to help you."

"But—"

Tillett held up a finger to silence him. "I'm on good terms with Captain Hazelton, and I'm in a position to talk to him. I think we should approach him and ask him if he knows what the commission wants from you. I believe he will tell me what he knows. I can talk to him today if you wish."

Sullivan hesitated. Talking to Hazelton would mean another delay. He would have to set aside his plan to attempt to board a train to Dover and a ferry to France.

He felt the sudden intrusion of his grandfather's rasping voice, with its recitation of the injustice that still haunted the family. He heard his own voice, childish at first, promising to bring justice. The promise had been delayed into adulthood. Could it be delayed again?

"It's up to you to put it right. Find that woman and clear my name. Clear the family's name."

The decision came easily. His grandfather had been wronged, but so had the men in the boiler rooms. The old man had lived, but they had not. His promise to his grandfather would keep, but the voices that cried out to him from the scalding horror of the boiler room demanded to be heard now.

He looked at Tillett. "I don't know what they want of me, but I'll talk to them. I'll tell them everything I know."

Kensington Gardens
London
Alvin Towson

Towson counted last night's winnings, decrying the fact that he had not been able to find a high-stakes game. He was a nothing now. Until it was safe to use his own name again, he would have to settle for playing for shillings and half crowns in London's backroom bars. He could not find words to express his frustration. He had been so close. If he had been allowed to go ashore at Plymouth, he would have been able to find her. She could keep the other winnings. The money clips and the gold watches meant nothing, but retrieving the Matryoshka would make the difference between a life in hiding and a return to being one of the high-stakes fraternity, the brotherhood of gamblers who worked the oceangoing liners of the world.

Of course, he knew now that he should never have stopped working his trade on oceangoing liners. If he had not decided to take his chances on land, none of this would have happened. There was something about shipboard life that made a naive man reckless, and thus an easy mark. Perhaps it was the boredom of a long ocean passage, or perhaps it was the feeling that money lost one day could be recouped the next—after all, no one was going anywhere—that persuaded men to bet with money they could not afford to lose.

Towson had turned his back on the ocean and taken rooms in Biarritz in the fall of 1911 on the strength of nothing more than a hunch and boredom with his usual routine. He had picked up a rumor that a killing was to be made at the tables in France, and so that was where he had settled for the winter. It was said that players in the fashionable French resort were being unusually reckless, spurred on by rumors of war, trouble in Mexico, and an American presidential election.

All went well in the beginning, but by March of 1912, he knew he was in deep trouble. The cards were not going his way, and nothing in his very well-stocked bag of tricks would turn them in his favor. He began to throw money about like a rank amateur, always counting on the next deal or roll of the dice to turn his way, and before he knew it, he was as deep in debt as any green college boy on his first outing. And then the threats began to arrive—whispers, then messages, and then the physical presence of men in dark coats. He knew that his credit, and therefore his life, was in the hands of a man who would never allow a debt to go unpaid. The only way to be free of him was to be dead, and that was something the messengers would be happy to arrange as an example to others. Towson needed a great deal of money, and he needed it immediately.

Desperation took him to a rendezvous on a cold, windswept beach with nothing but a handful of seagulls to overhear the whispered words of the informant, and for the first time, he heard of the fabulous Siberian discovery, the Matryoshka.

"Where is it now?"

"It is in the hands of a courier who is taking it to America to sell to a collector, a man who will pay not for its size but because it is unique. It is the only one in the world."

"But why should this interest me?"

" The courier is a big man, monsieur, but he has two weaknesses, vodka and cards, and you are a gambler ..."

Towson shook his head. "Men gamble on impulse. If he has this jewel, he will place it in the purser's safe. He won't gamble with it."

"No, it will not be in the safe. He is instructed to keep it on his person at all times. If he sits at the card table, the jewel will be in his pocket. It will be a temptation, and if you add vodka ... well ..."

"And he sails on the Titanic?"

"Oui, monsieur."

"And you are sure of the value of this jewel?"

"No, monsieur. No one is sure of the value. It is the only one in the world. It is priceless."

All in all, Towson thought as he dressed for the day, the sinking of the *Titanic* had not been such a bad thing for him. People had died, of course, but he had not, and in those last few minutes, as death had stared him in the face, the courier had reached into his vest pocket and pulled out the Matryoshka.

Towson knotted his cravat with care. He dressed for respectability but not for attention. He would attend the inquiry again today, and he should present himself as a safe, reliable, but unremarkable man. Perhaps he had been wrong to keep asking the constable about the expected appearance of the stewardesses. He would not do that again.

He doubted that anyone would discover him in this shabby London backwater, but he would have to surface sometime soon. He could not keep himself alive on penny-ante card games in London's backstreet pubs. His only comfort was that the ignorant stewardess would never discover the true value of the jewel she had stolen. It would take an expert to look beyond the flawed heart of the stone and see what was beneath. The stewardess would probably try to sell it, and he would have to find her before she sold it to some second-rate jeweler who would send it to be recut and polished.

The landlady knocked on his door. Her London accent grated on his ears. "Breakfast, Mr. Rotherhithe, and I brought up your newspaper."

Towson opened the door and stooped to pick up the paper. He studied the headline: white star officers flee ahead of subpoena. He gave a passing thought to the officer who had no doubt saved his life and the lives of all the men who had passed the night on the hull of the upturned collapsible. He had little room in his heart for gratitude, but he thought that Officer Lightoller did not deserve to be disrespected. He was a breed apart who made Towson momentarily ashamed of his own behavior.

He skimmed over the daily twaddle from Interrogantum. Why couldn't the man use his own name? Maybe he was ashamed to be writing such rubbish. Towson thought of sending an anonymous letter to the editor, suggesting that Interrogantum was a meddling fool. With so many new rumors arising every day, it would soon be impossible to discover even a kernel of truth. He paused for a moment to consider that fact. Maybe that was the purpose of the rumors. He shrugged. He had nothing to say and no intention of appearing before the inquiry.

He flipped over to the next page and came close to dropping the newspaper. He turned back into his bedroom and slammed the door behind him. Was this even possible? He took the paper to the window to study it in the morning sunlight.

Socialite Lady Marguerite Melville, daughter of the Earl of Riddlesdown, poses outside the Dulwich Club as she tells of her journey on the Titanic. *"It was all for fun," she says, speaking of her service as a first-class stewardess on the doomed White Star liner.*

Towson flung the newspaper onto the bed and went to the window. His heart was pounding; his stomach was churning. He felt as though his whole being were on fire. He had always been lucky, but never this lucky. He pushed up on the sash window and gulped in cool morning air. He knew her name!

He stepped away from the window. The thief was not an ignorant slut of a girl from the backstreets of Southampton who would not know a diamond from a glass chip; she was an aristocrat. How much would she know about diamonds? She would know enough to recognize that the Matryoshka was a diamond, but would she discard it as flawed? Had she already discarded it or sold it for next to nothing? He had to find her.

London Scottish Drill Hall
Harry Hazelton

Although Shackleton was Harry's friend, and although his appearance at the *Titanic* inquiry had created a storm of interest, Harry was growing impatient.

It's not enough, he thought. Questions were posed and replies were received without emotion. Even Shackleton was finding it impossible to stir the lawyers into righteous anger. Reports from the American inquiry described US senators expressing fury and disbelief at what they heard. They were not expert seamen, but they knew enough to know when something was very wrong.

Unfortunately, the lawyers holding court in the Drill Hall showed no such indignation. They would take a witness and pose the same question a dozen different ways and would then quarrel with each other as to their understanding of the answer, and then one of them would simply ask the question again. This process was repeated endlessly as each lawyer attempted to gain an advantage for the party he represented.

Shackleton fidgeted in his seat as he was asked yet again if he thought it wise to slow down in an area of icebergs.

"I would take the ordinary precaution of slowing down whether I was in a ship equipped for ice or any other, compatible with keeping steerageway for the size of the ship."

"You would slow down?"

"I would slow down, yes."

"And supposing you were going twenty-one to twenty-two knots, I suppose that would be the better reason for slowing down?"

Shackleton's voice crackled. "You have no right to go at that speed in an ice zone."

Lord Mersey looked down from his high seat. "And you think that all these liners are wrong in going at this speed in regions where ice has been reported?"

"I think the possibility of accident is greatly enhanced by the speed the ship goes."

A buzz of conversation drowned out the questions that followed as the lawyers moved in to parse Shackleton's response and apply it to their own individual interests. Inquiries on both sides of the Atlantic had focused on the speed the *Titanic* was making on the night she had struck the iceberg, the reason for the speed, and who had ordered the speed. Shackleton was now suggesting that all ships should reduce their speed. He had already told the inquiry that his ship would do no more than four knots in an ice region. He'd certainly given them something to think about. Some of them would be wishing they had not asked him to appear. Shackleton's opinion carried weight, but no shipping line could make a profit creeping timidly across the Atlantic at four knots.

Harry was already on his feet when he saw that he was not the only person about to leave. A man had risen from a seat in the front row and was making his way to the back of the hall. Harry recognized him immediately as one of the reporters he had seen in Plymouth. He thought back to that overheard breakfast conversation. Charlie had been the reporter with the large stomach and a vestige of conscience about printing outright lies. The man now leaving the room was Dan, the reporter who had been Charlie's companion.

He assumed that Dan was on his way to report the latest speculations to Interrogantum. He wondered what the persistent rumormonger would make of Shackleton's statements.

Are transatlantic ships to be limited to four knots per hour?

Will this be the end of British shipping?

Did Titanic *captain ignore the advice of a polar hero?*

Harry stepped out, closed the door behind him, and retreated to his office. He sighed as he looked at the stack of crew depositions. He had now read every word of every deposition many times over. He had read them so frequently that he felt he could recite some of the evidence by heart, and yet he still did not know what he was looking for. Added to the confusion was the fact that some of the crewmen who had been detained in the United States had now returned to England and were adding their own memories to the sworn statements. The tragedy itself was still feeding newspaper headlines, but time was passing. Almost a month had gone by, and with every day that passed, each witness that faced the Wreck Commissioner added another layer of confusion.

Facts that had seemed indisputable were now in dispute as memory faded and made its own preferred alterations. Even the instructions given at the moment of impact were under question. Had Murdoch's order of "hard a-starboard" been misinterpreted by Hichens at the wheel? Had it even been a wrong order?

As time wore on, the surviving crewmen grew irritable and unresponsive, unable to answer the endless questions of what they had or had not done as their lives had hung in the balance. No, they did not know what officer had given what order. They could not say how many ladies had refused to get in the lifeboats. They could not say what the captain had been doing—they had not seen him.

Lord Mersey, in his high seat, dignified and distant, seemed unaware that the witnesses brought before him were suffering mentally and physically. Harry had seen the same behavior in his own men after battle. The mind can only absorb so much horror before it begins to build protective walls around the worst of the memories. A year after the event, Harry knew that he had an incomplete memory of the boar hunt that had cost him his career. As for his memory of the birth of the general's son, that wall was growing higher and wider every day. He could no longer see Eloise as he had first seen her, an English rose beneath an Indian sun. All that was left was a fading watercolor of a woman whose eyes were forever closed.

Harry picked up the morning paper to see what questions Interrogantum was already asking. Bigham read the *Daily Mail*; Lord Mersey read *The Times*; but Harry preferred the *Daily Inquirer* for the sake of Interrogantum. He already knew that at least one of the two reporters he'd overheard in Plymouth was feeding information to the unknown columnist, and he wondered how many more aspiring reporters were feeding Interrogantum's rumor mill.

He glanced at the headline: WHITE STAR OFFICERS FLEE AHEAD OF SUBPOENA. He felt a stab of sympathy for the men who had already faced the US inquiry. He understood the burden of command. He studied Interrogantum's questions of the day. Today Interrogantum had Captain Lord of the Leyland liner *Californian* in his sights. The Americans had already lined up enough evidence to say that the *Californian* had been the ship closest to the *Titanic*. She had been so close that her lights had been seen from the deck of the sinking ship, and they had confirmation that the *Titanic*'s lights had been seen by the *Californian*'s crew and reported to Captain Lord. The captain had, apparently, responded by going to bed and sleeping peacefully all night. Now Interrogantum was asking if Captain Lord had been instructed to stay away. Had he been told to linger on the horizon and make sure that the *Titanic* went down with no survivors? Harry smiled. That was one of the questions he'd overheard Dan asking in the breakfast room at the Duke of Cornwall Hotel.

"Why would White Star have a ship waiting just over the horizon?"

"What ship?"

"There was a ship. The survivors saw its lights. It didn't approach. It just waited."

Interrogantum's timing was perfect. Tomorrow Captain Stanley Lord would appear in front of Lord Mersey to explain why the *Californian* had not moved. He had already been destroyed in the American newspapers, and now the British papers would have their turn, and the *Daily Inquirer* had already made a start.

Harry stopped reading when the door opened and Clive Bigham strolled in.

"Morning, Hazelton. What does Interrogantum have for us today?"

"I thought you only read the *Daily Mail*."

"I only *buy* the *Daily Mail*. Don't want to be seen buying the

Inquirer, but I'm not above reading it."

"It's nothing new," Harry said. "Rumors about Captain Lord of the *Californian*."

"The man's a sniveling coward afraid to move in the ice," Bigham said, "but that's not why I came to see you. You have a visitor, a man with a dueling scar on his face. Says his name is Sullivan."

"Sullivan?" Harry queried. "Is he an Australian?"

"Yes."

"He was a fireman on the *Titanic*," Harry said.

"Yes, I know. In fact, we've been looking for him. He failed to give us a deposition in Plymouth, and he failed to pick up his pay. We lost track of him in Southampton and—"

"Do you mean that you were following him?"

"Yes."

"Why?"

"He was in a boiler room very close to the point of impact. We would like to know what he saw."

"And he didn't want to tell you?" Harry asked.

"No, he didn't, but he may have told someone else," Bigham said. "He's got some money from somewhere, and he's spent it on dressing like a gentleman."

Harry thought back to the moment on the train when Sullivan had given Poppy his address.

"It's the address of his bank."

"I don't think he needs anyone's money," Harry said.

"Well, we'll soon find out," Bigham said. "He's waiting in the lobby." He turned toward the door and then stopped. He laughed. "Well, apparently, he's not waiting. He's here."

Ernie Sullivan appeared in the doorway. His hands were no longer bandaged, and he was wearing a dark suit, a high starched collar, and a paisley waistcoat. His neatly trimmed beard and mustache did little to conceal his most prominent feature—the scar. Now that Bigham had pointed it out, Harry could see the possibility that the slash was a dueling scar or a sword stroke and not just the result of a barroom brawl. He agreed with Bigham that Sullivan now looked like a gentleman, but there was no escaping the fact that he still looked dangerous.

Surprise brought him to his feet. He had not expected to see

Sullivan again, and certainly not like this. He was about to extend his hand when Sullivan dropped a copy of the *Daily Inquirer* onto the desktop.

"Have you seen this?"

Harry nodded. "I read it every day. I know a little about where he's getting his information."

"Who?"

"Interrogantum."

Sullivan retrieved the newspaper impatiently. "I'm not talking about that troublemaking fool." He opened the paper and stabbed his finger down on a photograph. "I'm talking about her!"

Harry stared down at a picture of Daisy Melville posing provocatively outside the Dulwich Club.

Sullivan looked from Harry to Bigham and then back to the picture. "That young lady is in more trouble than she knows. I know you want something from me, and I want something from you. I want an assurance that Daisy will be protected, and in return I'll give you my deposition."

Bigham shook his head. "It doesn't work like that. First, you tell us what you know. Then you tell us why she needs to be protected, and then I'll tell you whether she'll be protected."

Sullivan scowled. "Call off your watchdogs, and I'll protect her myself."

Harry studied the two men, who bristled at each other like fighting dogs. He stepped forward and extended a hand to Sullivan. "Will my word be sufficient?"

CHAPTER FOURTEEN

London Scottish Drill Hall
Harry Hazelton

Sullivan's face underwent a physical change as he told his story. His eyes were shadowed, and his expression was distant. Harry could not even imagine the horror of the memories that must have surfaced with every word the Australian uttered.

The story was not what he had expected. With the newspaper opened to the picture of Daisy Melville, Sullivan spoke impatiently, and Harry began to understand why Daisy needed protection.

Sullivan described what he had seen in the first-class smoking room: some men drinking, some praying, and four men engaged in a drunken brawl over a game of cards. Harry would find the story hard to believe except for the fact that he had witnessed Daisy's impulsiveness at first hand. *No, not just impulsive—reckless and greedy.* He had seen the decaying splendor of Riddlesdown Court for himself and witnessed the earl's disdain for the welfare of his daughters, so perhaps he should not be surprised to find Daisy grasping for any money that would help her run from her home.

It would require a cool head and a ruthless determination to steal from drunken, angry men so far gone in their gambling fever that they did not even care that the ship was sinking beneath them.

"She grabbed the winnings and took off," Sullivan said, "and the man with the pistol—it was a Mauser—took off after her. The other men were drunk, but I don't think he was. He was sober enough to know what she was doing."

"Spunky little minx," Bigham said with a flash of a smile showing beneath his mustache. "I thought she was quite a goer."

Sullivan cast an unfriendly look in Bigham's direction and

continued with his story. "I lost sight of Daisy and the gambler once I was out on the boat deck. They were loading the last of the lifeboats with women and children. I assumed Daisy went looking for a boat, but I don't know what happened to the man who was following her."

Harry glanced at the pile of depositions. "Well, that explains something," he said. "It's obvious that Daisy was not telling the truth in her deposition; now I know why."

"Did you know she was a thief?" Bigham asked.

Harry shook his head. "No, of course not. I knew nothing about any of what Sullivan is telling us, but I knew she was lying in her deposition. She says that she was in lifeboat four with Mrs. Astor, but no one remembers her being there. Of course, it was dark by then, with just starlight—"

"I know," Sullivan growled. "You don't have to remind me. I was there."

"And you didn't see her get into a lifeboat?" Bigham asked.

"I've already told you that I don't know where she went. Once it was obvious that there were not enough lifeboats, it was chaos. The captain said it was every man for himself, and that's what it was."

"What did you do?" Bigham asked.

"I went over the side without a boat," Sullivan said grimly. "All I had was a piece of floating wreckage. I think it was the remains of a staircase. There was nothing to hold on to, and my hands were burned. I was almost done when Lowe came along and picked me up. Everything after that is a blur. I only vaguely remember Lowe gathering the boats together and moving people around to even out the numbers. I know Daisy was in one of those boats, because Poppy found her. Poppy was … she was kind … and …"

Sullivan fell silent, seemingly lost in thought.

Bigham broke the silence. "We made a deal," he said. "You tell us what you know, and we—"

"I'm telling you what I know," Sullivan snapped. "Lowe was moving people around. I was next to Poppy, although I suppose that's not her real name … Anyway, I was next to her and heard her calling out to her sister. I don't see that any of this matters. Obviously, the girl got herself into a boat one way or another, but what about the man who was chasing her? If he's alive—"

"He's alive," Harry said with sudden certainty, "and he's looking for her."

Bigham frowned at him. "How do you know?"

"I was told yesterday that a man has been hanging around the Drill Hall and asking when the stewardesses will be giving their testimony." He looked at Sullivan. "The constable pointed him out to me. Red face, protruding eyes, bald head. Is that him?"

"I don't know. Do you think I took time to study his face?"

He's not just worried, Harry thought. *He's furious. He can barely hold it in.*

When he had met Sullivan on the train in Southampton, he had not given this same impression of anger boiling just below the surface. In Southampton he'd seemed full of devil-may-care jauntiness, winking at Daisy, declaring he did not want to be paid, and then giving Poppy the address of his bank. He was different now. Something was frustrating him, and it was not the fact that the girls he'd flirted with had turned out to be the daughters of an aristocrat.

Harry gestured to the newspaper. "Daisy's picture in the paper changes everything."

"That's what I'm trying to tell you," Sullivan hissed. "He won't need to hang around in London, waiting for the stewardesses to show up. He can go straight to her father's castle."

"It's not a castle," Harry said, "but you're right. She'll be easy to find."

Bigham leaned back in his chair. "She's a little firecracker, isn't she? What do you think she stole?"

"What does it matter?" Sullivan asked.

Bigham ignored him. "It has to be something more than money or a couple of gold watches," he said. "The transatlantic trade attracts gamblers. All the shipping companies put out notices to passengers, warning them not to engage in games of chance, but it makes no difference. The professionals know they can find easy targets on board, so they buy themselves a first-class ticket and start making friends." He shook his head. "Your average gambler would be glad to have got off the *Titanic* alive, and he'd write off the loss and wait for the dust to settle. He would not take the next boat back to England and start a search for his lost winnings. There's something more behind this. Lady Daisy has something he really wants."

Sullivan scowled. "I didn't look. I just gave it back to her. Are you going to do something about this gambler or not?"

Harry wondered how long it would be before Sullivan took a swing at someone. He had no doubt that he and Bigham between them could hold him off, but he wished he knew what lay behind Sullivan's angry impatience.

Bigham either had not noticed or did not care that the Australian's anger teetered on a knife edge. "You gave it back to her?" he queried. "What do you mean?"

Sullivan's eyes slid sideways as he realized what he had said. He looked at Harry. "Plymouth," he explained. "There was talk of searching Daisy's bag, and so I helped her out. I didn't want to see her accused of stealing. I don't want to see anyone accused of stealing. I know about the English idea of justice."

Harry thought he could detect a lifetime of meaning behind Sullivan's statement, but now was not the time to explore it.

"So you had your hands on the winnings?" Bigham asked.

"I returned them."

"And you've no idea what you were holding."

Sullivan shook his head. "It was knotted into a handkerchief. If I had to guess, I'd say some paper money, and maybe a couple of watches."

"So nothing of real value?" Bigham asked.

Sullivan ignored him and turned to Harry. "Are you going to do something about this? Are you going to warn them, or do I have to do it myself?"

Harry thought of the family at Riddlesdown Court, a couple of little girls, a pregnant woman, old Nanny Catchpole, and the earl himself, oblivious to everything except his desire for a son. Maybe they employed an estate worker or two—the big house would not take care of itself. The village was at least a mile away and probably contained nothing more dangerous than a flat-footed village policeman and a couple of poachers. Sullivan was right. They had to be warned. In fact, the whole family should be removed to a safer place.

"We'll telephone them," Bigham said magnanimously, "just as soon as you finish telling us everything you know."

Sullivan fixed Harry with a furious stare. "You gave me your word."

"And my word is good," Harry said. "Let's be practical. The first thing is to warn them."

"Use the telephone," Bigham said.

"I'm not sure we can," Harry said. He searched his memory. Had he seen a telephone at Riddlesdown Court? Nanny Catchpole had used a telephone to phone the Bishop of Fordingbridge, which meant a telephone existed somewhere nearby. He thought back to his meeting with the earl's pregnant wife. The parlor had shown the same signs of neglect as everything else at Riddlesdown Court, and he was quite certain that the few lighting fixtures were gas-mantle lamps and not the new electric lights. Was it possible to have a telephone if the house had no electricity? Perhaps the earl, who showed every sign of being as self-centered as his daughter Daisy, had electric lights installed in his study or his bedroom, or perhaps Nanny Catchpole had taken herself down to the village post office to make her call.

Bigham leaned back in his chair, regarding Sullivan through half-closed eyes. He did not shift his gaze as he spoke to Harry. "There is such a thing as a telephone directory," he said.

Harry knew he should not be hesitating, but he was painfully aware that he did not know what to do. He had been away from Europe and London for a long time. The business he conducted on behalf of the British Empire had taken him to small, hidden corners of bazaars and taverns, where messages were written in code or whispered in ears and not shouted down telephones. He knew that the garrison office in Lucknow was equipped with telephones, but an officer wishing to make a telephone call simply told a desk wallah to do whatever was necessary.

Harry imagined that hundreds, maybe thousands of telephones were being operated at this moment in London. Of course there would have to be a directory. On the other hand, Riddlesdown Court was not in London.

His response was driven by nothing but wounded pride. "Riddlesdown Court is in Hampshire. I don't think it will be covered by the London directory."

Bigham shrugged. "Maybe not. You could try sending a telegram."

"I assume that a telegram would be delivered to the earl," Harry said defensively, "and I doubt he would do anything."

He imagined the earl shredding the telegram and sending the telegraph boy on his way with a clip round the ear. Did the earl even remember or care what his daughters had been doing on the *Titanic?*

An uncomfortable silence settled over the room, and Harry knew he was failing. He had given his word to Sullivan, but this went beyond his word. He knew that he would never forgive himself if anything happened to the family at Riddlesdown Court simply because he did not know how to function without the help of a desk wallah to make a phone call.

"You could call your club," Bigham said. "I'm sure they have a list of members and—"

"Of course," Harry interrupted, feeling the wheels of his mind beginning to turn. "They can give me the number for their uncle, the Bishop of Fordingbridge. He'll know how to reach them."

"Bloody Pommies," Sullivan said furiously. "Go ahead. Just sit there on your arses. I'll take care of it myself."

Bigham sat up straight, no longer languid and disinterested. "Be very careful, Mr. Sullivan. We bloody Pommies don't take kindly to insults. Captain Hazelton will take care of this matter. The young ladies are none of your concern."

Harry was silently cursing the wild boar that had savaged his leg and sent him home to live in a civilian world he no longer understood. He should be buttoning his uniform and calling for his horse and a squad of native soldiers. At the very least, he should be sprinting to the train station to catch the first train to Winchester, instead of which he was fussing around with telephone numbers. He was a soldier, not a damned telephone operator.

Bigham was still speaking. "We made a deal. Hazelton takes care of the problem with your lady friends, and you tell me what you know."

"I've told you."

"You've told me about Daisy. You haven't told me about yourself. You haven't told me what you did."

Sullivan rested his hands on the arms of Bigham's chair and loomed over him. "What I did?" he repeated. "I bloody nearly drowned. That's what I did."

Bigham did not move, did not even blink. Harry waited for the inevitable explosion of fury, not sure which one would throw the first punch. He did not have time for this. A thought began to grow in the back of his mind, something that would break the impasse. He teased at the memory, and there it was.

"Sullivan."

The Australian kept his eyes on Bigham. "What?"

"You were hired on in the black gang."

"So what?"

"Shoveling burning coal," Harry said. "That's how you burned your hands."

Sullivan eased back, although his gaze was still locked on Bigham.

Harry took a step forward. He knew! At long last, after days of reading depositions, he had found an answer. Why hadn't he realized what Arthur Scarrott had been saying?

"Sometimes a bunker will be on fire, and if the ship's in a hurry to leave, you have to get a black gang to come on board and shovel it."

"Shovel it where? Over the side?"

"Lord love you, no! How would you do that? No, best thing to do is to shovel it into the furnaces."

Harry looked at Bigham, who reluctantly turned toward him as Sullivan took a step back.

"You were with me," Harry said. "We talked to a seaman and asked him about a black gang. Do you remember?"

Bigham's voice was cold. "I remember."

"So according to Mr. Sullivan, one of the coal bunkers on the *Titanic* was on fire before she left Southampton," Harry said, "and White Star hired a last-minute crew to take care of it."

Bigham shrugged. "I don't see—"

"It's impossible to shovel the burning coal over the side, so it has to be shoveled into the furnace," Harry said. "Is that what you were doing, Mr. Sullivan?"

Sullivan nodded.

"And you were still shoveling when the *Titanic* entered the Labrador Current?"

"Yeah, bloody oath we were."

" So," Harry said, "according to Shackleton's testimony, when they crossed out of the Gulf Stream and into the Labrador Current, any competent captain would know that icebergs were a possibility, but what should they do about the burning bunker? If the black gang stopped shoveling, the fire could spread and burn out of control. The only alternative was to keep up the *Titanic*'s speed and keep shoveling. You want to know why they were doing twenty-two knots in the ice field? That's the reason why."

Bigham looked at Sullivan. "Is this true?"

"It's true I was shoveling," Sullivan said. "The fire in bunker six was barely contained."

"And you say you went aboard in Southampton?" Bigham confirmed.

Sullivan nodded.

"And the fire was already burning?"

"It was."

Harry looked at Bigham. "How in the hell did White Star get a certificate of seaworthiness while there was a fire in the bunker?".

"Don't waste your time asking him," Sullivan said. "We already know the answer." His anger was visibly fading, replaced by understanding. "That's why they've been looking for me. Someone is trying to silence me."

"Who?" Harry asked.

Sullivan shrugged and gestured to Bigham. "Don't ask me. Ask him."

Bigham curled his upper lip as he spoke. "You failed to give your deposition and pick up your pay. It was a matter of record-keeping, that's all. We had no idea that—"

"That what?" Sullivan asked. "No idea that the ship was on fire?"

Bigham remained silent.

The scar tugged at the corner of Sullivan's mouth as he returned Bigham's disdainful expression. "Your inquiry is a sham, and I won't be involved. Maybe the Americans will reach the truth, but you never will, because you don't want to. You have my deposition. Do what you like with it. You can call off your watchdogs. I've said my piece."

Bigham remained silent, and Sullivan turned to Harry. "I believe I'm free to leave now, so I'm coming with you. You need all the help you can get."

Riddlesdown Court
Poppy Melville

Poppy followed Daisy up the carved oak Tudor staircase and across the landing toward the bedroom they shared. The voices of her sisters drifted up from the breakfast room. Neither Nanny Catchpole nor Agnes had been present at breakfast, and the unsupervised girls were now giggling wildly.

Daisy paused to listen. "So where is our beloved stepmother?"

"Maybe she's still in bed."

"Maybe she's too fat to stand up," Daisy said.

According to Nanny Catchpole, the child could come any day now, and Agnes was not feeling well. The old lady had already taken Poppy aside.

"It won't be much longer. Will you mind if it's a boy to take your inheritance?"

Poppy shook her head violently. "If it's a boy, I will dance for joy."

"You really don't want to be the countess?"

Poppy hugged her old nanny. "No, I don't. I'm tired of seeing disappointment on his face every time he looks at me."

Nanny Catchpole returned Poppy's hug. "God bless you, poppet. It hurts me to see the way he treats you."

Poppy looked into the old woman's eyes and saw her own unhappiness mirrored there. "When I was on the Titanic—*"*

"Oh, don't talk about it," Nanny Catchpole said. "It's too awful to think about."

"Before the sinking," Poppy continued, "when we were looking forward to New York, I realized that I was happy. We were going to California, and we were never coming back. I knew I wouldn't be a film star—that was Daisy's dream—but I felt light and free." She waved a hand to encompass the dusty vastness of the Tudor building. "I can't ever be what my father wants, so why should I stay here?"

Nanny Catchpole took a step back and studied Poppy. "You won't run away again, will you? You won't leave without saying goodbye."

"If Daisy—"

"No, don't say that. You can't stop Lady Daisy doing whatever she wants, but you don't have to go along with it."

"If I'm not with her, she'll get into all kinds of trouble."

"You being there won't make any difference," Nanny Catchpole said. "That girl was born for trouble."

Poppy was thoughtful as she followed Daisy up the stairs. For the first time, she had put her thoughts into words. If she knew for certain that she would inherit the estate, perhaps she would find pleasure in planning for the future. She had so many ideas on how the land could be improved and how the tenant farmers could be encouraged, but it was a waste of time for her even to suggest them. Her father would never listen to her, and he could not bear the thought of her being his heir.

Daisy turned on the top step. Her mouth was set in a sullen pout. "I asked for coffee, and they don't have any."

"We've never had coffee before."

"That's what I mean," Daisy said. "We're different now. We've seen the world."

"We've seen the Atlantic," Poppy said, "but not much of anything else."

"We should be given coffee," Daisy insisted. "We're not children, and so what if Father hates coffee? It doesn't mean we all have to hate it."

Daisy stepped into the bedroom and shook dust from the moth-eaten bed curtains. "I'm not going to live like this. Even working on the *Titanic* was better than staying here in this moldering ruin." Her eyes took on a faraway, dreamy expression. "It was clean, and everything was new." She flopped down onto her bed, raising a small cloud of dust as she flung out her arms. "I can't stay here another moment."

Poppy opened the windows to let in the cool air of a cloudy May morning. "We can't leave yet. We should wait until the baby's born and until we know if it's a boy."

"It's not going to make any difference," Daisy said petulantly.

"If it's a girl, Father will have to try again." She paused and threw a disgusted look at Poppy. "Can you even imagine?" she asked.

"Father and Agnes making babies. Oh, it's too awful to think about."

"Then don't think about it," Poppy said.

Daisy shivered. "I've already thought, and I can't get the picture out of my mind. It's disgusting."

"You shouldn't be having those kinds of thoughts," Poppy said. "What happens between Father and Agnes is private."

Daisy laughed. "It may be private, but we know what it is. We both had Nanny's lecture about where babies come from. I haven't been able to look at Agnes the same way since. It's disgusting."

"If we all thought like that," Poppy said, "there would never be any babies."

Daisy waved a dismissive hand. "I don't mean that the whole

thing is disgusting. I was just thinking of Father and Agnes. They're so old and ugly. I'm sure it's very different when the man is, well ... you know." She gave Poppy a sly glance. "Someone like Captain Hazelton."

Poppy felt the blush rising in her cheeks.

"Or Sullivan," Daisy said. "That scar on his face is very intriguing, don't you think?"

"No, I don't."

"What about Captain Bigham? He was very dashing, wasn't he?"

"You shouldn't be thinking that way about men."

Daisy laughed. "Why not? Don't you ever wonder what it will be like?"

Poppy shook her head, and Daisy laughed again. "Yes, you do. I saw you when we were at the Dulwich Club. Every time Captain Hazelton looked at you, your face turned bright red. You even blushed when Captain Bigham looked at you. So which one is it?"

"It's not anyone," Poppy said. "I'm not thinking about marriage."

"And I'm not talking about marriage," Daisy said. "Who said you have to be married?"

"Daisy!"

"If I'm going to be a movie star, I will have to do a lot more than blush and giggle," Daisy said.

Poppy stared down at her sister, and Daisy stared back. She pressed a finger to her cheek and fluttered her eyelashes. "Sullivan knows what I mean."

"Sullivan! You didn't ... you wouldn't ..."

"No, I didn't. He wasn't interested, or he was too much of a gentleman. I thought he would jump at the chance. I really did. I wanted him to help me get on the next boat back to America, and I offered to ... well, anyway, I offered, and he wouldn't do it. Maybe he has his eye on you."

Poppy's heart jumped, and a little flutter of warmth expanded somewhere deep inside her in a way that was totally inappropriate for the daughter of an earl. The idea that Daisy had actually approached a man and offered ... Poppy's mind skipped away from whatever Daisy had offered, but the thought would not stay away. She could not do what Daisy had done and offer herself to a man, but what if a man approached her? What if Captain Hazelton ... She shook her head. She sensed that the captain was carrying a great weight of sadness. Something was preventing him from moving forward. She could not tell what was under his stiff exterior. As for Sullivan, like all men, he had spent most of his time looking at Daisy. However, there had been moments when she had found herself trapped by his gray-eyed gaze and wishing that she knew what he was thinking. The scar pulling at his mouth had made his expression unreadable, but she liked to believe that there was kindness behind his enigmatic expression.

"You're lucky Mr. Sullivan turned you down," she said, replacing her inappropriate thoughts with a renewed anger at Daisy. "You can't behave like that, Daisy. What if you become pregnant?"

"I'm sure there are ways to avoid that," Daisy replied.

"Do you know what they are?"

"No, but I'll have to find out, because I intend to become scandalous just as soon as I have the opportunity. I am not going to bury myself down here in the countryside while Agnes has one baby after another. I haven't changed my mind. I'm going to be a star. If you won't come with me to California, I'll go on my own."

"What will you use for money?"

"You know what I'll use."

Poppy's heart sank as she tried once again to persuade Daisy to part with the stolen money. "It's stealing, Daisy."

"How can I steal something that's already stolen? That man was cheating. They all said he was."

"But that doesn't mean the money is yours."

Daisy sat up, hugging her knees and looking at Poppy with eyes that were suddenly glacial. Her voice was cold. "It's mine because I say it's mine. I don't have to return it to anyone, because there is no one! Why can't you understand? They're all dead, Poppy. It's just as much mine as anyone else's."

"You could give it to a charity," Poppy suggested. "There's a fund for the widows and orphans of the *Titanic* crew. You know they need the money more than we do."

"That's not true. We need money just as much as anyone else. Father doesn't give us money, and we can't leave until we can buy our tickets. I'm not working as a stewardess again. The money is mine, Poppy, because I risked my life to get it. I'm keeping it, so stop telling me to give it away."

"But, Daisy—"

"But, Daisy," Daisy repeated in a mocking tone. "Just stop it, Poppy. You like the clothes I bought, don't you?"

Poppy was still ashamed of the pleasure she had taken in the beautiful blue hat and coat. She fought against the memory of how elegant she had felt shopping in Harrods and how pleased she had been on seeing her own reflection in the department store mirrors. She was overwhelmed with guilt knowing that the new clothes were still hanging in her wardrobe. She should give them away. Perhaps someone in the village would like to have them. No, that was ridiculous. They would not fit any of the sturdy young women who lived in the village.

Daisy bounced off the bed and pulled open the top drawer of her dresser. She set the knotted handkerchief on the bed. "I really don't want to go on my own," she said, "so here's what I suggest. We should keep the money, because no one can possibly know who that belongs to, but I'll let you sell the ugly diamond necklace. It has to be worth something."

"What ugly diamond necklace?" Poppy asked.

Daisy tightened her grip on the handkerchief. "First you have to agree that you will stop asking me about the money, because if you don't agree, I am going to take everything and disappear in the middle of the night. If I do that, the widows and orphans will have nothing."

"It's wrong," Poppy insisted.

Daisy grinned at her. "Take it or leave it."

"Let me see the necklace."

Daisy unknotted the handkerchief, opened a small velvet bag, and lifted out a chain with a diamond pendant. "It's a big stone," she said, "but there's something wrong with it. Take it over to the window and look. It doesn't sparkle. Maybe it's not even a diamond."

Poppy carried the necklace to the window. The stone was square and had been cut with only rudimentary facets. Although Poppy was no expert on diamonds, she had on occasion seen Agnes wearing the Riddlesdown heirloom jewelry. The small collection of necklaces and bracelets was of very little interest to Poppy, and she had never worn any of the pieces. The jewelry would be worn by her brother's wife, if she ever had a brother, and in the meantime, it was worn by Agnes on the rare occasions that she and the earl attended a formal function.

The stone in her hand was larger than any stone in the Riddlesdown collection, but it lacked sparkle. The light caught the facets that carved the stone into a square, but the center was dull. The setting was simple and did nothing to enhance whatever qualities the diamond did possess.

Poppy stared down at the smeared center of the stone. The sun broke through the clouds and sent a ray of light onto her hand. Poppy squinted and peered at the flaw in the stone and found that she was looking through the diamond—no, not through, *into*. She was looking into the diamond and seeing something at the center. She gave the pendant a tentative shake and thought she detected movement. Something was moving and rattling inside the stone.

She turned to Daisy. "Come and look at this. There's something inside here."

"No, there's not. What do you mean?"

"I don't know what I mean. Just come and look."

Daisy bounced off the bed and joined her at the window.

"Listen," Poppy said. "If I shake it, I can hear something rattling inside."

Daisy shook her head. "I didn't hear anything."

"If you hold it in the light, you can see there's something inside."

"It's a flaw," Daisy said. "That's why I don't think it's worth anything."

"And that's why you said I could have it?" Poppy asked.

"You could take it to a jeweler. Maybe it could be cut into smaller stones." Daisy shrugged. "It's up to you. You can have it because I'm keeping the rest. That's what we agreed."

Before Poppy could respond, the bedroom door opened with a bang, and Dianna, their half sister, strode into the room with a look of disgust on her face.

"He's coming," she said.

"Who is coming?" Poppy asked.

Dianna, forgetting her errand, stared distractedly at Poppy's hand. "What is that?"

Poppy closed her hand over the flawed jewel. Dianna turned her attention to Daisy. "Why is there money all over your bed? Is that what you earned when you ran away?"

"Mind your own business," Daisy said. "What do you want? You know you're not allowed to come in here."

"He's coming," Dianna repeated.

"Who?"

"The baby. Our brother. Agnes is making a terrible fuss just like last time, and Nanny sent me to tell you that you have to go to fetch the doctor."

"We're not errand boys," Daisy said. "The gardener can go."

"He's not here. Nanny says you must go."

Poppy slipped the diamond pendant into her pocket and studied Dianna's face. "Are you telling us the truth?"

Dianna's answer was preempted by a woman's scream from along the upstairs corridor, followed by the earl's thunderous complaining voice. "Will someone go and fetch the damned doctor!"

"He's very angry," Dianna said.

Poppy sympathized with the girl. The atmosphere in the house was taut with anticipation, and Poppy knew from repeated experience the terrible wrath that would accompany the birth of another daughter.

"He's not angry with you," Poppy said.

"I know," Dianna said spitefully. "He's angry with you for being a girl, because if you'd been a boy, none of this would be happening, and we could all be happy. That's what I heard."

Poppy stared down at the girl, completely lost for words.

Dianna tossed her head carelessly. "What did you put in your pocket?"

Daisy reached out and took hold of a handful of Dianna's hair, turning the girl's face away from Poppy. "Mind your own business. Nasty things happen to nosy little girls."

"I'll tell Nanny."

"Nanny's too busy to listen to you."

"I'll tell Father."

"Good luck with that," Daisy said as she gripped Dianna's shoulders and propelled her toward the door. "Father doesn't care what we do. Now go. Go on, get out of here, and tell Nanny that we're going to fetch the doctor."

Poppy waited to speak until the door closed behind their reluctant sister. "Why did you say that? It's not like you to offer to be an errand boy. We should have a telephone."

"I'm sure we'll get a gold-plated one," Daisy said, "just as soon as Father gets the boy he wants. Everything will change if it's a boy."

Poppy realized that her hands were trembling. *What if it isn't?*

Daisy tugged on her arm. "Hurry up. We'll take the shortcut through King Henry's Wood, and we'll be there in no time."

Poppy spoke her doubts aloud. "What if it's not a boy?"

"That's why we're leaving," Daisy said, "and that's why we're willing to be errand boys. We don't want to be here when he finds out. We'll tell the doctor to come, but I'm not coming back until it's all over." She gathered up the pile of money and winked at Poppy. "Or maybe I'm never coming back."

The door opened again, and Dianna approached cautiously, keeping one eye on Daisy. "Poppy, Nanny says to come now. Something has gone wrong, and you have to help."

"Tell her not to worry," Poppy said. "Daisy and I are going to fetch the doctor."

"She says to come now."

"I don't know anything about babies," Poppy argued, "and—"

Her words were cut short by the sudden appearance of the earl himself, standing in the doorway with a face like thunder.

"Where's the damned doctor?"

Poppy stared at her father in shock. He rarely even spoke to her, and he had certainly never appeared in her bedroom. Although the earl radiated hostility, she was surprised to find that she was not afraid of him. After the sinking of the *Titanic* and all that had followed, she thought it possible she would never be afraid again. She had coped with the icy Atlantic; she could cope with her father.

"We're going now," she said.

The earl shook his head. "Not you," he said. He pointed at Daisy. "That one goes."

"I have a name," Daisy said, and Poppy realized that Daisy was not afraid or even intimidated. When they left Riddlesdown and boarded the *Titanic*, they had left their old selves behind, and now they were home again, they had not fallen back into fearing their father.

"I don't care about your damned name," the earl said. "Go and fetch the doctor."

"What's happened?" Poppy asked.

Her father's voice was angry but tinged with panic. "Don't know. That Catchpole woman slammed the door in my face. Told me I couldn't come in. Told me to get the doctor." He ran a hand through his sparse ginger hair and glowered at Poppy. "Told me to fetch you."

"But I don't know anything about babies," Poppy said.

"And I'm not a damned errand boy," the earl replied. He turned to Daisy. "So you, missy, do as you're told, and go and fetch the doctor."

"We're going," Daisy said. She gave Poppy a pleading look as she picked up the knotted handkerchief and dropped it into her purse. "Are you coming, Poppy?"

Poppy stared into Daisy's eyes, realizing that they had arrived at a moment of decision. All these years, she had thought she understood Daisy, but she was wrong. Looking at her now, she realized that she did not know her at all. She didn't know if Daisy would deliver the message, but she did know that Daisy was leaving—leaving and never coming back.

"Are you coming?" Daisy asked again.

Poppy could not find the right words.

The earl broke the silence. "She stays here," he snapped. "You go."

Daisy raised herself on tiptoe as she confronted her father. "You go," she said. "You go and fetch the doctor. It's your damned baby."

The earl's hand shot out to slap Daisy's cheek, but Daisy danced lightly away.

The earl was left paralyzed by shock as Daisy slipped past him and out of the door.

Poppy sat down abruptly on the bed. She felt as though she were a puppet whose strings had suddenly been severed. All her life, she had danced to Daisy's tune, and Daisy was gone.

The earl was blustering now. He looked down at Dianna. "Go and fetch the doctor."

Dianna burst into tears of terror. "I don't know where he is," she sobbed.

Poppy rose from the bed and approached her father. She stared into his eyes, seeing the color of her own eyes mirrored in them and the color of her own hair in his meager beard. She was his height. She could look at him without raising her head. She knew what she had to do. Something had gone terribly wrong with the birth of the earl's baby, and she did not think Daisy would pause in her headlong flight to freedom and deliver a message for the doctor.

Filled with fury, Poppy poked her father's chest. "Dianna's not going. You go." She repeated Daisy's words. "It's your damned baby."

CHAPTER FIFTEEN

West of London
Ernie Sullivan

Sullivan savored the sheer energy of Ben Tillett's Vauxhall. The countryside flashed by in a blur of green hedges and scattered pedestrians while Harry Hazelton in the passenger seat wrestled with the road map and shouted directions.

Sullivan had not given Hazelton a chance to drive. He assumed that the army officer would be daring and dangerous on a horse, but he doubted he knew how to drive an automobile. *He probably had a driver who could be summoned at the flick of a finger.* A man who could not operate a telephone would surely be unable to operate a motor vehicle. Hazelton was, however, doing a fine job of reading the map. His directions had been clear and precise as they had left London on the Bath Road, and the Vauxhall's three-liter engine had growled contentedly while it ate up the miles. Now they had left the main roads behind, and Sullivan had been forced to slow down and change into a lower gear as they navigated narrow roads that rarely saw an automobile.

"Here," Hazelton shouted. "Turn here. See the signpost."

"I'm looking at the road," Sullivan growled, "not the signposts."

"Just turn," Hazelton said.

Hours had passed since they'd left Hazelton's office. A telephone call to the bishop in Fordingbridge had been fruitless. The bishop was away, and the bishop's chaplain did not know of a telephone at Riddlesdown Court. A study of the railway timetable told them they were too late to catch any of the connecting trains that would take them to their destination. Sullivan had known of only one other alternative—Ben Tillett.

Tillett was incensed that Sullivan had brought Hazelton to visit him at his secret love nest, but Eva Newton had sided with Sullivan as a fellow Australian. Eventually, Tillett had been persuaded to part with the Vauxhall on the condition that Sullivan was careful and returned it without a scratch.

Well, that would not be possible, Sullivan concluded as he drifted the Vauxhall around an abrupt right turn and onto a narrow, stony lane.

"Are you sure about this?" Sullivan asked.

"We're almost off the map," Hazelton said, "but I know there's a railway line between Lower Norton and Riddlesdown Halt, because I came by rail last time. So if necessary, we follow the railway."

"In this?" Sullivan asked. Ben Tillett's Vauxhall was not made for cross-country excursions.

"On foot if we have to," Hazelton said, "but there will probably be a lane. This map is the most up to date I could get, but new roads are being added almost daily. If only we could have talked to the bishop—"

"I don't understand," Sullivan said. "Why would the bishop suddenly take a trip to Germany?"

Hazelton folded the map and tossed it into the back seat. "It may not be sudden. Maybe it was planned."

Sullivan concentrated on navigating a sudden bend in the road, the wheels skidding as he flung the heavy car around the corner.

"I doubt it's a vacation," Harry said breathlessly, clinging to the door handle. "A bishop may go where a politician or a soldier may not go. His sudden visit to the expatriate Anglican flock in Berlin is no doubt more political than pastoral."

Sullivan took his eyes off the road and risked a sideways glance at Harry. "I heard a rumor about you and Bigham both doing some kind of secret work."

"Did you also hear that I've retired?"

"And yet you're helping Bigham with the *Titanic* inquiry."

"The bishop visiting Berlin has nothing to do with the Titanic inquiry," Harry insisted. Sullivan turned his eyes back to the narrow road and was surprised when Harry spoke again. "Maybe I'm wrong," he said. "In the final analysis, the *Titanic* may be at the center of everything. One of President Taft's vital aides went down with the ship. He was on his way back from a secret mission; some say to the Pope, and some say to Germany."

"But to sink a ship just to kill one man ..." Sullivan protested.

"Not just one man," Harry said. "Some of the world's richest men died on the *Titanic*, and as a result, the corporations they headed are foundering. The American stock exchange is depressed, and the British shipping industry is facing bankruptcy."

"You sound like that fool reporter in the *Daily Inquirer*," Sullivan said.

"That reporter," Harry replied, "is no fool. He can't be called a liar, because he makes no statements; he just asks questions."
Sullivan negotiated another turn in the road, frustrated by the fact that he had to reduce speed to little more than a crawl.

"Will Australia fight?" Harry asked suddenly.

"Fight? What do you mean?"

"If there's a war, will Australia fight?"

"Is there going to be a war?"

"I think a world war is inevitable."

Sullivan spared another glance at his companion. He didn't speak like a man who had retired from his army career and opened a private investigation agency. He spoke like a man who knew state secrets.

Will Australia fight? Of course it will. The whole empire would fight if the king commanded, but how could there be a world war? The whole world at war! What about the Americans?

Harry's voice penetrated his thoughts. "Stop!"

What side would America take in a world war?

"Stop!" Harry bellowed.

Sullivan stamped on the brakes as a five-bar gate suddenly appeared in front of them. A flock of fat English sheep stared at him from the other side of the gate, and beyond the inquisitive sheep lay a broad green pasture.

Sullivan glanced to left and right. The road did not turn. This was it. This was as far as the Vauxhall could go. They had missed a turning somewhere and arrived at a dead end. Sullivan cursed inwardly as he turned off the ignition. The big engine sputtered a couple of times and then backfired. The sheep scattered with a chorus of astonished bleats. The sound of the agitated sheep reminded him of home. He closed his eyes, and for a moment, he was at Goolagong at muster time. His grandfather intruded on the memory and held out his wrists.

"Look at my scars."

I have my own scars now. I have my own life.

"Clear my name."

Your name has been forgotten.

Harry climbed out of the car. "We walk," he said.

Sullivan looked at him dubiously. It was quite possible that Harry knew military secrets. It was also likely that he was a crack shot with a pistol and that he was deadly with a sword, but he limped and walked with a cane.

Harry leaned into the back of the car and retrieved a silver-embellished Malacca cane. "We walk," he said again.

"Walk where?" Sullivan asked.

Harry gestured with the walking stick. Sullivan could discern a path that meandered for some distance across the field and arrived at a small building. He looked to his left and saw puffs of steam rising up into a clear blue sky.

"That's the station," Harry said. "Train's coming. We'd better get a move on. Did you bring a weapon of any kind?"

"I've seen the bloke," Sullivan said, remembering the undersized man who had chased Daisy. "We won't need a weapon."

Harry nodded and patted his walking stick. "Just in case."

"You'll hit him with your walking stick?"

Harry shook his head. "No. I'll spear him with my sword stick. It's what I'm good at."

Sullivan followed Harry to the gate and over the stile while the sheep eyed them balefully from a distance. The drifting puffs of smoke changed to a steady stream. The train was close. If the gambler was coming to find Daisy, he would be on this train. Sullivan was surprisingly glad to have Harry with him.

Riddlesdown Halt Train Station
Alvin Towson

The train came to a halt. Towson sprang from his seat and jumped down from the carriage onto the platform. He was momentarily blinded by a cloud of steam that erupted from the locomotive as it prepared to move on in its slow, winding journey across the English countryside. In a moment of temporary confusion, Towson felt a hand pushing him aside. He pushed back.

A voice scolded him from within the cloud. "Hey there, we'll be having none of that."

The steam began to dissipate, and Towson saw that his attacker was a small man in a brass-buttoned uniform. The man, obviously a railway official, blew a sharp blast on a whistle and waved a green flag. The train pulled forward and chuffed away, leaving Towson and the railway guard alone on the platform.

"Attacking a railway official in the course of his duties is an offense punishable by a fine or imprisonment or both," the official said.

"I didn't attack you. You were in my way."

The railway official was a small man, but apparently, he thought his brass buttons made up for his lack of size. "No, sir. You were in *my* way. You did not close the carriage door behind you, and so it was my duty to do so."

"Well, that's your job, isn't it?" Towson said.

He knew he should not draw attention to himself by becoming embroiled in an argument with a railway official, but he had run out of patience several hours earlier. The idiot ticket clerk at Victoria station in London had sold him a ticket to Riddlesdown Halt, the station closest to the home of the Earl of Riddlesdown. The clerk had failed to explain that getting there would mean changing trains three times and waiting at increasingly isolated country railway stations for the arrival of increasingly uncomfortable trains.

He was hot, tired, impatient, and angry. He clenched and unclenched his fists. *Not here. Not now. Save it for the girl. Teach her a lesson she won't forget in a hurry.* He had managed to acquire an Enfield revolver in London, and its weight dragging on his pocket reminded him that he was not going to need his fists. He missed his old Mauser, which had fitted comfortably into an inside pocket or up his sleeve. It was the girl's fault that it was gone. It was the girl's fault that he was cowering in England under a false name.

April 15, 1912
On Board the Carpathia

Four professional gamblers had survived the sinking, and once they were aboard the Carpathia, *they formed a prickly alliance. They had barely acknowledged each other when the* Titanic *had set sail from Southampton. The* Titanic *had promised fine pickings, enough for everyone and no need to be in each other's space. The* Carpathia *was a different story and presented a need for the usual unwritten and unspoken rules to be discussed.*

They huddled together in a sheltered corner of the promenade deck, where they were out of the wind. The Carpathia *was clear of the ice field, but it was hemmed in by cold, penetrating fog and making only slow progress toward New York. The weather forecast warned of storm clouds building ahead of them. It seemed there was to be no mercy for the* Titanic *survivors nursing their wounds and their grief. Up on the deck, those who were uninjured wrapped themselves in blankets and stared at the sea with dull, uncaring eyes. Towson could guess what pictures played behind those glazed eyes, but he was not interested in replaying the past. He had made no progress in his attempts to find the girl who had stolen his winnings. The stewardesses were beyond his reach, taking care of the injured and, of course, the moneyed. They were not to be disturbed.*

Towson, shivering and impatient, had little time for pleasantries. He kept his hands in his pockets, protecting the few valuables he still possessed.

Charles Romaine, stocky and blond and sporting a bandage around his forehead, gave Towson a quizzical look. "I heard tell you played until the last minute," he drawled. "The very last minute."

Kid Homer, whose boyish features had brought about his nickname, cocked his head to one side as he looked at Towson. "Seems like you were desperate." He sucked his teeth for a moment. "As I heard it, you might not want to arrive in New York without a decent number of dollars in your pocket, but I didn't see you making any big wins."

"What I did or didn't do is none of your damned business," Towson said.

Boy Brereton, yet another gambler with an innocent baby face, started to speak and was stopped by a sudden spate of coughing. He banged his chest and swore quietly. "Doc says it's pneumonia."

If he was looking for sympathy, he was looking in the wrong place. His companions were still concentrating on Towson. He knew they sensed his vulnerability, and they took pleasure in kicking a man when he was down.

"Seemed to me you were after that big Russki fellow," Homer said.

Towson was annoyed with himself. He thought he'd been subtle. Had his interest really been that obvious? The Russian had been hard to break—a cool and careful player whose copious intake of vodka had not seemed to cloud his judgment. If Towson had not been in such desperate need of a big win, he would have abandoned the guy and looked elsewhere for funds. If it were not for the iceberg, he would never have broken him.

"How you gonna settle things in New York?" Brereton asked. "I hear you're in deep."

"Mind your own damned business," Towson snapped. He did not need to be reminded of what awaited him in New York.

Romaine held up a hand for silence. "I got something to say. Don't want you to think me soft, but, well, there are people on this boat who are in a bad way, lost everything. I think we should leave them alone. You know, keep to ourselves."

"Keep to ourselves," Homer repeated. "When did you become so high-minded?"

Romaine shrugged. "I don't know. Something about being given a second lease on life, I suppose. I just think these people have been through enough."

Boy Brereton shook his head. "Some of them still have money. I have one lined up."

"Who is he?"

"First-class survivor, and we're not talking penny-ante poker; we're talking horses."

"Can you keep him on the back burner until New York?" Romaine asked.

"I suppose so."

Romaine looked at Towson. "What about you?"

Towson nodded. "Yeah, sure, whatever you say." His mind was elsewhere. Even with the fog and the increasing ocean swell that promised a storm, the Carpathia *would be in port in a couple of days. He had to find the stewardess who had stolen his winnings, or at least find her name, but so far he'd found nothing. So far as he was concerned, nothing else mattered.*

"Ticket, please." The guard was holding out his hand. When Towson felt in his pocket, his fingers brushed against the Enfield. He caressed it briefly and then located his ticket.

"Here."

The guard studied the slip of paper. "This is a single."

"So?"

"How are you getting back?"

"I'm not going back," Towson growled.

"Ticket office closes at six."

Towson ignored the remark. He didn't give a damn about the hours of the dinky little ticket office. So far as he was concerned, nothing existed beyond the next few hours, or even minutes, when he would find Lady Marguerite Melville and retrieve the Matryoshka.

The sound of the steam locomotive faded into the distance, and the railway employee tucked his flag under his arm and walked away. Towson took stock of his surroundings. He had assumed that if he purchased a ticket to Riddlesdown, it would be a simple matter to find the home of the earl, which would no doubt be a castle that dominated the landscape. He did not expect the train to set him down on the outskirts of a village where the only thing that dominated the landscape was a dusty street bordered by thatched cottages, a stone church, and a pub.

He whistled at the retreating guard. "Hey, you."

The man turned.

"Riddlesdown Castle. Where is it?"

"No castle here."

"I'm looking for the earl."

The man's face twisted into a cynical smile. "Are you indeed?"

"Yes, I am. Where will I find him?"

"Through the village and up the hill."

"How far?"

"A mile or so, maybe more."

The morning clouds had vanished, and the sun was high in the sky. Just a few short weeks ago, when he had been fighting for a hold on the icy keel of the upturned lifeboat, Towson had thought that he would never be warm again. Now, as sweat trickled down his collar, Towson could not even summon a memory of that freezing water. He could only think of one thing—the Matryoshka.

Poppy Melville
Riddlesdown Court
Poppy Melville
Riddlesdown Court was not short of bedrooms. At one time, it had been the home of a favored Tudor courtier and had been built to a scale that would allow King Henry VIII himself to visit as he made his summer peregrinations around his kingdom. With the deer in the sycophantically named King Henry's Wood available for sport, the walled gardens available for dalliances, and the attraction of a heated orangery wall to provide exotic fruit, Riddlesdown Court had once been a splendid place.

The only remaining remnant of that splendor was the number of bedrooms and the number of four-poster beds. The Countess of Riddlesdown was now installed in one of those many beds. Poppy slipped into the room and closed the door behind her. She saw that the bed hangings had been pulled aside, and the brocade bedcovers were heaped on the floor alongside a pile of bloodstained sheets. Agnes lay in the middle of the bed with a white sheet pulled to her chin. Her face was as pale as the sheet that covered her, and her eyes were closed.

"Has anyone gone for the doctor?" Nanny Catchpole whispered.

"I don't know," Poppy said distractedly. "I'm not sure if Daisy or ... What's going on here, Nanny? I thought she was in labor."

"Not anymore."

Nanny Catchpole lifted a corner of the sheet, and Poppy saw a small blanket-wrapped bundle set beside Agnes.

"Is he ...?"

"No, not dead, and not a boy." The old nurse looked at Poppy with desperation in her eyes. "It's another girl. I can't tell your father."

Poppy fought back a vast disappointment. She was not free. She would never be free. "We have to tell him, Nanny. I'll do it if you like." *I've already sworn at him. I have nothing to lose, and I'm still his heir whether he likes it or not.*

Nanny Catchpole shook her head. "If you tell him it's a girl, he won't let the doctor come." She looked at the pale figure on the bed. "Lady Riddlesdown needs a doctor, but he won't allow it if he knows she's birthed a girl. He'll want her dead so he can find another, younger wife, one who will give him a son."

Poppy silently acknowledged the cold, hard truth of the old lady's words. "Do you really think she'll die? Can't you do something?"

"No, I can't." Nanny Catchpole was angry now. "If I knew what to do, I would do it instead of standing here and watching the poor woman bleed to death. Where is the doctor? That's what I'd like to know."

Poppy suppressed a moment of panic, took a deep, steadying breath, and faced her own uncertainty. She didn't know if Daisy would call on the doctor and deliver the message that he was needed at Riddlesdown Court, but she knew that she and her sister had said their final goodbye and Daisy would never return. There was nothing to prevent Daisy from stopping by the doctor's house, but there was also nothing to prevent her continuing with her headlong flight toward the life she so desperately wanted.

If Poppy doubted Daisy, she had even greater doubts about her father. She thought it most likely that he had locked himself away in his study to mull over the fact that his oldest child, his biggest disappointment, had poked him in the chest and sworn at him.

"I'll go myself," Poppy said. "I'm no use here."

Nanny Catchpole grasped Poppy's arm. "No, don't leave me. What do I tell your father if he forces his way in? He might. He's very impatient."

"He won't do that," Poppy said. "He won't want to see this." She lifted the sheet again and saw that the blood had seeped into the mattress and was staining the baby's blanket. She turned on the old nurse. "Why are you leaving the baby there? I know she's not wanted, but you can't just leave her there. You can't abandon her."

Nanny Catchpole's anger was a match for Poppy's frustration. "I haven't abandoned her. You're the one who abandoned all of us and ran away on a lark."

Poppy drew in a sharp, shocked breath. Nanny Catchpole had

never spoken that way before. She had scolded, of course, but never shown such deep resentment.

"I didn't abandon you. I was trying to help Daisy."

"She's not your only sister. What about the other two? What did you think would happen to them?"

"I didn't think—"

"No, you didn't." Nanny Catchpole heaved a sigh. "Lady Daisy has you wound around her little finger, and she's all you ever think about."

Poppy lowered her head, overcome with shame at the truth of Nanny Catchpole's words. She had not given even a passing thought to Dianna and little Olivia as she had followed Daisy onto the *Titanic*.

"As for abandoning the baby," Nanny Catchpole said huffily, "I put her beside her mother because I thought that Lady Riddlesdown would rouse herself if she felt the baby moving." She shook her head. "It hasn't helped. I think the poor soul has lost too much blood. She hasn't even opened her eyes. Someone has to fetch the doctor."

"Daisy said—"

Nanny Catchpole was still angry. "It doesn't matter what Lady Daisy said. I don't trust her to do anything but please herself."

Poppy's mind tried to shy away from the truth of Nanny Catchpole's accusations. Daisy had only ever pleased herself, and now that Poppy would not go along with her plans, she had left Poppy behind. A lifetime of pleasing Daisy had resulted in this moment of painful revelation. Stopping at the doctor's house was a simple task that should not even slow Daisy's headlong flight, but Poppy doubted that she would do it. Agnes and the baby, the future of the estate, the welfare of the little sisters, even Poppy herself, did not matter to Daisy. Only Daisy mattered to Daisy.

Poppy felt a prickling of tears forming in her eyes and swiped at them with the back of her hand. She opened the door a crack and slipped outside.

Her father stood with folded arms. "Well?"

"You have to get the doctor."

"What about my son?"

"There's no baby yet," Poppy lied. "It's a difficult birth, and she'll need the doctor, so you will have to go and get him."

"You want me to go to the village?"

"Yes, I do," Poppy said firmly. "If you want to see your son alive, you will have to go for the doctor. Nanny Catchpole needs me here to help her."

The earl snorted impatiently. His teeth were clenched as if biting off angry words. *He'll never forgive me for this,* Poppy thought, *but I don't care.*

"Do you expect me to walk?"

Any man worth his salt would run.

"The gardener's bicycle is in the greenhouse."

"I'm not riding that blasted thing."

Poppy was amazed at the way the depth of her outrage swept aside the last of her restraints. "Then damned well walk, Father. Just go before your wife dies."

The earl curled his lip. "You haven't heard the last of this."

Poppy turned her back on him and slipped back into the bedroom, closing the door firmly behind her.

"He's going."

"Did you tell him it's a girl?"

"No, not yet."

Nanny Catchpole lifted the sheet, extracted the blanket-wrapped baby, and put her into Poppy's arms. Poppy looked down at the baby's pink-and-white face, remembering how it had been to hold each of her newborn sisters. Each little girl had been expertly wrapped by Nanny Catchpole and presented to the glowering earl, who had dismissed her with a wave of his hand.

Nanny Catchpole turned away and bent over to study Agnes's pale face. She lifted the sheet. "So much blood," she said, shaking her head. "Whatever shall we do?"

Daisy Melville

Daisy took a shortcut through King Henry's Wood and emerged from the trees in time to see the afternoon train steaming away from the station. She was disappointed but not discouraged. Taking the train would be the easiest way to leave Riddlesdown Court behind, but it was not the only way. With no real time to plan, she had not been able to pack a suitcase, and she hated to leave her beautiful new clothes behind. However, she had the money she had taken from the gambler on the *Titanic*. She didn't have the necklace, but she doubted it had any real worth. The money she had in her purse would buy her everything she needed. All she had to do was find a way to leave the village.

She looked along the deserted village street and picked out the new petrol pumps outside the livery stable. Frank Meredith and his son had expanded their business, and now they were repairing motorcycles and automobiles. The barn doors stood open, and she could make out the shape of at least two automobiles inside. Excellent—better than the train. Frank Meredith would surely be willing to drive her to Uncle Hugh in Fordingbridge. She could go back to that lovely dress shop in Winchester and replenish her wardrobe and then onto London or maybe directly to Southampton and a ship to ... well, really, a ship to anywhere.

She turned toward the livery stable and then paused. *The doctor!* Everyone had seemed very agitated about the condition of Agnes and the new baby. She had never seen her father quite so engaged in what was happening in the house. Obviously, the problem with the birth was serious. She turned toward the doctor's substantial house, which stood foursquare facing the church in the center of the village. She owed nothing to her father and stepmother, but she owed this much to Poppy and Nanny Catchpole. The least she could do was pass on the message.

She felt unaccountably cheered by the display of spring blossoms in the front garden of the doctor's house. She had not been aware that she needed to have her spirits lifted, but perhaps she had indeed been a little sad. This village had always been her home, but she would not come back here ever again, or at least not until her father died and Poppy became the countess, and that might never happen, because there was always the possibility of a brother. She had no idea how Poppy could stand to be so quiet and so patient while the earl fathered one baby after another, each one potentially capable of stealing Poppy's inheritance.

And if anything happens to Poppy, it will be my inheritance, and that will be a very different story.

The door to the waiting room was unlocked, and a bell on the door rang as Daisy stepped inside the sparsely furnished room. The doctor's wife arrived from somewhere in the back of the house and greeted Daisy with a surprised little curtsy.

"The doctor is needed at the house," Daisy said briefly. "The baby is coming."

"Well," said the doctor's wife, "my husband isn't here. He's gone down to Coombe Farm. Nasty plowing accident. Stitches required."

"I see. When will he be back?"

"There's no saying."

"Oh well," Daisy said. "I've delivered the message. I'm sure there's no real hurry. My stepmothers keep having babies, and Nanny Catchpole takes care of everything."

"She does indeed," said the doctor's wife.

"So that's all right, then," Daisy said.

The doctor's wife nodded. "Yes, that's all right."

Daisy stepped outside again and stood for a moment among the tulips and early rosebuds. Perhaps she should have been more forceful and insisted someone go to tell the doctor that whatever he was doing at Coombe Farm could wait because he was needed at Riddlesdown Court. She should send a boy, but for once there were no boys in sight. Usually there would be three or four half-wits lounging outside the pub and staring at her, but today the bench outside was empty.

She looked back toward the train station. A man emerged and looked both ways along the street. The stationmaster followed him and made a pointing gesture toward the road that led up to Riddlesdown Court. Daisy squinted at the two men. She knew the stationmaster by his polished buttons reflecting the spring sunlight, but the other man was not someone she recognized. He was taller than the stationmaster but not as tall as Captain Hazelton and Captain Bigham, and he certainly did not stand like either of the soldiers. He stood like a man about to pick a fight, with his shoulders hunched and his chin jutting forward. His dark suit and fedora marked him as someone who had not dressed for the unexpected warmth of the spring day. Perhaps he had come a long way and left home before the skies had cleared and the sun had broken through.

The stationmaster pointed again, and the stranger turned away from him and began to trudge along the road in the direction of Riddlesdown Court. After only a few steps, he took off his dark fedora and ran a hand over his head. Daisy gasped and instinctively ducked down behind a brightly flowering azalea bush. Without the hat to hide the shape of his head, she knew him immediately. He was the gambler from the *Titanic*. She squinted again. What was he doing here? Was it some dreadful coincidence, or had he tracked her down?

She had stolen a considerable sum of money from him, but surely there were better ways of recouping his loss than chasing all over England, looking for her. How had he even found her?

She peeked out from behind the azalea bush. This was too much of a coincidence. The only reason for anyone to come to Riddlesdown was to visit Riddlesdown Court. She felt the first welcome flush of excitement. Life had been so dull since they had arrived back in England. The only break in the tedium had been their visit to the Dulwich Club and meeting Captain Bigham and Captain Hazelton, and of course, the opportunity to be photographed by the newspaper photographer. That was it! Her picture had been in the newspaper.

Her heart began to race. This was like the plot of a movie, with the villain prowling the street and the innocent heroine trembling behind the shrubbery. Well, she was not actually trembling, and she was not exactly innocent, but she still felt like a movie heroine. This story was better than anything vapid Dorothy Gibson could dream up. Now she would have to make a daring escape.

The gambler was walking away, fanning himself with his hat. Daisy crept out from behind the bush and made a dash for the livery stable. Once inside she could make out the figure of Jacko, Frank Meredith's son, leaning in under the bonnet of one of the cars. She teased out several tendrils of hair and presented herself beside him with her bosom heaving dramatically.

"Oh, Jacko, please, you have to help me."

Alvin Towson

He had only walked a short distance up the hill and away from the station, but he was already hot and tired. He was also very doubtful that the railway official had given him honest directions. The man had resented him, and he would not be surprised if he'd sent him in the wrong direction. He was probably relaxing in his pathetic little railway office now with nothing to do but think about how he had gotten the better of the foreign visitor. Alvin hadn't set out to offend the officious little man. How was he to know that passengers were expected to close their own carriage doors?

He looked back down the hill. He no longer trusted the directions he'd been given. He didn't like the man's eyes. He was very good at spotting the smallest signs of deception, and the man in the brass buttons had blinked once too often and shifted his gaze sideways. At the card table, those small signs would have been a dead giveaway. He couldn't believe he had allowed himself to be so distracted that he had not realized what that meant.

He surveyed the village. It looked for all the world like an illustration for the lid of a chocolate box, complete with thatched cottages and a church with a stone tower. Only the two petrol pumps outside the livery stable gave any hint that he had not been transported back to the seventeenth century.

He was still hesitating and wondering whether he should retrace his footsteps when a man emerged from a thick coppice of oak trees and staggered out onto the road.

This man was tall and thin, with wild wisps of ginger hair scattered around his bald head. His face was flushed and red, and he stared at Alvin with pale, agitated eyes. "Who are you?" he demanded. "I don't know you."

"I'm looking for Riddlesdown Court," Alvin said.

"Riddlesdown Court, yes, well … yes …"

Alvin had heard that England was famously full of eccentrics, and it occurred to him that this might be one of that breed. He certainly seemed to be on the point of incoherence. He was, however, the only person in sight, and Alvin was more certain than ever that the railway official had sent him on a wild-goose chase.

Alvin stared into the man's face until he saw his eyes snap into focus. "Riddlesdown Court," he repeated. "Home of the Earl of Riddlesdown."

"I know whose home it is, damn it. It's my home. I'm the earl, and I am not at home, so go away. I have to find the doctor."

You have to find the men in white coats, Alvin thought.

"The doctor," the earl repeated. "I have to find the damned doctor. Get out of my way."

"If you could just tell me how to reach Riddlesdown Court …"

"Oh, you don't want to go there. It's full of screeching women."

"Your daughters?"

"Yes, my daughters. They're all there."

"Lady Marguerite?" Alvin asked.

The earl's eyes bulged in fury. "She swore at me. My own daughter swore at me. If you want her, you can have her. She's no use to me. None of them are any use to me. Out of my way. I have to get the doctor."

Alvin stood squarely in the earl's path with no intention of moving until he had the information he needed. "If you could just show me which way to go," he repeated.

"Go the way I came," the earl said angrily. "Through the wood. Follow the shortcut through the wood. Now, get out of my way."

Alvin bowed and stepped out of the way with a feeling of relief. Without intending to, the crazed earl had provided reassurance. Alvin had envisaged the earl's residence as a fortress bristling with servants, but it seemed it was only full of "screeching women." The biggest danger would have been the earl himself, but the scarecrow figure now running agitatedly away from him would be no obstacle. Alvin planned to be in and out of the house before the earl returned with the doctor. He patted his pocket and felt the reassuring weight of the Enfield.

He was about to enter the wood when he heard the roar of an engine. He turned in time to see two figures on a motorcycle burst from the shelter of the livery stable. The earl, who had been running distractedly down the center of the road, flung himself aside at the very last moment and landed in the dust as the motorcycle roared away. Alvin caught a glimpse of a woman's skirt fluttering as the motorcycle rounded a curve and disappeared from sight.

All along the street, cottage doors were flung open, and women in aprons hurried toward the earl, who was trying to regain his feet. The sound of the women's voices and the earl's bellowing curses followed him as he entered the deep shade of the oak wood.

CHAPTER SIXTEEN

Riddlesdown Village
Harry Hazelton

The sheep remained at a distance as Harry and Sullivan traversed the pasture toward the station building. The field was rutted with old plow furrows and pitted with deep, treacherous ditches. Sullivan, leading the way, stumbled and cursed, and Harry's injured leg was on fire with a pain that threatened to overwhelm him.

One night in the hospital in Lucknow, he was overwhelmed by the pain in his leg and the ache in his heart, and he cursed aloud into the darkness. Fortunately for his pride, his cursing did not bring an orderly with a lamp to see his shame and fuss with his bedclothes and bandages. The room remained in semidarkness, illumined only by fitful moonlight shining through the ornate shutters. He gritted his teeth and resolved to endure the night in silence. Tomorrow he would ask Cardrew Worthington to bring a bottle of Scotch.

When he heard a slight rustle from the darkened corridor outside his room, he pulled himself upright. Soon he heard the patter of bare feet. Someone was entering his room, and he was helpless.

"Who's there?"

A small figure emerged and allowed the moonlight to play across dark skin and a ragged turban. "It is me, sahib, the broom wallah."

"What do you want?"

"To help your pain."

Humiliation made him angry. "Go away. Get out."

"I can help you."

Harry knew what would happen. The boy would offer to bring illegal opium. He almost wished he could accept it and allow the pain and the grief to drift away in puffs of perfumed smoke. No. He was not that far gone in misery. He still had his pride.

"Go away. I don't need your help."

"It is words, sahib. Only words. I will teach you words."

"I don't understand."

"Mantra to remove the pain."

"You can't remove my pain with words."

"You can remove your own pain, sahib. You say the words many, many times, and then it will be morning, and all is better in the morning."

Harry had never asked the meaning of the words that he had recited over and over again throughout the long night—he was not even sure that he pronounced them correctly or even remembered them correctly, but he did know that concentrating on reciting the mantra gave him control over the pain. He let the words run through his mind now as he followed Sullivan's stumbling path across the sheep pasture. The recitation freed his mind from his body, allowing him to isolate the pain in his leg and send it to a place where it could be ignored.

Om shrim klim aim indrakshyai nama.

Om shrim klim aim indrakshyai nama.

Sullivan stopped for a moment and turned to look at him. "What did you say?"

Harry realized he had spoken aloud. "Nothing. Just singing to myself."

Sullivan shook his head. "Bloody Pommies."

At last they reached the barbed wire fence that separated the pasture from the railway tracks. Harry searched along the fence line for a stile but saw nothing, only strands of wire and clumps of wool where the sheep had grazed along the wire.

Sullivan flung himself down on his stomach and squirmed under the bottom strand. Harry followed behind him. The mantra deserted him. He could only clench his teeth and pull himself through.

They emerged onto a narrow paved road. The railway station was deserted, but a group of women had gathered a few hundred yards down the road, and they were helping a man to his feet.

Harry recognized him at once. He grabbed Sullivan's arm. "That's the earl. Something's happened."

"Where's the house?"

Harry gestured to the road that led uphill from behind the village church. "It's up there. I came here on the train once before." He looked back at the earl, who was standing now and brushing dust from his clothes. At home at Riddlesdown Court, he had been an unusual but commanding figure with his air of disdain for the common man and contempt for his wife and daughters. Standing in the middle of the village street, he presented a sorry picture.

His voice carried above the chatter of the village women. "The doctor. Need the doctor."

One woman, who was gripping the earl's arm and holding him upright, shook her head. "No need for the doctor, Your Lordship. You come in and have a bit of a sit-down, and you'll be right as rain. Doctor's up at Coombe Farm."

The earl shook himself free of the woman's grip. "Not for me, you silly woman. Lady Riddlesdown. Lady Riddlesdown needs the doctor."

"Sounds like something's happening at the house," Sullivan said. "We should go."

Harry nodded and took a firm grasp of his cane. It had been of no use crossing the pasture, and it would not make the journey up the hill any less painful. It was not the cane that mattered; it was the fine Toledo blade concealed inside.

Riddlesdown Court
Poppy Melville

"Can I hold him?"

Poppy turned to see that Dianna had entered the bedroom where Agnes lay white and still beneath a bloodstained sheet.

"You can't be in here," Poppy said.

"I want to hold the baby. Is it a boy?"

Poppy did not know if she could trust Dianna with the answer. So long as the earl believed that Agnes was in labor and had not yet delivered the baby, he would move heaven and earth to fetch the doctor. On the other hand, if he knew the baby had arrived and was, in fact, another girl …

Daisy had been right. If Agnes could only produce girl babies, the earl would want a new wife. Almost four hundred years after his death, the spirit of Henry VIII still haunted the old Tudor house. It made no difference that King Henry's daughter had become Queen Elizabeth, the greatest of English queens. The earl was Henry reincarnated, and he wanted a son. Of course, King Henry had had the authority to behead wives who did not please him. Horace Melville had no such authority, but he would find a way of ridding himself of Agnes, if only by lack of action. If the doctor did not come, Agnes would surely bleed to death.

Poppy looked down at Dianna, realizing that this child, no more than twelve years old, was the closest thing to another adult in the house. Daisy was gone, and the earl was gone, sent on his way by Poppy's curses. Only Nanny Catchpole remained, and she was fully occupied with trying to drip beef broth through Agnes's pale lips. The broth dribbled down Agnes's chin and stained the white sheet. The baby in Poppy's arms turned her face toward Poppy's breasts, rooting blindly for a nipple.

"Dianna," Poppy asked, "where is your sister? Where's Olivia?"

Dianna shrugged. "Don't know."

Poppy leaned down toward Dianna. The house had been suspiciously quiet for some time. "Did she go outside?"

"Don't know."

"You have to go and find her. You're the only one here."

"No, I'm not. Where's Daisy?"

"She's gone, and she's not coming back."

Dianna's mouth flew open in shock. "Has she run away again? Are you going with her?"

"No, I'm not going with her."

Dianna's mouth settled into a pout. "She didn't say goodbye."

"I know, and I'm sorry. Please, Dianna, go and find Olivia. She's too young to be left on her own."

Dianna shook her head. "I want to hold the baby."

Poppy searched her sister's face, and there, in the set of the girl's mouth and the toss of her head, she found what she did not want to find. Dianna was Daisy all over again, and she would not move until she had what she wanted.

"You can hold the baby for just a moment, and then you have to go and see to Olivia."

Dianna pursed her lips thoughtfully. "All right."

Poppy placed the squirming, blanket-wrapped bundle in Dianna's arms. The baby uttered a thin wail and turned her head toward Dianna's barely developed breasts.

"What's it doing?"

"She's looking for milk," Poppy said.

Dianna curled her lip. "Ugh!"

"It's only natural. She's hungry."

Dianna's eyes were wide. "Is it a girl?"

Poppy nodded. "Yes, it is. You have another sister."

Dianna pushed the baby back toward Poppy. "We don't want another girl."

Poppy could not control her anger as she clasped the unwanted child. "There's nothing wrong with being a girl. You're a girl."

"Father wants a boy. He's going to be very angry with Agnes, because Agnes only makes girls."

Nanny Catchpole spoke quietly from the bedside. "Perhaps it's the earl himself that's at fault. Perhaps he's the one who only makes girls."

Poppy stared at the old nurse. "What did you say?"

"You heard me."

"Is that possible?"

Nanny Catchpole set down the cup of beef broth and stroked Agnes's hair for a moment. "Could be. She's his third wife, and not one of them has given birth to a boy, so maybe it's up to him and not up to them."

Poppy was suddenly very glad that she had sworn at her father. In fact, when he finally returned, she might do it again. She had always lived under his accusatory gaze. The whole house had waited time and again with bated breath for the birth of a son, and all that time, it had never occurred to her to think that the biological fault lay with her father. She looked at the still figure of the earl's third wife and felt a wave of sympathy that extended not just to her but to her own mother, and to all of her sisters.

"Someone's coming," Dianna said.

Poppy set aside her anger and went to join Dianna at the window. "Is it the doctor?"

"Don't know," Dianna said. "Don't know the doctor."

Poppy stared down at a man in a dark suit who was walking determinedly up the driveway. He seemed flushed and was breathing heavily like a man in a hurry.

"It's not the old doctor," Poppy said, "but perhaps he's a new one, or a helper. You'd better go down and let him in. Send him up here, and after that, go and find your sister."

Dianna scampered away, and Poppy turned to Nanny Catchpole. "Do we have a new doctor?"

"I don't think so."

Poppy turned back to the window and studied the approaching figure. Something was wrong. He disappeared from sight under the portico.

Poppy grasped at an elusive thought. What was wrong? *The bag!* Doctors always carried a bag. This man had been empty-handed. She made an attempt to calm herself. So what if he wasn't the doctor? That didn't make him a dangerous criminal. He was probably a traveling salesman. *No, a salesman would have a sample bag.* He wasn't from the village, not with that dark suit and hat, and a man from the village would not walk up to the front door; he would go around to the kitchen door. She clasped her hands together to calm herself. She did not know his intentions, but that didn't mean he had bad intentions.

She walked out onto the landing with the baby in her arms. Standing at the top of the staircase, she could see down into the hall, and she saw Dianna skipping lightly across the black and white tiles to open the front door. The sound of a child giggling came from somewhere in the region of the kitchen. Olivia was too little to be left alone, and she was up to some kind of mischief.

Dianna opened the front door, and sunlight flooded across the tiled floor. "Hello."

"Well, hello there." The man sounded out of breath and unreasonably hearty. "I'm here to see your sister."

"I have a lot of sisters," Dianna informed him.

"Your sister Lady Marguerite."

"You mean Daisy."

"Perhaps I do. Did your sister Daisy sail on the *Titanic*?"

Poppy gasped. Who was this man? What did he want? His accent told her he was an American. She clasped the baby tightly, uncertain whether to return her to Nanny Catchpole or take her downstairs to confront the stranger.

"Your sister has something that belongs to me," the stranger said.

A chill ran up Poppy's spine as she realized what the stranger had said. Now she knew who he was, and now she knew what he wanted.

"Daisy's not here," Dianna said blithely. "She's gone away."

The newcomer took a step forward into the hall. "Gone, you say? That's most … inconvenient. Maybe I should come in and look around, just in case. Are there any other adults in the house?"

"Of course there are," Poppy said firmly, drawing the stranger's attention away from Dianna and causing him to look up the stairs.

Although she was wearing an old morning dress and clasping a newborn baby, she held herself with dignity. Queen Elizabeth had descended these stairs. She had been a woman, but she had not been weak. Poppy would not be weak. "What do you want with my sister?" Poppy asked.

The man pushed past Dianna. "I want what she stole."

Poppy took only one step down the staircase and remained there, looking down on the flushed and angry American. "I don't know what you're talking about."

"I'm talking about your sister stealing something from me and running off into a lifeboat."

"I think you're mistaken," Poppy said.

"No," the American said, "I am not mistaken. I know what she did, and I've been looking for her ever since she went ashore in Plymouth."

The words were out of Poppy's mouth before she could stop herself. "How could you have been in Plymouth if you were on the *Titanic*? Why weren't you in New York?"

"Because I sailed on the *Lapland*. I followed her."

"Just for some stolen money?" Poppy asked.

"No, not for the money."

The stranger dipped his hand into his pocket, and suddenly Poppy was staring into the barrel of a pistol. She froze. She did not dare to look at Dianna, who was standing behind the gambler. It would be so easy for the intruder to turn on her, and there would be nothing Poppy could do with the baby in her arms. She locked eyes with the gunman.

"Who are you?"

"Alvin Towson. Who are you?"

"I'm Lady Penelope Melville, and you are trespassing in my house."

"Give me what I want, and I'll leave."

"I don't have any money."

"Yeah," said Towson, "I noticed. This is a shabby old place, ain't it?"

"Yes, it is," Poppy agreed. "So you will believe me when I say we have no money."

"And I don't see any servants," Towson said.

Poppy remained silent. Of course there were no servants. The earl did not think a household of women had need of additional servants. She caught a flicker of movement behind the gambler. Dianna was moving, but where was she going? She dared not look away from Towson's face, but she listened for sounds from the kitchen. Olivia was no longer giggling. Did that mean that Dianna had led her away from the house? Surely she would do that. Surely she wasn't running away by herself, Daisy all over again.

Alvin advanced up the stairs. "That your baby?"

"No."

"Give it to me."

"I will not."

"If I shoot you, you'll drop the baby. Best give it to me now. Don't want the baby to get hurt."

"Shooting me won't help you. I don't have your money. If I did, I'd give it to you. Please just leave. My sister isn't here. She's gone away, and she's not coming back."

"Did she take it with her?"

"Take what?" Poppy asked.

"The Matryoshka."

"I don't know what that is," Poppy replied.

Towson advanced to the next step and shook his head in mock sympathy. "Now that I see this place, I understand. You need money just like the rest of us, and that was your plan. Your sister knew all along, didn't she? She knew the courier was sailing on the *Titanic*, so she got work as a stewardess so she'd have the key to all the cabins, and she could just go in and take it. Didn't work, did it? He had to keep it on him at all times."

"You're talking nonsense," Poppy said, backing away up the stairs. "She's not here. Just go away."

On the corridor above, a door banged, and floorboards creaked as someone approached. It could only be Nanny Catchpole.

"Lady Poppy, is that the doctor?"

"No, it's not. Go back inside, Nanny."

Nanny Catchpole was coming closer. "Someone has to go for him."

"My father has gone," Poppy said. "Go back inside, Nanny."

Enough talking, Towson said. "Let's get this settled before the doctor arrives. You wouldn't want me to delay him, would you?"

"There's nothing to settle. I don't have your money."

Towson climbed another step. "I don't want money. I want what your sister stole."

Poppy heard Nanny Catchpole's sudden catch of breath and heard the rustle of her apron just behind her. "He has a gun."

"I know."

"What does he want?"

"He wants Daisy."

Nanny stepped around Poppy and glared at Towson. "You put that thing away. Lady Daisy's not here, and you won't bring her back by waving that gun around."

Towson climbed another step. Poppy could see sweat trickling down from his forehead, but his hand on the gun was steady and aimed at the baby. "Where has she gone?"

"How would I know?" Nanny Catchpole asked. "That one does whatever she wants."

"There's no point in looking for her," Poppy added. "She will have spent your money by now."

"I didn't come for the money. I came for the diamond."

The diamond! The diamond is in my pocket.

Poppy reached into her pocket and felt the weight of the gold chain, so much heavier than the diamond itself. She pulled it out and held it at arm's length.

"Is this what you're looking for?"

Towson's eyes lit up. The gun wavered in his grasp. Poppy hurled the necklace over his head and down into the entrance hall. Towson turned and raced back down the stairs. Poppy thrust the baby into Nanny Catchpole's arms and pushed the startled old woman back into the bedroom.

"Bolt the door and don't come out."

Poppy stepped away from the door. She had just reached the top of the stairs when she heard the first gunshot.

Ernie Sullivan

When the first shot split the air, Sullivan was already running. Hazelton was doing his best, but he couldn't keep up, and Sullivan couldn't wait. If the Englishman was offended by being shown up, then so be it. Maybe that kind of tomfoolery worked for Pommies, but the gambler wouldn't be playing by those rules, and neither would Sullivan.

As he sprinted along the curving, weed-choked driveway to the old house, he saw movement in the trees ahead, and a shambling figure in a tweed suit broke free of the thicket that paralleled the driveway, shouting incoherently. Another shot rang out, and the figure fell. Who the hell was firing?

Sullivan rounded a curve, and the ancient brick house came into sight. The front door was open, and a man stood on the front steps. Sullivan could make out the pistol in his hand as he took aim again at the man who had fallen. *What the hell?* He redoubled his speed. The man on the ground was the eccentric old earl. Obviously, he knew a shortcut back from the village and had arrived ahead of them. The man on the steps must surely be the gambler. Was he going to fire again? The earl was already on the ground. The gambler was in no danger from that quarter. In Sullivan's experience, the firing frenzy marked the gambler as an amateur who wasted bullets. He hadn't killed the earl with the first two shots, but given enough chances, he surely would. Hazelton had a sword, but Hazelton was a hundred yards behind. The gambler had not yet seen Sullivan, but when he did, he surely wouldn't miss now that he was getting the hang of the weapon.

Sullivan couldn't believe it. He, Richard Sullivan's grandson, was about to make a noble gesture and risk his life for an aristocrat. If he lived to tell the tale, his grandfather was never going to forgive him.

He gave a bloodcurdling shout as he ran. The gambler turned toward him, and then something inexplicable occurred. Two girls in flowered dresses emerged from behind the house. The bigger of the two girls was shouting angrily, and the little one was crying. The gambler whirled around to look at them, and Sullivan saw a sudden movement from within the house. A figure loomed behind the gambler and pushed. The gambler stumbled and fell forward to lie sprawled across the steps.

As Sullivan panted to a halt, Harry Hazelton passed him, gasping and limping but moving steadily ahead. Sullivan doubled over, sucking in lungfuls of air, and watched in amazement as Poppy Melville stepped out of the shadowy interior of the house and made a hesitant approach to the man sprawled on the steps.

He heard Hazelton's shouted instruction from close behind. "Stay away from him. He has a gun."

Sullivan rolled his eyes heavenward. *Talk about stating the obvious.* But then he saw the gambler's hand move. He still had the gun, and he intended to use it. Hazelton leaped past him, discarding the outer cover of his cane as he ran. The sword blade flickered in the sunlight, and then the sword was at the gambler's throat.

Well, Sullivan thought as he steadied his breathing, *this is going to take a lot of explaining, and who will be the hero here?*

Without even glancing in her father's direction, Poppy ran past Hazelton and fell on her knees to gather the younger girls into her arms.

Sullivan turned at the sound of hoofbeats and saw a pony and trap rattling up the drive. He looked at the man sprawled on the steps, at the earl lying on his back in the grass, and at the old lady who was now walking out of the house with a baby in her arms, and wondered where the doctor would begin.

CHAPTER SEVENTEEN

Riddlesdown Court
Harry Hazelton

The sun was setting behind the oak trees and painting the sky with stripes of pink and purple. A swallow swooped low above his head, and a pair of collared doves exchanged melancholy good-nights as they fluttered into the dovecote. Harry's mind touched briefly on the jasmine-scented gardens of India, but the comparison no longer mattered. For a year, he had drifted, a prisoner of pain and memory, but the events of the day had finally dispelled the ghosts of the past.

Sullivan came to stand beside him. "I was wondering where you had gone."

"It was a madhouse in there," Harry said, "and they didn't need me to tell them what to do."

Sullivan handed him a glass tumbler. "The old earl has some good Scotch put by. He won't be needing it for a while, so I helped myself."

Harry allowed the liquor to rest on his tongue for a moment before he swallowed. "Has everyone gone?"

"Not everyone," Sullivan said. "There are still two of the little sisters, the old nanny, and of course, Poppy. Mother and baby have gone to the hospital, and the doctor is staying with the earl until the ambulance arrives to take him to the hospital in Winchester."

"What about the gunman?"

Sullivan took a long swallow of the earl's Scotch before he replied. "Bloke by the name of Alvin Towson, professional gambler. Daisy took something that he wanted." He laughed. "I saw her do it. She snatched it off the table and ran for the lifeboats."

"Where is Lady Daisy now?"

"Gone," said Sullivan. "Poppy says that she won't come back."

Harry was surprised to find himself correcting Sullivan. "She's not Poppy," he said. "She's Lady Penelope." A sudden stab of unreasonable jealousy made his voice stiff and cold.

Sullivan laughed aloud. "My God, you Pommies! All right. *Lady Penelope* says that her sister has flown the coop, taking the money with her, but she has left behind the real prize. Towson didn't care about the money; he was after a very rare diamond being carried by a courier from Russia. Daisy didn't know its value, and so she left it behind. Poppy, *Lady Penelope*, showed it to me. It doesn't look like much, but Towson says it's the only one of its kind ever found. It's a diamond trapped inside another diamond. Damnedest thing I've ever seen. If you shake it, it rattles. Apparently, it's priceless."

"What will happen to it?"

Sullivan shrugged. "I assume it will be returned to the people in Russia who found it in the first place. If Lady Daisy had known its worth, she would never have left it behind."

Sullivan walked to the low brick wall that surrounded the terrace and stood for a moment, staring out at the wide expanse of lawn and the lake beyond. "So this is what it's all about," he said.

"What do you mean?"

The scar pulled at Sullivan's face, making his expression unreadable, but his words, spoken with his casual Australian accent, lacked anger. "Everything you Pommies do, the whole bloody empire, it's all done to preserve this."

"I suppose it is," Harry said eventually. He turned to look up at the old house, noting the crumbling chimneys and the blind, empty spaces where attic windows were devoid of glass. "I don't think we can keep it up much longer."

"Do you think Poppy will try?" Sullivan asked.

Harry closed his eyes for a moment. What was the point of reprimanding Sullivan for his renewed use of Poppy's name? Obviously, his relationship with Poppy had come to a point where titles were not important.

"She's the heir now, isn't she?" Sullivan said. "I had a word with the doctor, and ..."

Harry did not want to listen. While he had been out on the terrace, mooning over the woods and the lawns and the centuries of history accumulated in the Tudor house, Sullivan had been with Poppy, no doubt holding her hand while the doctor explained ... Explained what?

"The old man won't be fathering any more children," Sullivan said. "I don't know what Towson was aiming for, but I know what he hit." He gave a grin that even his scar could not defeat. "A fate worse than death."

"So there'll be no son and heir," Harry said. He tried to imagine what this would mean for Poppy. She had lived her entire life in the shadow of a brother yet to be born, and now the shadow had been removed. Poppy knew her future. She would be Countess of Riddlesdown.

"How did she take the news?" Harry asked. He hated that he was relying on Sullivan for information, but what else could he do? He couldn't go barging into the house and talking to Poppy about her feelings. Obviously, she would prefer to share those feelings with Sullivan.

"Hard to tell," Sullivan said. "At first she had no idea what the doctor was saying. The old fellow was beating around the bush, trying to find a polite way to say that the earl had taken a bullet in the donger, so I told her myself. No point in coming at it sideways. There have been enough babies born in this house; she has to know where they come from."

"What did she say?"

"She thanked me for the information," Sullivan replied, "and informed me that she would make arrangements for Tillett's car to be retrieved, and meantime, we are to be her guests for the night."

Harry stared out at the darkening landscape. An owl hooted from the shelter of the oak trees, and a flight of bats rose in a dark cloud from the dovecote. In the distance, a fox barked a long, lonely mating call. History was written into every inch of the landscape: Druids, Romans, conquering Normans, and a king who had killed his wives, and all of this would be placed into Poppy's keeping.

A sudden flare of light brought him back to reality. Someone had lit the gas lamps in the dining room. It was time to go inside.

Victoria Station
London
Daisy Melville

Daisy listened to the babble of voices rising from the passengers as they boarded the train. She heard French, of course—after all, she was boarding the train to Paris. French did not excite her. French was too ordinary. She wanted to hear other, more exotic tongues. The boat train, timed to arrive in Dover and connect passengers to the night ferry, was just the first step in a long journey that could lead to … She didn't know where. The journey could lead to anywhere she wanted to go. Europe awaited her, and if she tired of Europe, she could board the *Orient Express* and journey to Istanbul and across into Asia.

She showed her ticket to the guard, who looked at her suspiciously as he gestured to a first-class carriage. She knew she appeared disheveled, and the fact that she had no luggage would certainly arouse even more suspicion, but there had been no time. Jacko had delivered her to Winchester station just in time to catch the London train, but she'd had no time to go shopping in London. She was not yet far enough away from Poppy, the bishop, her father, and all the other people who had tried to tame her over the years. To be free of them, she would have to leave England immediately, not just because she was carrying stolen money but because she might lose her nerve and change her mind.

She told herself that she would not miss Poppy, with her constant instructions to be careful and to act like a lady. It was not as though she would never see her again. She would always know where to find her. Without Daisy to spur her on, Poppy would probably never leave Riddlesdown again. She would cling to the old house and wait for the earl to die. Their father would probably marry her off to some boring local landowner whose fumblings in the bedroom would no doubt result in a handful of children. She thought that Poppy would be a good mother. She was the only mother Daisy had ever known. She was surprised to feel a tear trickling down her cheek. She wiped it away angrily. Now was not the time to think kindly of anyone at Riddlesdown. She had to tell herself that she was well rid of all of them.

She settled into her seat and stared out the window at the activity on the platform, fearful that someone would arrive at the last minute to drag her from the train. She was a thief. The fact that she had stolen from dead men would not matter to the police. She would not be surprised if Poppy had reported her, or maybe Captain Hazelton. He was very strict and upright, and he would take a dim view of robbing men who were about to die. Sullivan was the only one who would understand what she had done and why.

She pouted a little. She wished Sullivan had not turned her down. Was it possible that he actually preferred Poppy? This was a new and unwelcome thought, and it led to a momentary lack of self-confidence. She was still struggling with the idea that any man would find Poppy's cool self-control more attractive than Daisy's own fire and excitement when the carriage door opened and a man entered. As he took the seat opposite her, she noticed that he was darkly handsome with mesmerizing brown eyes. He gave her an appraising glance before he opened a copy of *Le Temps* and pretended to read.

The newspaper remained open until the train had pulled out of the station, and no one else had come to join them in the carriage.

He folded the newspaper. "Madame," he said.

"Monsieur."

"Why are you not in the ladies-only carriage?"

Daisy fluttered her eyelashes. "Are you telling me, monsieur, that I am not safe in here … with you?"

Riddlesdown Court
Poppy Melville

Poppy was awake and dressed before the dawn chorus of birds had heralded a new day. She hovered in the kitchen doorway, watching as two women from the village arrived to prepare breakfast for the guests. Last night's dinner had been a shambles—there had been no time to prepare and very little food in the pantry. This morning would be different. The women had brought their own supplies: bread from the village bakery, bacon from the village butcher, and coffee donated by the doctor's wife.

The gardener's boy sat on the back step, staining his fingers green from the polish he was using on the long-neglected silver coffee service. Nanny Catchpole was hard at work heating a flatiron on the kitchen range and applying it vigorously to a tablecloth and a set of linen napkins. She looked up at Poppy.

"Your first morning as mistress of Riddlesdown," she said.

Poppy shook her head. "Lady Riddlesdown is the mistress of Riddlesdown."

"Well, Lady Riddlesdown is not here, and neither is your father," the old lady replied, "so it's all in your hands, pet."

"You appear to have everything in *your* hands," Poppy corrected.

"I wasn't sure you'd remember how it was in the old days," Nanny said. She paused to spit on the flatiron and test its temperature. "Things were very different in your mother's time," she said as she resumed her ironing. "In those days, before your father became a … well, never mind what he became. In those days, we would have visitors for breakfast, lunch, and dinner, and of course, your father had a valet."

Poppy was surprised by a faint memory of an upright, humorless man who had been her father's valet. He had been dismissed not long after Daisy had been born. Since that time, the earl had dressed himself, which accounted for his shabby appearance.

She didn't know what he would make of the hubbub in the kitchen or the profligate use of the household money to hire village women to cook an enormous breakfast. Well, for once his opinion did not matter. He was gone from the house now, dosed with morphine and taken away in an ambulance in the small hours of the morning.

She was still trying to accustom herself to the news of her father's condition. The doctor had told her that the wound was severe and that … well … there could be no more births in the family.

"Because of Lady Riddlesdown's condition?"

The doctor shook his head. "No, no. Because of your father."

"You mean he does not wish to put Lady Riddlesdown through that ordeal again."

"No. Your father's wound is … um … delicate … and …"

Sullivan had chosen that moment to sweep the doctor aside and tell Poppy the truth. There would be no more babies because the bullet had struck her father's "donger."

"Donger? What on earth is a donger?"

She still could not believe that Sullivan had thought it appropriate to give her so many details of her father's injury and how that would affect the birth of any future children. He had spoken words aloud that she had only overheard used by farmers in reference to animals. Nonetheless, when he was finished and she finally understood why her father would have no more heirs, she felt an overwhelming sense of relief. It was over.

All those years of telling me that Riddlesdown would never be mine, and now there is nothing more he can do about it. It's mine. Riddlesdown is mine.

"If you want to help," Nanny said, "you could go to the henhouse and see what they have for us this morning."

Glad to be given a task, Poppy picked up the willow egg basket and set off across the kitchen garden toward the chicken coop. All around her, life was stirring. A thrush lifted its head in song; a blackbird flitted overhead with a worm in its beak; sheep bleated in the distance; and the primroses along the fence opened their petals to the sunlight.

She was almost at the door of the chicken coop when she saw that one of her visitors was up and about. Harry Hazelton was leaning on the fence that enclosed the stable paddock, stroking the gray muzzle of Dobby, the dapple plow horse. She wondered what they were saying to each other, because it was obvious that they were saying something, although not with words.

Dobby nickered softly as he stretched his neck to lay his head on the captain's shoulder, and Poppy realized that she was watching a moment of perfect contentment—a moment she was suddenly able to share. For weeks, she had thought that the icy chill of the Atlantic would stay with her forever and she would never again be warm, and never again feel truly safe. Now, as the morning light crept across the paddock and bathed the man and horse in a golden glow, she was finally able to feel warmth and comfort.

She dropped the egg basket and turned away from the chicken coop. Although she walked slowly, almost as if she walked in a dream, the soldier and the horse heard her approach. Dobby lifted his head from Harry's shoulder as Harry turned to face her. The captain was different this morning. He had not shaved, and a dark shadow lay across his chin and cheeks. His hair, showing flecks of gray, was uncombed, and rebellious curls fell across his forehead. His brown eyes were wide and unguarded.

Poppy looked deep into her heart and found no doubt, not even a flicker of uncertainty. *I want this. I want him.*

When he spoke, she wondered if she was still dreaming. Surely he would not speak this way in the real world. His hand grasped Dobby's mane as if to draw strength, and his voice was husky.

"There was a woman," he said.

Poppy waited. It was as though, in this waking dream, he had read her thoughts.

He released Dobby's mane and let his hand rest on the fence. "The general brought a wife to India. She was very young and he was not." He lifted his eyes for a moment, as if looking into another world. "India is a hard place for an Englishwoman, and a general's wife cannot have friends. It was a cruel thing to do, but the general wanted a child."

A son, Poppy thought. *The general wanted a son.*
Harry's eyes were still fixed on that other world that Poppy could not imagine. Heat? Dust? Danger?

"Her name was Eloise, and for me, she was England," Harry said.

"Did you ...?"

"No!"

"I'm sorry. I shouldn't ..."

"The child came early," Harry said. "The general was not there. The regimental doctor came for me to ask me what he should do. I told him to bring an Indian midwife." Harry was still looking away from her, still trapped in a memory. "The midwife saved the baby," he said. "She could not save Eloise. Her loss has haunted me."

Harry's eyes came back into focus. He looked down and slapped his leg. "And then this."

"A bullet wound?" Poppy asked.

Harry shook his head. "A wild boar. My own fault. I was not paying attention." His hand crept up and grasped Dobby's mane again. "I have been haunted by the memory of a woman I hardly knew." He looked at her intently. "You have banished that memory."

Poppy had a sudden flash of her own unwanted memory: men and women fighting to hold on to their lives as the *Titanic* plunged beneath the waves. They had done nothing to deserve this fate, but life was not guaranteed. It could be cut short at any time. All she had was *now*, this very moment. If he would not come to her, she would have to go to him.

She stepped toward him.

He released Dobby's mane. For a moment, she knew her future, and then a man's voice shattered the silence that had been wound as tightly as a watch spring.

She turned her head and saw Sullivan striding across the paddock and waving a newspaper. "Have you seen this?" he shouted. Poppy turned away from Harry and did not turn back to look at him again as Sullivan drew close. She knew what had been about to happen, and even the thought made her blush. She stepped away and bent to retrieve the egg basket. She heard Harry speaking to Sullivan in an irritated tone.

"Couldn't this wait until after breakfast?"

"No, it couldn't."

Harry Hazelton

Harry leaned against the sun-warmed fence post and studied the newspaper with the plow horse looking over his shoulder. He shifted the paper slightly as the horse's breath ruffled the pages.

"Interrogantum's column," Sullivan said angrily. "Read that."

Harry looked up one more time and saw Poppy crossing the kitchen garden. She was walking away from him and from whatever had so nearly happened.

Sullivan snatched back the paper and started to read aloud. "'Was the *Titanic* on fire before she sank? Was a black gang hired to extinguish a coal fire in the bunkers? Where are they now? Did their secret die with them?'"

Harry retrieved the newspaper and read the words again. "I don't understand. You spoke to Clive Bigham in confidence yesterday morning. How could Interrogantum get hold of what you said?"

"He couldn't," Sullivan said, "and yet he did."

Harry looked up and caught a glimpse of Poppy as she opened the kitchen door and went inside.

"What's the point of all this?" Sullivan asked. "This bloke asks questions that can't be answered and gets everyone stirred up. Now there'll be a wild-goose chase of reporters looking for the black gang, but they're not going to find me. I'm done."

Harry banished Poppy from his thoughts and concentrated on the problem. The solution was as unlikely as it was obvious. "We spoke to Bigham yesterday and not to anyone else. Now today these questions are in the morning paper. What does that tell you?"

Sullivan stared at him. "Strewth, mate! Are you saying that Bigham …?"

Harry felt a cold, reluctant anger. He liked Bigham. They were brother officers, and yet it was obvious that Bigham had been playing him for a fool. "Yes," Harry said, "that is exactly what I'm saying. Clive Bigham is feeding information to Interrogantum. Maybe he even *is* Interrogantum. Yesterday morning I saw a reporter who has a very active imagination arriving at his office. I should have put two and two together."

Sullivan shook his head. "I don't see the point. Are you suggesting he doesn't want the truth?"

"No one wants the truth."

"Why do you say that?"

Harry jabbed the newspaper with a finger. "I should have realized. The inquiry drags on day after day, with the lawyers poking and prodding at each other, and day after day this damnable Interrogantum spews out questions that cast doubt on every word spoken. These are questions that will never go away. They'll take on a life of their own, and forever after, people will believe rumors and falsehoods."

"But why?"

Harry knew the answer, although he had arrived at it reluctantly, along with the knowledge that he had been played for a patriotic fool. Bigham had told him what needed to be done, and he, like a good little soldier, had done what he had been told.

"You should start with the crew's depositions. You may find that words have been spoken that should not have been spoken."

He understood everything now, from the Drill Hall, where the words of the witnesses could not be heard clearly beyond the front row, to the admission of innumerable lawyers acting on behalf of unions, passengers, and shipping lines, and all asking questions of each other as much as of the witnesses.

Bigham had even told him what was at stake.

"If we are not careful, the loss of the Titanic *will go down in history as a lesson in total incompetence … A bad day for British shipping … It will lose us*

the transatlantic trade ... If it comes to war, we will need those ships to transport our troops."

He looked up at Sullivan. "Bigham thinks he's doing the right thing for the empire."

Sullivan fixed Harry with a steady gray-eyed gaze. "Is he?"

Harry shook his head. "I don't know. You tell me. Australia is in the empire. What do you want from us?"

Sullivan's voice was harsh and angry enough to send the plow horse trotting away across the paddock. "My family has already had more than enough from the mother country," Sullivan said. "We are Australian because my grandfather was transported in chains for a crime he didn't commit. The daughter of a petty local squire accused him of fathering her child. I suppose it was safer to accuse him and call it rape than admit she'd let things get out of hand with someone of her own class.

"The old man is one of the richest men in Australia now, but all he can see is the scars of the manacles. I was raised to be his vengeance, so don't ask me what I think of the empire. I was sent here, to the heart of the whole bloody thing, to find the people who wronged him."

"Did you find them?" he asked.

"The magistrate is long dead, and the girl who accused him is an old woman now. I followed her onto the *Titanic.*"

"So she's gone?" Harry said.

"No. I put her in a lifeboat."

"Why?"

Sullivan shrugged. "I didn't want her to die. I wanted her to live with the knowledge that I was still looking for her."

"And are you?"

Sullivan thought before he spoke. "Whatever happened, right or wrong, the old man has had a good life in Australia. Maybe it was tough in the beginning, but in the end, it's better than the life he would have had here. I can't change the past."

He shook his head. "I've seen England now, and I understand my grandfather was no more important than the boy who brought me this newspaper. If he'd stayed here, he would have been no one, and I would be no one. No, I'm not going to look for her. I'm going to get on with my life."

Before Harry could comment, the gardener's boy came running

across the kitchen garden. "Breakfast is ready, and they've brung the Vauxhall, sir. She's a beauty, ain't she?"

"Yes, she is," Harry agreed.

The boy ran back across the field. Harry waited for Sullivan to speak.

"London?" Sullivan said.

Harry nodded. "I'm afraid so. The sooner the better. We can't let him get away with this."

"Shame about breakfast," Sullivan muttered.

Harry looked up and saw Poppy hovering in the kitchen doorway. He wanted nothing more than to stay right where he was. Something rare and precious had passed between them. They were two wounded souls who had the power to heal each other, but the healing would have to wait.

Sullivan strode ahead of him and spoke to Poppy as he passed her. She turned her head toward Harry and waited for him just inside the door. "Mr. Sullivan says you're going to London," she said.

He had no response beyond words that were bland, ordinary, and apologetic. "I'm sorry. I wish we could stay for breakfast."

I wish I could stay forever.

She walked with him across the black-and-white-tiled foyer. He explained what he could. "It's the *Titanic* inquiry. Something has come up."

I love you, Poppy Melville. You have banished my ghosts.

She stepped aside to allow him to leave by the front door. Sullivan was already in the driver's seat of the Vauxhall. Harry took her hand. "I'll come back."

CHAPTER EIGHTEEN

On the road to London
Harry Hazelton

They were close to London. Its presence was marked by a gray smudge of coal smoke against the bright midday sky. Harry set aside the map. He wouldn't need it in order to give Sullivan directions to the Drill Hall.

He still had no plan as to how to make use of his realization that Bigham was the driving force behind Interrogantum's rumormongering. After his initial flash of anger, he had made a determined effort to look at Bigham's actions in the best possible light. Would Bigham really abuse the implicit trust existing between officers in the king's service and use Harry to perpetrate lies? He wanted to think better of his fellow officer. There had to be a reason why Bigham had asked him to study the crew's depositions. Was it because he knew Harry would not be easily fooled?

"What am I looking for?"

"I don't know, but I trust you will know it when you find it."

"And if I do find something?"

"Leave it to me."

Thinking about Bigham kept him from thinking about Poppy. More than anything, he wanted to tell Sullivan to turn the Vauxhall around and take him back to Riddlesdown. He had so much he wanted to say to the woman who had rescued him from his melancholy.

A thunderous boom interrupted his daydream. It took a moment for him to realize that he was not under enemy fire. Some monstrous motor vehicle had backfired, sending startled pigeons into the air and causing Sullivan to stand on the brakes. The Vauxhall swerved off the road, coming to rest with its nose in a hedge. Harry's first thought was that Sullivan would have to pay a hefty repair bill for the damage he'd done to Ben Tillett's shiny motorcar. That thought vanished immediately as Sullivan turned toward him, his face pale with shock.

"Well, stone the crows," the Australian said softly. "How did I forget?"

Harry waited. Sullivan, who had displayed almost no emotion when he had spoken of the loss of the *Titanic*, was now in the grip of a fierce memory.

"Strewth," he muttered.

"What?"

Sullivan waved a hand in the direction of the retreating lorry. "Why now?" he asked. "Why can I remember now? Why didn't I remember it before? I should have remembered."

"Shock does strange things to the memory, and then something will trigger a memory, and it all comes back."

"I suppose you'd had some experience of that," Sullivan said.

Harry resisted the temptation to share even one of the memories that he kept locked away. He had seen his own share of death and violence, but now was not the time. It was Sullivan's sudden memory that mattered.

"It was that lorry—the backfire," Sullivan said. "Not the same, but it reminded me."

Harry waited while Sullivan struggled to put words to his memory.

"Before anything," Sullivan said at last. "Before the alarms, before the watertight bulkhead doors coming down, before the water came boiling up around our feet, there was a sharp crack." He hesitated. "Not a scraping, a crack, like a rifle shot, and then the water came in."

He looked at Harry hopefully. "Do you understand?"

Harry shook his head. "No, I don't. It obviously means something to you, but I don't understand the significance."

"We'd been shoveling burning coal for days," Sullivan said. "It didn't take an officer to tell us to put our backs into it. We all knew what was at stake. I heard it from a bloke called Dilley when I first went aboard. He'd been with the *Titanic* when they brought her around from Belfast, and he said she been on fire when they started out. They shoveled out one of the bunkers on the way round and rubbed a bit of oil on the place where the bulkhead was dinged. That's what he said—rubbed it so the inspectors wouldn't notice, but they didn't put out the fire; it had moved to bunker five, and it was still smoldering."

Harry was hardly able to believe his own ears. "Are you saying that someone was told to rub oil over the burn marks to conceal the damage done by the fire?"

"That's what Dilley said."

"And I don't suppose Dilley has been asked to testify," Harry muttered angrily.

"He came back with us on the *Lapland*," Sullivan said. "I don't know what's happened to him since."

Harry thought of the stack of papers on his desk at the Drill Hall. No one by the name of Dilley had given a deposition. He amended that thought. Maybe Dilley had been deposed, and maybe he had said something about the fire damage. All Harry could say for certain was that Dilley's deposition was not on his desk.

Sullivan slapped the steering wheel in frustration. "I should have said something in Plymouth," he growled. "I didn't think it would matter, and I wanted to get out of there and back to New York. I didn't know the inquiry would be so ..."

" So what?" Harry asked.

"So bloody crook," Sullivan said. "I didn't think the whole bloody thing would be a sham. Some good blokes died down there in the engine room." He leaned back in his seat and looked up at the sky almost as if he were beseeching heaven to listen to him.

"I soon found out that we were in a three-way race. If we couldn't load the burning coal into the boilers fast enough, the fire would spread, and the *Titanic* would burn to the waterline before we reached New York, but if we shoveled too fast, we'd run out of coal and not have enough to keep the boilers fed, and the third leg was not much better.

"Too fast through the ice, and you risked a collision," Harry said.

"That's right. We heard talk that the only way to put out the fire was to wait for New York and use the harbor fireboats." Sullivan gave a cynical chuckle. "Turns out we didn't need them."

"What about the rifle crack?" Harry asked.

"It wasn't a rifle," Sullivan said, "just a sound like a rifle, and then a crackling. Bunker five was already empty, and the fire had moved into bunker six. When we emptied bunker five, the bulkheads were glowing red hot. The metal was warped. None of us said anything. What was the point? We were in hell and we knew it. If we didn't do our job, the whole ship would be red hot, so we shoveled and we kept quiet." He gave a derisive snort. "White Star's been trying to keep us quiet ever since."

Harry nodded. "Yes, I know. If they can't keep you quiet, they'll make sure you're discredited. It's obvious that Interrogantum's job is to come up with anything and everything he can to divert attention. So what was the noise you heard?"

"I think it was the ship's bulkhead cracking like an egg," Sullivan said. "The iceberg didn't just scrape along the side; it pierced at the point where the metal had been red hot. That's why it was so quick. We never stood a chance."

Sullivan replaced his hands on the steering wheel and turned the car back toward the road. "I'm going to see Bigham," he said.

"And do what?"

"Tell him what I know."

"And then what?" Harry asked.

"I'll give evidence."

Harry shook his head. "He'll never let you. The Wreck Commissioner, who just happens to be Bigham's father, has compiled his list of witnesses on the basis of the depositions they collected in Plymouth. You're not on the list."

"What about Fred Barrett?" Sullivan asked. "He knows what happened, and he's a leading fireman. They put him on the stand in the States."

"And what did he say?" Harry asked. "Did he talk about the bulkheads being red hot and the fact that the *Titanic* was racing against time before she burned to the waterline?"

Sullivan's knuckles were white as he gripped the steering wheel. "I don't know," he said. "The papers haven't said."

"If the papers in the States had caught hold of this story, we would know about it," Harry said. "Barrett hasn't given the game away. You say he's a leading fireman?"

"Yes."

"A company man with a long career with White Star," Harry guessed. "He'll know what side his bread is buttered."

"Then what do we do?" Sullivan asked.

"You'll have to tell what you know."

"You just said Bigham—"

"Not Bigham," Harry interrupted. "I don't trust Bigham." His heart was pounding as he began to plan. He would have to put his trust in what he'd overheard in Plymouth.

"Fleet Street."

Sullivan gave him a puzzled frown. "What's on Fleet Street?"

"All the London newspaper offices."

Sullivan glanced sideways. "You want me to tell that story to the newspapers?"

Harry shook his head. "No, I don't. I don't know how many reporters are in the pay of the White Star Line. I don't know if Bigham has set me up to learn the truth or made sure I can't learn the truth. This is a complicated game, and you, Mr. Sullivan, hold one of the very few trump cards. I don't know what will happen to you if you talk, but I hope you'll take the risk."

"And do what?"

"Tell your story to a reporter who can be trusted."

"And who is that?"

Harry hesitated for just a moment. All he had to go on was scraps of an overheard conversation and his own instincts honed and sharpened in the king's service.

"I don't care what this Interrogantum fellow pays, our job is to report news and not rumors. I don't want any part of it ... I have standards, and I won't stoop to outright lies."

"He's a reporter called Charlie."

"What newspaper does he work for?"

"I don't know. I don't even know his last name, but I think I know where to find him."

"I'd rather be warming a seat in the Cheshire Cheese than peddling lies."

Harry pointed toward the distant dome of St. Paul's. "Head that way."

The traffic increased as they approached the city, and Harry concentrated on giving Sullivan directions. The Vauxhall was soon absorbed into the city's flow of automobiles, lorries, horse-drawn carts, and rattling, crowded omnibuses. Keeping his eye always on St. Paul's Cathedral, Harry managed to direct Sullivan from the Strand onto Fleet Street.

"Is this it?" Sullivan asked as he edged the Vauxhall onto the narrow street. Tall office buildings crowded out the sky, and young men with ink-stained hands and frantic faces dashed from one side of the street to the other. The very air hummed with activity and urgency. Looking around, Harry could see the names of all the world's great newspapers displayed on the four- and five-story buildings. Between the buildings, smaller and very much older, were the pubs and coffee houses that had long been the meeting places of London's writing community.

Sullivan blew a blast on the Vauxhall's horn as a boy stepped heedlessly into the street. The Australian's face was taut with concentration. Harry imagined that a man who had spent his boyhood on an Australian sheep station would never have seen anything like the chaos of the automobile-choked streets of London.

"I'm going to park this bloody thing and walk," Sullivan declared. "Where the hell is this place?"

A break in the rush of pedestrians showed Harry what he was looking for. "Pull over here," he said. "I can see it."

Ye Olde Cheshire Cheese was crammed in between the commercial buildings with only a hanging sign and a small expanse of lattice windows to reveal its presence. The door opened to a crowded, dimly lit bar.

"Well, where is he?" Sullivan barked as he pushed in behind Harry.

Harry searched through the fug of tobacco smoke and located the man he had last seen at the Duke of Cornwall Hotel.

Charlie looked up as they approached. "Saw you in Plymouth," he said. He laughed at the surprise on Harry's face. "I'm paid to observe," he said.

"So am I," Harry countered. "My friend and I have a story for you."

Charlie used his formidable stomach to clear a path through the crowd and into a secluded corner.

"I listened to your breakfast conversation in Plymouth," Harry said, "and I heard you declaring that you would only report the truth.

It seemed that your associate had other ideas. I assume that he is behind Interrogantum's rumormongering."

"He's one of many," Charlie said.

"But you are not involved?"

Charlie shook his head. "No, I am not, and I must admit that I'm paying a high price for my principles." He gestured toward his empty tankard. "The price of beer these days …"

Harry took the hint and picked up the glass. "I'll go," he said. "I'll leave Mr. Sullivan to tell you his story."

By the time Harry had fought his way to the bar and returned with three sloppily filled glasses, Sullivan had finished telling his story, and Charlie was slumped despondently with his head down.

Sullivan shook his head. "He won't do it."

Harry's heart sank as he set the beer down. Charlie looked into the glass with sad spaniel eyes. "No one will print it. It's just another rumor, and Interrogantum has cornered the market in rumors. Your only hope of having this story believed is to have it printed in *The Times*."

"So take it to *The Times*," Harry said impatiently.

"I don't have the credentials." Charlie spread his hands. "Look at me. I'm just a sad-sack hack reporter. The only extraordinary thing I've ever done is stand up to Interrogantum and refuse to report irresponsible lies." He looked at Sullivan. "For what it's worth, Mr. Sullivan, I believe you, but the only way you'll get your story into a real newspaper is to tell it to the Wreck Commissioner's Inquiry and make it part of the official record. I assume you have not been called."

Sullivan shook his head. "White Star will make sure I'm not called. In fact, White Star would be relieved if I was silenced permanently."

"You exaggerate," Charlie said.

There was an edge to Sullivan's voice as he replied. "No, I don't."

Charlie looked at Harry and raised his eyebrows as if to ask for confirmation.

"Mr. Sullivan is lucky to be alive," Harry said grimly.

"Tell that to Interrogantum," Charlie suggested. "He'd print that." He held up a hand as if to make a headline appear in the smoky air. "Are *Titanic* Crew Members Receiving Death Threats?"

"Would you like to know who Interrogantum is?" Harry asked.

Charlie rose to his feet and picked up his glass. "No, I would not. I may not have much of a life, but I would like to keep it." He gave them an apologetic smile. "I wish I could help you, but I can't." He fixed his eyes on Sullivan. "You would be wise to leave the country." He glanced quickly at Harry. "Find a way to tell the world," he said. "The dead deserve the truth."

London
Ernie Sullivan

Sullivan was glad that he could still draw on his grandfather's letters of credit. When the old man found out that Sullivan had allowed his quarry to escape, he would surely regret his generosity, but in the meantime, Sullivan was going to need a few pounds, shillings, and pence to take care of Ben Tillett's Vauxhall.

Tillett scowled as he looked at the damage Sullivan had wrought on the automobile's shining paint. "What the hell did you do with her?" he demanded.

Eva Newton's four children, arrayed on the doorstep of her fashionable London home, drew in a concerted gasp of shock. Apparently, they were not accustomed to such language from their father.

Tillett shooed them away. "Go back inside."

The children scampered back into the house, and Tillett turned to follow them. "You'd best come into my study," he said. He glared at Sullivan. "I'll be sending you a bill for the repairs."

"It's just a few scratches," Sullivan said.

"It was necessary," Hazelton said grimly. "Lives were at stake."

Tillett nodded. "Yes, I heard the story. The earl's daughter turned out to be a diamond thief."

Sullivan could not resist coming to Daisy's defense. "She's an opportunist, not a thief. The thief is in custody."

"And what about the girl?" Tillett asked.

"She no longer matters," Hazelton said.

Sullivan followed the two men into Tillett's study and sat quietly as Hazelton told the labor leader what they had discovered about the fire in the bunkers. He allowed his mind to wander back to what Hazelton had said about Daisy. *She no longer matters.* He was wrong.

Daisy Melville mattered. She could not be so easily dismissed. When the inquiry was over, when the story of the fire was written into the official record, he would—

"Sullivan!" He looked up to see that Hazelton was glaring at him impatiently.

"What?"

"Do you know this man?"

"What man?"

"The man that Mr. Tillett is speaking of."

Sullivan vanquished the memory of Daisy's blue eyes and shook his head at Hazelton. "Tell me again."

"Hendrickson, Charles Hendrickson."

Sullivan nodded. "Fireman," he said. "Big, surly bloke. He went to get the lamps so the engineers could see the gauges. Dropped them off and scarpered. I heard he was one of the first into the lifeboats."

He fought against a sudden surge of anger. What was done was done. So Hendrickson had been among the first rats to leave the sinking ship, but he was not the only rat. Reports from the United States inquiry made it quite clear that the rule of "women and children first" had only applied to first- and maybe second-class passengers, and after that it had been every man for himself, with third-class passengers fighting for their lives. If he allowed himself to be angry with Hendrickson, he would soon be angry at the whole world.

Tillett steepled his fingers as he looked down at the papers strewn across his desk; some appeared to have been typed, but many were handwritten.

"So Hendrickson would know about the fire?" Tillett asked.

"He was shoveling alongside me," Sullivan said, recalling the heat and horror of the burning bunker, "but he won't talk. He's a White Star man. They'll pay him not to talk about the fire."

"I'm sure that's the case," Tillett said grimly, "but they don't know we have an ace up our sleeve." He grinned, his teeth gleaming white beneath his luxuriant mustache. "We have you, Mr. Sullivan."

"They won't call me," Sullivan said impatiently. He looked at Hazelton. "Didn't you explain? I'm not on the witness list."

"But Hendrickson is," Tillett said, stabbing his finger at a list of names. "He's due to appear tomorrow. White Star will use his testimony of what happened in his lifeboat as a distraction and a way to refocus the public interest. Everyone is looking for a villain. The Americans are focusing on Bruce Ismay, the chairman of the line, who had the sheer effrontery to save his own life and not go down with the ship. They'll never prove anything against him, but he'll be destroyed."

Tillett smoothed his mustache for a moment, very much like a music-hall villain. "The British, on the other hand, have chosen a different victim to distract the general public. Instead of Bruce Ismay, they are set on destroying Sir Cosmo Duff-Gordon, and they'll use Hendrickson to do it."

"What did Duff-Gordon do?" Sullivan asked.

Tillett shrugged. "He let the side down," he said. "He loaded himself and his wife and a couple of other first-class passengers, mostly male, into one of the emergency lifeboats, commandeered five crew members, and rowed away with twelve people in a boat that would take forty. It was not the behavior of a gentleman, and the British public will never forgive him. As luck would have it, Charles Hendrickson was one of the men he bribed."

"Bribed?" Sullivan repeated. "You mean he bribed him to get into the boat and row?"

"No. He bribed him not to turn back and pick up people who were waiting on the deck. There was still time to save them, but Duff-Gordon wouldn't do it."

Sullivan felt suddenly out of his depth. A complicated game was being played out in front of the Wreck Commissioner. It was a game of national pride and corporate greed, with the crew of *Titanic* as the unwitting pawns.

He looked at Hazelton and saw that the soldier's eyes were gleaming with understanding. This was meat and drink for Hazelton—a return to the shadowy world of half-truth and rumor that he had played for so long on behalf of the empire. Hazelton understood every subtle nuance of the plan Tillett was preparing, and he looked forward to seeing the game played out to the end. Sullivan liked Hazelton, even admired him, but he could not admire the game. He was suddenly homesick for Goolagong and the uncomplicated rhythm of life on the sheep station.

"Hendrickson will be called and asked to point the finger of blame at Duff-Gordon for rowing away in an empty boat," Tillett said.

"They have his deposition," Hazelton agreed. "They won't expect any surprises."

Tillett grinned. "The British Seafarers' Union has been allowed one lawyer," he said. "I think it's time he earned his fee."

Riddlesdown Court
Poppy Melville

The telegrams arrived at midday, while Poppy was in her father's study, examining the estate account books. She had decided not to call in the estate manager—not yet. Jack Renfrew had known her since she was a child, and he called her Miss Poppy as if she were still in short petticoats. Her father, of course, had done nothing to encourage Renfrew to respect her. The earl had no place on the estate for his daughter and had encouraged the same attitude in his estate manager. Poppy knew that she would be in for a battle of wills when the time came for her to inherit. Now, having read the accounts, she was ready.

Glancing out the window, she saw the post-office boy riding up the drive on his red bicycle. There was no doubting who he was or why he was coming to the door. He had a telegram, and telegrams were never good news.

Daisy! Who else could it be? She tried to remain calm. Perhaps it was a telegram from the bishop. She was desperate to talk to her uncle, a voice of reason in a sea of chaos. He was not yet back from Berlin, but perhaps this was news of his impending arrival.

She opened the door herself, calling to the boy as he made his way toward the back of the house. "Bring it here. No need to go to the kitchen."

The boy looked crestfallen. He wanted to go to the kitchen. Poppy took not one but two envelopes from his hand and directed him to the back. "Get yourself some tea and cake, and I'll read these and see if I need to give you a reply."

He tipped his cap and disappeared. Poppy walked back into the study and picked up her father's letter opener. She hesitated for only a moment. Bad news was never improved by waiting. Whatever words were in the telegrams would not be magically altered by a delay on her part. On the other hand, the fact that she had two telegrams presented a chance that at least one of them would be from her uncle and would not be bad news.

She laid the envelopes on the desk. They were identical. No hint as to the sender. *Just pick up the first one and read it.* She allowed her hand to hover for a moment and then pulled an envelope toward her. She slit it open, and the yellow telegram form with its pasted white message fluttered onto the desk.

BIG DAY AT TITANIC HEARING TOMORROW STOP PLEASE COME STOP REPLY TO DULWICH CLUB STOP WILL MEET TRAIN STOP REGARDS HAZELTON (CAPTAIN) STOP

She stared down at the paper. It was impossible to read any emotion into the simple message. She hovered over the word regards. The word could mean anything or nothing, and he had not even used his Christian name, simply his surname and his rank. Of course, he had said please, and that was good, but what did he mean by Big day at Titanic hearing? Had some new evidence come to light? He and Sullivan had certainly left in a hurry. Perhaps this was the reason he had scorned her lavish breakfast and left without any reference to what had passed between them in the paddock. She should go. She should take some of Agnes's housekeeping money and buy a train ticket. He would meet her at the station and ... Her heart skipped a beat. She could not get beyond the idea of meeting him at the station.

She looked down at the other envelope. Could this be from Uncle Hugh? It was possible but unlikely. *Oh, Daisy, please don't ruin this for me. Let me be happy.*

COME AT ONCE BRING MONEY CLOTHES STATION HOTEL DOVER

The fact that the telegram had no signature and no unnecessary words told Poppy that this missive was from Daisy, and Daisy had run completely out of money. She must have spent her last few pennies on sending this cry for help.

She pushed the account books aside and filled out two reply forms, one for Harry Hazelton and one for Daisy, and then she walked back to the kitchen and handed them to the telegraph boy.

CHAPTER NINETEEN

London Scottish Drill Hall
Harry Hazelton

Sir Ernest Shackleton joined Harry and Sullivan as they walked from the Dulwich Club to the Drill Hall, where Charles Hendrickson was due to testify immediately after the lunch break. When they emerged onto the Mall and Buckingham Palace came into view, Sullivan paused. He looked up at the royal standard flying above the front portico.

"It means the king is in residence," Shackleton said.

"What does he do all day?" Sullivan asked.

Shackleton shook his head. "I don't know. It's a big empire, almost half the world. I'm sure he has plenty to do. He's visited Australia, you know."

Sullivan's lips quirked, with the scar making it impossible to know if he was smiling or merely offering a sardonic grin. "The old king's brother came on an imperial visit, and one of our blokes shot him. Didn't kill him, but gave it a good try. Some of us can understand why."

Harry looked up at the lions and harp of the brilliantly colored flag and thought of the many times he had put his life at risk for the sake of that flag. The discontent behind Ernie Sullivan's words came as a welcome distraction. Pondering the fate of the far-flung empire kept his mind from the paper he had crumpled into his pocket. The telegram was brief. She was not coming; Daisy needed her. *Daisy will always need her.*

Shackleton tapped him on the shoulder. "Come on, Hazelton. Can't stand there staring all day."

When they reached the London Scottish Drill Hall, they found the usual crowd of reporters and photographers milling around the entrance. The reporters always had an eye out for the rich and famous or for anyone who looked like they might be a survivor. Shackleton was naturally a person of interest, and the reporters who crowded around him did not even glance at his companions. Harry was not known to them at all. He had always remained on the periphery of the inquiry, slipping in and out through a side door and rarely taking a seat to listen to the evidence. Ernie Sullivan was equally unknown. In a well-tailored suit, with his beard trimmed and a homburg hat casting a slight shadow over his face, he could not be readily identified as a man who had shoveled and sweated over the *Titanic*'s boilers.

Shackleton waved the reporters away. He had nothing new to say. He was still of the opinion that four knots was a safe speed through ice, and anything faster was an invitation to disaster.

They found Ben Tillett waiting for them inside the Drill Hall, where the hearings were already underway. Clive Bigham's acoustic curtains had done little to improve the sound quality, and Harry was relieved when Tillett told them that he had reserved seats in the front row.

Harry pulled Tillett aside before they sat down. "Does the lawyer know what to ask?"

"He does."

"Will he do it?"

"He says he'll try. It's not easy to get a word in against the White Star lawyers."

As Harry walked toward his reserved seat, he paused to observe the players in White Star's high-stakes game. Lord Mersey sat on the highest platform, looking judicial but bored. His only concession to the idea that this was not an actual court of law was the fact that he was not wearing his wig or robes. The lawyers surrounding him on lower platforms were equally informal in dress but not in manner. Clive Bigham had insisted that this was not a court of law, but nothing could dispel the feeling that the man standing to one side and penned in by railings was, in fact, a prisoner in the dock.

Charles Osker Hendrickson, the man who had been bribed to row away with an almost empty lifeboat, had dark hair and a ruddy complexion that belied his Swedish name. Sullivan, who was also making his way along the front row of seats, stopped abruptly and stared at him. Hendrickson returned the stare long enough to register that they had once been shipmates.

Harry poked Sullivan's arm. "Sit down. You're drawing attention."

Sullivan sat and satisfied himself with glowering at the witness. Hendrickson returned his attention to the group of lawyers who were firing questions at him.

Harry caught a glimpse of Clive Bigham hovering in the doorway behind the platform. *Why is he here? Does he suspect that we're about to put an end to the game? Will he try to stop us, or are we doing what he really wants?* Bigham was a soldier, and he would obey orders, but he didn't have to like the orders.

Harry wished that Poppy were here to see his moment of triumph. He was a wounded soldier with no fortune and few prospects, but he had gone up against some of the most powerful men in British commerce, and he was about to prevail. At least one witness was going to tell the truth. He hoped that he was correct in his assessment that Bigham had given him this assignment because he knew that they shared a skill. They were both practiced in the art of looking beyond written words to find the words that had not been written.

He glanced around and saw Charlie's large figure overflowing onto two chairs set beside the wall close to the model of the *Titanic*. He was ready. If Tillett's lawyer could ask the right questions, Charlie would know what to do with the answers. This was Charlie's big day. He was about to get his foot in the door at *The Times*.

Harry turned his attention to the lawyer who was questioning Hendrickson. He was a small man with untidy hair and an ill-fitting suit who paced restlessly and peppered Hendrickson with questions. Harry turned to Tillett.

"Is that our man?"

"No. That's Harbinson, appearing for the third-class passengers. He's doing a fine job of blackening Duff-Gordon's name. It won't help us, but it's a delight to watch."

Harbinson stepped close to the witness. "So, you say that lifeboat number one was launched with seven crew members to row and only five passengers?"

Hendrickson nodded. "Yes, five passengers."

Harbinson raised his eyebrows. "It is the duty of the crew to exhaust every resource in order to rescue passengers, is it not?"

"Yes."

"What I do not quite understand is that there being seven of the crew, why you did not, despite the protests of these first-class passengers, go back to some of the dying people?"

Hendrickson's mumbled reply was inaudible even in the front row.

Lord Mersey leaned down from his high seat. "Speak up so that I can hear!"

Harry reminded himself that this was why he had so far been reluctant to attend the hearings. The acoustics of the hall made for difficult listening.

Hendrickson raised his voice. "There was a man in charge of the boat; he should know what to do best. It would not do for everybody to be in charge of a boat that is in her. When a man gets in a boat, the coxswain takes charge and does everything."

Lord Mersey nodded. "And you say that the coxswain in charge of your boat showed no inclination to pull back."

"No, none whatsoever."

Harbinson stepped up again. His voice was needle sharp. "And this attitude of his was due to the protests of the Duff-Gordons?"

"Yes, sir."

"And you heard cries?"

"Yes."

"Agonizing cries?"

"Yes, terrible cries."

"At what distance?"

"About two hundred yards away."

Harry saw Sullivan's shoulders stiffen. He was remembering. He had heard those agonizing cries.

Harbinson drove his point home. "And yet despite that fact, no effort was made to move in the direction of those cries?"

"No, none at all."

Lord Mersey leaned forward again. Despite listening to day after day of testimony about the night of the sinking, he still seemed capable of genuine shock. "I cannot understand this," he declared. "Was there any discussion on board this boat as to whether you should go to these dying people—any talk?"

Hendrickson shook his head. "Only when I proposed going

back, that's all."

Lord Mersey scowled. "Do you mean to tell me that you were the only person that proposed to go back?"

"I never heard any others," Hendrickson said truculently. "I spoke to everyone. I shouted out in the boat. They said it would be too dangerous to go back; we might be swamped."

"And who said that?"

"Sir Cosmo Duff-Gordon."

"Did anyone else say anything?"

"His wife. She agreed."

"Am I to understand that because two of the passengers said it would be dangerous, you all kept your mouths shut and made no attempt to rescue anybody?"

"Yes, sir."

Harry sensed movement around him. Journalists were scratching pens on paper. Sir Cosmo Duff-Gordon was about to lose all the appointments in his social calendar.

Another lawyer took advantage of the momentary lull to step forward. Harry leaned toward Tillett. "Is that our man?"

Tillett shook his head. "That's Edwards—Dock, Wharf, Riverside and General Workers' Union. He'll just be seeking attention. Wants his name in the papers."

Edwards was a much larger man, with slicked-back hair and a dark, brooding gaze. "Mr. Hendrickson, was any money given to you by any passengers when you got on the *Carpathia*?"

Hendrickson nodded.

"And what did you receive?"

"An order for five pounds."

"And who was that from?"

"Sir Cosmo Duff-Gordon."

"And what did the other members of the crew get?"

"The same."

Harry saw, to his dismay, that lawyers were lining up to ask Hendrickson for details of his gift from Sir Cosmo Duff-Gordon. Was it a bribe? Was it given as a reward for not turning back? Was it just a gesture of gratitude? The lawyers tied themselves and the Wreck Commissioner into knots with the same question asked a dozen different ways. Harry was now more than ever convinced that the inquiry was not intended to produce a result.

Harry glanced at his watch. Lord Mersey was a stickler for routine. The hearings ended every day promptly at four thirty, and the time now was four twenty-five. If the union lawyer did not interrupt now, he would have to wait until the next day, and Harry was not even certain that Hendrickson would be recalled the next day. The seaman had already performed above and beyond expectations and blackened the name of Sir Cosmo Duff-Gordon for generations to come.

The shadowy figures who were steering the course of the hearings would be very satisfied with Hendrickson's performance so far. They would not risk him saying anything unexpected. Clive Bigham had said it himself: *When in court, never ask a question to which you do not already know the answer.*

Lord Mersey began to gather up the papers on his desk. Harry's heart sank. Sullivan leaned across to speak to Tillett. "Too damned late," he hissed.

Tillett shook his head. "No, just in time. Here he comes."

The man who was pushing through the mass of lawyers was built like a tree stump, with wide shoulders and a barrel chest. His freckled face might have belonged to an Irish leprechaun, but there was nothing impish about his booming voice.

"Thomas Scanlan, Member of Parliament for North Sligo, appearing for the Seamen's and Firemen's Union," he said.

Lord Mersey glared at him impatiently. "Not now. Bring your questions tomorrow."

Scanlan's Irish voice was filled with scorn. "We all know, don't we," he said, "that this man won't be appearing tomorrow? I'll ask my questions now."

"Well, be quick about it," Lord Mersey snapped. "I have heard quite enough for one day."

Scanlan bowed and turned to Hendrickson. "Mr. Hendrickson, do you remember a fire in a coal bunker on board this boat?"

The other lawyers raised their voices in protest. This was not the line of questioning that they were following; Scanlan should wait his turn. What did this have to do with the matter of Sir Cosmo Duff-Gordon?

Scanlan persisted. "Mr. Hendrickson, I ask you again. Do you remember a fire in a coal bunker on board this boat?"

Hendrickson seemed relieved at the change of subject. In

blackening Duff-Gordon's character, he had done nothing for his own character.

He nodded. "Yes, I do."

"And did you help to get the coal out of the bunker?"

"I did."

"Did you hear when the fire commenced?"

Hendrickson's eyes roved around the room.

He's looking for someone to tell him what to say, Harry thought. *He's been receiving signals from someone in the audience, and now they've stopped signaling.*

Hendrickson's eyes finally came to rest on Sullivan. His face twisted in a rueful grin.

"I heard it commenced in Belfast," he said.

Scanlan nodded. "And when did you start getting the coal out?"

Hendrickson looked at Sullivan, back at Scanlan, and then at the Wreck Commissioner. He was a man without a script. He was on his own.

"When did you start getting the coal out?"

"On the first watch from Southampton."

The Wreck Commissioner leaned forward, and Harry came to understand that Clive Bigham's father was no fool. He was a small man with a high-pitched voice, and without his robes, he did not cut a very imposing figure. He was, however, not a man to be taken lightly. It appeared that he was no longer concerned about ending on time.

"How many days would that be after you left Belfast?" he asked.

"I do not know when she left Belfast, not to the very day," Hendrickson stammered.

"It would be two or three days, I suppose," Scanlan suggested.

Hendrickson nodded. "Yes, I suppose so."

"And how long did it take to put the fire itself out?"

Hendrickson shrugged with a poor attempt at nonchalance. "The fire was not out much before all the coal was out. I finished the bunker out myself, me and three or four men. We worked everything out."

Scanlan held up a finger to silence the other lawyers, who were now anxious to join in the new line of questioning.

"The bulkhead forms part of the bunker, does it not?" he asked.

"It forms part of the side."

"Yes." Hendrickson stared up at the vaulted ceiling for a moment.

Harry shook his head. Hendrickson was trapped. Thanks to Sullivan, Scanlan was not fishing blindly in the dark. Like any good lawyer, he already knew the answers to his questions.

"Did you look at the side after the coal had been taken out?" Scanlan asked.

Hendrickson nodded.

"And what condition was it in?"

"You could see where it had been red hot—all the paint and everything was off." Hendrickson shuffled his feet. "It was dented a bit."

"It was damaged?"

"Yes, warped."

"And was much notice taken of it?" Scanlan asked. "Was anything done about the damaged bulkhead? Anything at all?"

Hendrickson stared at his tormentor and then looked at Sullivan. Sullivan's scarred lips quirked up into a smile, and Harry was surprised to see an expression of relief on Hendrickson's face. The secret was about to be revealed, and Hendrickson could do nothing about it. Perhaps he had wanted to tell the truth all along.

Hendrickson shook his head. "Well, we—I just brushed it off and got some black oil and rubbed it over."

"To give it an ordinary appearance?"

"Yes."

"To disguise the damage?"

Hendrickson said nothing. There was no need.

Harry looked across and saw Charlie rising to his feet. He moved quickly for such a large man. His report for *The Times* was already written. While the other reporters were still trying to work out what exactly they had heard, Charlie would be well on his way to Fleet Street.

Dover
Poppy Melville

Poppy's journey to Dover had been long and frustrating and made even more so by the restricted schedule resulting from the coal strike. The stationmaster at Riddlesdown had even been reluctant to sell her a ticket.

"I can't guarantee anything, Your Ladyship. The Winchester train will be coming through shortly if it comes at all, but from Winchester you will have to go to London and change from the Great Western to the South Eastern." He shook his head discouragingly. "No guarantees on that line. You may have to wait at Victoria for the boat train, because there are no other trains running, and I've heard there's a shortage of first-class carriages. Are you sure you want to do this, Your Ladyship?"

I'm sure I don't want to do it, but I have to. One more time, Daisy. This is your last chance.

Poppy thanked the stationmaster for his advice and handed over money for a third-class ticket.

"Third class, Your Ladyship?"

"You said it yourself, first class may not be available."

I'm using the housekeeping money, and I can't afford to waste it.

When the Dover train, delayed by two hours, finally steamed out of Victoria station, the sky had begun to darken with rain clouds. By the time they were crossing the exposed North Downs, the wind had grown to gale force, and rain slashed at the windows of the third-class carriage, finding every weak spot in the battered wooden frames. As additional passengers joined the train on its journey across Kent, Poppy found herself crammed into a corner of the carriage with no way to avoid leaning against the leaking window.

She shifted uncomfortably as water dripped onto her shoulder and down her neck. When a large man who was taking up far more than his fair share of space on the bench apologized to her, she gave him a genuine smile. He wasn't to know that she had survived the *Titanic*. A few drops of cold water were nothing, nothing at all.

At long last the train pulled into Dover Priory, the end of the line. Poppy pulled her portmanteau down from the luggage rack without the assistance of a porter and stepped out onto the platform. The salt-laden wind, bitingly cold, tugged at her hat and skirt, but she was surprised at how easily she shrugged off the discomfort. She had changed. She was still Lady Penelope Melville of Riddlesdown Court, but she was also Poppy, first-class stewardess and survivor of the *Titanic*. She was capable of anything. *Anything except refusing Daisy's demands.*

Her portmanteau was not heavy. She had brought a change of clothes for Daisy, but she had not packed any of the new frivolous and expensive items Daisy had bought with the stolen money. What she had brought would be enough for one night, and tomorrow Daisy would have to return to Riddlesdown. Poppy could not imagine what had happened to the large sum of money Daisy had taken with her, but obviously, she had spent it or lost it somehow, and there would be no more. Daisy would have to learn that actions had consequences.

She handed her ticket to a collector and stepped through the gate into the station concourse, where she was sheltered from the rain if not from the wind. The journey had taken far longer than she had expected, but presumably, Daisy was still waiting at the Station Hotel. *Unless she's found someone to give her money and I've come all this way for nothing.*

As she walked toward the exit, a figure stirred in the shadows. A woman had risen from a bench and was running to meet her. Poppy staggered back as Daisy flung herself into Poppy's arms, clinging to her neck and sobbing.

"Poppy, oh, Poppy, where have you been? What took you so long? I've been waiting."

Poppy put her arms around her sister but could not keep irritation from her voice. "You should have waited at the hotel. I told you in my telegram."

Daisy stamped her foot, and Poppy felt a surge of impatience. *She's still doing that.*

"They wouldn't let me wait," Daisy wailed. "I told them you were coming, but I didn't have money for the room, so they said I had to leave. I've waited all day. I thought you had changed your mind."

Poppy sloughed off her initial anger and put her arm around her sister's shoulders. She was quite sure that Daisy had passed a truly miserable day in the grimy train station.

"No money at all?" she asked.

"No, none. I'm so hungry."

"What happened?"

"I'll tell you in a minute. Look, there's a café. Can we get something to eat?"

The station café was almost deserted. Daisy flung herself into a chair and looked up at Poppy beseechingly. "Tea. I want a cup of tea, and then ..." She looked at the chalked menu on the rear wall. "Eggs, bacon, and toast. It'll be a kind of breakfast because I didn't have breakfast. What took you so long?"

"You're lucky I'm here at all," Poppy said. "How could you just leave us like that?"

Daisy ignored her, leaning back in her chair and waving at the waitress.

"Daisy!" Poppy snapped. "I'm talking to you."

Daisy gave her order to the waitress, adding an additional cup of tea for Poppy.

" What happened?" Poppy asked again.

"I met a man on the train."

"Daisy!"

"Don't look at me like that. You know it's not my fault that men find me attractive. I can't help it."

"You don't have to encourage it."

Daisy raised her eyes to the ceiling in exasperation. "We're not all like you, Poppy. I see you mooning over Captain Hazelton, but have you done anything to let him know you're interested?"

Poppy looked down at the scarred wooden table, trying to hide the sudden warmth of her cheeks. By Daisy's standards, she had done nothing to encourage the captain, but by her own standards, she had been very receptive to his advances, although she was not sure he had actually been advancing.

"We're not talking about me," Poppy said firmly. "We're talking about you, Daisy. You had a large amount of money, and now you have none. Explain that."

"I was going to take the ferry last night," Daisy said, "but the train arrived in Dover, and we were told the ferry would not sail, for lack of coal. I didn't know what to do, but this very kind gentleman walked me to the Station Hotel, and I obtained a room for the night." She looked at Poppy. "On my own," she said. "A room on my own."

"I wasn't suggesting—"

"Yes, you were. You thought I shared a room with my new gentleman friend, and you're wrong. I didn't." She looked up as the waitress brought a teapot and two cups. "The gentleman invited me to have dinner with him, and so I accepted, and then he told me that he knew where we could find some entertainment."

"What kind of entertainment?"

"Just cards. Gentlemen playing cards. They had all planned to take the ferry. They were playing *vingt-et-un*, which is a really simple game and just a matter of luck. They said we'd play for money to make it more interesting, and I was very lucky at the beginning."

"And at the end?" Poppy asked.

"I started to lose, but everyone said I'd get my luck back if I kept playing, and so I did. We played for hours."

"And you lost all your money?" Poppy asked.

Daisy poured tea into her teacup and looked at Poppy in frustration. "You don't understand. It wasn't my fault. It's just a matter of luck. They all said that they couldn't believe I could be so unlucky."

Poppy took the teapot from Daisy and set it down on the table. "Daisy, look at me."

"I'm looking," Daisy said. "You're quite a mess. You need to comb your hair."

"Don't change the subject," Poppy replied. "You may think I'm naive, and I don't understand how to attract the attention of gentlemen, and I don't have any great ambition to see the world or become famous, but I know that you were played for a fool—"

"I was not," Daisy hissed. "It was just bad luck, and I don't want to talk about it." She turned her head and looked at the door that led to the kitchen. "What's happened to my food? I am so hungry. I'm so hungry I could eat a horse."

Horse—a dappled plow horse with a gray muzzle. Poppy's mind took on a will of its own, leaving behind the seedy café and the willful girl, and returning to early morning by the paddock at Riddlesdown. She saw Harry's hand grasping Dobby's mane and heard his whispered words.

"I have been haunted by the memory of a woman I hardly knew. You have banished that memory."

Daisy's voice impinged on her thoughts. "I had already paid for my room, so I was allowed to stay last night, but I only had enough to send a telegram. If you had not come, I don't know what I would have done."

"What about your gentleman friend?" Poppy asked, not even trying to keep icy anger from her voice.

Daisy lowered her head. "I don't know what happened to him. I thought he would help me, but I couldn't find him anywhere." She looked up eagerly as the waitress delivered a plate of eggs and bacon. "I knew I could count on you, Poppy. How much money did you bring?"

"Just enough," Poppy said.

"Enough for what?"

"To get us home. I have enough money for a hotel tonight, and I brought you a change of clothes."

"Is that all? Nothing for emergencies?"

"Yes, of course I have emergency money," Poppy said. "Unlike you, Daisy, I plan ahead. I don't just run away and hope that someone will help me. I've had to use some of the housekeeping money, and I will need to return it when we get home. Now eat your dinner or breakfast or whatever meal that is, and we'll go to the hotel. Tomorrow we're going home. Do you understand me?"

Daisy nodded obediently and spread butter on her toast.

The Dulwich Club
Ernie Sullivan

Sullivan looked around at the battered furnishings of the Dulwich Club and shook his head in amazement. With the *Titanic* hearings over for the day, Harry and Shackleton had invited Sullivan to dine with them at their club and promised him a room for the night. It was an offer he could hardly refuse.

He had no plans for the evening. In fact, he had no plans at all. For the first time in his life, he was completely free. Now that he had decided that he would not follow the path his grandfather had set for him, he was unsure what path he should follow. Part of him longed to return to the wide-open skies of Goolagong, but he knew that if he returned, he would not leave again. He was here now, on the other side of the world, and there must be something better to do than simply sail home and confront his angry old grandfather.

He could be dead. It was not the first time he had considered the possibility. Richard Sullivan was an old man, and messages from Australia were few and far between. Even if someone at Goolagong wanted to send him a message, they would not know where to send it. For the time being, until he could decide on a poste restante address, he would have to remain ignorant of any developments on the sheep station.

Harry had turned his back and was arranging for the club to give Sullivan a room for the night, so Sullivan addressed his question to Shackleton.

"So this is one of the famed London gentlemen's clubs?" he asked.

Shackleton grinned. "Well, old chap, it's not White's or Boodle's, but it's a club. I don't think the established clubs would let us through the door."

"They'd let *you* in," Harry said over his shoulder. "Internationally famous polar explorer and Knight Commander of the Royal Victorian Order."

"They'd get one whiff of my Irish accent and throw me out," Shackleton said amiably. He turned back to Sullivan. "It's a school club. We all went to Dulwich College."

"Is that one of your famous boarding schools?" Sullivan asked. He found that his right hand had moved involuntarily across his face to finger the scar that had disfigured him for so long.

Shackleton shook his head. "Old, but not famous," he said. "But the school has turned out some fine gentlemen." He glanced at Sullivan's hand as it rested on the scar. "Someone did that to you at school?"

For one brief moment, memory kept him silent. He could only nod his head as he fingered the long scar.

"That wouldn't happen at Dulwich," Shackleton said.

Sullivan found his voice. "I was given this at the best school in Australia. My grandfather thought they would make a gentleman of me, but all they saw was a convict's grandson. I've grown better with a blade since then. I don't have style, but I can take care of myself."

Harry turned away from the desk. "I have you booked in," he said, "and they'll send someone to Eva Newton's house to collect your bags. I'm afraid our Mr. Tillett, man of the people, couldn't join us to celebrate. He won't risk being seen in a privileged place like this."

"It's amazing how he keeps his opera singer and his second family out of the newspapers," Sullivan said.

"No one would believe them if they printed it," Harry said. "He's a popular figure with the working classes, and they won't let him be smeared."

"Unlike Sir Cosmo Duff-Gordon," Shackleton said.

"No more than he deserves," Sullivan said. "He had room for forty in his boat. That would have been forty people who wouldn't have had to go in the water."

"I'm amazed anyone survived the water," Shackleton said. "I've seen a man die in less than a minute."

"It felt like death," Sullivan said.

When he plunged into the water, the icy shock stabbed him like a thousand knives and momentarily paralyzed his lungs. He had to find something that would float. He shivered as he clung to his precarious perch. It had taken every last vestige of his strength to heave himself out of the water and onto the floating remains of a staircase.

The staircase drifted with the current, carrying him away from the death throes of the great ship. She was low in the water now, with waves washing across her bow, but her lights were still blazing. Someone was still down there. Some brave soul was still tending to the steam and generating power to the lights and providing a spark for the radio operators to send out their cries for help.

Another wave washed over the bow, and then abruptly, and with great finality, the lights winked out as if a curtain had closed to hide the final scene of the nightmare. Sullivan was blind now but not deaf. The night was filled with cries and whimpers, and the staircase teetered precariously, jostled by unseen debris. Slowly his eyes adjusted. Cold starlight showed him that he was adrift in a field of floating bodies, and beyond the bodies, the Titanic *was a great dark shape with her bow buried in the water and her stern slowly rising.*

Sullivan tried to concentrate on the moment he was now enjoying. He was warm and dry, and he had gained entry to a gentlemen's club, the most sacred of British fortresses. He should be satisfied, but he could not drag his mind away from the thought of Sir Cosmo Duff-Gordon in a lifeboat that contained only twelve people, bribing sailors to steer clear of reaching arms and beseeching voices. He knew that he himself had been just moments from death. If Officer Lowe and Poppy Melville in lifeboat fourteen had not picked him up, he, too, would have died.

"What will they do with him?" Sullivan asked.

"Unfortunately, Duff-Gordon's actions were not criminal," Shackleton said. "I've been at sea most of my adult life, and I can tell you that some of the rules we all rely on are unwritten; they are matters of conscience. Women and children first, the captain goes down with his ship, they are not matters of law.

Sir Cosmo Duff-Gordon rowed away to safety. Bruce Ismay, chairman of the White Star Line, saved himself. They are both alive, and they won't go to jail, but they are dead to society. Captain Smith, on the other hand, went down with his ship, and someone will surely erect a statue to him."

Sullivan followed Harry and Shackleton into the club bar, where they settled into threadbare wing chairs in front of a blazing fire. The spring weather had given way to a harsh north wind and driving rain. He looked at Shackleton, who had stretched his hands out to the warmth of the fire.

"I didn't think you would feel the cold."

Shackleton laughed. "Oh, I feel it. I even have a touch of frostbite in my fingers. Cold doesn't really bother me, but rain is a different matter. It doesn't rain in the Antarctic. It either snows or it doesn't, but at least it doesn't pour cold water down your neck."

Sullivan accepted a glass of brandy from an elderly waiter and lifted it in a salute to Harry. "Well done, mate. We got what we wanted."

Harry raised his glass in return, but his face was serious. "It will be in the record," he said, "and that's what I wanted. If it's printed in *The Times*, perhaps someone will take notice."

A man's voice spoiled the moment. "I'm afraid they won't have a chance.""

Sullivan looked up and saw Clive Bigham standing in the doorway with two waiters hovering uncertainly beside him.

Harry waved his hand. "Let him in. I know he's not a member, but let him in."

Bigham stepped into the room. "Sorry, old man," he said.

Harry was on his feet. "Sorry about what?" he asked through gritted teeth.

"Sorry that *The Times* will not be printing the article your journalist friend is writing. You did a damned fine job of finding the weak spot in White Star's armor, but I can't let you tell the world."

Sullivan studied the two men, equal in height and military

bearing, Harry's brown eyes boring into Bigham's steady gray gaze. He turned to Shackleton. "What the hell's going on here?"

"Damned if I know," Shackleton replied, "but I think we need to stay out of it."

"Why in blue blazes should we?" Sullivan asked.

"Because it's not our fight."

"I shoveled that coal," Sullivan said. "Don't tell me there was no fire."

Bigham tore his gaze away from Harry's face and turned to Sullivan. "I believe you, Mr. Sullivan," he said. "I believe there was a fire in the bunkers, and I believe White Star should not have been given a certificate of seaworthiness in Southampton, but there'll be nothing in the newspapers." He hesitated and then smiled dismissively. "I'll rephrase that. The fire will be subjected to the irresponsible musings of Interrogantum, musings designed to tangle the reader in a web of conspiracy and conjecture where the truth can be easily dismissed."

Sullivan did not dare get to his feet. He knew that if he came within reach of Bigham, he would make his very best attempt to beat the man to a pulp. How dare he suppress the truth?

He set his glass aside as a wave of memory threatened to swamp him.

As the Titanic*'s bow slid beneath the waves, the stern rose into the air, higher and higher, until it stood upright with its massive rudder and propellers clearly visible. A mass of people had scrambled and fought their way up the steep incline until they clung to the stern rail like a swarm of bees clinging to a tree branch. Unlike bees, these people had no wings, and so they fell singly and in clusters, plummeting like obscene rotted fruit into the water far below. They screamed as they fell until the bitter cold Atlantic paralyzed their lungs, and then all they could do was whimper.*

He rose slowly, knowing he had to bring his anger under control. He was the only survivor in the room. Shackleton knew of the cold, but only Sullivan knew of the horror. Only Sullivan could speak for the dead, but what could he say? Who could be blamed?

Bigham watched him. His face betrayed no emotion, but his stance told him that Bigham was ready for him.

"Someone in Belfast signed a certificate of seaworthiness," Sullivan said.

Bigham nodded his agreement.

"And yet the coal in her bunkers was on fire."

"Probably."

"And someone in Southampton inspected the ship again and signed a certificate of seaworthiness."

"Yes."

"And they could not see that the bunkers were still burning?"

"Apparently."

"And they failed to notice Hendrickson's attempt to hide the damage where the bulkhead had been red hot?"

"Hard to believe," Bigham said, "but we will have to try."

"Why?"

"For the good of the empire," Bigham said. "We are leaving it to the Americans to point the finger of blame, and my agents in Washington tell me that they are most likely to blame Captain Smith. He's dead, you see. He can't defend himself. They are letting us off lightly."

"Fifteen hundred people are dead," Sullivan hissed. "They did not get off lightly."

Bigham acknowledged the point with another nod of his head. "No, they didn't. Unfortunately, there is worse to come, and we have to be ready. Captain Smith will take the blame from the Americans, and we in Britain will blame God."

"God?"

"'They that go down to the sea in ships and occupy their business in great water; they see the works of the Lord and his wonders in the deep.'"

Sullivan tried to interrupt, but Bigham merely shook his head. "Psalm 107, old chap. God made the iceberg."

CHAPTER TWENTY

The Station Hotel, Dover
Daisy Melville

"I'm going to bed."

Daisy looked at her sister. "Not yet," she said. "Don't go to bed yet. We have to talk."

"No, we don't," Poppy said, climbing into one of the narrow beds in their small, shabby room. "I've had a very long day, and I'm going to sleep. We'll have plenty of time to talk tomorrow on the way home."

"Will Father be at home?"

"I don't know. His wound is serious, and I think he'll need hospital care for a while."

"Tell me again where he was wounded," Daisy said. She grinned as she watched color spread across Poppy's cheeks. "Go on, you can say it."

"Mr. Sullivan referred to it as his '*donger.*' If we have to talk about it, that's what we'll call it, but I see no reason to talk about it."

"But Father's *donger* has changed everything," Daisy said. "You're going to inherit Riddlesdown. No more waiting, no more babies. It's all going to be yours."

"Yes, it is," Poppy said, "but not for a long time. Father's not going to die from this wound to his ... from this wound."

Daisy opened Poppy's portmanteau and inspected the contents.

"I can't believe that ugly diamond necklace was worth a fortune," she said as she lifted out the clothes that Poppy had brought for her.

"It's the only one of its kind in the world. We were all nearly killed for it."

349

"So was I," Daisy said.

"You stole it," Poppy said angrily, "but we were completely innocent. What if the baby had died, or Dianna, or Nanny Catchpole, just because you stole from Alvin Towson? What would you have done then?"

Daisy tried to imagine the scene as Poppy had described it, with her father rushing out of the woods and being shot in the *donger* while Poppy tried to save the baby and their stepmother did her best to bleed to death. The most exciting part, and she could tell from Poppy's breathless tone that she agreed, was the fact that Captain Hazelton and Ernie Sullivan had come out of nowhere to rescue them all.

She had watched Poppy's face as she had described Harry Hazelton flourishing his sword, and her expression had told her all she needed to know about Poppy's feelings for the dashing captain. *Not that the silly goose will ever do anything about it. She'll bury herself in the country and say nothing, and he'll be all gentlemanly and say nothing, and so no one will do anything.*

She rummaged her way to the bottom of the portmanteau and discovered that Poppy had not brought a nightdress for her. She looked up to complain and saw that Poppy was already asleep. Apparently, a simple train journey from Riddlesdown to Dover had worn her out. Poppy had always been that way. She took life too seriously and wore herself out with worry.

Daisy stripped off the clothes that she had now been wearing for three days, and stepped into the underwear that Poppy had provided: clean, serviceable, but completely devoid of ribbons and lace. That was so typical of Poppy. Sometimes she wondered how they could both have been born of the same mother. Of course, she had no memory of her mother at all, but she was convinced that she took after her mother, because she most certainly did not take after her father. On the other hand, maybe Poppy was a little like her father. She didn't have his mean spirit, but she did like things to be predictable.

Daisy sat down on the second bed and looked at her sleeping sister. She knew she should apologize, not just for stealing the jewel and creating so much trouble but for almost everything she had done in her entire life. She'd had so many scrapes, so many near disasters, and Poppy had always been there to bail her out. She knew Poppy had not wanted to go to America, but she wouldn't have let Daisy go on her own. Of course, if they had not had their entire adventure, including the sinking of the *Titanic*, Poppy would never have met Captain Hazelton, and Daisy would never have met Ernie Sullivan. She shook her head. Why on earth was she thinking about that scarred Australian oaf?

She looked at the narrow bed awaiting her in the corner of the room. She didn't want to go to bed. Climbing into that bed would be an admission of defeat. If she slept in that bed tonight, she would eat breakfast at the hotel tomorrow, and then she would follow Poppy home like a good little girl.

And then what? She couldn't bear the thought of returning to Riddlesdown. For as long as she could remember, Riddlesdown had felt like a prison. It wasn't just the presence of her domineering father or the boredom of living in a tiny village where nothing exciting ever happened. The problem was the trees! Yes, that was it. That was the problem. Riddlesdown was surrounded by ancient oaks that cut off any possibility of seeing the horizon. Without really thinking what she was doing, Daisy began to dress in the clothes Poppy had brought her. Why hadn't she thought of this before? She needed to see the horizon. In fact, she needed to see what was beyond the horizon, and once she had seen beyond one horizon, she would need to know what was beyond the next horizon.

She began to feel strangely and unpleasantly warm and constricted. She was being closed in, not by the clothes that Poppy had brought and not by the walls of the bedroom but by the life that lay ahead. Poppy turned in her sleep and flung her arm out free of the bedclothes. That was all Poppy needed, Daisy thought. Poppy needed just a tiny amount of freedom, just a small amount of room, but Daisy needed space, a wide horizon leading to a great unknown.

With her mind made up, Daisy finished dressing. She folded her discarded clothes into the portmanteau and, ignoring a twinge of guilt, opened Poppy's purse. Her sister had brought very little money, but she had spoken of emergency money.

Poppy made another restless turn, half-awake, her hand over her eyes. "Turn out the light."

Daisy turned down the flame in the gas-mantle and waited for Poppy to settle back into sleep. When her sister emitted a slight snuffling snore, Daisy felt safe to move. She picked up the portmanteau and Poppy's purse and slipped out of the door. She padded quietly to the end of the corridor and opened the door to the ladies' lavatory, where a small candle burned on the shelf above the toilet. She sat down on the toilet and rifled through Poppy's purse until she found two five-pound notes tucked into the lining. Was ten pounds enough? It was, she knew, more than some families earned in an entire year, but was it enough for her? Would ten pounds take her beyond the horizon?

The Dulwich Club
Harry Hazelton

Bigham spoke softly. "A word in your ear, old man."

"I don't think—"

"But I do," Bigham said. "Can we find a quiet spot?"

Harry reluctantly drained his brandy. "Follow me."

Bigham followed him across the lounge and into the small, oak-paneled room that had served for years as a place where members could exchange confidences, make deals, settle debts, and just occasionally change the fate of nations. From the tone of Bigham's voice, Harry suspected that this was a moment of the last type. Bigham had something to say that could not be said in front of the openly hostile Sullivan or in front of Shackleton, whose interest lay only in Antarctica.

Before they reached the room, one of the waiters, sprightly for his years, darted ahead of them, opened the door, and put a light to the gas-mantle .

"Will you be requiring any refreshments, Captain Hazelton?"

Harry shook his head. "No, I think not."

"Close the door behind you," Bigham said.

When the waiter failed to move, Harry repeated the instruction, and the waiter departed, closing the door behind him.

Although the room contained a table and several chairs, Harry resisted the temptation to sit and take the weight off his leg.

"Sorry for the deception," Bigham said.

"Don't apologize to me; apologize to the families of the dead. What's it all about, Bigham? Why did you hire me if you didn't want me to find anything? Was it charity? Did you think I needed the job?"

Bigham's expression was hard to read, and Harry reminded

himself that Bigham was practiced in the art of deception. He, too, had spied for the empire.

"Well, I thought you might be short of money," Bigham said, "but that wasn't why I asked you to come on board. I asked you because I knew that if anything was to be found, you would find it."

"Then why not use it?" Harry asked.

"Remember what I told you in the very beginning," Bigham replied. "My father's creed?"

"When in court, never ask a question to which you do not already know the answer," Harry replied.

"Exactly, and that's why I needed you. I had questions, but I had no answers, so the questions could not be asked. You managed to catch us by surprise when you had Scanlan ask Hendrickson about the fire. We weren't ready for that revelation, but I think I've managed to limit the damage."

"You knew the ship was on fire," Harry said.

"I knew it had been on fire, but I didn't know about the damage to the bulkhead." Bigham sighed and sat down abruptly. "Don't stand there like a wooden soldier, Hazelton. For God's sake, sit down. I'm not your enemy, and I haven't deceived you. You may not believe this, but you've been one step ahead of me all the way, especially today."

Harry remained standing. "You played me for a fool."

"You're no fool," Bigham said. "I needed your help, Hazelton, but I couldn't ask directly. I needed to test you. The White Star lawyers were way ahead of me in Plymouth. I knew that evidence had been suppressed and the depositions had been doctored. I told you the truth at the time, that I wanted you to find what was missing, and that's what you did, and because you did, I have been able to limit a good deal of damage. Now it's time to talk about something else. While the gutter press and Interrogantum have been keeping the masses entertained with—"

"Entertained!" Harry interrupted. "I find nothing entertaining about such a tragedy."

"You're right," Bigham said. "It's a tragedy, and I should not call it entertainment. Let me call it a distraction. The general population has been distracted by the stories coming out of the inquiries on both sides of the Atlantic, but the world did not stop turning, and our trade did not come to a halt."

"Our trade?"

"Whispers in dark corners, words overheard, a slip of paper found in a pocket, a walk in the park to see, and yet not see, an old acquaintance. You know very well what trade I speak of."

Bigham's expression had become conciliatory. He stretched out a long leg and hooked a chair, pushing it toward Harry. "Sit down, Harry, please."

Harry sat, suppressing a sigh of relief at taking the weight off his leg. Bigham obviously had more to say, and there was little point in Harry torturing himself by standing in stiff-backed offense.

"I'm sure you've heard the whispers," Bigham said. "War in Europe is inevitable."

"Inevitable?" Harry asked. "What makes you so sure?"

"I've already told you," Bigham said. "Whispers in dark corners. Taft, the American president, had a special envoy on board the *Titanic*. We believe he was returning from Europe with a private message from the German kaiser to the Americans. We will never know what the message contained, but the presence of Major Butt implies that war, when it comes, will involve America."

"On which side?" Harry asked.

"That's the question, isn't it?" Bigham said. "Perhaps we should also ask what side Britain will take. The German kaiser and our king are cousins; in fact, half the crowned heads of Europe are grandchildren of Queen Victoria. It will be the family squabble to end all family squabbles, and men will die. I can assure you that the *Titanic* disaster will be forgotten in the bloodshed yet to come."

"Can it be avoided?"

"It's up to people like us to find that answer," Bigham said.

"People like us?"

"Agents of the empire."

"Spies."

Bigham nodded. "Yes, spies. I'm asking you to go back to work."

"I've been invalided out," Harry said. "I'm unfit for service. I can't go back to my regiment."

"You can't go back to India," Bigham agreed, "and you can't be a soldier, but you can still serve your country."

A tingle ran up Harry's spine as he took in the full import of Bigham's words. He had resigned himself to a future as a figure to be pitied, a wounded soldier trying to make ends meet as a private investigator. He had imagined accepting sordid little commissions following faithless husbands or thieving employees. He had even wondered where Lady Penelope Melville would fit into that life, but of course, she wouldn't. She was far beyond his reach.

Bigham was still speaking. "Berlin at first," he said. "A post at the embassy—military liaison or some such title. When would you be able to leave? How long will you need to put your affairs in order?"

"You assume I will accept."

"Will you?"

Harry's answer was preempted by a tap on the door and a rusty old voice calling Harry's name. "Captain Hazelton, you have an urgent telephone call."

Bigham scowled. "Tell him it can wait."

Harry rose to his feet and walked to the door.

"I need your answer," Bigham said.

"I will answer when I'm ready," Harry replied as he opened the door.

Dover
Poppy Melville

Poppy opened her eyes to dull gray morning light. Rain tapping on the window told her that yesterday's storm had not yet abated and their journey home would be cold and dreary. Daisy hated rain. Even as a small child, she had refused to go for a walk if the sun had not been shining. No doubt the complaining would begin as soon as they stepped outside, and would continue all the way to Riddlesdown.

Poppy made up her mind to break into her emergency money and buy an umbrella for Daisy. Buying two umbrellas would be an extravagance, but one umbrella could be justified on the grounds that Daisy was "different" and needed to be kept dry. A few shillings spent on keeping Daisy in a good mood would be a good investment.

She stretched her arms and looked across at Daisy's bed. Her morning greeting died before it was spoken. Daisy's bed was empty. In fact, it was obvious that Daisy's bed had not been slept in.

A quick glance around the room showed Poppy that Daisy had taken the portmanteau, leaving Poppy with just a small pile of clothing. Poppy's heart raced in sudden alarm as she sprang out of bed and took her purse from the dressing table. She opened it with frantic fingers and spread out the contents. She was not a vain woman, and she carried very few personal items: a comb, two handkerchiefs—one to use and one for emergencies—a small mirror, a notebook and pencil, gloves, and a coin purse. She lifted the coin purse to feel its weight, but she already knew that it would have no weight. Daisy had taken the coins.

With a feeling of dread, she thrust her hand into the depths of her purse, and her fingers contacted the place where a pleat concealed a small slit in the lining. She probed desperately, her fingers seeking the crinkling paper of two five-pound notes. There was nothing. Daisy had taken everything. How could she? It had to be a mistake. Surely Daisy had not intended to leave Poppy stranded. Even Daisy could not be so selfish.

Poppy returned to feeling around in the bottom of the bag. Perhaps she would find a few coins that had slipped from her purse. It could happen very easily, and a few coins would be sufficient to send a telegram.

Nothing! The bag was empty. Poppy turned to the window. The wind had died down, but the rain was still heavy, drenching the pedestrians on the street below. The window gave her a view of the sea, leaden gray with small, sullen waves. She caught a glimpse of a ferry plowing a steady path past the protective bulk of Dover Castle and out into the English Channel. Poppy stepped back. She knew without a shadow of a doubt that Daisy, with stolen money and not an ounce of guilt, was on that ferry, making her way toward France and whatever lay beyond.

She returned to the dressing table and picked up her comb. She studied her reflection in the foxed mirror. Her hair had come loose from its nighttime braid and fell in tangled curls to her shoulders. Her face was creased with sleep, but her eyes were surprisingly bright, and her heart was now beating at a steady, unperturbed pace.

She continued to stare at her reflection. The girl in the mirror stared back with calm, untroubled blue eyes. Was it possible that she was relieved? Did she secretly welcome the fact that Daisy had vanished over the horizon? By taking Poppy's money and leaving her stranded, Daisy had finally achieved the freedom she had been looking for—freedom from Poppy's smothering love and guilt.

Poppy continued to stare at the woman in the mirror, marveling at the sudden realization that she, too, was free. She had spent her entire life under the shadow of her mother's last whispered words: *Look after your sister.* The dying woman had not known that she had given birth to a wild child who could not be tamed or that Poppy would be forced to sacrifice herself to obey that impossible final instruction.

"I really have to make a plan," Poppy said aloud as she rose from the dressing table and picked up her clothes. She tried to corral her wandering thoughts. *One thing at a time.* She should get dressed. She could achieve nothing in her nightgown. When she picked up her discarded clothes, a piece of paper fluttered to the floor. She recognized it as a leaf from her own notebook. She read the familiar scrawl of Daisy's handwriting.

"Get dressed and comb your hair and stop thinking I abandoned you. I took your money so you wouldn't run away (and anyway, I need the money more than you do). Now you can't leave until he comes. I phoned him. I told him to come at eight in the morning. I love you. Be happy. Daisy.

Poppy stared at the note. What did it mean? Who was coming? Who had been told to come at eight? She felt as though Daisy were in the room, sitting on the bed and laughing at her as she dragged her skirt over her head and fumbled with the buttons on her blouse. Daisy's words tumbled around in her mind.

"Every time Captain Hazelton looked at you, your face turned bright red."

Poppy paused with her blouse still unbuttoned.

"I see you mooning over Captain Hazelton, but have you done anything to let him know you're interested?"

"I told him to come at eight."

Poppy buttoned her blouse and ran back to the window. She pushed up the sash and looked down at the pedestrians hurrying through the rain with umbrellas to hide their identity. In the distance, a clock began to chime. She stood transfixed by fear and yearning and counted the chimes.

A car swished by, its passengers invisible behind steam-smeared windows.

Six chimes.

A man and woman walked arm in arm under the shelter of an umbrella.

Seven chimes.

A woman in a raincoat tugged on the leash of a reluctant dog.

Eight chimes.

Someone tapped on the bedroom door. She turned from the window, patted her hair, and opened the door.

Harry's hair and coat were wet, and his face was creased with worry. "Lady Daisy said …"

She walked into his arms. "What did Daisy say?"

"She said that you were—"

She interrupted him, her lips inches from his mouth. "She said I was what?"

"Waiting for me."

"I am," she said.

Cold rainwater from his hair ran down her cheeks, and still he had not kissed her. She reached her arms around to the back of his neck and pulled his head down.

She felt the warmth of his breath as he still tried to speak. "Lady Daisy said—"

She kissed away any further mention of her sister. *Thank you, Daisy. I know what to do now.*

She stepped out of his damp embrace and pulled him into the warmth of the bedroom. He was wet; she was wet. She could almost hear Nanny Catchpole chiding her: *Take off those wet clothes before you catch your death of cold.* Nanny had always given her good advice.

EPILOGUE

Hydrographic Office
July 17, 1912

New York: The White Star liner *Oceanic* arrived today from Southampton over the old route, which has not been used by a White Star ship since the *Titanic* struck an iceberg.

Reports sighting two small icebergs on the morning of July 15. Captain states either berg might do considerable damage to a ship in case of collision.

CHAPTER TWENTY-ONE

Monte Carlo
Daisy Melville

Daisy stared down at the cards in her hand and tried to control her sense of foreboding. This was not the magical unbeatable *vingt et un,* but surely it was a lifeline. She looked at the small pile of chips set on the green baize table in front of her. She had started so well, but most days she started well, and most nights she finished with just enough money for a room and a stake for tomorrow's game.

In Dover where she had first discovered *vingt-et-un,* she had believed what she had been told, that winning was just a matter of luck. Perhaps luck was still an element, but she no longer trusted that luck was on her side.

She looked around at the magnificent trappings of the casino, marble, gilt, plush carpeting and men and women dressed in the height of fashion. She could hear whispered conversations in a myriad of languages, the soft click of the roulette wheel, and the music of a string quartet. Perhaps it was the music that had brought on this sudden lack of confidence. The band on the *Titanic* had played even when the ship was sinking. She could not trust that the strains of violin music meant that all was well.

Her vision blurred and tears prickled at the back of her eyes. She shook her head. What did she have to cry about? She had a jack and a ten — a good hand, almost unbeatable except that the dealer was displaying an ace. She could still be beaten. An inner voice, sounding very much like Poppy told her to leave. Don't walk, run! She pushed her chair back, gathered up her remaining chips and fled precipitously from the room.

Once outside, she leaned against the warm stones of the ornate terrace and watched the play of sunlight on the blue Mediterranean far below. Yachts with white sails danced across the gentle waves winging away toward the place where the sky met the sea and the horizon beckoned. How could she have forgotten? She had embarked on a journey to find lands beyond the horizon and instead she had found herself here trapped by a delusion that all she needed was luck.

She closed her eyes against the prickling of tears. She should not have read the newspaper. If she had not seen the notice of her sister's marriage perhaps she would have staked her remaining chips and come away with a big win – or at least security for a few days. She still could not understand why the the newspaper had been discarded at the doorway of her modest *pension* or why the marriage notice had been circled in blue ink. Apparently someone knew who she was and someone thought she would want to hear about the marriage.

A tear trickled down her cheek and she wiped it away with the back of her hand. She should be happy – happy because Poppy was to be married and happy because she, Daisy, had made sure the marriage would happen. By stealing Poppy's money and running away, she had ensured that Harry would ride in a like a knight in shining armor. She hoped that Poppy would understand that her motives had been purely altruistic.

So now Poppy was married with a small ceremony conducted by Uncle Hugh at the chapel of Fordingbridge Cathedral. According to the newspaper, Poppy had been attended by her sister Dianna as bridesmaid and Captain Hazelton had been attended by Sir Ernest Shackleton as best-man. After a European honeymoon the happy couple would take up residence in the Ambassadorial compound in Berlin where Captain Hazelton had been appointed military attaché.

Daisy was suddenly aware that a man was standing beside her and he was far too close for comfort. She shook her head as she edged away. She had fallen, but she had not fallen that far. She knew what happened to women who went down that road.

"Are you ready to leave now?" the man beside her asked.

She drew herself up into a haughty posture. How dare he presume? Just because she had made a spectacle of herself by running out of the room, did not mean that she was desperate. She was emphatically not desperate – not yet.

She summoned up a withering, scornful stare and turned to face the unfortunate man who had dared to proposition Lady Marguerite

Melville. The withering stare died before it was born and scorn stood no chance. The scar, a white slash across his cheek, still produced an unreadable expression but his eyes were brimming with amusement.

"You?" she said.

"You expected me, didn't you?"

"No, why should I —"

"I left the newspaper for you."

"How did you find me?"

"It wasn't easy, but I was determined."

"Did Poppy send you?"

His smile was so broad that even the scar could not disguise it. "No one had to send me. I always intended to come. I'm on my way home now, so I thought you might like to come with me."

"Why would I want to come with you?"

"Because you can't stay here, and you can't go home again."

For a moment Daisy was back on the deck of the *Lapland* facing the worse rejection of her life. She had offered herself to this oaf and he had rejected her and now he wanted to change his mind. Now he wanted to take advantage of her temporary run of bad luck to persuade her to go with him to the back of beyond. She didn't need his help. Any day now, the cards would turn in her favor. On the other hand, even the very best run of cards could not make her heart pound the way it was pounding now.

He was still talking. "We could go the long way round; take a ship to Cape Town, and over to India."

She looked past him and was in time to see the white sails of a yacht blink out of sight as it sailed beyond the horizon.

"Fiji, Tahiti, Samoa." His voice caressed the words and Daisy stared at the place where the yacht had vanished and thought of the islands far beyond.

"Would you have to be in the engine room?" she asked.

She thought she heard him laugh although she could not imagine why.

"I could be a steward," he said, "but the passengers may not like my face. I've been told my scar gives me a dangerous look."

Daisy turned from the view and studied his face. She reached up and touched the scar. "I like it."

He nodded. "I suppose I could work in third class," he said. "What about you?"

What about me? Could I do it again?

"I'd prefer to work in first-class."

He was laughing again. What was so funny?

"Perhaps you'd prefer to be a passenger."

She stamped her foot. "Of course I would, but that's not possible so we will just have to make the best of it."

"Why do you say it's not possible?"

"Because we have no money."

His face was suddenly serious. "Would you really come with me, even if I have no money?"

He was such a fool. Didn't he know?

"Of course I would."

He pulled her into his arms and she made no resistance. Why would she? He was what she'd wanted from the moment he pulled her from the harbor in New York.

THE END

Turn the page for additional information on the Titanic Inquiry
Sign up for Eileen Enwright Hodgetts' newsletter at
www.eileenenwrighthodgetts.com
Find other books by this author at Amaon.com and other online outlets.

The Girl in the Lifeboat is a work of fiction based on testimony given by survivors at both the U.S. and British inquiries. In both cases much of the questioning was repetitive and spread over a number of weeks. For this reason I have used some of the testimony out of its correct order, and also used some of the original words in conversations to convey the truth and avoid tedium.

Readers may be familiar with some of the names I have included in *The Girl in the Lifeboat*. My cast of characters contains many people who truly existed and were involved in the Titanic sinking and its aftermath Only a few of my characters are fictional. You may be surprised.

WHO IS NOT REAL
Poppy Melville
Daisy Melville
Captain Harry Hazelton
Ernie Sullivan
The Earl of Riddlesdown
The Bishop of Fordingbridge
Nanny Catchpole
Alvin Towson

WHO IS REAL
From the Titanic
Captain Smith
Second Officer Charles Lightoller
Fifth Officer Harold Lowe
Frederick Clench
Alfred Crawford
Frederick Fleet
Quartermaster Robert Hitchens
Violet Jessup
Agnes Stap
Charles Joughin
Edward Brown

Archie Jewell
John Hesketh
Johnathan Shepard
Thomas Andrews
Madeleine Astor
Victorine, the maid
Charles Romaine
Kid Homer
Boy Brereton
Fred Barret
John Dilley
Dorothy Gibson
Charles Hendrickson

In London
Lord Mersey
Clive Bigham
Ben Tillet
Eva Newton
Ernest Shackleton

Dulwich College founded in 1619 is real. The Dulwich Club is fictional

The Ships

RMS Carpathia During World War I the Carpathia transported Allied troops and supplies. On July 17, 1918, it was part of a convoy traveling from Liverpool to Boston. Off the southern coast of Ireland, the ship was struck by three torpedoes from a German U-boat and sank. Five people were killed; the rest of the passengers and crew were rescued by the HMS Snowdrop. In 1999 the wreck of the Carpathia was discovered intact and lying upright . Due to its remote location and extreme depth the Carpathia has only been visited twice by scuba divers. The wreck is owned by RMS Titanic Inc.

SS Lapland. In 1914 The Lapland began Liverpool – New York City crossings under the UK flag. She sailed from Halifax to

Liverpool on 29th September, 1916 with Canadian troops of the 150th Battalion of the Canadian Expeditionary Force. In April 1917 she struck a naval mine off the Mersey Bar Lightship, but managed to reach Liverpool. In June 1917 she was requisitioned and converted into a troop ship. Among her passengers in August 1917 were aviators of the 1st Aero Squadron, the first unit of the United States Army Air Service to reach France. She was broken up for scrap in Osaka in 1934.

SS Californian continued in normal commercial service until World War I when the British government took control of her. She was responsible for transporting equipment and troops for the Allies mired in the Battle of Gallipoli. On 9 November 1915, while *en route* from Salonica to Marseilles, she was torpedoed by the German U-boat SM U-34. While she was under tow by a French patrol boat, she was torpedoed again and sank in 10–13,000 feet of water, approximately 60 miles south-southwest of Cape Matapan, Greece. The wreck remains undiscovered

The Diamond: The only known matrryoshka diamond was found in Siberia. It was not taken aboard the Titanic.

REPORT OF THE COURT.

The Court, having carefully inquired into the circumstances of the above mentioned shipping casualty, finds that the loss of the said ship was due to collision with an iceberg, brought about by the excessive speed at which the ship was being navigated.

Dated this 30th day of July, 1912.
MERSEY.
Wreck Commissioner.

The British Inquiry sough to answer 26 questions. Here are the published answers to those questions.

1. When the "Titanic" left Queenstown on or about 11th April last: -

(a.) What was the total number of persons employed in any capacity on board her, and what were their respective ratings?

(b.) What was the total number of her passengers, distinguishing sexes and classes, and discriminating between adults and children?

Answer:

(a) The total number of persons employed in any capacity on board the "Titanic" was: 885

(b) (b.) The total number of passengers was 1,316.

2. Before leaving Queenstown on or about 11th April last did the "Titanic" comply with the requirements of the Merchant Shipping Acts, 1894-1906, and the rules and regulations made thereunder with regard to the safety and otherwise of "passenger steamers" and "emigrant ships"?

Answer: Yes.

3. In the actual design and construction of the "Titanic" what special provisions were made for the safety of the vessel and the lives of those on board in the event of collisions and other casualties?

Answer: These have been already described.

4. (a.) Was the "Titanic" sufficiently and efficiently officered and manned? (b.) Were the watches of the officers and crew usual and proper? (c.) Was the "Titanic" supplied with proper charts?

Answer:

(a.) Yes.

(b.) Yes.

(c.) Yes.

5. (a.) What was the number of the boats of any kind on board the "Titanic"? (b.) Were the arrangements for manning and launching the boats on board the "Titanic" in case of emergency proper and sufficient? (c.) Had a boat drill been held on board, and, if so, when? (d.) What was the carrying capacity of the respective boats?

Answer:

(a.) 2 Emergency boats.

... 14 lifeboats.... 4 Engelhardt boats.

(b.) No, but see page 38.

(c.) No.

(d.) The carrying capacity of the:

.... 2 Emergency boats was for 80 persons.

... 14 Lifeboats was for 910 persons.

... 4 Engelhardt boats was for 188 persons.

... or a total of 1,178 "

6. (a.) What installations for receiving and transmitting messages by wireless telegraphy were on board the "Titanic"? (b.) How many operators were employed on working such installations? (c.) Were the installations in good and effective working order, and were the number of operators sufficient to enable messages to be received and transmitted continuously by day and night?

Answer:

(a.) A Marconi 5 Kilowatt motor generator with two complete sets of apparatus supplied from the ship's dynamos, with an independent storage battery and coil for emergency, was fitted in a house on the Boat Deck.

(b.) Two.

(c.) Yes.

7. (a.) At or prior to the sailing of the "Titanic" what, if any, instructions as to navigation were given to the Master or known by him to apply to her voyage? (b.) Were such instructions, if any, safe, proper and adequate, having regard to the time of year and dangers likely to be encountered during the voyage?

Answer:

(a.) No special instructions were given, but he had general instructions contained in the book of Rules and Regulations supplied by the Company. (see "Sailing Orders.")

(b.) Yes, but having regard to subsequent events they would have been better if a reference had to be adopted in the event of reaching the region of ice.

8. (a.) What was in fact the track taken by the "Titanic" in crossing the Atlantic Ocean? (b.) Did she keep to the track usually followed by liners on voyages from the United Kingdom to New York in the month of April? (c.) Are such tracks safe tracks at that time of year? (d.) Had the Master any, and, if so, what, discretion as regards the track to be taken?

Answer:

(a.) The Outward Southern Track from Queenstown to New York, usually followed in April by large steam vessels. (see)"Route Followed.")

(b.) Yes, with the exception that instead of altering her course on approaching the position 42° N., 47° W. she stood on her previous course for some 10 miles further South West, turning to S. 86° W. true at 5.50 p.m.

(c.) The Outward and Homeward bound Southern tracks were decided on as the outcome of many years' experience of the normal movement of ice. They were reasonably safe tracks for the time of year, provided, of course, that great caution and vigilance when crossing the ice region were observed.

(d.) Yes. Captain Smith was not fettered by any orders and to remain on the track should information as to position of ice make it in his opinion undesirable to adhere to it. The fact, however, of Lane Routes having been laid down for the common safety of all, would necessarily influence him to keep on (or very near) the accepted route, unless circumstances as indicated above should induce him to deviate largely from it.

9. (a.) After leaving Queenstown on or about the 11th April last, did information reach the "Titanic" by wireless messages or otherwise by signals of the existence of ice in certain latitudes? (b.) If so, what were such messages or signals and when were they received, and in what position or positions was the ice reported to be, and was the ice reported in or near the track actually being followed by the "Titanic"? (c.) Was her course altered in consequence of receiving such information, and, if so, in what way? (d.) What replies to such messages or signals did the "Titanic" send, and at what times?

Answer:

(a.) Yes.

(b.) See particulars of ice messages already set out (see) "Ice Messages Received.")

(c.) No. Her course was altered as hereinbefore described, but not in consequence of the information received as to ice.

(d.) The material answers were: -

At 12.55 p.m. s.s. "Titanic." "To Commander, 'Baltic.' Thanks for your message and good wishes. Had fine weather since leaving. Smith."

At 1.26 p.m. s.s. "Titanic." "To Captain, 'Caronia.' Thanks for message and information. Have had variable weather throughout. Smith."

10. (a.) If at the times referred to in the last preceding question or later the "Titanic" was warned of or had reason to suppose she would encounter ice, at what time might she have reasonably expected to encounter it? (b.) Was a good and proper look-out for ice kept on board? (c.) Were any, and, if so, what directions given to vary the speed - if so, were they carried out?

Answer:

(a.) At, or even before, 9.30 p.m. ship's time, on the night of the disaster.

(b.) No. The men in the crow's-nest were warned at 9.30 p.m. to keep a sharp look-out for ice; the officer of the watch was then aware that he had reached the reported ice region, and so also was the officer who relieved him at 10 p.m. Without implying that those actually on duty were not keeping a good look-out, in view of the night being moonless, there being no wind and perhaps very little swell, and especially in view of the high speed at which the vessel was running, it is not considered that the look-out was sufficient. An extra look-out should, under the circumstances, have been placed at the stemhead, and a sharp look-out should have been kept from both sides of the bridge by an officer.

(c.) No directions were given to reduce speed.

11. (a.) Were binoculars provided for and used by the look-out men? (b.) Is the use of them necessary or usual in such circumstances? (c.) Had the "Titanic" the means of throwing searchlights around her? (d.) If so, did she make use of them to discover ice? (e.) Should searchlights have been provided and used?

Answer:

(a.) No.

(b.) No.

(c.) No.

(d.) No.

(e.) No, but searchlights may at times be of service. The evidence before the Court does not allow of a more precise answer.

12. (a.) What other precautions were taken by the "Titanic" in anticipation of meeting ice? (b.) Were they such as are usually adopted by vessels being

navigated in waters where ice may be expected to be encountered?

Answer:

(a.) Special orders were given to the men in the crow's-nest to keep a sharp look-out for ice, particularly small ice and growlers. The fore scuttle hatch was closed to keep everything dark before the bridge.

(b.) Yes, though there is evidence to show that some Masters would have placed a look-out at the stemhead of the ship.

13. (a.) Was ice seen and reported by anybody on board the "Titanic" before the casualty occurred? (b.) If so, what measures were taken by the officer on watch to avoid it? (c.) Were they proper measures and were they promptly taken?

Answer:

(a.) Yes, immediately before the collision.

(b.) The helm was put hard-a-starboard and the engines were stopped and put full speed astern.

(c.) Yes.

14. (a.) What was the speed of the "Titanic" shortly before and at the moment of the casualty? (b.) Was such speed excessive under the circumstances?

Answer:

(a.) About 22 knots.

(b.) Yes.

15. (a.) What was the nature of the casualty which happened to the "Titanic" at or about 11.45 p.m. on the 14th April last? (b.) In what latitude and longitude did the casualty occur?

Answer:

(a.) A collision with an iceberg which pierced the starboard side of the vessel in several places below the waterline between the forepeak tank and No. 4 boiler room.

(b.) In latitude 41° 46′ N., longitude 50° 14′ W.

16. (a.) What steps were taken immediately on the happening of the casualty? (b.) How long after the casualty was its seriousness realised by those in charge of the vessel? (c.) What steps were then taken? (d.) What endeavours were made to save the lives of those on board, and to prevent the vessel from sinking?

Answer:

(a.) The 12 watertight doors in the engine and boiler rooms were closed from the bridge, some of the boiler fires were drawn, and the bilge pumps abaft No. 6 boiler room were started.

(b.) About 15 - 20 minutes.

(c.) and (d.) The boats were ordered to be cleared away. The passengers were roused and orders given to get them on deck, and lifebelts were served out. Some of the watertight doors, other than those in the boiler and engine rooms, were closed. Marconigrams were sent out asking for help. Distress signals (rockets) were fired, and attempts were made to call up by Morse a ship whose lights were seen. Eighteen of the boats were swung out and lowered, and the remaining two floated off the ship and were subsequently utilized as rafts.

17. Was proper discipline maintained on board after the casualty occurred?

Answer:

Yes.

18. (a.) What messages for assistance were sent by the "Titanic" after the casualty and, at what times respectively? (b.) What messages were received by her in response and, at what times respectively? (c.) By what vessels were the messages that were sent by the "Titanic" received, and from what vessels did she receive answers? (d.) What vessels other than the "Titanic" sent or received the messages at or shortly after the casualty in connection with such casualty? (e.) What were the vessels that sent or received such messages? (f.) Were any vessels prevented from going to the assistance of the "Titanic" or her boats owing to messages received from the "Titanic" or owing to any erroneous messages being sent or received? (g.) In regard to such erroneous messages,

from what vessels were they sent and by what vessels were they received and at what times respectively?

Answer:

(a.) (b.) (c.) (d.) and (e.) are answered together.

(f.) Several vessels did not go owing to their distance.

(g.) There were no erroneous messages.

[Submitted - Wireless messages in connection with "Titanic" sent the evening of April 14-15, 1912.]

19. (a.) Was the apparatus for lowering the boats on the "Titanic" at the time of the casualty in good working order? (b.) Were the boats swung out, filled, lowered, or otherwise put into the water and got away under proper superintendence? (c.) Were the boats sent away in seaworthy condition and properly manned, equipped and provisioned? (d.) Did the boats, whether those under davits or otherwise, prove to be efficient and serviceable for the purpose of saving life?

Answer:

(a.) Yes.

(b.) Yes.

(c.) The fourteen lifeboats, two emergency boats, and C and D collapsible boats were sent away in a seaworthy condition, but some of them were possibly undermanned. The evidence on this point was unsatisfactory. The total number of crew taken on board the "Carpathia" exceeded the number which would be required for manning the boats. The collapsible boats A and B appeared to have floated off the ship at the time she foundered. The necessary equipment and provisions for the boats were carried in the ship, but some of the boats, nevertheless, left without having their full equipment in them.

(d.) Yes.

20. (a.)What was the number of (a) passengers, (b) crew taken away in each boat on leaving the vessel? (b.) How was this number made up, having regard to: -

1 Sex.

2 Class.

3 Rating.

(c.) How many were children and how many adults? (d.) Did each boat carry its full load and, if not, why not?

Answer:

(a.) (b.) (c.) It is impossible exactly to say how many persons were carried in each boat or what was their sex, class and rating, as the totals given evidence do not correspond with the numbers taken on board the "Carpathia."

(d.) No.

At least 8 boats did not carry their full loads for the following reasons: -

1. Many people did not realise the danger or care to leave the ship at first.

2. Some boats were ordered to be lowered with an idea of then coming round to the gangway doors to complete loading.

3. The officers were not certain of the strength and capacity of the boats in all cases (and see Testimony re Buckling.).

21. (a.) How many persons on board the "Titanic" at the time of the casualty were ultimately rescued and by what means? (b.) How many lost their lives prior to the arrival of the ss. "Carpathia" in New York? (c.) What was the number of passengers, distinguishing between men and women and adults and children of the 1st, 2nd, and 3rd classes respectively who were saved? (d.) What was the number of the crew, discriminating their ratings and sex, that were saved? (e.) What is the proportion which each of these numbers bears to the corresponding total number on board immediately before the casualty? (f.) What reason is there for the disproportion, if any?

Answer:

(a.) 712, rescued by "Carpathia" from the boats.

(b.) One.

(c.) (d.) and (e.) are answered together.

The following is a list of the saved: -

[List - Persons saved, by class and rating.]

(f.) The disproportion between the numbers of the passengers saved in the first, second, and third classes is due to various causes, among which the difference in the position of their quarters and the fact that many of the third class passengers were foreigners, are perhaps the most important. Of the Irish emigrants in the third class a large proportion was saved. The disproportion was certainly not due to any discrimination by the officers or crew in assisting the passengers to the boats. The disproportion between the numbers of the passengers and crew saved is due to the fact that the crew, for the most part, all attended to their duties to the last, and until all the boats were gone.

22. What happened to the vessel from the happening of the casualty until she foundered?

Answer:

A detailed description has already been given (see "Description of Damage")

23. Where and at what time did the "Titanic" founder?

Answer:

2.20 a.m. (ship's time) 15th April.

Latitude 41° 46' N., 50° 14' W.

24. (a.)What was the cause of the loss of the "Titanic," and of the loss of life which thereby ensued or occurred? (b.) What vessels had the opportunity of rendering assistance to the "Titanic" and, if any, how was it that assistance did not reach the "Titanic" before the ss. "Carpathia" arrived? (c.) Was the construction of the vessel and its arrangements such as to make it difficult for any class of passenger or any portion of the crew to take full advantage of any the existing provisions for safety?

Answer:

(a.) Collision with an iceberg and the subsequent foundering of the ship.

(b.)The "Californian." She could have reached the "Titanic" if she had made the attempt when she saw the first rocket. She made no attempt.

(c.) No.

25. When the "Titanic" left Queenstown on or about 11th April last was she properly constructed and adequately equipped as a passenger steamer and emigrant ship for the Atlantic service?

Answer:

Yes.

26. The Court is invited to report upon the Rules and Regulations made under the Merchant Shipping Acts, 1894 -1906, and the administration of those Acts and of such Rules and Regulations, so far as the

consideration thereof is material to this casualty, and to make any recommendations or suggestions that it may think fit, having regard to the circumstances of the casualty, with a view to promoting the safety of vessels and persons at sea.

Answer:

An account of the Board of Trade's Administration has already been given and certain recommendations are subsequently made.

Please continue to next page for Book Club Questions

BOOK CLUB QUESTIONS

Here are a few suggestions to spark discussion in your book club or library group.

1. After 110 years and so many books and movies, why is there still so much interest in the Titanic?

2. Did reading this book change your opinion as to what happened?

3. What was your favorite part of the book?

4. Did you race to the end or was it more of a slow burn?

5. Who was your favorite character and why?

6. What was your biggest surprise?

7. What is your "take away" from this story?

8.. What did you think of the actual writing?

8.. Would you read another book by this author?